"WHAT DO YOU WANT ME

"Call an air stri[k]

"Call an air stri[k]

"Ask the Turks [...] [d]oesn't matter who blows the hill as long as it gets blown."

Brognola knew he was sticking his neck out. "Mr. President, my team is on-site at this minute and is more than ready to go in and do its best—"

"Then send them in. Take some prisoners."

"That isn't their primary goal. The men they're up against are sititng on a United States Patriot missile, ready to launch at the touch of a button. My men can get into the valley, take down some of the terrorists and come away with living, breathing prisoners. But I can't promise you they can stop that missile from flying. We're worried about Turkish civilian casualties."

"Do I have to remind you that we're talking about just one of fifteen missiles remaining at large in Turkey?"

DON PENDLETON'S

MACK BOLAN.

STONY MAN.

COUNTDOWN TO TERROR

A GOLD EAGLE BOOK FROM

WORLDWIDE.

TORONTO • NEW YORK • LONDON
AMSTERDAM • PARIS • SYDNEY • HAMBURG
STOCKHOLM • ATHENS • TOKYO • MILAN
MADRID • WARSAW • BUDAPEST • AUCKLAND

If you purchased this book without a cover you should be aware
that this book is stolen property. It was reported as "unsold and
destroyed" to the publisher, and neither the author nor the
publisher has received any payment for this "stripped book."

First edition June 2001

ISBN 0-373-61937-5

Special thanks and acknowledgment to
Tim Somheil for his contribution to this work.

COUNTDOWN TO TERROR

Copyright © 2001 by Worldwide Library.

All rights reserved. Except for use in any review, the
reproduction or utilization of this work in whole or in part
in any form by any electronic, mechanical or other means,
now known or hereafter invented, including xerography,
photocopying and recording, or in any information storage
or retrieval system, is forbidden without the written permission
of the publisher, Worldwide Library, 225 Duncan Mill Road,
Don Mills, Ontario, Canada M3B 3K9.

All characters in this book have no existence outside the
imagination of the author and have no relation whatsoever to
anyone bearing the same name or names. They are not even
distantly inspired by any individual known or unknown to the
author, and all incidents are pure invention.

® and TM are trademarks of Harlequin Enterprises Limited.
Trademarks indicated with ® are registered in the United States
Patent and Trademark Office, the Canadian Trade Marks Office
and in other countries.

Printed in U.S.A.

COUNTDOWN
TO TERROR

Printed in U.S.A.

CHAPTER ONE

Stony Man Farm Annex

Aaron Kurtzman's fingers froze over the keyboard when, without warning, a small window with bright red letters appeared on his screen. It said simply, "Alert."

He stopped what he was doing.

The alert signal was generated by software written by the Stony Man cybernetics master himself, and its nature was to make some of the most "human" decisions of any of the software pieces in the vast new Stony Man Farm Annex computer center. The Alert software tied itself in to the array of communications constantly being fed into the Farm—everything from high-security U.S. military intelligence to online news services and media feeds—listening and reading for key words and codes that would be of interest to the Farm. The software was self-evolving: it improved itself. Every time an alert code was generated, Kurtzman graded the software on the pertinence of the Alert. The software used that grade to build in more-precise quantifying parameters for subsequent decision making.

Still, the Alert tended to generate more false alarms than actual, useful alerts, so many that sometimes the computer expert considered just turning the application off.

This wasn't a false alarm.

Kurtzman found the communications feed that had generated the alarm and turned on an audio feed from U.S.-European military operations, where a tumult of audio and electronic data signals was being relayed. "Security system is breached. Grid layout six and seven. And eight and nine and ten! They've got the north end. Are we reaching you?"

Kurtzman heard a note of panic in the radio operator's voice. He wondered whom the young man was in contact with. The data screen coming through was from an Air Force security system, feeding sensor information on a large-scale security breach somewhere. The list was growing line by line as one after another secure systems at a U.S. military facility was tripped. Kurtzman scanned the window for an identifier, then saw the word "Incirlik."

Footsteps behind him, heavy and hurried. "Wow."

"It's Incirlik, Hunt," Kurtzman told Huntington Wethers. The tall, dignified black man leaned at the waist to look more closely at Kurtzman's screen. "All hell is breaking loose, but I can't tell what's actually going on."

"I'll see what I can find out."

Wethers strode to another seat at a terminal in the new computer center. He began accessing communications links and opening new ones.

"You finding anything?" Kurtzman asked.

"Not yet."

"Damn."

Whatever was going down was going down right now.

Nobody was bothering to stop long enough to brief the world's digital onlookers on the situation.

"I'm seeing crazy stuff here," Kurtzman said out loud. "Unauthorized-deployment alarms of all types. Everything from aircraft to high-security hangar access. It's like every automatic system is going berserk."

"Could it be a large-scale system failure?" Wethers asked aloud. It was a rhetorical question. The former Berkeley computer professor knew the answer as well as Kurtzman did: possible, but not likely.

A young Japanese man entered the room, headphones plugged into a tiny MP3 player in his pocket, and sensed the mood at once. Without a word Akira Tokaido pulled out the earphones and plopped into another terminal seat to begin his own search of the incoming reams of data.

The radio operator was talking urgently again, and Kurtzman adjusted the volume so that the voice of the young man, speaking into a microphone at Incirlik Air Force Base on the other side of the world in Turkey, sounded as if he were in the room with them.

"I don't know if anybody is hearing this because the whole place is shot to hell! We have been infiltrated and are under attack! I repeat, we are under attack! We've got a bunch of people dead already. We have twenty guys on the grounds, shooting the place up! They've blown up five aircraft already! I have no idea where my CO is. I'm telling you this, though—we're not able to defend ourselves right now! We could use a freaking assist!"

"Check it out!" Tokaido spoke for the first time, and he was pointing at one of the big displays on the wall above Kurtzman. Eight small windows filled the screen with news channels from around the world. One of them showed a shaky ground-based image of an airport hangar billowing black smoke. With a stab of a button Kurtzman brought up the sound on the BBC News channel.

"...identity is unknown! This all just started fifteen minutes ago! We heard a large explosion, and then we saw smoke from the airfield and came to the scene as fast as we could!"

The speaker was British, and when he appeared on the picture briefly he wore a crooked tie and a rumpled suit jacket.

"We see no evidence of attacking aircraft." The reporter was panting as he ran. They even heard the cameraman breathing hard. "We have been inside the air base since yesterday doing a human-interest piece, and there was no indication of impending danger or alerts. I have to say the base was totally unprepared for this attack, no matter where it is coming from— Bloody hell!"

An explosion erupted, and for a fraction of a second the video camera recorded the image of a blast bursting to life under the wing of a OA-10 Thunderbolt II, jumping it into the air. The Thunderbolt aircraft stood up on one wing, the broken stub where the other wing had been pointing into the sky, hanging there for a long moment. Before the Thunderbolt collapsed, the camera image turned to chaos and went black.

For a moment there was nothing.

A voice-over came on. "It appears we have lost the signal temporarily. That was BBC's Terence Taylor in Incirlik, Turkey, where at this moment the Air Force base that is shared by the Turkish air force and the U.S. Air Force is under some kind of bombing attack. Details are almost nonexistent so far...."

Kurtzman scanned his massive amounts of data flowing into the Stony Man mainframes from Incirlik. Very little of it answered his immediate questions. Who?

How? Why? He was aware of others coming into the Annex computer center. Carmen Delahunt, a vivacious and attractive redhead, was standing next to an older man, Yakov Katzenelenbogen, whose prosthetic hand was tucked into the front pocket of his jeans. Everyone in the room was staring at the BBC screen and listening to the dispassionate voice of the English news anchor.

"...is apparently at Incirlik to produce a news piece in cooperation with American Forces Network in Europe, which was scheduled to be aired next week—"

"Are we back? We're back! Do we know if they're getting this? Keep shooting anyway!" The image from Turkey appeared again. "This is Terence Taylor, BBC, and we're at Incirlik Air Base in Turkey, which at this moment is under attack by persons unknown. We were knocked flat a moment ago by debris from a nearby explosion, but neither of us are hurt badly."

The camera panned shakily onto the dirty, bloodied face of the reporter, whose tie was now twisted almost to his shoulder and dangled on his back. "We've seen the soldiers responsible for the attack, and all I can say so far is that they appear to be in U.S. Air Force uniforms—but I haven't got close enough to tell for certain. There are bodies littered throughout the air base. I've counted at least five dead personally, and I believe there are more...now there's something happening! Jonathan, come on!"

The camera image shook wildly as the men ran toward a low yellow building, then peered around it, sneaking a peek at the activity on the tarmac.

A long line of heavy trucks was accelerating across the blacktop surface, with armed soldiers perched atop every one of them, assault rifles in hand. When they spotted the video camera they began to cheer and wave.

Emboldened, the cameraman jogged into the open, ignoring a bloodied corpse and getting a close-up on the faces of the terrorists.

The last two trucks in the convoy came to a halt without warning. The cameraman stopped in his tracks.

One of the terrorists shouted to the cameraman, "Watch this!"

In a matter of minutes the machinery on the rear of the last truck was activated, and a heavy black shape was elevated on the bed.

"Who are you people?" the BBC reporter demanded.

"Shut up and watch! Get this on TV!"

There was a flash and a puff of smoke, and suddenly a missile ejected itself from the black cartridge, flinging itself into the air and disappearing. There was an explosion seconds later.

"Jesus!" the BBC reported exclaimed. "They've just launched the missile into the air base! Can you get that, Jonathan?"

The camera turned toward a growing billow of black smoke just a few hundred yards away.

"I think they've just blown up more fighter aircraft!"

Kurtzman stared at his monitor screen, where a new window had suddenly displayed the word "Alert."

There had to be some sort of malfunction in the application. It had to be giving him an alert on the ongoing Incirlik condition. Right? He traced back the source of the alert to an Air Force base emergency code, and for a moment it all made sense—just some sort of a duplicate reading. He'd debug it later.

Then he realized that the Air Force base in question wasn't Incirlik. He brought the radio feed online from Hickam Air Force Base, Oahu, Hawaii. Out of his monitor speakers he heard a woman shouting, "...multiple casualties and our medics can't get at them. They're just laying there dying! Give me some response, over!''

"We're working on it, but we're in the same situation," answered a boyish voice. "We go out there we're as good as dead! Where are the damn MPs, over!''

"The MPs are the ones dying, over," the woman shouted back. "Who's in charge here, anyway?''

Before Kurtzman announced his new discovery, he heard Tokaido issue an incredibly vulgar expletive. "Look at this!''

Tokaido brought up the sound on a second news feed. It was CNN, with the Breaking News banner at the bottom of the screen and, above it, an eerily familiar scene: a U.S. Air Force base under attack. It was as if someone took the video from Incirlik air base disaster and placed it on a background with palm trees and a green mountain in the background.

"This is CNN correspondent Warren Bowles reporting live from Hickam Air Force Base in Hawaii on the island of Oahu, where we're in the midst of a battle that erupted just five minutes ago. As you can see, the first wave of violence has already left several airplanes destroyed, including an unknown number of fighter aircraft. There have been casualties. I don't want to speculate how many, but there are some dead and many wounded. The identity of the enemy is also a mystery right at this moment. Shit!''

An explosion behind a nearby building blasted through the speakers and sent a wall of dark debris up in a curtain behind the correspondent.

"I can't tell you who's responsible. I can say this— from what little I did witness, it appeared as if the attackers were in military uniforms. The shooting and bombing started when they were already inside the compound. This is a ground-based attack only—there have been no aircraft actually flying. Now what?''

As the cameraman moved around a building, he focused his camera on another familiar scene, directly out of the Incirlik news feed.

''Déjà freaking vu,'' Tokaido muttered.

A line of trucks was moving away from a smoking hangar. Most were enclosed in tarpaulins, but the last was exposed, revealing the skeletal steel supports of a launch system, cradling the square black mass of a missile cartridge. The men hustling around the launch bed had assault rifles draped over their shoulders. They were moving fast, wasting no time or effort.

The cartridge elevated and the missile came to life, sliding out of the launch framework on a pillow of fire and leaving the field of vision of the video shot within a fraction of a second. The smoke billowed around the launcher, floating over the corpses scattered in the foreground while the operators jogged to another of the nearby waiting trucks and jumped aboard.

''Can you get that? Can you get it?'' the correspondent was shouting.

The cameraman turned his lens into the sky, and for a moment only he was able to focus on the arc of the missile's exhaust. Then it became insubstantial and disappeared.

''It looks like the attackers are leaving with their trucks. Get that! Get the trucks!''

Kurtzman heard the door to the new Computer Room burst open, and when he glanced around he saw Barbara Price. When her eyes met his they looked hollow, but they went back to the news feeds on the screen. She stepped up behind his wheelchair and put her hands on his big shoulders. He grasped one of them and they continued watching in silence.

Price had missed most of the action. On the screen the convoy of missiles was leaving the air base, devastation and death in its wake.

The phone buzzed on his desk. Kurtzman grabbed it and said nothing, but heard a Stony Man communications officer state simply, "Call for Ms. Price."

She took the phone absently from Kurtzman. "Price," she said into it.

There was a sound on the other end like the growl of an angry dog. "I'm on my way."

"We'll be ready," Price said.

HAL BROGNOLA ARRIVED within the hour, but he was the last one to walk into the Stony Man Farm War Room. He wasn't smiling and no one else was, either. During the time it took him to get to his seat at the head of the huge table, he took attendance. Everyone he wanted was there, minus one.

"Striker?"

"Mexico City."

Brognola nodded and landed heavily in his chair. He was a big man whose entire existence was situated between a rock and a hard place. As director of the covert Sensitive Operations Group, he was the one and only liaison between the President of the United States of America and Stony Man Farm.

The Farm wasn't legal. The role it played was clandestine. The measures it took were above and beyond the efforts of other federal agencies such as the FBI and CIA.

A curious sequence of events occurred whenever there was a new United States President. Brognola had witnessed it several times during the changes in administrations. When the new Man came into power and initially learned about the existence of the nebulous entity known as Stony Man Farm, he was initially taken aback—sometimes even outraged—that the Constitution-loving U.S.A. could sponsor an organization of beyond-the-law commandos. Every single President declared that *he* was above using such extreme measures.

But then a crisis occurred, one that was beyond the capabilities of his other agencies to handle. Stony Man Farm would have the opportunity to justify its existence one more time.

There was never a shortage of opportunities.

The first U.S. President elected in the twenty-first century was no exception.

"I have the word from the Man," Brognola said simply. "We're authorized to proceed on both fronts."

"That was quick work," Kurtzman observed.

"He called me. Took all of fifteen minutes," Brognola replied. "This is a bad situation. It gets worse with every minute. What do we know now?"

Kurtzman pressed a button on the table in front of him, and the big screen along one wall came to life. A pair of images showed the now familiar scenes of destruction.

"At 19:13 hours local time, a series of explosions initiated an attack at Incirlik Air Force Base in Turkey. The explosions were carefully planned to disrupt communications and isolate sections of the base. The base commander was killed, other officers were isolated and the result was a high level of confusion.

"Amid this, a group of highly trained gunmen in U.S. military uniforms materialized, swept through the base, causing further substantial property damage and loss of life. Their target was a storage facility for PAC-3-type Patriot missiles and their ground-based vehicular launch systems. They breached the security of this storage facility and launched one of the missiles into the Turkish section of the Incirlik air base, destroying three Turkish fighter jets, damaging many more and killing an unknown number of Turkish airmen. They left with fifteen—repeat, fifteen—functional Patriot missiles and four launch systems, each with four launch breeches.''

For many of the men and women around the table, this was all brand-new information. They glanced at one another uneasily while Kurtzman continued, the videotapes of the destruction playing silently on the screen behind him.

''At 07:21 hours local time, an almost identical scenario occurred at Hickam Air Force Base in Hawaii. The base commander was killed instantly, other officers were isolated by the firepower employed by the terrorists and the attackers headed directly to a missile-storage site. Again they got away with fifteen functional missiles, including four vehicular launch units. That's after they launched one of the missiles on the spot.''

''Launched it at what?''

Kurtzman paled slightly. ''Four U.S. Air Force Cobra gunships were responding. They were minutes away from engaging the terrorists. The Patriot took down two Cobras, killing their crews. The third crashed without loss of life.''

Gary Manning, a barrel-chested Canadian, shook his head slowly. ''The implication is that these people went in with an extremely high degree of intelligence, not to mention support. Getting a large number of men inside an Air Force base with substantial explosives and weaponry isn't an easy task.''

"That's an understatement. Their intelligence was superb," Brognola admitted.

"They also knew where to find the cache of Patriots they were after, and when and how to strike to plunge the base into momentary chaos," Price said, ticking off the items on her fingers. "They knew how to not only bypass the safety protocols on the Patriots, but also how to target and fire them."

"Patriots are for ground-to-air support," Thomas Jackson "T. J." Hawkins observed. He was the youngest man in the room and a Phoenix Force commando who had proved himself in a number of missions. "These guys even know how to target them at motionless ground targets."

"Getting that far required help from the inside," Katzenelenbogen stated.

"But not necessarily high-level help," Kurtzman added. "They must have had false ID to get past the gates. Once inside all they needed to know was where the missiles were stored and what kind of resistance to anticipate. The Patriots weren't kept in a secret location. There must be hundreds of airmen at the bases who would know that information. Some grunt sold out."

"Even the ability to operate the missiles couldn't have been all that difficult to come by," Price said. "There have to be hundreds of U.S. military personnel trained to fire Patriots from ground-based launchers."

"At aircraft, yes, but not at nonstandard targets on the ground," Hermann "Gadgets" Schwarz argued.

"So who the hell is responsible?" Brognola demanded, his teeth grinding at the stub of an unlit cigar.

"That's still unknown," Kurtzman admitted.

"Not anymore, sir." The man in the doorway was a communications officer, charged with running the smaller auxiliary communications center in the farmhouse building. "They've just outed themselves, sir. Try CNN."

Kurtzman stabbed at the controls on the table. The twin images of the air bases were replaced with a full-screen image of a news anchor. Above her left shoulder appeared the words "Global Missile Crisis."

"The message was delivered to our office in Washington, D.C. just minutes ago, claiming responsibility for the twin attacks in Hawaii and in Turkey. The message is signed by Asad Cakmak, supreme general of the True Army of Kurdistan. Unfortunately, that is about all the message says. It makes no demands or further threats, although further violence is clearly implied...."

"Hunt, Carmen?" Kurtzman said.

"We're on it," Delahunt said as she pushed back her chair and headed for the door with Wethers.

"Meanwhile?"

Brognola looked meaningfully at Price. "We put Able in the field in Hawaii and Phoenix in Turkey."

"What do we have to go on?" the big Fed asked.

"Not much," the mission controller admitted. "But it'll take us hours to get on-site. By then I hope to have *something*."

Brognola nodded. "And Striker?"

"Mack's been out of contact for the last twelve hours," Price admitted. "Last we heard he was in Mexico City. We'll bring him in as soon as we hear from him, if he's willing."

Brognola nodded. He understood. He didn't like it, but he understood.

BROGNOLA AND Mack Bolan had a curious history together that stretched back years.

When he came back from his term of military service to attend the funeral of his mother, father and sister, Bolan was an Army sniper with a stellar record. But he ran amok, declaring a single-handed war on the Mafia, which he held responsible for wiping out his family. Brognola was the man from Justice who tracked the Executioner and, after innumerable battles, ran him down.

Bolan began working with and for Brognola, and the two men had a mutual respect for each other. But the Executioner was no longer an Army man accustomed to taking orders. He had come to obey one law only: his own moral code, which gave him plenty of leeway to commit the murders of those he saw as the slaughterers of the innocent.

He helped Brognola put together the commando complex known as Stony Man Farm, and it still served as his occasional base of operations. He made use of the facilities here, especially the vast realm of cybernetic intelligence under Kurtzman's jurisdiction. But Bolan distanced himself from the day-to-day operations. He chose his own missions, set his own agenda and he was the one person connected to the Farm who didn't—wouldn't—answer to Hal Brognola.

But Bolan never failed to come to the aid of the Farm when asked.

"We'll send Mack to Hawaii as backup to Able, unless another target presents itself," Price said.

Carl "Ironman" Lyons, Able Team leader, leaned on his elbows and clasped his hands. "Do we know the Patriots are still in Hawaii?"

Price grimaced. "Ironman, we don't know jack."

CHAPTER TWO

Island of Oahu, Hawaii

The wraith materialized out of the jungle. One moment the guard was alone; the next he was watching the bizarre predator shape disengage itself from the undergrowth and face him on two legs.

The apparition had darkness where his face should have been, as dark as the eye socket of a skull. He cocked his head and held a black-gloved finger to his unseen lips, ordering the guard to stay silent.

The spell broke, and the guard yanked at the M-16 with one hand while grabbing the radio from his belt with the other. A sound erupted from his mouth, but he never formed the words. He never targeted the weapon and he never activated the radio.

The wraith moved with preternatural speed. Out of nowhere a suppressed pistol appeared in his hands. Coughing three times in such rapid succession, it sounded like a quick stutter. The guard's sternum and rib cage were blasted to shrapnel by the machine-fired triburst of 9 mm Parabellum rounds. Before the sound of the shots reached him, the guard was dead on his feet and toppling to the ground.

Carl Lyons touched the side of his head.

"I heard that all the way over here, Ironman," came the voice of Rosario Blancanales through the helmet headset.

Lyons didn't answer immediately. He stood silent against the wall of fern and undergrowth at the edge of the jungle, listening for sounds of alarm. The Beretta 93-R he had just fired was fitted with a precision silencer, but there was nothing silent about it. The retort from such a firing was loud enough to travel for hundreds of feet over open terrain. Whether it would reach more guards in the vicinity was a big unknown. There was no reaction apparent—not yet.

"One down," he reported succinctly into the radio.

"Copy that, Able One," answered a woman with a voice of authority. "Position check."

"Able Two in position," Rosario Blancanales stated.

"Able Three in position," Hermann Schwarz reported.

"I'm set, Stony One," Lyons informed the woman.

"You call it, Able One," the woman said. Barbara Price, sitting in the Stony Man Farm command center half a world away, was Sensitive Operations Group's mission controller. She usually called the shots, but sometimes left decision-making to the leaders of her team. She didn't explain why she suddenly placed this judgment call in Lyons's lap. Maybe she had read hesitancy in the tone of his voice. If there was something bothering him, he should be the one to make the call.

For almost a minute nothing happened, no one spoke and the sensitive creatures of the jungle, which had grown still at the retort of the handgun, began making their noises again.

"Carl?" Price asked finally, concerned.

"I don't like this one, Stony," Lyons said. "Something's not right here."

Price didn't ask him for an explanation. He'd give her a better answer when he had one.

"Let's move in," Lyons stated. "Able One and Two, be extrasharp."

"Understood."

"Ten-four."

Lyons moved out of the jungle and into the trap.

DESPITE HIS BULL-LIKE build, the commando managed to move with the stealth that came of intense special-forces training, and he emerged from the Hawaiian rain forest with all the uproar of a panther stalking a gazelle. He watched the ground, littered with rusting metal and rubber parts among the knee-high grass, but at the same time he kept an eye on the scum-covered windows twenty feet above his head in the warehouse wall. Without a sound he reached the guard who leaned against the wall, smoking a cigarette while facing the other direction.

The man never knew what hit him. His head was suddenly cocked to one side, exposing his throat, and before he could croak in alarm there was an impact. When the edge of Blancanales's stiffened hand slammed into his exposed neck with the power of a crowbar, the guard went out. Blancanales sat him against the wall with his face on his knees. Maybe it would look as if he were taking a nap.

Blancanales's senses were tuned as tight as a guitar string. He'd heard the note of concern in Lyons's voice, and it had affected him, as well. He felt the same sense of disquiet.

This all seemed just a little too easy.

HERMANN SCHWARZ USED the butt of his Randall fighting knife. The crack of the guard's skull was as loud as a suppressed gunshot. The guard slithered down the tree trunk like an intoxicated serpent, but Schwarz grabbed him by the shoulders before he toppled to the side. It took seconds to yank the unconscious man's hands backward around the tree and secure the wrists with plastic handcuffs, nudging the fallen M-16 into the underbrush. Then Schwarz moved through the grass to the edge of the loading ramp. The weeds growing through the concrete were crushed, as if the ramp had been used for a delivery in recent hours. He walked across the narrow retaining wall, then jumped onto the ramp and placed his ear and one hand against the steel roll-up door. He heard and felt nothing. None of the hum that would come from the machinery of a functional warehouse, and no sound of human inhabitants.

He squeaked through the entrance door, which stood frozen open on rusty hinges, and crouched in the darkness to allow his eyes to accommodate the change in light before making his way across the loading bay. Assorted machinery dangled from the ceiling, and old junk was piled on the floor.

He paused to examine the floor, and spotted fresh scrape marks in the grime.

As he walked farther inside the loading bay, the ceiling suddenly gave way to the massive interior of the warehouse. It was filled with giant scaffoldlike shelving units, their feet anchored into the concrete floor, their top supports bolted into the black ceiling. They were empty, as were the aisles between them.

Logic told Schwarz that three men with U.S. military-issue assault rifles wouldn't protect an old building with nothing inside. Something had to be here.

He saw movement, but he had expected it. A hundred yards across the darkness, entering through the front door, was Rosario Blancanales.

The commandos stared at each other across the vastness of the warehouse for a moment. They didn't even need the radio to communicate their thoughts to one another. *What the hell was going on around here?*

Then Schwarz caught a glimmer of red light out of the corner of his eye. He followed it to a tiny control box mounted to the wall—electronics. Battery powered, obviously. The readouts were just numbers. Could be anything, he thought as his gaze followed the electronic cabling that went from the box, up along the wall into the darkness forty feet above him.

There was something wrong with the ceiling. For some reason, Schwarz had a flashback to a visit with an old girlfriend to the Smithsonian, where they'd seen a stuffed gray whale suspended from the ceiling. Schwarz had been more interested at the time in how they suspended the whale than in the creature itself.

Then the memory was gone and he recognized what he was seeing.

It wasn't a dead whale, but it looked almost as big.

"Holy crap."

"Whatcha got, Gadgets?" Blancanales asked quietly over the radio.

Before he could answer, the walls started opening up.

"SOUTH WALL!" Lyons stated succinctly from his perch. He'd gone in through a side door and made his way up to the warehouse office, with a balcony, some eighteen feet above the floor of the storage area. He landed in a crouch on the balcony, placing the business end of his M-16 A-2 on the tubular safety rail with a clink of metal.

The lights came on brilliantly, and he saw Blancanales and Schwarz retreating suddenly, blinded, as figures emerged from a bank of cabinets.

Lyons squinted hard, but he'd entered the building last and hadn't fully accustomed his vision to the gloom. It was lucky he'd been able to notice the movement when it happened. Those gunners had been staged in the cabinets, waiting there, in ambush.

The Able Team leader would consider the implications later. The gunmen rushed out of their hiding places, splitting into teams. Schwarz was in the most immediate danger, and Lyons triggered a long burst of automatic fire that brought Schwarz's attackers to a halt. One had been tagged and fell to the ground, unmoving, while the rest looked around wildly, confused by the sounds of rounds ricocheting off the equipment.

When they spotted him, Lyons triggered again, cutting into two more of the gunners before they took flight and evaded his fire. The Able Team leader spun to send another sustained burst into the more distant team of hardmen chasing down Blancanales. He managed to slap a pair of them to the floor before the others realized they were under attack from behind. Lyons counted them as they scrambled for cover behind a crane operator's podium: three remained standing. If they stayed put for another few seconds, he could plant a grenade at their feet and Blancanales would be out of danger.

The impact of the first bullet hurtled him to the floor of the balcony, and more rounds sizzled in the air above his head, in the spot he had been kneeling.

As soon as his pursuers were sent clambering away by Lyons's shots, Schwarz went on the offensive, racing at the enemy with a shout that took them off guard. The survivors saw him coming while they were still trying to take cover from the sniper, but their reaction time wasn't shabby. One of the hardmen triggered his assault rifle first, trying to swing an arc of flying lead across Schwarz's path, but the Able Team commando fired a precise burst on the run, ripping the gunner's chest open. A stray round found his neighbor, who grunted in surprise at the bloody blossom on the ball of a muscular shoulder. He recovered from the wound, but not soon enough. As he brought his weapon into play again, Schwarz already had him targeted, and a short burst tore open his gut.

The survivor had achieved his status through luck and cowardice more than skill and daring, and as he witnessed the fall of his last companion he turned and ran, heading the way Schwarz had entered, into the loading bay. Schwarz was after him, but the runner was too fast.

By the time Schwarz reached the door, the man was crashing away through the rain forest, his M-16 discarded on the grass.

BLANCANALES HAD BEEN the first to enter the warehouse, and his eyes weren't yet accustomed to the new brightness when the quartet of gunners responded to a yell from the balcony by exiting from their cover. "*That* guy!" someone shouted from above.

That guy was him. Blancanales let loose a wild, sweeping burst at the shout and retreated. He made it into a hallway, then a couple more paces took him to a dingy entrance vestibule with boarded-up windows. The gunners hadn't thought to include this when they wired their lights. Blancanales was once again able to see clearly.

What was even better was that when the gunners pursued him into the darkness, the tables had been turned. Now they were unable to see. Blancanales cut the forerunners across the chest before they even knew he was there, then, as the final pair retreated from his blast, he kicked open the door to the outside and fell against the wall.

There was a scramble at the end of the hallway, then a hushed discussion.

"He ran away."

"We gotta get him!"

"You want to go looking for him in the woods, man?"

"We gotta!"

There was a sign of exasperation. "Come on."

The pair advanced into the hall, then into the vestibule, and it seemed to occur to both of them at the same instant that they had walked into a trap. They whirled on Blancanales at the same instant. He was already firing, cutting their legs out from under them.

LYONS USED three or four torturous seconds assessing the damage. Had the bullet impacted his flesh? No. It hit Kevlar. No open wounds. But he'd have a bruise, and he couldn't be sure he'd get hundred percent capability out of his right arm. The man who shot him was coming out of the office, where he been waiting in hiding for the Able Team probe.

Lyons twisted onto his back, transferred the M-16 to his left hand and drew a figure eight of continuous fire in the air above him. The weapon cycled empty, but the desired result was achieved. The man was a corpse.

Lyons pushed himself to his feet.

"Status?" he asked.

"This is Able Two. I think we're clear."

"Able Three here. The immediate threat is gone—"

The warehouse was suddenly overwhelmingly quiet. Lyons winced as the throbbing pain in his shoulder took on a life of its own, and he descended the stairs to find Blancanales crossing toward him anxiously.

"Hit?"

"Not bad."

"Explain 'immediate threat,' Able Three," Price said. It was the first time she had spoken since the probe began. She knew when not to be a distraction.

Ignoring the corpses around him, Schwarz stared at a box of electronics on the wall that had been holding his attention when the shooting started. Several flashing LEDs told them the electronics were doing something.

Schwarz glanced meaningfully at the ceiling. Blancanales and Lyons followed his gaze and stared in shock at the monstrous device dangling on the crane forty feet above their heads.

"Stony One, this is Able Three," Schwarz said. "We have a PAC-3, wired to blow."

"Repeat that, Gadgets."

"It's a damned Patriot missile, Stony. They've patched into the on-board CPU and monkey rigged it like a time bomb."

Blancanales craned his head at the missile, wrapped in steel chains and dangling from the ceiling-mounted warehouse crane. It was 520 centimeters long, forty centimeters in diameter, with four delta-shaped fins at the base. A small panel on the warhead had been removed, and a trail of wires dangled out and snaked down the wall to the control electronics.

"If it's wired like a time bomb," Lyons asked in a low voice, "how much time until it blows?"

"My question exactly, Able Three," Price demanded.

Schwarz didn't answer at once. Using his fighting knife and a steady hand, he sliced into the soft, semi-translucent plastic covering on the electronics and peeled it away with a yank. Under the plastic was another display—the countdown timer, which had been hidden from view.

It read 00:00:14.

"Time to go," Schwarz said.

"THE RAVINE!" Lyons shouted.

"What's going on?" Price demanded.

The three of them slammed through the side entrance one after another.

"Not enough protection!" Schwarz retorted. He pictured the ravine they traversed in the rain forest during their approach to the warehouse grounds, and in his memory it was no more than a shallow crease in the jungle floor.

"Got any better ideas?" Lyons demanded as they crashed into the Hawaiian rain forest.

"The ravine will work!" Blancanales insisted. Somehow, automatically, the countdown was continuing in his head, and he added, "We have seven seconds."

"How far was it?" Schwarz demanded.

"Not far!" Lyons said.

"Report, Able One," Price commanded.

"Three seconds!" Blancanales warned.

"Here!" Lyons said as he descended into the forest ravine. "Hit the deck!"

They flattened among the rocky streambed. Their mission controller had suddenly gone silent. The rain forest was eerily still. For a fraction of a second, Schwarz thought he could hear, like a whisper, the sound of the surf on the beach thirteen miles away.

Then the jungle cracked open like a new volcano god being born.

CHAPTER THREE

Island of Oahu, Hawaii

"Able One, I'd love a report," Price said in his headset. Carl Lyons raised his head and saw that the warehouse was obliterated, as if it had never existed. There was a crater in the earth where it once had stood, and the concrete foundation had been transformed to powder during the explosion and blown in every direction. The building had literally been wiped off the face of the earth.

Much of the jungle had been, too. The blast and the scouring, high-velocity remains of the warehouse had flattened trees for a hundred yards. The air was still filled with the fluttering green confetti of plant life that was tossed in the buffeting breeze.

Lyons's teammates rose slowly to their knees and pushed themselves to their feet. "You guys live through that?" Lyons asked.

"Not sure yet," Schwarz asked, hands on his knees and swaying slightly.

Blancanales shook off the shock more easily. "Looks like an Amazon clear-cut," he muttered.

"Able?" Price said, her voice edged with impatience.

"Sorry, Stony. Able One here," Lyons said. "The warehouse just blew up in a big, big way."

"Everybody survived it, I take it?"

"Just barely. We were lucky. We got out and into cover, such as it was, before the place went up."

"Was it the Patriot?"

"Affirmative," Lyons said.

"Negative," Schwarz insinuated. "I mean, the Patriot started it all. But that blast was more than just ninety pounds of high explosive."

"Explain, Able Three."

"We've got a crater here, Stony. Maybe five feet deep in the center, blasted through the concrete floor of the warehouse, end to end, maybe two hundred feet. The Patriot had been suspended off the floor. It wouldn't have created that blast pattern without a lot of help."

As they paced back in the direction of the ruin, Blancanales nodded. "You're right, Gadgets. Look at the shape of this thing."

Blancanales stepped into the depressions that had once been the middle of the warehouse floor. Now they could see there was two more craters in the depression at either end. "I'd say three explosions occurred here, all at one time so we couldn't make them out."

"Three Patriots?" Price suggested.

"Maybe," Schwarz said.

"You sound doubtful," Lyons stated.

"We didn't see them. If there were other Patriots in the warehouse, where were they?" Schwarz asked. "Why weren't they hung up with the one we saw? They had to be buried or hidden under the floor or on the roof, and that doesn't make sense."

"I saw steel access panels on the warehouse floor,"

Lyons told them. "Not long enough to hold the entire missile but big enough for the warheads."

"I don't think so," Schwarz said. "I think that may be where the other explosives were, but they weren't from other Patriots. If you want to know my theory, we were meant to find this place. This was a setup. Whoever took the Patriots led us here, put up just enough manpower to make the place look heavily guarded and even watched to make sure that we got inside. Then the timing mechanism was started. Maybe they gave us one minute, maybe two. Long enough for us to report finding one of the Patriot missiles. When the place blows up, we go with it, along with most of the evidence. The force of the explosion is so large it could have been all the stolen missiles. The conclusion by the outside world—the Hawaii missiles are no longer a threat."

"The truth would be uncovered," Blancanales argued. "The Air Force will come in and sift through the rubble. They'll figure out all the missiles weren't here, and they'll identify it if a different type of explosives was used."

"Our bad guys don't need a permanent fix," Schwarz said. "All they need is a little time. Long enough for them to get them out of the Islands."

"That was an expensive purchase," Lyons said. "They sacrificed some of their own men."

"You had better bet those guys had no clue they were scheduled for termination by explosion even before we showed up," Schwarz stated.

Lyons said, "If you're right, Gadgets, then the people who did this think they succeeded. They think they've bought the time they needed to get the missiles out of Hawaii."

"So maybe they'll be careless," Price finished the thought. "And we'll be there when they slip up."

"Which will be where, exactly?" Blancanales asked.

*Pacific Ocean, North-Northwest
of Mendocino, California*

THE PILOT LOOKED up and grinned.

"Didn't you and I drink Cuervo in a Mendocino bar one time, Gadgets?"

Schwarz nodded. "I vaguely recall something like that. Gives me a headache just remembering it. What's our ETA, Jack?"

"Mendocino in thirty minutes," said Grimaldi. The Stony Man pilot had dark, close-cropped hair and dark eyes under bushy eyebrows. He wasn't a short man, but his slim build made him look boyishly small, especially when he wasn't standing. There was nothing immature about his skills. Jack Grimaldi could fly any vehicle made by man—everything from eighty-year-old antique biplanes to a space shuttle. As ace pilot for Stony Man Farm, he had plenty of opportunity to try various aircraft. Right now he was at the helm of an Airbus Industrie A300-600.

"If you're in a hurry, I can get you there in twenty," Grimaldi added, growing a mischievous grin.

"I'll let you know," Schwarz said.

Schwarz returned to his seat in the passenger cabin of the transport jet, where Lyons and Blancanales were sitting at an oblong table that jutted from one side of the cabin wall. The thin monitor on the wall showed a Secure Transmission notice at the bottom.

"Everybody online?" asked Barbara Price.

"Able's all here," Lyons reported.

"I'm hearing you," said Grimaldi's voice over the speaker.

"I'm on, Barb," Aaron Kurtzman added.

"Okay. I'll start," Price said. "First the back story on the group known as the True Army Of Kurdistan.

"You all know the demands of the Kurdistanis. They're a Middle East ethnic group who want their own nation, made up of traditionally Kurdish-inhabited lands in Iran, Iraq, Syria and mostly Turkey. Naturally, those nations have no interest in surrendering the real estate. Thus the conflict. There have been fervent anti-Kurdish measures taken over the years—the most extreme by Saddam Hussein. He used chemical weapons on thousands of Kurdish citizens of northern Iraq prior to Operation Desert Storm, and he's never stopped tormenting them. In Turkey, violent clashes between the Kurds and the Muslims have erupted regularly for years.

"The Turkish People's Liberation Army of Kurdistan, or ARGK, was the armed wing of Kurdistan Labor Party, or PKK. The ARGK agreed to a cease-fire in 1999 that essentially put itself out of business, much to the dismay of some of its more fervent members. They went on to form their own violent pro-Kurdistan movements, one of which was the True Army of Kurdistan, known to English-speaking supporters as TAK, headed by a terrorist named Asad Cakmak."

"Terrorist?" Blancanales asked.

"I don't use that term lightly. Terrorism has been the stated aim of TAK since its beginning, and every act attributed to TAK has been violent and often targeted at innocent people or political targets. Often the targets are just everyday Turkish citizens. As you might guess, Cakmak's goal is the formation of the state of Kurdistan at all costs.''

"Can you be more specific about the activities TAK has been involved in?'' Blancanales asked.

"Restaurant and mosque bombs, mostly. Threats against all kinds of Turkish and visiting government officials, although they've never gotten close to anybody high profile.''

"They don't sound like major players,'' Blancanales suggested.

"They've also never been caught, despite significant taunting of the police and military in Turkey. They're a vocal group, the kind of guys the government would like very much to shut up,'' Price explained. "But not one of them has been imprisoned in the past eighteen months. They've demonstrated a high degree of training and some highly intelligent planning. That can all be attributed to Cakmak. It's thought that he went underground for three years and trained with groups in Afghanistan and Algeria, maybe even Hamas. There are unsubstantiated stories of Cakmak using his newly honed terrorist and military skills to murder fourteen of his teachers and fellow Muslim classmates at the conclusion of a training session at a Saharan camp.''

"So he's good,'' Blancanales said. "But what's changed about him?''

"What do you mean, Pol?'' Lyons asked. Blancanales was known as "Politician'' to his friends for his understanding of the human animal and his ability to say the right thing to bring people around to his point of view. "Politician'' was a mouthful, so it was usually shortened to "Pol.''

"I mean, he's been in Turkey using small-time measures to get attention for himself. Nothing large scale.

All of a sudden he's gone big time. After his raids in Hickam and Incirlik, we're talking about a terrorist superpower. How did he make that jump? He must have a network of intelligence and a lot of funding to do what he's doing now.''

"You're right," Aaron Kurtzman chimed in. "There was a radical shift in the personality of the True Army of Kurdistan in recent months, although it went unnoticed. The petty terrorism halted and big-time training efforts were under way. Military training consultants were called in from around the world to hone TAK soldiers. This was all suspected by various international intelligence agencies. In hindsight somebody should have known something was up."

"The other question remains—who's bankrolling TAK?" Price asked.

There was a moment of silence, and Blancanales could almost picture Kurtzman grimacing and shrugging. "We're working on it," he said with genuine regret in his voice.

If there was one thing Kurtzman hated, it was not having the answers.

"So what's in Mendocino?" Lyons asked, eager to get back to what was known.

"That I can tell you about. It is a very curious fishing boat called the *First Fathom*," Kurtzman said, and the flat screen on the wall of the cabin showed a photograph of a dingy, rugged-looking fishing boat tied to a concrete pier.

"The *First Fathom* looks like a run-of-the-mill fishing vessel. She's fifteen years old and until recently did good business supplying fresh-seafood wholesalers in northern California," Kurtzman explained. "She was purchased by parties unknown three months ago and outfitted with new motors and electronics.''

"Why?" Lyons asked.

"Good question, considering she's been tied to the pier since the refit was completed. That's the report we get from the local police. But she made a strange run last night.''

The photo of the fishing trawler disappeared and was replaced by a computer-generated image of the Pacific Ocean between Hawaii and the California coast. A small blue line started moving away from the Islands as the time-lapse monitor showed the passage of an hour every ten seconds.

"We don't know what aircraft this is," Kurtzman said. "As you can imagine, we've been keeping a pretty close watch on all air and water traffic out of the Islands for the past twenty-four hours. So has the FBI, Air Force and just about any other agency. But this is the only aircraft that wasn't identified. It called itself in as a single-engine water-landing pleasure craft.''

"It's beyond the range of aircraft like that," Lyons noted.

"Yes. A little trickery went into this one. There actually was a small, single-engine aircraft taking off from a private Oahu airfield. At some point another aircraft with much better range literally took off underneath it, so close that radar couldn't distinguish the separate aircraft. That's what we're guessing, anyway," Kurtzman said.

"So what happened to the small single-engine plane?" Blancanales asked. "Did they just ditch it in the ocean?''

"A pretty good ruse," Kurtzman said.

"An expensive one.''

"Not as expensive as the next step in the plan. Now watch. The red line is our fishing boat, *First Fathom.*"

As they watched the computer animation, the blue line stopped suddenly in the ocean off the California coast on top of the intersecting line with the fishing boat. The *First Fathom* turned and headed directly back to Mendocino.

"They drop the launchers on pontoons to keep them floating, then pull them onto the *First Fathom.*"

"Then dump the transport plane, too?" Blancanales asked.

"Why not?" Price asked. "It's too hot to stick with. Factor in the cost of a couple of aircraft, and it's still a pretty cheap price to pay for a boatload of eight Patriot missiles."

The three members of Able Team watched grimly as the slower-moving blue dots that signified the path of the *First Fathom* touched the shore. The time register told them it had occurred almost one hour ago.

"The *First Fathom* docked already. There's nobody but locals in the immediate area. They're tourist-town cops. Good at their job but unprepared for an army of terrorists," Price said.

"So it's just the three of us. We can handle it," Lyons said without the slightest hesitation.

"Make that four," Price said. "Striker is already minding the store."

Mendocino, California

MACK BOLAN MOVED along the wharf as if he belonged there. In dirty jeans and a greasy red sweatshirt, he looked as if he could have stepped off any of the fishing vessels. He moved fast, his eyes scanning the wharf for signs of furious activity that had to be the hallmark of the vessel he was looking for.

He had a feeling he was already too late.

A minute ago, as he parked on the city street and made his way onto the wharf, he saw a couple of semi trucks rumble out and head in opposite directions. They could have been transporting just about anything. Including the Patriot missile launchers.

Another pair of trucks was waiting on the wharf ahead, and he recognized the profile of the *First Fathom.* One of the trucks pulled out and quickly accelerated away from him, toward the other exit. Bolan evaluated his chances of catching up to the truck and knew they weren't good.

He would have to leave it for later.

Right now he needed to get close enough to be certain that the cargo going onto those semi trucks was what he thought it was, and get some answers from the men in charge of loading them.

The soldiers watched from around the corner as a steel shipping container the size of a city bus rose on a crane from the bowels of the *First Fathom* and hung in the air as if defying gravity. The container was unmarked. Bolan moved in closer, watching the bed of the truck sink under the weight of the steel box, and as soon as it was in place the workmen rushed to clamp it down securely.

"Hey, buddy!" shouted the guy who had waved in the load. "What do you think you're doing here?"

"I'm supposed to be working this job," Bolan said. "Frank said to show up here."

"I don't think so."

"Yeah, yeah, Frank gave me the job."

"There ain't no Frank here and this ain't the job you're looking for. Beat it."

"This is the place, I'm sure of it."

"Listen, asshole—"

Bolan grabbed the guy as he came in close, twisting his arm up hard behind his back, in the same movement lifting the handgun out of the other guy's underarm holster and allowing it to fall to the pavement. The man shouted as his arm bent well beyond its limits. In the moment it took for the others to react with their own shouts of surprise, the Executioner drew the .44 Magnum Desert Eagle, leveled the big handgun at the truck and triggered it four times as the workmen fled in a panic. The truck descended as several tires abruptly deflated.

This truck, at least, wasn't going anywhere.

"Son of a bitch!" the big foreman shouted as he tried to duck away from the shooter. Recovering some of his wits, he lashed out at his adversary's shin with his heavy boot. Bolan let go of the foreman's wrist and hooked the foot with his own and pulled it into the air, sending the foreman collapsing heavily on his face with a grunt.

Bolan didn't wait for the man to recover. His peripheral vision had spotted the familiar outlines of automatic weapons coming into play aboard the *First Fathom.* He put down a suppressing fire from the Desert Eagle that slammed through the glass of the deckhouse and chopped at a wooden deck railing as he put the front end of the semi between himself and the shooters.

A burst of autofire pinged into the steel sides of the crate. Bolan waited them out, listening to the fleeing footsteps of the dock workers. Let them go. Maybe they were in on the deal, or maybe they were innocent hired help. Better to let them get free than involve them without knowing their status. He made use of the time, reloading the magazine in the Desert Eagle, then holstering it and dragging the canvas knapsack off his shoulder and

withdrawing the Heckler & Koch MP-5/10A3 submachine gun.

He slapped home the straight 30-round magazine as
he made his way in quick bolts toward the rear of the
truck, using the wheels to keep his legs protected from
the gunners on the fishing vessel. He looked for a gap
in the steel panels of the crate, trying to get a glimpse
of the contents, and found none. It didn't matter. He
harbored no doubts about what was inside.

He had one job now: get all the intelligence he could
about the destination of those trucks. If he was only
wired to the Farm at the moment, he might have had
them call in tails on the trucks, but he had gone into the
field on his own business weeks before, and much of his
communications gear had been rendered useless during
an especially brutal altercation with a handful of Mexican drug lords a few days earlier.

They were death merchants who manufactured meth-
amphetamines in the deserts of central Mexico, then
wholesaled and distributed them from a ceramics store
near a pair of old churches in the small, picturesque town
of San Luis Potosi. From there the meth made its way
into the hands of people throughout northern Mexico and
the U.S. West Coast and Southwest. Bolan had personally witnessed meth being sold in small packets to gram-
mar school children in a soccer park in Monterrey, Mexico. That distributor was now out of business.

But the manufacturing was continuing, and Bolan's
black notebook contained the name Manuel Santoso, the
mastermind behind the Mexican meth manufacturing.

Manny the Meth Maker would have to wait. Bolan
had answered a call from Barbara Price, asking him to
come to the assistance of Stony Man Farm. When he

was told the story of the Patriot missile thefts Bolan was uncharacteristically surprised.

"I guess the Air Force has holes in its security," he growled.

"To say the least," Price agreed. "Now it's up to us to clean it up."

He spoke to her again hours later, during his Mexicana flight from Monterrey, Mexico, to San Francisco and while he was in the car headed up the coast. She had sent him on an intercept with the aircraft that was being traced from Hawaii to California. She told him it had disappeared after a flyover with a Mendocino-based fishing vessel named *First Fathom*. He headed for Mendocino.

Too late.

The Patriots were distributed.

If they didn't stop those trucks soon, they'd slip through the net. They could end up anywhere in the U.S., and they could threaten anyone in the U.S. who was a passenger on virtually any aircraft, not to mention anyone on whom the bombed aircraft might fall on. Who knew whom TAK would target?

Bolan didn't have to consider the implications or the morality of his actions. Terrorists who threatened the innocent people of the world, no matter how noble their political aims, were no better than Manny the Meth Maker, who profited on the ruined lives of schoolchildren.

They were all targets for the Executioner.

Now there were new names in the black leather notebook he called his War Book: Asad Cakmak, and the True Army of Kurdistan.

All he had to do was find them.

Bolan stepped out from behind the crippled semi truck

and squeezed the trigger on the MP-5/10A3 as the gunners on the boat reacted to his bold appearance with surprise. The 10 mm rounds crashed through their flesh and bone with uncompromising power, dropping the first two gunners where they stood and sending the third to the deck with a shout.

The foreman was crab-walking for cover and Bolan fired a short burst that kicked asphalt in his face, sending him to ground with his hands over his head, then the warrior triggered a burst at the fishing boat. The gunner was jumping up for a shot, but he was dead before he knew it, the 10 mm round piercing his face and brain. His Kalashnikov rifle clattered to the deck.

Bolan used the momentary silence to drag plastic handcuffs around the wrists of the petrified foreman, then strode up the gangplank onto the boat, convinced there were more players on hand. The heavy cargo work performed by this group in the past several hours took substantial manpower. When he stepped on the deck he saw nothing except bodies. Just a cursory glance at each of them was enough to convince the Executioner that all three gunners were dead.

The MP-5/10A3's 10 mm round had almost twice the projectile energy of the 9 mm version, which was commonly used by the Navy SEALs and antiterrorists groups worldwide. Bolan himself had used the 9 mm version a time or three.

Bolan crept to the lip of the cargo opening, and almost reeled from the stench of rotting fish parts, but the hold was empty. No fish. No missiles. But there was a scrape of movement. Somebody was down there, trying to stay out of sight.

The Executioner drew back and stepped briskly for the deckhouse, where he found a ladder. Two steps up revealed that the deckhouse was empty. He grabbed the phone off the brushed aluminum control panel and punched in a number that connected him via a series of cutouts to Stony Man Farm. In seconds he reached the communications center in the Annex and was patched through to Barbara Price.

"I'm on-site," he said in a low voice, "aboard the *First Fathom,* along with an unknown number of crew. How long until Able's arrival?"

"Sorry, Mack, it's going to be another twenty minutes at least," Price said. "The only support I've got to offer is the local PD."

"That's worse than nothing," Bolan answered. "I'm sure they're quite capable, but they don't have the firepower to compete with these terrorists." Then he paused. "They're on their way anyway."

"We didn't call them," Price started to say.

"My problem. I've been raising a racket since I arrived. A local citizen must have called in a disturbance of the peace." Bolan scanned the controls in front of him, then said, "I'm getting out of here."

Price said nothing at first. She quite simply didn't believe what she had just heard.

"Repeat that, Striker?"

"I'm getting out of here. Out of the harbor. All of us are."

Now Price understood. Mack Bolan wasn't leaving the job unfinished; he was taking the job with him. He reached to the control panel and fired up the fishing trawler's diesel engines.

CHAPTER FOUR

Massoud Gozeh looked over his men in confusion. All were accounted for. One of the gunners he had thought was killed on the open deck had to still be alive. But why was he starting the ship?

What the hell was going on around here, anyway? How had they been targeted so quickly upon landing on North American soil?

The only thing he knew for certain was that the operation had attracted major attention. Cakmak's order to get in and out absolutely unnoticed hadn't been obeyed. Gozeh was going to pay for that error.

What was worse was that one of the trucks was stuck on the wharf. With several flat tires, it wasn't going anywhere soon. Which meant it would be opened up, its contents revealed.

He tried to look at the bright side. Three of the trucks had managed to get away before the U.S. forces retaliated.

It occurred to him that it had to be the American attackers who had started the ship. For what reason?

He cursed the blank monitor. In his command center, deep in the bowels of the ship near the engine room, his series of monitors had been watching every step of the operation from cameras mounted in the deckhouse, at several points along the deck and in the cargo hold. But the system had gone off-line when shooting from the wharf slammed through the deckhouse windows, and now the only image he was still getting was from the cargo hold. The one monitor he didn't need. He was too damned dependent on all this equipment!

He still had seven men down here. How many military types would the U.S. have on deck and on the wharf? What were the odds that they could repel the Americans and make their escape?

Gunfire! Now what in the name of God were the Americans shooting at?

Then he felt the shifting of the boat beneath his feet, and he knew.

BOLAN SCRAMBLED OUT the window and dragged himself onto the roof of the deckhouse, where he raised the MP-5/10A3 and triggered off seven rounds that chewed into thick line that stretched between the gunwale and the wharf. The rounds ate into it ineffectualy, chewing at the fat rope like blunt teeth worrying a strand of yarn, but then the weight of the trawler leaned against it, tightening the slack, and the frayed rope tore and parted with a lurch. The trawler's bow began to drift away from the concrete wall of the wharf. Bolan turned to the stern, where the aft line was closer and now strained taut. When the 10 mm rounds chomped at the rope, it parted quickly and the vessel drifted away from shore.

Bolan dropped the MP-5/10A3 on its nylon shoulder rig and stepped quickly down to the window, swinging into the deckhouse. He shoved hard on the throttle control. The high-powered engines belowdeck rumbled to higher revolutions and the air filled with the smell of diesel as the water churned as the *First Fathom* moved away from Mendocino.

The soldier didn't wait long. He knew the players belowdeck would be coming up to investigate any moment. But he kept his eye on the shore, until he was sure the vessel was distant enough from the wharf to make returning to dry land an inconvenient swim. He radioed Stony Man, then dropped the phone with the connection still open.

With the stock of the MP-5/10A3 in the closed position the weapon was a stubby twenty-two inches in length, so Bolan could tuck it comfortably into his shoulder while he swept a room. In his other hand he grabbed his second handgun, the Beretta 93-R, which he wielded equally well left-handed or right. Thus armed he was a walking one-man army.

He stepped down the ladder into the belly of the *First Fathom*, in search of the terrorists. He found himself in a corridor just three paces long. The engines throbbed behind the door in back of him, which meant ahead lay the crew bunk rooms, the galley and access to the cargo hold.

Bolan knew he was one man against any number of killers. He'd faced huge and indeterminate odds in the past, and had survived through a combination of skill, brains and instinct. Right now he wanted to clear out the room behind him before he moved on, and he crouched before springing through the engine-room door and rolling like a ball of tumbleweed that came to a sudden stop against a rusted steel girder serving as an engine support. His eyes scanned the shadows created by a single overhead bright bulb. It took him seconds to satisfy himself that the room was empty, and then he heard voices coming from down the hall. Bolan eased the door closed in a hurry.

He waited with the patience of a trapdoor spider.

"I'm not going up there alone!" an American-accented voice protested.

"He's gone, I know it!" another said in an accent that was clearly Middle Eastern, but strangely difficult for Bolan to place, even with his vast experience interacting with the world's cultures. He assumed it was Kurdish. He'd know soon, but he waited still, hoping for better indication of the number of gunners outside his hole.

"Then you go up," the American argued.

There was an exasperated heave. "Farhad, go with him! Bulut, check out the engine room."

Bulut depressed the comma-shaped aluminum latch to the engine-room door and opened it, looked into the darkness, then stepped inside. Bolan grabbed him from behind the wall and hauled him in with intense pressure applied to his trachea, crushing it closed, and nudging the door shut with his foot as he manhandled his victim bodily into the huge cast-steel block of the engine. The impact of his head on the engine was a death blow.

The seconds of waiting were over—Bolan wasn't going to listen at the door again to find out if he had been noticed. He snatched the door open, swinging the submachine gun into play as he did so. Two men were in the narrow hallway, one just an arm's length away, and Bolan triggered a pair of 10 mm rounds into his chest before the man could do more than grunt in wild-eyed protest. The rounds slammed through him and splashed blood on the man behind him, who possessed the presence of mind to throw himself to the wall and slip through a doorway as his lifeless companion dropped.

Bolan turned his attention up the ladder, where a pair

of legs now scrambled to get up and out. The climber was too slow, and the MP-5/10A3 drilled a deadly pair of 10 mm high-energy rounds through the back of his upper legs, ripping through his thighs, pulverizing the bone. The climber dropped hard.

The Executioner stepped between the ruined legs of the body to sight up the porthole and was ready when a man leaned into view with his AK aimed down. Bolan fired first, then stepped out of the way as another corpse wriggled through the ladder opening and flopped to the deck.

The sudden quiet lasted for no longer than a three-count, ending when the occupant of the nearest room opened the door and unloaded a full magazine of 7.62 mm rounds. Bolan waited out the fire, heard the magazine cycle empty, then returned fire into the darkness. He was probably wasting rounds and stopped after a triburst. There was a shout from inside, but it was panic, not pain.

"Help me! He's got me trapped in here!"

Help could come from one direction only—the cargo hold. When the door at the end of the hall banged open, the warrior laid down a cover fire for himself as he retreated over the bloody corpses into the engine room again.

As he leaned against the wall, he was getting frustrated at being stuck in this section of the boat's insides. Time to fight his way free.

When he guessed the timing was right, he fired through the passageway at the dark square of a door at the other end. There was a squawk and a thump in the cargo hold, but more autofire followed immediately. Bolan watched it rip up the walls.

He sensed the changing aspect of the fire, broadcasting the hidden movement of one of the gunners. Bolan pulled back. The autofire tore through the open door where he had been standing and clanked against the steel mass of the diesel engine, which took it in stride, never changing its heavy thrum.

"Coming to my right!" the Kurd leader shouted.

Bolan moved as he heard the ruined door swing open and the man slipped out, hugging the wall to his right as a gunner aimed carefully past him and triggered at the warrior, who reacted to the immediate threat first, dodging the first round with a sharpshooter's instinct before it was fired. Then he placed the cold, unused 93-R across his right wrist and triggered a single round that took the gunner in the chin. The round forced his head to nod forward in a strange, grotesque salute before it continued into his neck and dropped him to the deck, where he thrashed for air that would never again enter his lungs. By then the Kurd leader had dived into the darkness of the cargo hold.

A standoff. Bolan's enemies were stuck in one room. He was trapped in another. He still was clueless as to their numbers, and he wondered if some of them were already making their escape by climbing the bulkhead-mounted rungs out of the cargo hold.

But even if they reached the upper deck, they'd be trapped. They were by now a good half mile out into the Pacific Ocean. They'd have to be confident swimmers to risk escaping overboard.

Even as he considered this he heard shouts from through the door and above. Some of them were up and out already, and he heard the word *overboard*. He hadn't counted on the terrorists' careful planning, and he realized that even now they were bringing escape boats out of their top-deck storage.

If these men got away, then Stony Man got no intelligence on the destination of the Patriots.

If those missiles were fired at carefully chosen civilian targets, hundreds of innocent Americans would die.

That was simply unacceptable to Mack Bolan, and he stepped into harm's way without further consideration of the consequences. He leaped over the corpses and sprinted through the door into the cargo hold, turning as he did to find the gunners and discovering none on the deck. Four were scrambling up the rungs to the upper deck, and a pair of guards with AKs watched from above. They raised their weapons when Bolan appeared in their line of sight, but he took out one with a quick burst from the MP-5/10A3 and halted at the bottom of the ladder. The second gunner held his fire for fear of hitting his comrades, and the pause was long enough for Bolan to get off a shot. But the guard retreated, disappearing beyond the lip of the cargo hold.

Then Bolan aimed the weapon almost straight up. The men scrambling up the rungs were in a panic, shouting and defenseless. When the warrior triggered a pair of rounds from the submachine gun, they punched into the buttocks of the man at the top of the ladder, even as he was clawing his way out. He screamed then plummeted, crashing into the man below him before swinging into open space and flying end over end. He hit the deck with a sickening crunch, while the second man grabbed at the third as he fell, taking both of them down in a twisting mass of limbs and weaponry that slammed into the rust-covered deck.

The bottom man on the ladder was unscathed. He looked at Bolan, who shook his head. The man stepped down to the deck and raised his hands.

Bolan's eyes did double duty, monitoring the deck

above for a sign of more gunners as he disarmed his prisoner and cuffed his wrists around one of the rungs. He heard the shouts of activity, then the voice of the Kurd leader, speaking English for the benefit of his American mercenaries.

"Who's still down there?"

Somebody shouted out a bunch of names in rapid succession, then he heard the Kurd again. He didn't know the language the man used, but something alerted Bolan and he watched the square of sky twenty feet above his head with hawk eyes that missed nothing. Something was happening.

The tiny dark spot appeared, wobbling in the square of sky as it traversed its arc and descended into the cargo hold.

Bolan was running already, and he flew into the passageway and dived, slamming into the deck with nothing protecting him from the projectiles of the fragmentation grenade except the pair of corpses. When the blast came, it was powerful. There was a strange metallic ring as the walls of the hold absorbed the bulk of the impact of the shrapnel.

Bolan felt a sudden chord of pain from his back and he tried to count the cuts—three or four, at least, but the target he had presented had been small, and the pieces had sped over the tops of the dead men and skidded along his flesh instead of burrowing into it. The cuts were long, but shallow.

His prisoners in the cargo hold had been sacrificed.

In the ringing aftermath Bolan heard a splash, far away, and receding voices.

He mounted the ladder and emerged cautiously on the upper deck, then followed the thrum of outboard motors.

A pair of inflatables raced away from the vessel, already out of shooting range.

Bolan happened to glance into the cargo hold.

They were all dead. He'd had no doubts about that. But the man he had handcuffed to the rungs was still held up by his bound wrists. He had to have hidden his face from the grenade blast, because now, as it flopped into Bolan's view, it was curiously unmarred. But the rest of his body looked as if it had been skinned with a scaling knife.

Bolan wasn't remorseful. The man was a killer, and he'd received no worse than he deserved.

Instead, the warrior experienced seething bitterness. If he had arrived an hour sooner, he could have halted the madness that was now just commencing.

If he hadn't been cheated out of his prisoners by his murderous adversary, he would have had some clue as to how to proceed.

But he had nothing.

CHAPTER FIVE

Barbara Price realized that Bolan hadn't disconnected the phone call. He had left the line open. She sat at a desk, with the ambient sound from the fishing vessel thousands of miles away feeding through her tiny headset earphones. She heard gunshots, with a feeling of helplessness that was strange to her.

She'd been in this situation before, listening to the sounds of deadly battle far away. But typically she was involved, calling at least some of the shots, lending some kind of support. Now, as the battle on the *First Fathom* raged with increasing intensity, she felt less like a mission controller and more like an eavesdropper, spying on Bolan's private crusade.

Then the shouts, and the sound of an explosion, the thrum of small gasoline engines that faded into silence.

Her hearing searched for sounds of more movement— anything that would tell her Bolan was still alive.

"Stony?" Bolan's voice said so suddenly it startled Price and she raised her hand to her face.

"Striker! Yes. Go ahead."

"I'm in pursuit. Where's Able?"

Price had been monitoring Able Team's position minute by minute, and she knew they were on the ground in Mendocino, racing to the scene. She relayed the information. "Where are the terrorists?"

"Right now they're in two inflatable escape boats and they're splitting up. One boat appears to be heading back to the wharf. They'll reach it in under five minutes," Bolan said.

"They'll be a minute or two ahead of Able, then," Price stated flatly.

Bolan spit out the descriptions and license plates of the three automobiles he'd seen parked at the wharf. "Get the local PD to help if they're not on the scene already. And get the Air Force alerted. They've got a least one truck full of Patriot missiles to collect at the scene. The others are on the road already."

"Affirmative. You're after the second escape raft?" Price asked.

"Yeah."

"Pursuing them in what?"

"A fishing trawler," Bolan said flatly. "You did tell me this thing was clocked by recon going faster than your average work boat."

Bolan pushed the engine throttle to its stops, felt the vibration under his feet grow to a smooth whine.

"I'm going to see exactly how fast she is."

Littleriver Airport

THE TURBO DIESEL Hummer was a four-door hardtop industrial model, but it fit the bill perfectly. Jack Grimaldi slipped behind the wheel as the trio of commandos hustled into the vehicle with their packs of gear, leaving the Stony Man copilot to mind the parked Airbus Industrie A300-600 jet. Grimaldi put the vehicle into gear and stomped on the gas. Lyons's head jerked back from the acceleration as he pulled on his combat headset.

"Stony, we're on the ground," Grimaldi stated.

"ETA?" Price said, her voice coming over the speaker on the console, as well as the headphones.

"Four and a half, maybe five minutes" Grimaldi answered.

"Not good enough," Price replied before Lyons could speak. "The situation's gone bad for Striker. Can you cut that time?"

"Yes." Grimaldi said with utter confidence, scanning the mental map he had made of their route before the landing. "I know some shortcuts."

The pilot-turned-chauffeur twisted the wheel quickly to the right and sent the big wheels barreling over a curb, swiping a bus stop bench off its metal bolts and sending it flying across the sidewalk. He sped across the open acreage of an office building lawn and laid on the horn to clear a path of pedestrians.

"The trick is to think like a pilot," Grimaldi called above the roar of the 6.5-liter turbocharged diesel V-8, not known for its quiet operation. "We don't go around obstacles—we go over them."

Price was describing the situation at the wharf, and Lyons found himself struggling to concentrate as he simultaneously prepared his hardware and tried not to watch the world spinning by outside at reckless speed.

"Got that?" he demanded of his companions in the back seat as Price completed her briefing.

"Got it," Schwarz answered coolly, snapping a magazine into the M-16 on his lap.

"We're ready," Blancanales assured him.

"Remember, there could be a heavy civilian presence.

I don't want bystanders caught in our cross fire," Lyons stressed.

"Shots fired at the wharf," Price interjected. "The local PD is on the scene, taking fire."

"Does the law know we're the good guys?" Lyons asked.

"They're expecting military advisers, Able One—officer down!" Price exclaimed. "They need some reinforcements who know how to handle this situation. ETA?"

"Two minutes!" Lyons said.

"Another officer down," Price said with an intake of breath. "They need help."

"One minute," Grimaldi said. "Count on it." He yanked the wheel hard, sending the Hummer up the side of a retaining wall, flying into empty space five feet over the lower level of the adjoining lot. It landed on all fours with a crash, like a big cat made of junkyard parts, crushing a chain-link fence beneath it.

They found themselves on the other side of the block. Grimaldi had indeed found a shortcut, although few vehicles besides the Hummer would have been able to make use of it. It barreled at an angle across a strip-mall parking lot, swerving and honking through strolling civilians and accelerating at the queue of vehicles waiting at a stoplight in the street. Grimaldi scraped the paint off a fire hydrant, then shoved his way past the front fender of a blue minivan like a schoolyard bully, tires squealing as he sighted the wharf entrance and headed for it.

"Shots!" Lyons said. "Jack, put her halfway between that squad car and the water, facing west."

Grimaldi didn't appear to have heard the Able Team leader. In fact, he was still accelerating, then he braked hard and fast, spun the wheel and allowed the Hummer to skid to a stop on the pavement. On target.

"I aim to please," he stated.

"There they are," Schwarz said.

The others had missed it. "Where?" Lyons demanded.

At that moment a man with an AK-74 stood up from below the edge of the wharf, as if he were standing on air. He was momentarily surprised to see the Hummer, but didn't hesitate when he aimed his weapon and squeezed the trigger, riding out half the magazine. The first couple of rounds slammed into the ground in front of it, but the others stitched their way down the bright yellow body of the vehicle, cracking into the bullet-resistant windows and descending into the rear tires. With a quick duck the gunner disappeared.

"Those are their escape vehicles," Lyons said, nodding at the three parked cars fifty paces down the wharf. "Pol, disable them. Gadgets, you and I are going to try to attract their attention while Jack tends to the wounded."

"Understood."

"Let's go," Lyons said, jerking open the bullet-riddled door and flopping to the pavement on all fours. From the rear passenger-side door Schwarz hit the asphalt in a similar fashion while Blancanales stood up on the protected side of the Hummer and covered the spot where the gunner had appeared. There was no further sign of him.

Schwarz, bent at the waist, sprinted away from the water, then turned north when the pair of police squad cars was between himself and the gunner. He could see a single police office sprawled behind the squad car, watching him suspiciously with one leg stretched out in front of him. The second downed officer was out in the open, fully exposed and motionless.

Schwarz jogged north until he was opposite the three cars. A Chrysler 300M and a pair of Lincolns, all black, probably all armored. Once the cars were out of commission there was no easy escape route left for the terrorists. He kept an eye on the scene of the gun battle. No bad guys were in evidence, so he moved into the open fast and low, hugging the Beretta 92-F handgun to his chest as a defensive weapon as he rummaged on his belt for car-killing munitions.

He pulled out a high-explosive grenade. One of these planted between the first two cars would crack their shells. Another on the third car. Then they'd be going nowhere.

Then a hardman appeared in a flurry of movement from below the edge of the wharf, flopping to the pavement and rolling out of sight behind the protection of the 300M before Schwarz could bring the Beretta into play. There was a click of metal against pavement, and Schwarz didn't hesitate. The hardman had been holding on to an assault rifle, and now he had a clear shot of the commando's feet and legs. The Able Team commando tossed one of the grenades and ran fast zigzagging wildly as gunshots zipped across the asphalt, parallel to the ground at just five inches' altitude.

Something that felt like a crowbar slammed into Schwarz's ankle and jerked the leg violently to one side. He twisted his body to spin with the fall, conscious that he was now putting his entire body and head into the path of those low-flying rounds.

He hit the pavement at the same instant the grenade rolled to a stop under the Chrysler and blew, tossing the front end of the vehicle five feet into the air, cutting a crater into the blacktop and blowing off the head and arms of the prone gunman. The rest of the body was thrust backward, sending it out into the empty space trailing blood, then arcing to the water's surface, thirty feet below.

LYONS DIDN'T HAVE TIME to worry about what the explosion meant but he did have time to use it to his own advantage.

"Go, Pol!"

Blancanales raced ten paces, dropping to the pavement with his M-16 extended. Lyons ran after him, watching the spot on the edge of the wharf where the gunner had been, then dropped himself. Blancanales rose fast and raced to the edge, looking down. He found nothing.

Lyons came alongside him and they stared down at the empty raft, the corroded ladder from the water's edge and the thick black rubber bumper that protected watercraft from hitting the concrete wall.

"Underneath," Blancanales said. "There are support shafts."

"Will they take those guys all the way down to the cars?" Lyons asked.

"Maybe."

He bit his lower lip, considering this. "They'll be hanging by both hands. That's no way to shoot a gun. I'm going down. I can pick them right off."

"You'll be a sitting duck."

"They'll be the sitting ducks. As soon as I start taking potshots at them, they'll try to get back up on top where they can free their hands to shoot back. That's when you take them."

"Understood," Blancanales said without further argument, although he didn't like the plan.

The ladder that was bolted to the side of the wharf was rusted and flimsy as if it had been there for decades. Lyons grabbed the rails and descended a half-dozen rungs before coming to a halt. When he looked back up, Blancanales had already moved out of sight. He switched to the radio.

"Able One here. They're moving hand over hand, just as we thought, and the going isn't easy."

"Able Two here. They see you yet, Ironman?"

"Negative. I'm going to get down to the inflatable. Able Three, you still with us?"

"Affirmative, Able One. I was surprised by one of them, though. Where the hell did he come from?"

"They're hanging from the supports under the bumpers. Be ready for more to come over the top."

"Understood."

"WHO ARE YOU GUYS?" the cop demanded.

"Local gun club," Grimaldi said with a grimace. "How's your friend?"

"I don't know. I got it in the knee when I was trying to get to him. Then I got it again in the back when I tried to get to cover."

Grimaldi pulled the cop forward and inspected his bloody back. Just a flesh scrape. No bullet penetration there. The knee was pulverized and would have to be replaced. None of the damage was life-threatening. Grimaldi crawled into the open, keeping an eye on the pair of Able Team warriors for signs of danger, and sprawled next to the fallen man. He was about to put a finger to the officer's throat when he realized the cop's eyes were open.

"Is that what the modern army calls camouflage these days?" the cop demanded, glaring at the Hummer.

Grimaldi glanced back at the Hummer in surprise. For the first time he realized the thing was bright yellow, the color of construction equipment. Stony had to have arranged to borrow it from a nearby construction site. It could probably be seen from miles away. He chuckled as he overcame his surprise and turned back to the officer. "That's what happens when you let military bureaucrats specify equipment," he lamented. "Where are you hurt, friend?"

"Spine," the officer said more quietly.

Grimaldi's smile faded. "Move something."

"I've been laying here trying. I can blink and that's about it."

"Your buddy's called for an ambulance. I'll make sure they know to expect a spinal injury." There wasn't much more Grimaldi could say or do for the man.

"Shouldn't you be helping your friends?" the cops asked.

"No way. I'm just the chauffeur."

CARL LYONS THOUGHT he'd seen few sights as unusual as this one. There were four of the gunmen underneath the wharf bumpers, hanging from the rusty supports as they tried to go hand over hand to a protected place behind their cars to crawl to the wharf.

One of the men was plainly out of shape and exhausted, and he dangled with the metal supports under his armpits, looking pained. The others were making progress by swinging laboriously on the supports, their weapons dangling from their shoulders. One of them was already at his destination, and was resting before making the dangerous crawl over the top of the bumper and then onto the wharf. A dangling strand of rope was there to make the climb easier.

"Able One here. Able Three, what's your position?"

"Still holding back, Able One. Safe for me to move in and take out the other getaway vehicles?"

Lyons told Schwarz about the man just below the cars' position. "He'll make his move up at any second."

"I'm getting into position, Able One. Tell me when."

The man hung there another ten seconds, panting, before deciding he had enough of his strength back. He reached out, grabbing the rope, and allowed himself to swing out, away from the steel supports.

"Go, Able Three," Lyons said.

Out of their sight, Schwarz had approached the bumper in a run, and on Lyons's command he swiped at the rope with his fighting knife. It parted instantly, and the hanging man shouted in terror as he plummeted to the sea. He held on to the rope with both hands all the way down.

Lyons started the inflatable raft's outboard and throttled it up, allowing it to putter slowly along the base of the concrete wall. The men hanging from the supports hadn't overcome their alarm at their comrade's sudden swim when they were shocked by the appearance of the commando in their boat. Only one of them tried to go on the offensive. When he grabbed for his rifle he lost his grip with his other hand and slammed into the wall before hitting the surface of the water.

The rest of them hung there, angry and helpless as Lyons covered them.

"Able One here. This altercation is over."

CHAPTER SIX

"Gozeh, look!"

Massoud Gozeh saw the eruption of white foam at the bow of the *First Fathom*, watching the angle of the trawler change until he was staring down the prow.

"It's coming right at us. I thought you killed that man!" Osman Karim shouted.

"I did kill one of them. He couldn't have made it out of the hold," Gozeh retorted. "There must have been more than one man on board."

"You said there was just one man."

"So I was wrong—shoot that devil!"

Two of his men began firing into the wide-open sea, aiming high in an attempt to score on the pilot of the trawler in the too-distant wheelhouse.

"We need more speed."

"I've been at full speed since we took off," Karim replied.

Gozeh glanced at the boulder-strewn stretch of beach they were heading for. It crept in their direction with agonizing slowness. "He's going to try to swamp us—prepare to evade him!"

The *First Fathom* somehow found the extra reserves of speed their boat didn't have. It grew into a monster of metal plates that towered on top of them with tremendous rapidity.

"Turn now—ride it out!" Gozeh ordered when they had just seconds to spare. Karim spun the outboard motor and leaned the small vessel through a ninety-degree turn, then drove the little vessel away from the path of the *First Fathom* as fast as possible. Gozeh turned to watch the bulk of the trawler pass within twenty feet of their position.

Then he saw the sudden movement as a figure appeared on the rail outside the deckhouse. Geysers sprung to life on the sea surface an arm's length from the raft, then one of Gozeh's gunners gurgled and slipped over the side.

"Return fire!" Gozeh ordered. He raised his own weapon and triggered a steady burst as the remaining pair of gunners commenced to fire. The rounds went wild on the swell of the ocean surface, and then the *First Fathom* was carried past the raft and the wake hit. It swelled underneath them like a surfacing whale, and Gozeh dropped his weapon and grabbed at the rubber side as one end rose more rapidly than the other. Hundreds of gallons of whitecapped water flowed into the raft, then left carrying another gunner. The ocean fell away beneath them and Gozeh's stomach flopped. The raft slammed into the water again and somehow managed to stay afloat, right side up.

Gozeh's guts heaved and he tasted bile in his throat. His decision to leave the trawler had seemed perfectly logical at the time, the most rapid way of escape. How had it all been turned against him so completely?

"What are you doing?" he demanded suddenly.

"Going back for Ahmet," Karim said.

"Let him swim home. Look!"

Gozeh's finger stabbed at the fishing trawler, which was suddenly broadside to them, circling fast.

"He's going to come at us again," Karim shouted, straightening the raft. "We can make it to the rocks."

Gozeh saw this was true. The beach was littered with boulders that stuck out of the water for a fifty yards from the shore. Once they were among them the fishing boat wouldn't be able to get close.

The *First Fathom* had already aimed itself at them and was increasing speed.

"There—get to that boulder," Gozeh ordered, pointing to a car-sized table of black rock. It stood less than a foot above the water and was nearly level on top. Occasional waves splashed onto it, but with the current tide level it was mostly dry. "We can make our stand there," Gozeh explained.

"We'll be entirely exposed," Karim protested.

"We are three guns. He is just one. He will be on a moving platform. We can stand on that rock and aim carefully and end his miserable life. If he doesn't simply turn tail and run like a dog."

As Karim slowed the engine, Gozeh was the first to jump onto the surface of the rock. His gunner was right behind him, and helped Karim pull the raft onto the rock until only the motor end hung over the end.

They *First Fathom* was homed in on them. At three hundred yards they saw their adversary, the American gunner, come to the prow and observe them, then jog out of their range of vision.

"He's going to turn and run," Gozeh predicted.

The distant thrum of the diesel engines increased in pitch. The foam on the prow rose higher.

At two hundred yards Karim whined, "He's going to ram the rock."

"It would be suicide. He's just trying to scare us back into the boat."

At one hundred yards Karim and the other gunner began stepping back involuntarily.

At fifty yards it was the point of no return, and Karim jumped into the raft, his body weight carrying it partially off the rock. The gunner followed him as the noise of the diesel engines increased to thunder. Gozeh dived into the wildly skewing boat just as Karim throttled up the outboard motors and steered them across the agitated incoming tide. Gozeh found himself sprawled on his face and pushed himself up as the *First Fathom*'s pilot altered her course by mere feet. Then the terrorist saw the man run to the rail and fling himself into the sea. The *First Fathom* came at the raft and Gozeh screamed.

When the fishing trawler slammed into the table of rock, her bow sang a song of tortured, collapsing metal as her momentum drove her over the rock, twisting wildly, so that she slammed on top of the tiny raft like a meaty hand smacking a gnat.

BOLAN PUSHED the pack ahead of him at a careful pace, resting a moment to allow the tide to take them through a gap in the rocks. The surge swept him into the tiny bay created by the rocks, where the water was calmer. With one hand on the pack, made buoyant by its inflatable compartment, he stroked with the other and soon felt the gravelly ocean bottom rise up under his feet. It was then that he heard the coughing.

There was a man on all fours, retching into the sand like a sick dog. The tide swept around him, carrying away the bile, and he retched again.

The Executioner strode out of the sea and waited for the terrorist to notice him. He grunted when he saw Bolan standing there, terrified as if he had witnessed something supernatural. When he tried to leap to his feet Bolan reached out with his own bare foot and kicked the man's legs out from under him. The terrorist landed on his back and lay there gasping for breath.

"Your name?" Bolan demanded.

"Massoud Gozeh. Who are you?"

"You're with the True Army of Kurdistan."

Gozeh, sullen eyed, said nothing.

"I need information."

"I have nothing to tell you."

"I disagree."

Gozeh examined the man before him. The dark-haired American had shed his shirt and shoes when he entered the water. Even barefoot he stood over six feet. He wasn't a slim man, maybe exceeding the two-hundred-pound mark, and that weight was molded into a body that was somewhere between a gymnast and a bodybuilder—a proportioned, powerful physique with a feline litheness. His eyes were cold and blue, turned steely in the reflection of the gray Pacific Ocean. He exuded a self-confidence that came from an extreme level of capability, and a perfect understanding of that capability. He was a man who could do just about anything. Include kill, mercilessly, as needed.

But he was unarmed. If he'd been wearing a holster for his handguns, it was gone now. There was no evidence of a knife sheathed beneath the fabric of the trousers clinging to his ankles. His pack was lying on the sand several paces away. They were on equal terms, and Gozeh was a good fighter.

"You get nothing from me, American," he said, spitting out a last cheek full of bile and climbing to his feet.

Then he was flipped sideways abruptly, and he landed

on the sand on his hand, twisting the wrist violently underneath him and hearing something inside crack. Gozeh shouted and twisted sideways to face Bolan from the sand.

"You broke my wrist!"

"I need a list of destinations for each of the trucks."

"What trucks?"

Bolan was on him like a striking snake, twisting him onto his stomach and wrenching his good arm behind his back in a move that was so fast and so powerful Gozeh didn't even have the time to harden his body to the attack. There was another crunch, this time in his shoulder, and the vibration echoed sickeningly throughout his skeletal system.

By the time he was shouting again, his attacker was standing still on the rocky beach a few paces away, as if he had never moved.

"I want you to provide me with a list of destinations. And I don't have time for game-playing."

The words were oddly chilling. The big American was working him like a cougar working a dazed hare, which he may or may not eventually decide to chew to pieces.

Gozeh's pitiful helplessness dissolved into sudden rage. He wouldn't be treated like that by anyone, anywhere, at any time. With a bellow of bull-like anger he surged to his feet, even using his shattered arms, allowing the shrill pain to thrust him to higher levels of fury. He moved at the big American like a whirlwind out of the desert.

But when he slammed into the American, something odd happened. The man had somehow descended into a crouch and now straightened. Gozeh was airborne, flying end over end like a suicide out of a skyscraper.

Before he experienced the shock of these wounds,

Gozeh felt his head moving, and it took a moment to realize the American was holding his head by the hair, forcing his face into the sand, dragging his head back and forth. Gozeh's face was being used like the paw of an animal to burrow into the earth. When the hole was made, his face was forced into it, and Gozeh couldn't breathe.

His lungs spasmed as he fought for breath, and the pain in his broken chest was excruciating.

When, after a long minute, he was allowed to breathe again, he heard the infuriatingly calm voice of the American.

"I need a list of destinations for the trucks."

"I will give it to you," Gozeh said.

THE VEHICLE PULLED to a stop on the shoulder of California State Road 1 and the driver's window opened on Mack Bolan.

Bolan was still wearing nothing but trousers, and he'd been smeared with dirt and sand during his climb out of the secluded cove where he'd found himself. His hair was plastered to his skull, and an ugly bruise discolored his right shoulder, yellow and sickly.

"My mom told me not to pick up hitchhikers, but I guess you look okay," the driver said.

"Your mother should have taught you to be a better judge of character," Bolan growled. "This hitchhiker is about to appropriate your airplane."

"Just don't take the car." Grimaldi grinned. "We're out chasing bad guys and you're what, swimming on the beach?"

"Exactly." Bolan didn't return the smile as he slid into the rear seat alongside Blancanales, but he wasn't offended by Jack Grimaldi's levity. The man was one of his best friends.

"Barbara says you had better luck than we did," Carl Lyons said from the front seat.

"I got answers," Bolan answered. "I think I convinced my man to tell the truth, but the only way we can be sure is to actually check them out."

Bolan had left Massoud Gozeh secured in plastic cuffs and unconscious from pain on the beach below. After climbing out of the cove, he reached the road and hiked to a pay phone, where he got in touch with the Farm and arranged for Able Team to give him a ride. After a quick review of the pair of targets Gozeh provided, Price and Kurtzman came up with a strategy. They would send Able Team along the coast, and Bolan would head inland, after the truck heading into the Rockies.

Grimaldi pulled a U-turn and drove the Hummer back into the city of Mendocino, where the cleanup was proceeding. They bypassed the downtown area and headed for the small airport, where Stony Man Farm's Airbus Industrie A300-600 was refueled and ready to fly.

"Stay cool, Striker," Schwarz said with a brief wave as Bolan and Grimaldi hustled out of the Hummer. Minutes later they watched the big jet rumble down the runway. As soon as the ground released its hold on the unmarked jet, Grimaldi was banking over the ocean to the south.

ABLE TEAM DIDN'T WAIT to watch it disappear. Carl Lyons, taking the wheel of the Hummer, was already thinking ahead, to their own destination. He was feeling the burden of responsibility weigh heavily on his shoulders, and he allowed himself the luxury of a little introspection.

Bolan's intelligence placed one of the Patriot missiles on its way south on the interstate, heading into the central part of the state just south of San Francisco, to the town of Gilroy. That wasn't the final stop on its journey, just the end of the first step to its staging area. Where it would ultimately end up wasn't known. That's what Massoud Gozeh told Bolan, which meant it was probably true. Bolan was an effective interrogator when he needed to be.

So they would go to Gilroy, California, and find what they could.

But what if they found nothing? That's what worried Lyons. This True Army was clearly a highly professional bunch of lunatics, with the benefits of a careful plan and extensive funding. Its leadership would have built in safeguards against discovery. They would have known there would be many agencies searching for them and would guard against discovery in any and every way they could.

What if they were too good? What if even one of those Patriots was fired? How many innocent people would die then?

No one would blame Able Team if it failed to locate and disable the weapon, but the death of the innocents would be on Lyons's conscience, and he would have to live with that burden.

Enough of that crap, he thought angrily, steering the Hummer onto the highway. Self-pity was beneath him. He and his team would give this search everything they had, and that was saying a lot. Able Team was as experienced an antiterrorist force as existed anywhere in the world, with superlative investigative skills and the backing of the most extensive resources available. If the Patriot could be found, the commandos of Able Team would find it.

CHAPTER SEVEN

Massoud Gozeh, before the agony of his wounds sent him spiraling into unconsciousness, had named the ski resort town of Evergreen, Colorado. He had even named the location a couple of miles outside the city limits where the Patriot might be staged.

Gozeh had admitted that maybe Asad Cakmak would be in residence at the Evergreen house. That would be a stroke of luck, and Bolan was distinctly uncomfortable with relying on luck. But if there was an opportunity to take down Cakmak, it couldn't be ignored.

He was in a race against time, but in this case he had an upper hand.

"ETA?" he asked Grimaldi from the door to the cabin.

"We'll be on the ground in Denver in an hour. From there we're twenty minutes away by chopper."

"McDonald?"

"En route," the pilot replied. "But they've got a lot more of the Land of the Free to traverse than we do. I'd guess they're at least four hours behind us."

McDonald was the leader of the Stony Man blacksuit team, an auxiliary force of commandos called into the field when the need arose. The team was a special group in its own right, its members culled from the ranks of the Army Rangers, the Navy SEALs and every other U.S. special-forces operational division, making the team as diverse as it was capable. Bolan had summoned them to the Rocky Mountains, knowing full well he would be up against an army in Evergreen, especially if this was Cakmak's U.S. headquarters.

"I think we can spare that much time," Bolan said.

Grimaldi glanced at his old friend over his shoulder. "You don't sound convinced of yourself."

"The True Army is sure to use ground transport to get the missiles to Evergreen," Bolan explained. "It left the wharf in Mendocino six hours ago, tops, which means it has to be at least eight more hours to get it into Evergreen."

"Why not send it by air?" Grimaldi asked.

"Too noticeable. Air-traffic security in the U.S. at this moment is probably higher than it's ever been. Ever. Everything that flies that's big enough to carry a Patriot is being watched."

Grimaldi considered that. "I don't think I'm comfortable with that assumption."

"I'm not, either," Bolan admitted.

Grimaldi turned and faced Bolan, trusting his copilot to keep the Airbus flying straight. "If I were Cakmak, I'd want to get those missiles into firing position as quickly as possible. A twelve-hour truck ride isn't quick."

"You're right. That's why I've been trying to figure out what other transport methods are open to him. Or combination of transport methods."

"Combination?" Grimaldi asked.

"Yeah. Right now every aircraft traveling out of northern California and throughout the western half of the United States is being watched. But what if Cakmak trucked the Patriot for several miles, then put it on a plane for a few hundred miles, then back on a truck? Not long enough to attract suspicion, but still a hell of a lot quicker than riding an eighteen-wheeler the whole distance.''

"And still virtually impossible to identify," Grimaldi said. "How do we figure this out?"

Bolan grimaced. "We don't. We get there as fast as we can and hope we're in time to take them down before the missiles arrive—or at least before they're flying.''

Dutch John, Utah

FAIK DIZAYEE STOOD looking toward the north. They were a stone's throw from the Wyoming border and the Flaming Gorge Indian Reservation. To the south rose the Uinta Mountains. The warm breeze brought with it a few sluggish mosquitoes, which Dizayee slapped at lazily.

Cakmak was pacing nervously, glancing at his watch again.

"Relax. They're on schedule," Dizayee said.

"In ten minutes they won't be," Cakmak retorted.

"In five minutes they'll be here," his companion answered with a reassuring calm.

"We didn't plan this well. We're traveling in too straight a line."

"Too straight a line?" Dizayee asked incredulously. "We've zigzagged all the way across three states. We've almost doubled the total distance between here and the West Coast."

"You're observing the route from a ground-based perspective," Cakmak said. "I'm thinking from the point of view of the satellite reconnaissance that's going on over this country right now."

Dizayee considered that, but he still didn't get it. He looked at his companion. "No, Asad, think about it. If you were to plot our course on a graph, it would look erratic, like scribbles."

"We've never strayed north of forty-one degrees and we've never strayed south of thirty-nine degrees since the cargo left Mendocino."

"It's impossible anyone could plot our course, Asad. You saw to that personally. You planned it too well."

Dizayee had been his comrade in the Kurdistan cause for twenty years, and Asad Cakmak knew the man wasn't trying to compliment him. He was simply speaking the plain truth. The planning was meticulous. The strategy was sound. There was simply no way the cargo could be tracked from Mendocino.

It had been driven across the coast ranges into the Sacramento Valley, where it joined the constant heavy flow of traffic on Interstate 5 through the city of Sacramento and out again on Interstate 80. Then, just before reaching the infamous Donner Pass, the first exchange took place.

On a private airfield outside Emigrant Gap the truck's cargo was loaded onto a transport prop plane, an old but well-maintained C-130. The Hercules flew north along the California-Nevada border, then veered due east, crossing the Smoke Creek Desert, then the Black Rock Desert, and continued east across the arid, scarcely populated northern top half of Nevada. The cargo was offloaded in the Great Salt Lake Desert outside the city of Clive. The truck with the missile was from Salt Lake City, and it returned there, passing through the city and beyond, heading for Dutch John. The plane refueled in Salt Lake City, where it was subject to inspection, as was any plane capable of carrying a Patriot missile. This wasn't like looking for drugs. A glance was enough to tell the FAA inspector that there was no such weapon on board.

It was a circuitous route, but it was designed to circumvent the security measures that would now be in place. It had worked so far. In a few hours, when the last stages were complete and the missiles were delivered, Cakmak would know the price tag for this stage of the operation—over one million dollars, including the refurbishment of the Hercules and the lease of the chopper—would be worth it.

There were two hundred miles left to travel.

"Here it is," Dizayee said.

The truck was pulling off the highway, passing in front of the setting sun, and they heard the engine rev up as the driver downshifted to ease its burden down the long incline. When it rolled to a chugging stop behind a rise in the scrubby earth, it was hidden from the highway, as was the transport chopper that was already waiting for it.

Dizayee grinned. "A minute early."

Cakmak grimaced, his mouth becoming a crooked, hideous line of taut flesh. He would save his delight for the moment they reached their final destination.

The team set to work removing the side panels from the truck trailer to reveal the armored crate holding the missiles and their launch system. The crate was already webbed in high-tension cables, and a series of four hooks was attached to these cables at all four top corners. The cables came together to a single line that snaked across the dry ground to the belly of the Skycrane chopper.

The Sikorsky S-64A helicopter was an ungainly-looking apparatus, really nothing more than an engine and a winch on a scrawny superstructure. With the capability to lift twenty thousand pounds, it typically was the kind of craft utilized to place large pieces of equipment, such as air movers and crane components, on building tops. This one had been leased for a different purpose. It would lift the launch system and carry it out of Dutch John and east into Colorado, then over the Danforth Hills southeast, making miles-wide swerves to avoid the few populated areas, finally entering the Rocky Mountains in the dark. The traverse through the Rockies would be the most dangerous part of the operation. Inevitably, the helicopter would have to pass within close proximity of a few towns. It couldn't be helped. Even with the big auxiliary tanks, the chopper could only go so far out of its way. But the risk was acceptable. So what if a few Americans heard a helicopter pass over? Cakmak was confident they would make it to their base outside Evergreen without incident.

The cables were attached. The pilot started the twin Pratt & Whitney JFTD12-4A engines to warm them up, but they had lots of time. They wouldn't take to the air until the sun was lower.

The operation was going perfectly smoothly, without a hitch. Cakmak's planning, plus the resources and connection provided by his sponsor, made it possible.

No reason to foresee any problems. And they had anticipated and planned for problems. They could deal with whatever situation arose without jeopardizing their mission.

So why, Cakmak wondered, was he filled with such foreboding?

CHAPTER EIGHT

Evergreen, Colorado

The big pine lodge was built into the steep side of the mountain, embraced by towering pines. It was four stories of rough-hewn pine, stained a rich golden color that looked almost white in the moonlight. The windows were bright eyes glowing in the night, and the men inside hadn't bothered to close the blinds. Not that they were involved in incriminating activity.

But Mack Bolan knew these men were the terrorists he sought. He intended to move in slow, see what he could see and pinpoint the Patriot he knew was staged somewhere nearby.

He had just determined how he was going to get inside.

The main house was a huge vacation home, which probably housed twenty skiers in luxury during the winter months, when this was a winter-sports paradise. There were dining areas, suites and hotel-like bedrooms, at least a couple of stocked bars that Bolan had spotted through his reconnoiter—unused at the moment. There were more patios and decks than he could count.

Nearby was a large carport that had room for five or six vehicles, and Bolan had examined it first. It was the most likely place for the missile and its launch system. He'd managed to get a glimpse inside when one of the garage doors opened. He saw enough of the interior to rule it out as the hiding place for the Patriot.

But where else would it be?

What if it wasn't even in Evergreen?

Bolan didn't believe it even as he thought it. He was sure the Patriot was scheduled to come to this place. It had everything the terrorists could ask for, including a high level of privacy. Evergreen was practically a ghost town at this time of the year. There were some summer vacationers, but with no other ski lodges in the area there wasn't much chance of anyone stumbling onto the TAK side of the mountain.

Another reason it was ideal, from a terrorist's point of view, was its thirty-mile proximity to Denver, which put it easily within the seventy-kilometer range of the Patriot missile system.

Bolan wasn't going to let it come to that.

He had determined to make the best use of the unusual terrain and the mountain-hugging position of the ski lodge. Skulking up and around the top of the lodge, he came down upon it, maneuvering through the pine forest as close as he dared. He paused for several long minutes to locate the guard duty. When he put on his night-vision goggles, he merely had to wait for these men to show themselves. A flicker of movement in a doorway or against a wall. Men simply can't remain perfectly still, even for just minutes, let alone for the monotonous hours of guard watch.

When he had their positions fixed, Bolan knew he wasn't going to successfully sneak inside at ground level. He had to come in from above.

At the closest approach he could make, he slung his pack on his shoulder and reached into the towering tree above him. Grabbing a low branch, he pulled himself up and crawled onto it, entering the dense foliage. A resinous odor rose from the needles he crushed. He moved carefully among the pliant branches, noise his major concern, moving ever upward. Once he loosened a seedless cone, which bounced among the branches but made almost no noise when it hit the needle-cushioned earth.

The tree was a blue spruce, nearly a hundred feet tall, and Bolan was one-third of the way up it before he was in an ideal position. He straddled the branch, gripping it like a horse between his knees, and inched out into open space. At first there was little visible below him except more of the evergreen branches, but then, as the branch began to narrow and gradually bend under his two hundred-pound weight, the greenery opened up. Now he was looking out at the roof of the ski lodge, at the moonlit vista of the mountainside and the brilliant expanse of the cloudless sky.

He didn't take time to admire the view. Pulling the nylon rope from the pack, he knotted it to the branch he was sitting on, tightening it behind a smaller branch so it wouldn't slide. Then he grabbed the rope, cinched it around his waist and dropped into the open air.

For a fraction of a second he was plummeting, the cool night air whistling in his ears, then the rope tightened, and he squeezed it hard. The rope slid several inches in his grip. The black leather gloves he was wearing saved his flesh from being abraded away, but he felt his palms grow hot. He was swinging wildly, causing the branch that supported him to shake. When his dangling body finally became still, he carefully began to let out the rope.

He rappelled twenty feet through the open night before he judged he was level with the sharply pitched roof of the ski lodge, and then he began again to swing.

The creaking of the nylon line rubbing against the skin of the tree branch twenty feet above him was so loud it was like the tree coming to life and groaning. In the quiet of the forest night it would surely be heard by someone inside the lodge. He had to make it stop soon. He swung harder and watched the roof swoop up under his black shoes, and then it fell away. As he swooped in on the roof again, he made the drop, reaching the apex of the swing and simultaneously letting go of the rope and reaching out with his hands and feet. The roof tiles were just inches away, but he fell on them heavily, and he crouched to lessen the sound even as his fingers gripped the corner of the roof. It was a weak hold and a precarious position, and for just a moment Bolan wasn't sure he was going to be able to hold it.

Then he was still. The tile he used as a handhold wasn't ripping out of its socket. The grip of his rubber-soled shoes wasn't failing against the rough surface. He breathed, long and low, waiting for equilibrium and listening for the silence he hoped would continue, not knowing how loud his landing might have sounded inside.

When there was no alarm he inched like a spider to the peak of the roof and manually embedded the claws of a grappling hook, then moved on the rope to the edge of the roof, finding himself looking down onto a top-floor balcony. There was a small wooden table with a ceramic tile top, and a pair of wooden outdoor chairs. A glass was on the table, containing the dregs of a beer. The room was inhabited. Bolan gave a mental shrug. This was his way in. He'd have to deal with the inhabitants if and when they became a problem.

He scooted over the roof and dangled until his toes found the railing, then he put his weight on it and stepped down to the balcony, collapsing into a crouch when he discovered himself in front of a glass patio door. Inside was a bed, occupied by a man who was facing him.

In a heartbeat Bolan had the Beretta 93-R in his fist and aimed at the man through the glass of the window, but he never squeezed the trigger. The man didn't move. His eyes were closed in sleep.

The room was dark except for the red glow from the digits on a clock radio, and when Bolan slid open the glass patio door he managed to do it in silence.

No one else was in the room. A Glock 9 mm handgun sat on the bedside table, and a Kalashnikov AK-47, the terrorists' standard issue for decades, was propped against the wall. The man was sleeping alone. This was as good a place to start as any.

He pulled a Model 14 Randall fighting knife, ripped the bedclothes off the sleeper and slashed a long red opening in his chest. The sleeper sprang into disoriented consciousness, his mouth opening to shout or scream. He was shocked to realize he was under attack and already wounded. The cold business end of a Beretta 93-R was inserted between his teeth, choking off the sound before it was made, and his eyes went wild when he recognized the flashing seven-inch blade of the Randall displayed inches from his face.

"You try to move and I splatter your brains on the

wall. You make a noise and I'll cut out your eyeballs. Understood?''

The man didn't know the warrior was playing up his own savagery. Not that Bolan would hesitate to carry out his threats if the need arose. But the combination of the glistening blood, the fresh pain and the vision of the unholy attacker rendered the Kurd terrorist helpless. He nodded, just barely.

"I'm going to remove the gun from your mouth. You'd better start using it to my satisfaction.''

Bolan pulled out the 93-R and said, "Start telling me what you know about this place. How many men?''

"Twenty, maybe twenty-five.''

"All Kurd?''

"No. Most of the men are mercenaries. Nine Kurds, including me.''

"All from the True Army of Kurdistan.''

"Yes.''

"What about your supreme general?''

The Kurd swallowed, his courage returning as he slowly gathered his wits. "Cakmak is in Turkey.''

Bolan flipped the blade in his hand and inserted it suddenly into the fleshy underside of the Kurd's chin. The terrorist froze, rock-hard in pain and fear, his eyes rolling to his forehead as the 93-R moved to it and pressed.

"That's one lie,'' Bolan said. "I won't tolerate another. You have three seconds.''

"Cakmak is here.'' the Kurd admitted. "He'll kill me for telling his secrets.''

"The missile?''

"In the woods. Up the mountain. No more than two hundred meters.''

"How many guards on the missile?"

"Four. Plus video security."

"Fine. Now, where *exactly* is Cakmak?"

The Kurd was afraid, but his momentary fear couldn't compare to the mixture of fervent admiration, loyalty and terror he had for his supreme general. He wasn't going to rat out the terrorist leader. As the Kurd snatched at the Glock on the bedside table Bolan reacted, yanking him forward with the Randall like a hooked fish being snatched out of the water. The Kurd was lightning fast. His hand swept at the Glock and it stuck to his fingers like glue. But he found himself stumbling off the bed and onto his feet, spun away from his attacker, facing the wide patio window and the dark forest outside. He tried to turn on the American, but it was far too late for that. Something like a hammer cracked against the base of his skull and his world became blackness.

Bolan stood in the darkness, touching the radio headset as he listened for noises of alarm from elsewhere in the house. So far there was nothing.

"Striker here."

Stony Man Farm, Virginia

"Go, STRIKER," Barbara Price said. The cool and confident honey-blond woman was dressed in worn jeans and a white blouse with Western-style lace accents, looking like the mistress of a well-to-do-ranch more than mission controller of an ultracovert government installation. She sat in the Stony Man Farm War Room, watching a monitor with an image of the house and the terrain, digitized from a previously taken satellite photo, wishing she had access to real-time satellite reconnaissance right now. A small blue cross on the screen showed her Bolan's exact position, information determined via Global Positioning Satellite data telemetered automatically from his radio. At the periphery of the screen, surrounding the image of the lodge, were eight stationary green crosses, each with a tiny name floating on the screen next to it.

"I'm inside," Bolan said. "I've been told the Patriot is in the woods, two hundred meters or less up the mountain from the house."

"Understood." Price tapped on her keyboard and a large circle appeared at that position.

"Wait on sending in the blacksuits. I want a chance to find Cakmak."

Price said nothing for a moment, then she spoke into the tiny microphone on her own headset. "That's not the plan, Striker. We need to get that Patriot disabled."

"We need to get this entire operation disabled, Stony. If Cakmak is taken out, then the True Army crumbles."

That made good sense, a fact that made no difference whatsoever. "Sorry, Striker, I'm sending in McDonald now. We can't risk a launch."

"Stony, if we loose Cakmak now, we effectively assume responsibility for any and every Patriot that gets launched from this moment on. And every life lost will be on our heads."

"Striker—"

Price stopped and raised her head.

"Allow me," Brognola said. He happened to be at the Farm, and had joined her in the War Room as an observer when the probe commenced. He pulled an unused headset microphone to his mouth. He didn't identify himself. He didn't need to.

"Striker, I understand your position on this, but I will not risk a launch of that missile. You know the terrorists' line of thinking as well as I do—Cakmak will have that damned thing prepped and ready to fire at a moment's notice, just so he can get off the shot should he feel threatened."

"Stony, you send in the blacksuits and this whole place will know about it instantly."

"So get the hell out, Striker," the big Fed retorted.

"The hell I will. I came here to take down Cakmak."

There was a sound like a rush of static, then nothing. Mack Bolan had gone off the air.

The warrior's GPS system continued to function, and on the screen the blue cross moved deeper into the interior of the lodge.

Price knew Bolan was right. There would be constant communication between the missile launcher and the lodge. The moment the missile's security was compromised the lodge would go on alert. Bolan would be a single lion in a den filled with hyenas.

She touched her radio and said, "Blacksuit One?"

McDonald, the current leader of the Stony Man Farm blacksuits, replied. "Blacksuit one here. Go, Stony."

"We've got a general location on the Patriot," she said, and gave him the description supplied by Bolan. "I want a cautious advance. If possible, let's stage ourselves prior to the assault."

"We'll do our best, Stony," McDonald said, a twinge of doubt in his voice. She knew what he left unsaid. They were tramping through dark woods in the night, looking for a target they had only a rough fix on. There would be a heavy population of guards and good electronics keeping an eye on things. Finding the missile and getting set up for a planned probe would be pretty highly unlikely.

Price listened as McDonald issued his orders, and the green crosses representing his highly trained commandos began floating across the screen, fanning out toward the large circle Price had placed in the spot where the missile lurked among the trees.

Her eyes were locked, however, on the blue cross, which moved through the graphical image of a hallway, added to the satellite image using the questionable blueprints from the lodge's original builder. The Executioner was still moving slow, undetected himself. Price knew how quickly that situation could change.

"Striker?" she said on his frequency. The word hung in the air, unanswered. She didn't look at Brognola, watching her impassively from across the room. Kurtzman was there, as well, on a remote monitor, helping maintain the integrity of her various radio and satellite links throughout the probe. None of them spoke.

"Blacksuit Three here." A quiet, measured voice. "Movement, ten meters to the northwest of my position."

"Blacksuit One here. Can't you do better than that, Furie?"

"Negative, One. Not much to see."

"Stony One here," Price said. "That position looks right."

"One here. Stay sharp, Suits. Anybody got a better view?"

No answer. The eight green crosses converged with infinite slowness, like green snails oozing across the glass surface of the huge wall screen. They had managed to form a near-perfect circle around the target, cutting it off from the lodge. Price could almost hear the rustle of the huge pine branches, smell the rich forest air with its slight tang of drying needles, feel the cushion of the endless carpet of brown needles underfoot.

Then, in utter silence, Price was amazed to see two of the green crosses abruptly cease to exist.

Evergreen, Colorado

THE NEXT BEDROOM DOOR was open, revealing in the moonlight a messed bed and half-open drawers. Trash littered the floor and nightstand. Cakmak had probably failed to hire a cleaning service for his group's stay at the lodge. Bolan stepped through the washroom and found a door to the next bedroom. He cracked it open and went through in a rush when the figure on the bed spotted him.

The Kurd twisted hard between the legs of the woman who had been straddling him. She squealed and flopped on the mattress, grabbing for the tangled bedclothes, but they couldn't keep her from rolling onto the floor with a thump. Her lover hit the floor on all fours, then stretched for the shoulder harness that rested amid the pile of hastily removed clothing. He got the harness but it came to him with the leg of his trousers snagged on it. He pulled them off hurriedly, then collapsed as Bolan reached him and kicked him in the side. The impact couldn't be dodged. Bolan's steel-reinforced toe damaged the soft flesh below the rib cage and threw the man into the wall. As the terrorist gasped for breath, he extracted the handgun, only to see it fly out of his hands and crack into the patio door, putting a crater in the glass. Bolan put the 93-R in his face.

"Don't say a word," the Executioner ordered the woman. She looked well used, with a collection of old and fresh needle bruises on the insides of her arms. Her hair was brilliant platinum with muddy roots, and she lay where she had fallen in a drugged daze.

"Where is Cakmak?"

"Who the hell are you?" the Kurd demanded with a sneer.

"I'm asking, you're telling. Where?"

"I am not telling you anything. What will you do? Shoot an unarmed man?"

Bolan fired. The retort of the round leaving the custom-made sound suppressor was the sound of a loud cough, and it nicked the hardman's shin. The terrorist's eyes glazed in shock. The hooker had risen to a sitting position, and she regarded the freely flowing blood with dawning horror.

"I've already had enough of the True Army's attitude to last me a lifetime," Bolan said. "Cakmak is where?"

"First floor. Southwest corner bedroom. That's where he sleep—"

The retort that came out of the woods was a thump. Some sort of explosion, although Bolan had seen no sign of a flash. It had been curiously muffled, as if it had gone off underground.

Suddenly Bolan knew what it was.

The wounded man made a desperate lunge for his fallen handgun, and Bolan nailed him in the chest with a single round from the 93-R. The Kurd stiffened and collapsed, his handgun clattering to the floor a second time.

The prostitute, finally, started to scream.

Stony Man Farm, Virginia

WHERE THERE HAD ONCE been two living, breathing men, there was now nothing except for the red letters, CF.

Catastrophic Failure.

"Blacksuit One here. We have an explosion. Report."

"Blacksuit Three here. Land mine. Four and Five are out of the picture."

"Blacksuit One here. Come around, Suits. You know this drill."

Price knew the drill, too, and it horrified her. She would deal with her emotions later. Right now she watched the sudden movement of the blacksuits as they circled to the north, converging on the spot where Blacksuit Four and Blacksuit Five—Doug Pierce and Randy Wedo—had just been blown to pieces.

The idea was to use the path that the dead man had cleared—approach directly *over* the bodies of their fallen comrades. Because that was the one perimeter access where they knew the land mines had been neutralized.

It made a kind of grotesque sense, and it somehow even gave an immediate purpose to the lives that had just ended.

Still, she was glad she didn't have to be one of the warriors marching into battle over the decimated bodies that had been their living, breathing brothers just seconds ago. She watched the remaining six green crosses pass between the two CF legends where Pierce and Wedo had spent their final moment of life.

"Stony One here. Are you getting any reaction from the guard around the Patriot?"

"Blacksuit One here. Here it comes now, Stony."

CAKMAK SAT STRAIGHT UP on his cot, eyes burning with sleep as he forced them to focus enough to grab his shirt and his handgun holster. He dragged both over the same arm as he strode into the security center that adjoined his room.

The Kurd loyalist manning the bank of monitors knew him well enough to offer a report before Cakmak even asked for it. "One of the land mines detonated. We're getting reports of movement sightings in the woods."

"What about the lasers?"

"They went off just before the mine blew."

"I knew we had them too close. What are they telling you now?"

"It is strange. The perimeter went quiet again everywhere but here."

The security man tapped the screen showing the graphic of the layout around the lodge. "That is where the mine blew, but maybe it missed," he suggested.

Cakmak rubbed his hands over his head, but his hair was gone, buzz cut prior to entrance into North America in an effort to change his appearance. He had a heavy forehead, a massive hawk's beak of a nose and a small, deformed, fishlike mouth.

As a boy in Tarsus he had been known as "the Girl Mouth," a nickname he bitterly resented. When the nickname followed him into his teen years, he became violent, fighting in countless battles against anyone, regardless of size, who called him that. Finally, when he was fifteen, he took on a group of Turkish Muslim boys in a single-handed battle that left him beaten nearly into unconsciousness. The Muslims had tied him down and burned his lips repeatedly with cheroots, then ground dung into the burns. The wounds and the resulting infection had left him with a grotesque mouth and a permanent, obsessive hatred of Muslims—even Kurd Muslims.

Cakmak soon found himself an outcast from the few fringe members of the Tarsus society who had once associated with him. Women cringed in his presence. His parents wouldn't have anything to do with him. Finally, he found a place for himself among the freedom fighters for Kurdistan. They preached violence toward the Turkish Muslims, a hatred with which Cakmak was sympathetic. The cause for a free Kurdistan was peripheral until Cakmak found himself regarded as a hero by his people for fighting the cause. He began to believe in the cause himself. The cause—and the satisfaction that came of the violence—became his life.

Americans made for especially satisfying targets.

"Give me the mike." Cakmak grabbed the small device out of the guard's hand. "Asad here. Do you hear me, Faik?"

"Dizayee here!" his longtime friend answered quickly. "One or more mines activated. They've bypassed the rest of the mines. They come in over their own dead!"

"How many?" Cakmak demanded.

"Unknown. Five, maybe ten. Impossible to tell. They've killed two of my men already."

"They will be using night vision. Turn on the lights," Cakmak ordered the security guard. "Faik, fire the missile."

"We are a little busy at the moment, Asad! We've got gunfire coming in from three sides now!"

Cakmak saw the sudden glow of lights come on as the floodlights planted in the woods ignited.

"They'll be blinded for a few seconds, Faik. Now get that missile fired!"

"Yes, Asad."

Dizayee's tone of voice was less than reassuring. Cakmak strode to the door, still holding the headset to his ears, and found pandemonium.

"What's going on?" he demanded from one of his mercenaries, grabbing the man by the collar as he rushed by.

"We're under attack!"

"What? Here in the building?" Then Cakmak heard one of the prostitutes they had shipped in from Denver screaming her fool head off on one of the floors above him. Then came the unmistakable sound of suppressed handgun fire.

SHOUTS FROM BELOW initiated a stampede of movement, and Bolan rushed into the hallway. Another Kurd emerged from the last bedroom on the floor, still inserting a magazine into his AK-47. He gaped when he saw Bolan, then seated the magazine with a shove and brought the weapon to bear, all too slowly. The big American triggered two rounds from the 93-R that ripped through his opponent's torso.

Bolan found himself looking over a railing into open space, with a good view of the third- and second-floor sleeping lofts and the ground-floor living room.

The confusion among the terrorists and their hired guns was quickly coalescing into order as the men appeared with their weapons and a voice out of sight called out that he was in contact with the guards.

"I don't care. I want all available men into the woods, now." The man giving the orders came out from under the overhanging floors, and Bolan saw him. The gash of a mouth told him it was Cakmak.

Bolan dropped the grenade on the unsuspecting band of terrorists, and at that instant something compelled the Kurdish leader to raise his head and look directly at Bolan.

There was a fraction of a second in which the Executioner and the terrorist stared directly at each other, and each knew his enemy instinctively. Bolan jerked the 93-R into target acquisition. He had intended to cover his head against the blast of the grenade, but he refused to allow this chance to slip away.

But Cakmak was too fast. He'd spotted the falling metal object, identified it and retreated from it all in the blink of an eye, disappearing from view. Bolan dived to the floor, his eyes squeezed shut, his wrists pushed against his ears, and the grenade sprung to life. The light flash was too far away, but the screech of sound filled the interior of the lodge to the bursting point, clawing at Bolan's eardrums. He jumped to his feet and raced down the exposed stairway, holstering the Beretta and freeing the Heckler & Koch MP-5/10A3 from the holster on his back.

Confused, moaning figures were scattered around the first floor. The ground-level door burst open as Bolan reached the second floor, and he spotted the AK-47 coming across the threshold before he spotted the man backing it up. He anticipated the gunner's advance, but the guy's instinct saved his life—he stopped short, and the 10 mm rounds slammed into the door frame. The gunner barreled through when Bolan's firing ceased, unleashing rounds from the AK that ran up the wall of the stairs, homing in on the warrior.

Bolan grabbed the rail and vaulted into open space, hearing the 7.62 mm rounds punch into the pine walls where he had been. As his feet slammed to the floor, he went into a shoulder roll that carried him across the floor to an antique oak desk. With a quick movement he yanked it away from the wall, giving himself cover, then rose just long enough to spot his opponent.

The man was a fool, ensconced behind a leather sofa. Bolan crouched, waiting as a barrage of AK rounds slammed into the desk above his head. When it ceased he rose onto his knees, laid the MP-5/10A3 on top of the desk and triggered a figure eight pattern into the sofa, tearing holes into the leather. There was a grunt and a clatter of metal as the gunner behind it died suddenly.

The dazed and deafened victims of the flash grenade were regaining their vision, and as two of them scrambled for the kitchen area of the great room, another gunner jumped to his feet and got off a burst from a mini-Uzi. Then shots went wild over Bolan's head, and he returned a short burst that cracked the gunner's skull open before he could scramble for cover. Bolan's machine-gun fire caught up to the two in the kitchen as they tried to scramble out the door, cutting into their legs and leaving them helpless on the cold ceramic tiles.

Where was Cakmak? Had he moved fast enough to escape the effects of the flash grenade? As he kept an eye on the moaning handful of surviving terrorists, watchful for any who might attempt a break for freedom, he quickly considered exactly where Cakmak had been standing when he reacted to the grenade. Bolan examined the great room for exit points Cakmak might have used in extreme haste. There was the front door, which took him out of the building, and another door into a side room. On second thought, Bolan's mental replay of the scene included another terrorist standing in the doorway. Cakmak would have had to fight his way past the man in order to escape. So, if he had time to actually make a decision, Cakmak would have headed through the second door.

Bolan stepped into it and kicked it open, falling back then to avoid a spray of bullets that never came. When he peered into the room, the warrior found a narrow library, with two walls crammed with shelved books, a computer monitor on a slide-away desktop and a leather reading chair.

And a wide-open window.

Cakmak's exit.

He gave the fallen terrorists in the main room no more thought. They were bit players. They'd all be neutered if Cakmak was taken down. Bolan rushed for the window and climbed through it, glancing to both sides before hitting the ground and rolling hard into the underbrush at the foot of the trees. He brought himself to a halt in the foliage. He was alone for the moment.

The forest up the mountainside was illuminated brightly, with glaring shafts of light coming through the trees like a scene in a horror movie. Monitoring the blacksuits' radio transmissions, he quickly determined the battle was a stalemate. Hemmed in on top of the bodies of their fallen comrades, the blacksuits were made highly visible in the spotlights, which pinned them to the spot, further advance impossible.

"Striker here," he said into his headset quietly. "Blacksuits, you reading me?"

"We're hearing you, Striker," McDonald answered. "Those of us who are left."

"Prepare to go to night-vision glasses."

"We've been aiming at the lights for five minutes, Striker. They're not going out."

"I'm not going to smash the bulbs, Blacksuit One, I'm going to pull the plug."

"Understood, Striker. Let us know when to go."

Bolan headed for the small outbuilding that he had spotted on his approach. Even in the nighttime it was clear the aluminum-sided shack was a new addition to the property, and it hadn't been built with the same attention to mountain aesthetics as the rest of the lodge. The power line that snaked up the mountain from the road came from a nearby pole, then descended to the roof of the shack. Bolan found the door wasn't even padlocked. Apparently, with all the manpower around, the Kurdish terrorists hadn't been worried about somebody breaking into their generator shed.

Inside he found a small glowing panel that told him the generator was in standby mode. No need to power up until electricity stopped flowing in from the utility company. It took him five seconds to locate the cables that descended into the ground and headed for the lodge. All the power went through these lines, whether they originated with the utility company or the generator.

"Striker here," he radioed. "Five seconds until darkness, Blacksuit One."

"Understood," McDonald radioed back.

The MP-5/10A3 wasn't designed to serve as a cable cutter, but it did an excellent job. When the shot was fired, the orange-insulated copper cables separated with a burst of sparks, and outside the world returned to the night. The generator display never changed. It was still getting power from the power lines, so as far as it was concerned everything was operational.

There were shouts from up the hill, followed by a short, controlled bursts of rapid gunfire. A shout, tinged with fear. The True Army was finding the tables turned against them. All of a sudden they were blind and helpless, while their enemy was tracking them down with catlike night vision. One of them had to have panicked and fled thoughtlessly, because he triggered one of his own land mines. The heavy thump echoed through the forest, cutting off a brief vocalization of surprise.

When the echo of the mine faded, Bolan heard the low-speed start-up revolutions of a dual-engine helicopter.

"Blacksuit One, send all available men after that chopper!"

"Understood, but we're meeting heavy resistance here, Striker."

Bolan followed the sound of the throbbing turboshaft engines, away from the lodge and the missile launch site. Ahead he saw a clearing in the forest, the stars becoming visible overhead and the faint lights glowing under the belly of a helicopter. Standing ready in the mountain prairie was a Sikorsky Aircraft S-76C+. It wasn't the military aircraft Bolan had expected, but the body could still be armored. He lined up his sights on the twin front windshields, hoping to take the pilot out of commission. The shot would have been a given with the precision of a sniper rifle, but that wasn't the kind of shooting the MP-5/10A3 was designed for. He fired, heard the tinkle of glass and triggered a burst into the nose of the aircraft. There was a pair of sudden bursts of gunfire from the helicopter, and Bolan heard the rounds chop into the nearby tree trunks. He found cover behind another trunk. They were lucky or damned good to have targeted him that well in the dark.

He sprinted to another tree, then dropped to the ground, making his way on all fours under the concealment of the waist-high prairie grass. He triggered a quick burst into the Sikorsky before dropping again and dodging, trying to get the aircraft facing him nose first, so he could shoot directly into its face. When he rose for the next burst, he found the low, sharp nose pointed directly at him. He clicked a fresh magazine into the MP-5/10A3 and bore down on the trigger, carving out a deadly figure eight that slammed into both windows, chopping fist-size holes into the already spiderwebbed glass and punching holes in the composite body.

The twin engines had to be warmed up by now, but the pilot was either dead or cowering behind the instrument panel. Bolan had to keep the helicopter from leaving the ground. Where the hell was McDonald?

A rush of another engine told Bolan he had unexpected company, and seconds later an SUV tore out from the trees at the far end of the clearing and careened in a wide circle around the Sikorsky. When it was coming directly at him, a quartet of roof-mounted floodlights flashed on, nearly blinding the Executioner as he dived out of the path of the oncoming vehicle.

Bolan rolled onto his feet and assessed his options in an eye blink—get to safety in the trees or make one more attempt at disabling the Sikorsky? He had no option at all really. The helicopter had to be grounded.

He fired the MP-5/10A3 on the run as he tried to blindly judge the location of the maneuvering SUV. Then the floodlights from the vehicle turned directly on him. Bolan knew that he was a perfect human target, dead in their sights.

But since he was between the SUV and the helicopter, the floodlights also illuminated the Sikorsky as it was throttling up to take off. Bolan found himself with a clean shot at both men in the pilot seats.

He flipped the off switch on the part of his brain that was shouting at him to jump out of the path of the on-coming SUV. He ignored his natural impulse to leap away from the sudden barrage of automatic gunfire that filled the mountain prairie, chopping at the nearby veg-etation like an impossibly rapid scythe. He targeted the pilots and fired.

The MP-5/10A3 thrummed in his hands, the voice of the suppressed weapon drowned under the turboshafts and the rattle of gunfire behind him. He watched the wide-eyed pilot drop out of sight, a spray of blood mark-ing the spot where he had been. Bolan aimed the sub-machine gun to take out the copilot, and then something like a cannonball slammed into his right shoulder blade, kicking his arm out in front of him and sending him sprawling on the ground.

Bolan rolled once, fast, then pushed himself through the low-lying prairie plants. One purpose dominated his thoughts now: find a hiding place before the paralyzing impact of the gunshot overcame him.

There was a pair of quick beeps from the SUV, fol-lowed immediately by the quick acceleration of the tur-boshafts, and then the wind from the Sikorsky washed over the prairie. In seconds it was gone.

Cakmak had escaped.

The pain hit him, not as bad as he had expected, but bad enough. Bolan twisted on his back, saw nothing above him but the brief silhouette of prairie grasses in the floodlights as the SUV rushed within arm's reach of him and was also gone.

Bolan realized the bullet, despite his expectations, hadn't bypassed the edge of his Kevlar vest. When he struggled to his feet, he flexed the arm. It had full range of motion, so nothing was broken, but he would have a hell of a bruise for a while.

With a fading rumble, the SUV accelerated onto the distant highway. Suddenly, the night was smothered in unearthly quiet.

For the first time it occurred to Bolan that the worst hadn't come to pass. The Patriot hadn't been fired. But somewhere in this forest, two Stony Man blacksuit warriors lay dead.

The man responsible had just escaped justice.

Bolan stood under the impassive stars, feeling the presence of the ghosts of the dead men as if they were real. He didn't even know their names. But the names didn't matter, and he made a life-or-death vow to them: Cakmak, sooner or later, would pay for their murders.

The Executioner would see to it.

CHAPTER NINE

Over the Tuz Gölü, Far-Eastern Turkey

David McCarter watched the tiny lights of the city of Ahlat on the shore of the huge salt lake. Tuz Gölü was a growing inland sea—more water poured into it than drained or evaporated out of it. Several peninsulas had become islands in the lake during the twentieth century, and McCarter wondered how long until the water flowed into the streets of Ahlat and drove its people away.

The small city came and went under the hull of the C-130 Hercules, which was transporting Phoenix Force from their Incirlik AFB base of operations, near the Turkish capital of Ankara. They had flown into the eastern end of Turkey and circled back west over the water to approach the tiny ghost town of Gecidi from over the mountains. The abandoned village was home to an ancient airstrip. A band of ARGK freedom fighters had been rousted from the enclave more than once, but the outpost was thought to have been permanently abandoned when the People's Liberation Army of Kurdistan agreed to the 1999 cease-fire. Somebody with TAK had apparently remembered it, and knew it would be useful.

The pilot was a recent Farm loan from the Air Force, a seasoned, competent flyer named Byarnsonn. He had come all the way from the Farm with them, first jetting them across the ocean from the U.S. to Incirlik, then taking them up in a borrowed U.S. Air Force Hercules, with the heavy cargo capacity Phoenix needed to get its equipment into the field for an operation such as this one.

"We're going in quiet here, mates, remember that," McCarter announced. "This isn't a search-and-destroy mission. We're not going to get so damned lucky as to find all our missing missiles parked in an old building in the desert. We need to find out where the missiles are and what their purpose is. This is a data-gathering probe. Understood?"

There was a chorus of murmured assents. McCarter knew he was wasting his words. His team was well briefed and highly professional. They knew their job and would perform it with the highest level of skill and conscientiousness.

McCarter knew all this and was confident. But there was still a combination of apprehension and disquiet that came over him just before the launch of a high-stakes insertion. Yet there also came with it a kind of nervous calm.

The big Briton had been with Phoenix Force from its inception, and prior to that had served in the British army for years. It was an understatement to say he had experience under fire. But he had only been serving as the leader of Phoenix for a short period. He might not be quick to admit it to the others, but he still wasn't entirely comfortable being the man in charge. There were times like this, when the incredible weight of the coming probe, and the lives that might hang in the balance, rested heavily on his shoulders. It had been difficult on those occasions when men under his command had been wounded. He couldn't imagine what it would be like if he lost a man—a distinct possibility each and every time Phoenix Force went into the field. No matter how highly trained and individually talented each man on the team was, it was impossible to avoid the reaper forever.

Enough. He sure didn't remember going through these prebattle self-examinations back in the old days, when Yakov Katzenelenbogen had been the man in charge of Phoenix Force. Being a grunt, even a Stony Man grunt, was a less stressful gig. He upended the plastic bottle and downed the last few ounces of Coca-Cola Classic, then stuffed the bottle into the trash bag in the wall. "We ready, mates?"

"We're ready," Rafael Encizo, the Cuban-born Phoenix Force commando, answered. There was an air of casualness, almost lethargy in his voice. McCarter would have envied Encizo his relaxed nature if he wasn't convinced it was a half-truth. The man came across as laidback, perhaps even as dull witted to some people. Nothing could be further from the truth. When he needed to, Encizo moved like lightning and fought with the intellect and instincts of a killer jaguar.

McCarter nodded vaguely at the rear cargo hold. "What about the minivans?"

Encizo's mouth drew up in a straight line of a grin. "Fully tuned and ready for a drive to the grocery store."

McCarter nodded and poked the button for the intercom to the cockpit. He reached the copilot, an Air Force man borrowed from the Incirlik base. He was handling himself like a professional, despite the fact that this unknown group of nonmilitary personnel—the man in charge not even an American—had waltzed into the base, requisitioned his aircraft and demoted him for the duration of the trip from pilot to copilot. McCarter was sure he was a competent flyer, but he wanted his own man at the controls. He'd flown with Byarnsonn on a handful of occasions.

McCarter asked to speak to Byarnsonn and was handed over to his man from the Farm.

"McCarter here. ETA?"

"I'll have you on target in five minutes, sir."

McCarter said, "Thanks," and clicked off. In five minutes the wait would be over. Once things were actually happening, he would feel better.

It was the waiting that got on his nerves.

THE TERRAIN in the drop-zone section of eastern Turkey was several thousand feet above sea level. It wasn't desert, as the rain fell year-round and the temperatures were moderated by the elevation. But the soil was poor. There wasn't much agriculture—a few fields of tea and tobacco and poppies for heroin—and there weren't many people. There was nobody for miles around to see the behemoth of an aircraft swoop down low over the hilly earth and disgorge a pair of shapeless black masses, which plummeted for less than a second each before a trio of chutes opened above them. Then they hung in the air almost motionless before floating gently to the ground.

Meanwhile, the ramp at the rear end of the big aircraft, which gaped open like the mouth of a Maori statue, swarmed with buglike figures that tossed themselves into the sky. But they, too, grew appendages that grabbed at the air, and soon there were five paragliders swooping through the silent Turkish sky and zeroing in on the first big mass.

Gary Manning was the first to come in for a landing, steering his paraglider in a steep bank before lining up on a slight rise in the land that allowed him to come in with almost no downward impact—he simply went from being airborne to sprinting across the hard-packed earth.

"Not too shabby," the barrel-chested commando said to nobody as he turned and gathered up the chute in a wad. The others quickly began making their own landings in his vicinity, then joined Manning in removing the protective canvas cover from the cargo packs that had come down with them.

Without wind, they had been given the luxury of attaching extra parachutes to their cargo, which meant they could give it a gentle landing without having to chase them on the breeze halfway across Turkey. In addition, the vehicles had landed on pillows of gas that were big enough to encompass the belly and sides of the vehicles. The air mattresses cushioned the impact of even a heavy landing. Manning had pulled the inflate cord on the cushions just as they were shoving the big packs out the back end of the Hercules. Now he unceremoniously and repeatedly stabbed them with his combat knife and watched the various inflated compartments burst. In seconds the cushions were reduced to saggy scrap material that they pulled off and flung away.

The vehicles that were revealed were Chenowth Advanced Light Strike Vehicles.

The ALSV was the follow-up to the Light Strike Vehicle used by U.S. special units, including the Rangers and Delta Force. The Chenowths had been used since Vietnam, and had proved themselves especially useful in the Gulf War, where special-forces units had relied on them for clandestine incursions into Iraqi-controlled desert.

The ALSV was manufactured with an all-wheel-drive system and a powerful diesel engine, designed to give it high-speed agility on the worst-possible terrain. It was configured with a primary weapons station with a 360-degree firing range. The standard configuration came mounted with either an M-2 .50-caliber machine gun or an MK-19 automatic grenade launcher.

Phoenix had one of each.

They mounted up in a prearranged configuration. McCarter took the wheel of the machine-gun-equipped ALSV. As a trained driver who participated in road rallies, he was a logical choice for driving in a situation that could require quick maneuvering. With him went the youngest member of Phoenix Force, T. J. Hawkins. Hawkins was a Texan, which became abundantly clear when he was off duty and relaxed into casual conversation. He had joined Phoenix upon the retirement of longtime leader Katzenelenbogen, and there had been plenty of opportunities for Hawkins to prove himself in combat situations. He had come through time and again with flying colors. Gary Manning, the Canadian-born commando, took the rear seat.

Behind the wheel of the second ALSV was a lanky black warrior, Calvin James. Tall and thin, with a pencil-thin mustache, he had a dapper look when dressed in civilian clothing and somehow managed to look clean-cut even in the tan-and-brown desert-camouflage clothing he now wore. But he could be a deadly adversary. He was an ex-SEAL, with all the proficiencies that came with that role, in addition to a black belt in tae kwon do. By his side sat the Cuban commando, Encizo.

Less than two minutes after the last of the warriors touched down, the Chenowths' diesels were rumbling quietly and the pair pulled away into the rocky hills around the Turkish ghost town of Gecidi.

As McCarter steered the ALSV steadily around boulders and rises in the landscape, unperturbed by the lack of a road or trail, he touched the radio on his headset. "Let's perform a radio check, mates."

"Phoenix Two here," Encizo radioed.

"Phoenix Three," Manning said quietly from the back seat, and McCarter heard his voice through the headphones.

"Phoenix Four," James said.

"Phoenix Five, ready to kick some ass."

"Stony, you with us?" McCarter asked.

"Stony One here," said the voice of Barbara Price, back in the Stony Man Farm Annex. Their radio transmission was being sent to the Hercules, which would be maintaining a position within range of their radios. The satellite uplink on the aircraft would keep them in contact with the Farm. "I've got a satellite update for you, Phoenix."

"Good. Go ahead, Stony."

"The look-see we were hoping to access came through in a big way. We got a good eyeful of the base camp outside Gecidi less than forty-five minutes ago. At that time, two semi-size trucks were departing the camp."

Manning cursed in the back seat of the Chenowth. "We're too late."

"No bloody way," McCarter said over his shoulder, then into the radio said, "Stony, you want us to go after those trucks?"

"Negative. They're moving slow. We think you'll be able to catch up with them later on."

"That's a pretty big maybe," Manning muttered.

McCarter ignored him. "Stony, what are we looking at inside the base at Gecidi?"

"Unknown. There's a lot of *something* there. We've

gone into the Pentagon archives for past satellite inspections of the base camp there. We think it is full of junk, which may have been done deliberately. They may very well have another Patriot missile on the site—or several—and we can't identify it from above."

"Understood."

"You think these guys are sharp enough to know how to confuse a satellite reconnaissance?" Hawkins asked.

"Yes," McCarter said without hesitation. "Let's hope that's what they have going on—that'll mean more Patriots will be on-site. The more we can take out of commission tonight, the better I'll feel about the whole thing."

CALVIN JAMES PARKED the ALSV on the side of a hillock, with just half of the distant abandoned town of Gecidi visible in the valley below. There was nothing more than a collection of 1960s-era buildings that truly looked as if they had been abandoned for more than three decades.

Gecidi owed its failure to a lack of infrastructure. When the only water source, a small stream from the hills, had vanished after a small localized tremor that sent the water flowing into the ground instead of over it, the people had no choice but to leave. Thirty-seven years later, most of the buildings had collapsed or fallen in on themselves, and the only structure still fully intact was a large, single-story, aluminum-paneled warehouse. There were few windows in the structure, but there were plenty of rips in the flimsy metal skin of the building, and through it they clearly saw the glow of light.

James glanced at his watch as he unfolded the tripod on the earth, withdrawing the telescopic legs to get a level mount. "It's thirteen minutes after midnight," he reported. "Somebody is up late."

"They're using the darkness to ship out the Patriots," Encizo stated.

James pulled a case from the rear of the vehicle. Inside was a foam cutout and an Orion refractive telescope, which he attached onto the quick-mount tripod gear with a snap. Then he donned his Integrated Helmet Assembly Subsystem headgear and plugged the dangling cord into the rear end of the Orion. With a flip of a power switch the Orion began feeding a blurred video image into the small display inside the helmet.

The IHAS was a part of the integrated fighting system developed by the U.S. Army for the information-age soldier. Stony Man Farm made use of the best of this equipment, even while it was still under development, putting together its own custom hybrids to integrate with its proprietary systems while removing bugs that existed due to poor design or cost-cutting.

Now Calvin James watched the image sharpen as he pulled the focus using a control on his helmet. When he had a sharp image he adjusted it using X and Y axis controls. The Orion locked on to the warehouse and refocused.

"So they lug those things all the way to the far end of Turkey, and then they decide to send them back again?" James asked incredulously as he observed the building, scanning the image smoothly.

"They got them into hiding. I don't think they cared about the convenience of the staging so much as getting them where they wouldn't be found, which they nearly succeeded in doing."

James nodded as he examined the building. No sign of movement. At one corner a five-foot-wide triangle of wall panel had been ripped off by the wind and dangled there, exposing a mass of old machinery. In the glow of the dim light inside the building, James thought he could make out a generator. Maybe not. Whatever it was, it had stopped working a long time ago. At the next gap in the walls he saw what had to be the front end of a truck. The front tires were intact. Interesting. He kept scanning, finding a sliding panel door that was a few feet ajar.

"Now they can take them wherever they want for a quick launch. They could reach Erzurum, Malatya, Diyarbakir, Elâzig, any number of large cities by morning. Any of them ripe with targets."

"We're assuming their missiles are actually here. We don't know that," Encizo said.

"We do now," James said. "Phoenix Four here. You getting this, Stony?"

"Affirmative, Phoenix Four," said the voice of Aaron Kurtzman from the other side of the planet. "Run it through the spectrum for me, will you, Cal?"

The Orion was equipped with its own radio, sending out high-resolution video images at a frame rate of four per second. Stony Man Farm was receiving them over the same satellite uplink as it was using for voice and other data from the Phoenix Force commandos. At the touch of a control James sent the Orion into a rotation of electronic and mechanically actuated optical image filter types: infrared, ultra-high-resolution grayscale, thermal, which reached the Farm virtually instantly.

"Stony Two here," Kurtzman said. "This is what Phoenix Four just spotted."

Encizo grunted as the grayscale image showed up on the video screen inside his own IHAS. Through a small gap in the doors of the building they spotted a large block mounted on hydraulics risers attaching it to the flat bed of a truck.

"Stony, are we getting anything audible?" McCarter asked. While James had been setting up the Orion, and Hawkins was setting up an identical telescope on the opposite side of the ghost town, Encizo and Manning were erecting portable long-range listening devices.

"Negative, Phoenix," Kurtzman said. He had been listening in on the feeds from the devices. "There are voices, but you're still too far off to hear it over the ambient noise."

"Okay, Phoenix," McCarter said. "Let's move in."

Encizo quickly packed up the tripod-mounted listening device. James left the telescope where it was. Stony could continue operating it remotely for as long as the uplink remained. Behind the wheel again, James drove the Chenowth ALSV over the hill and started down the incline into the Gecidi valley, using the night vision capability of his helmet to steer without lights. He avoided the dim light coming from within the building—it would have been blinding in his night-vision glasses—and steered around the far end of the warehouse.

They entered the remains of Gecidi on its one street, a wide dirt road that was now overgrown with weeds and ruts from rain runoff. The buildings were heaps of wood, corroded metal and flapping scraps. Encizo carefully scanned the ruins for movement, seeing nothing. James watched the tiny icons on his helmet display, superimposed onto a satellite image of the town. When they reached an agreed upon spot, he pulled the ALSV behind a wall of wide bricks. He watched the icon of the other approach vehicle, coming in from the opposite end of the town, reach its stopping point.

"Phoenix," McCarter said over the radios in a low but clear voice, "proceed on foot. Stay smart."

Stony Man Farm, Virginia

THE WALL-MOUNTED screen in the Computer Room was wide enough to accommodate the entire spectrum of the Gecidi probe. Kurtzman and Barbara Price watched as three small blue figures, representing McCarter, Manning and Hawkins, separated from the other white icon that was the second ALSV.

The Phoenix Force warriors and their vehicles were outfitted with GPS transponders that reported their positions in real time to Stony Man Farm, where the mission control monitoring computer system added the data to the electronically generated Gecidi map. Without battlefield monitoring from a drone aircraft or satellite, however, they couldn't monitor the positions of hostiles, as well. As potent an authority as Stony Man Farm was, it couldn't always get the satellite time it wanted to coincide with its missions. In addition, the global satellite net simply wasn't comprehensive enough to be in all places at all times. Such as now.

Kurtzman and Price didn't speak as their eyes moved from the electronic display, with its creeping blue icons, to the visual images provided by the twin Orion field telescopes.

Where nothing moved.

Gecidi, Turkey

ENCIZO SPOTTED what he could only call an anomaly—a flicker of odd movement. He held up a hand fast. James was a step in front of him, but heard the quickness in the movement, turned and saw the flat hand his partner held up.

Encizo eased the night-vision glasses attached to his helmet onto his forehead, and slowly bent, staring at James's left leg.

The pinpoint of red light was so dim as to be nearly invisible. Encizo poked at his radio control. "Phoenix Two here—hold up the approach."

"Copy that, Phoenix Two," McCarter replied. Then the Phoenix Force leader said nothing, waiting for the explanation that would be, he knew, forthcoming.

Encizo had spotted the flicker of light around the corner of his night-vision lenses as they passed over one of James's legs, stopping him when it was still on the second leg. He said in a low voice, "Animal."

James understood. As Encizo stepped through the beam and radioed a terse report to McCarter, James began waving his hand in and out of it, erratic behavior that an animal might be expected to engage in.

Somewhere an alarm was going off. Maybe those who heard it could be fooled into thinking they had nothing more dangerous than a wild dog roaming around their ghost town.

Of course, if the other three had already broken through the laser perimeter at their end, the tactic was a waste of time.

Stony Man Farm

PRICE SQUINTED. "Aaron, switch Camera Two to infrared."

Kurtzman's finger jerked on the keyboard, and the right-hand image from Turkey abruptly went green. Out of the hot bright insides of the warehouse they suddenly saw shadows of quick movement. Figures came to the door of the warehouse and looked out, obviously armed.

"The jig is up," Kurtzman muttered. Price was already on the radio to McCarter.

Gecidi, Turkey

PHOENIX, they know you are on-site."

"Bloody hell," McCarter muttered. The Kurd terrorists were either reacting to the alarm set off by James and Encizo or his group had passed through the laser perimeter guard without knowing it. He had to admit that was the likeliest scenario. So the Kurds knew they were being approached from two sides.

"So much for sneaking around in the shadows," Hawkins said, but he sounded just the slightest bit relieved.

"We drive in," McCarter announced.

He called the order to James and Encizo as his two companions fell back with him to the Chenowth ALSV. McCarter slid behind the wheel and Hawkins jumped into the rear, planting himself behind the primary weapons station and its M-2 .50-caliber machine gun, using it to keep from flying out of the side of the vehicle as McCarter stomped on the accelerator and whipped the ALSV into a tight spin, then bouncing across the rocky terrain.

"I've got four or five figures on the approach with automatic weapons," Manning reported, searching the distant building through his night-vision lenses. "Wait— two more emerging and coming this way."

"How many going after Cal and Rafe?" McCarter demanded.

"Unknown. The building's in the way."

"Not for long." McCarter twisted the wheel and took the Chenowth to the top of a short rise, where it stopped short as a hail of gunfire peppered the ground in front of them, then homed in on them.

"They see us," Manning commented.

"Master of the obvious," Hawkins grunted.

"Lights," McCarter ordered tersely.

Manning shoved the night-vision goggles onto his forehead, placed the oversize barrel of the flare gun onto the top of the windshield frame and aimed into the night sky. The device triggered with a short flare of a rocket, then exploded in brilliant fireworks forty feet above the heads of the gunners.

The closely bunched group of gunners stopped running and gaped at the descending flare.

Real amateurs, Hawkins thought, but he didn't hesitate. The M-2 vibrated in his two-handed grip, chopping through the bunch like a gigantic invisible scythe. The troop was cut down in seconds.

"Not the sharpest tools in the shed," McCarter announced.

"One o'clock, T.J.," Manning called.

Hawkins adjusted the big M-2 and fired off a burst of rounds that chased after the other trio of gunners as they fled back to a corner of the big building around which they had just come. There were loud clangs, and the first few rounds slammed into the sagging aluminum panels, then Hawkins's aim solidified and the three went down together. They wouldn't be getting up again.

The night was quiet, then came a distant metallic pop and a rattle of autofire. "Phoenix Four here," James said over the radio. "We engaged three bad men and took them down. They didn't have much fight in them."

"Phoenix One here," McCarter said. "We had a

larger number to deal with, but they laid down like tired dogs.''

"Stony here," Barbara Price spoke up. "Sounds like they sacrificed the lowest men on the totem pole to test you out."

"Yeah," McCarter agreed. "No honor among mass murderers, I guess."

"So what do we do?" Hawkins asked from the rear of the Chenowth. "Stand here and wait for the second wave?"

"No way," McCarter said. "But let's move with a purpose."

CHAPTER TEN

"You are clear to make your approaches, Phoenix," Price said emotionlessly over the radio.

"I sure hope Stony's getting good images," Manning said as he felt the Chenowth surge forward and accelerate down a short incline into the valley.

He leaned to the dashboard for enough room to tuck the M-16 into the sling on his back.

"Too late to worry about it," McCarter warned as he steered the vehicle over the leveling ground directly at the building, as if he meant to ram it.

"What, me worry?" Manning said, grasping the windshield frame as he stood and stepped onto his seat. His body swung out as McCarter sent the Chenowth into a hard turn to the left, bringing it alongside the end of the low warehouse. McCarter braked sharply under a section of the overhanging roof. The roofing materials had blown off, and the framework of steel bars was visible.

"Stony One here," Price said. "Company coming front and rear."

"Phoenix Four?" McCarter asked into the radio.

"Ready, Phoenix One," James said.

Manning stepped from the dashboard onto the windshield frame and grabbed the rusty steel supports, then curled his body to get a leg up onto the roof. He could feel the corroded steel bars and the ragged bits of remaining aluminum tearing at his combat camouflage, but he was up. "Go."

McCarter didn't look back. He stomped on the accelerator, and the big diesel powerhouse heaved the Chenowth forward as he shouted over his shoulder, "T.J.?"

"I'm on it!"

The young Texan spun the M-2 and had his hand on the trigger, so that in the instant the Chenowth reached the corner of the warehouse he was ready to fire. He squeezed the trigger and cut loose into an approaching horde of gunners unprepared for the assault. The big .50-caliber rounds decimated them. If a shot was fired before they went down, Hawkins didn't hear it. Then the Chenowth was powering away from the slaughter.

Behind him, from the opposite side of the building, a pair of topless Range Rovers spun into view. Hawkins twisted the weapon station 180 degrees on its axis, even as McCarter was steering the Chenowth through a sharp turn underneath him, and commenced a blazing barrage at the pair of new arrivals.

But one of the Range Rovers had come to a sudden halt. Hawkins knew why. The driver had spotted the second Chenowth, running dark, in his headlights.

JAMES FELT THE SWEEP of the headlights pass over him as the pair of Range Rovers came around the corner. One of the terrorist vehicles continued after McCarter's Chenowth, but the second one hesitated, and James knew they'd been spotted.

"Rafe?"

"Got 'em," Encizo answered calmly from the rear of

the Chenowth, and then James heard the thump of the grenade launcher. A moment later the ground at the nose of the second vehicle exploded in fire, launching it into the air and flinging out one of the occupants. The vehicle went over on its back with a crash.

Encizo rotated the weapon station, and there was a second thump from the MK-9 grenade launcher. His aim was good but the target didn't cooperate. The second Range Rover braked hard, the driver shocked by the sudden obliteration the other vehicle. The second 40 mm round exploded, creating a crater in the earth where the Range Rover would have been. That was enough for the driver. He twisted the wheel and hit the gas, getting the hell out despite the protests of his two passengers. In his haste he put himself broadside to Hawkins, who unleashed a three-second barrage that depopulated the vehicle.

Stony Man Farm, Virginia

AKIRA TOKAIDO WASN'T a person who made his presence known. He was more at home inside the cybernetic world than the real one. He had been moving like an electronic demon through global networks long before most people had even heard of the Internet.

Aaron Kurtzman wasn't even aware of him when the young Japanese computer whiz stood at his shoulder, squinting at the jerky, high-resolution displays coming in from the cameras placed by Phoenix Force. He could see Gary Manning's tiny form scrambling across the level roof of the low building. The man's shadow, dancing in the light from the burning Range Rover, passed over an object mounted on the roof.

What was that thing? A tent?

He jumped into the seat of his terminal and grabbed the image off the main feed, extracting the three-second video bite he'd just witnessed, then fed it onto his own monitor and played it forward and backward. The small, dark silhouette of Manning sprinted across the front of the strange object, then backed up, then sprinted again.

Tokaido slowed it down, grabbing a single frame just as Manning's shadow went over the object. There was a moment when the light was just right to show him what was inside.

There was a gap between the outside panels of the object. Tokaido saved the high-resolution image to the hard drive and a second later reopened it with image-processing software. He sharpened it, blinked to see better, sharpened it again.

Then, suddenly, Tokaido knew what he was staring at.

Gecidi, Turkey

"I CAN SEE IN," Manning said into the radio. "We've got one hell of an opening in the ceiling covered with paper camouflage. There's a launcher right below me, in position to launch—"

"Gary, this is Stony Three! Get off the damned roof!"

Stony *Three*? "Akira?"

"Get off the roof. Phoenix Four and Two, there's a square box on the east end of the roof—blow it up! Right now!"

Stony Man Farm, Virginia

PRICE AND KURTZMAN looked across the room in stunned silence. Neither of them could recall Tokaido ever breaking into their radio monitoring of a field combat situation.

"Akira, what's going on?" Kurtzman demanded.

"Radar," Tokaido shouted into the radio. "It's a dish. On the roof. Phoenix, blow it the hell up!"

It took Aaron Kurtzman less than a heartbeat to understand the implications. Then he whispered, "Jesus."

Gecidi, Turkey

"PHOENIX THREE, I don't care how you do it—just get off the roof now," Price was ordered tensely. "Phoenix Four, I want that dish taken out!"

"We're in position," James said. "Let me know when we have a clear shot."

"More gunners coming out of the bloody building," McCarter announced. "We're moving in to cover you, Phoenix Four."

"Phoenix Three?"

"I'm clear!"

"We're taking fire," Encizo announced calmly.

"We're there."

McCarter spun the Chenowth into the face of the gunners, who promptly ducked for cover behind the burning hulk of the first dead Range Rover. As Hawkins stood at the M-2 and launched a deadly barrage into the dying flames and wreckage, an equally steady barrage of machine-gun rounds were chopping into James and Encizo's parked vehicle, forcing them down.

Encizo, crouched in the Chenowth at the base of the grenade launcher, wasn't sure what was happening. There was a radar dish on the roof of the building. Sure, it needed to be taken out. But why the sudden need for speed?

But there was a sense of strident urgency in the voices coming out of Stony Man Farm. That had him concerned. A machine-gun round from outside ricocheted off the metal a few inches above his head with a loud ping.

"Phoenix Two here," Encizo radioed. "All I need is three seconds of cover and I can take out the dish."

"We're trying, Rafe!" McCarter shouted.

"STONY ONE HERE—more vehicles coming from inside the building," Price announced.

Hawkins drew a sideways figure eight through the burning wreck and suddenly the return fire stopped, but handheld automatic rifle fire commenced from a Jeep and two small automobiles careening into sight. Now it was McCarter's and Hawkins's turn to hug the floor as bullets tossed around them.

"Stony, they've got us hemmed in," McCarter radioed.

"Phoenix One, I can't tell you how important it is to neutralize that radar dish *right now*."

"Not bloody much we can do about it, Stony!"

There was a sudden change in the sound of the gunfire, and shouts of confusion came from the enclave of terrorist vehicles. McCarter heard the bursting of tires and a scream of pain. He pulled his head up over the dashboard. There was Manning, skipping sideways behind the vehicles as he peppered them with fire from his M-16.

Manning had their attention.

"PHOENIX TWO—you're clear!" McCarter shouted out of the headset.

"I'm on it!" Encizo replied, dragging himself to his

feet. He didn't waste time searching for gunners that might get him in their sights. He'd deal with that in a moment. He grabbed the rear end of the MK-19 grenade launcher, targeted the small, innocuous-looking gray square on the roof of the building.

And suddenly it was too late.

A flash filled the building with orange illumination, then the blazing Patriot MIM-104 missile emerged through the roof opening into the night sky. For a moment the building, the ghost town of Gecidi, and the entire valley were bathed in the warm light of the exhaust, and then the missile was gone.

Encizo triggered the MK-19 and the 40 mm grenade slammed into the roof of the low building and obliterated the dish.

It was a useless gesture. A wasted round.

The missile had a very short distance to travel and had already passed the point where it would require guidance commands or course corrections from the ground. With such a short distance to fly, it entered the terminal phase of its flight in under a second, and it had ceased communicating with its ground control center in an eye blink.

"...evasive maneuvers!" Kurtzman was shouting in the radio. To whom?

Encizo twisted his upper body violently, agitated, suddenly feeling somehow betrayed, even though he wasn't sure yet what had happened. What was targeted by the flying missile? He planted the next two 40 mm rounds on the hood of the Jeep and watched it become a ball of fire. The occupants of the two cars exited the vehicles and tried to flee. A second grenade landed on the ground and blasted them away. By that time Hawkins was firing the M-2 machine gun and took down the last man standing.

Encizo noticed a tiny flare of light, miles away and just over the horizon line. Then Encizo knew. It was the Hercules that had transported them there. The radar on the roof had discovered and targeted it, and the ninety-kilogram Patriot warhead had blown it away.

It blazed for a moment, as tiny and fiery as a paper match struck to life, burning brightly, flickering in the breeze, then suddenly dying out.

Suddenly, with no satellite uplink, their radio feed from Stony Man Farm was silenced.

David McCarter sat at the wheel of the Chenowth, watching the last orange glow of the burning aircraft tumbling out of the sky, feeling as helpless as he ever had during his long career.

"Thanks for your help, Mr. Byarnsonn," he said quietly.

As for the Air Force copilot, McCarter didn't even know his name.

CHAPTER ELEVEN

Gecidi, Turkey

A sense of dread descended over the five members of the Phoenix Force, but it wasn't apparent in their behavior. They moved with catlike silence through the dual entrances to the warehouse, then split up, moving cautiously. The place was filled with the smell of burned metal and the dissipating exhaust of the long-gone Patriot. Rusting scraps of machinery and junk filled the interior. Manning and McCarter started at one end, Hawkins and Encizo at the other, while Calvin James monitored the entrances for terrorists that might get flushed out.

McCarter heard a sharp cry of fear. He looked across the inside of the building at Manning, who shrugged. They both knew it wasn't one of their teammates who had made the sound.

"Report," McCarter said into the radio.

"Phoenix Five here," Hawkins said from the far end of the warehouse. Now McCarter could see him emerging from the clutter with a slim man, wrists handcuffed behind his back walking in front of Hawkins. "I just picked up a piece of trash."

Stony Man Farm, Virginia

THE ROOM WAS silent except for the sudden rush of static. The screens had transformed to snow, which had been replaced with the small red words, "Signal Terminated."

Barbara Price and Aaron Kurtzman glanced at each other briefly, then stared fixedly at the meaningless banks of computers and communications equipment. Tokaido glared at his screen, frozen with his final image grab from the video feed, in silent shock.

Then the phone rang.

It was the line designated for remote access to Stony Man when all other communications failed. "McCarter here," said the voice from the speakerphone.

"Report," Price said tonelessly.

"I think we cleaned out this nest. One survivor only. Get this—it's an airman."

"Say again?" Price asked.

"He's U.S. Army."

"Hostage?"

"No. He's a Patriot operator. He's one of the guys the True Army of Kurdistan paid off to help them fire the Patriots," McCarter explained, his voice full of bitterness. "He's the one who just downed our transport."

Behind them Price and Kurtzman heard Tokaido suppress something vulgar.

"I guess," Kurtzman said, sighing, "Incirlik will be glad to get their hands on him."

Cheyenne, Wyoming

THE KID WAS THE SIZE of a football player, with wide shoulders and a thick, powerful neck. In fact he had played football in high school, but he'd never taken it seriously. Never took much of anything seriously. How he managed to earn his bachelor's degree was a minor mystery, to his parents and to himself. He'd chosen journalism because being a television news reporter seemed like a cool job that would get him some respect without requiring that he actually know much of anything. He had more or less stumbled into a job as a producer and occasional reporter for a local station in Cheyenne.

Now he was being handed a major story on a silver platter. It was the kind of break that would get him some serious recognition.

"You okay, Randolph?" the driver asked.

"I'm fine," he answered.

Randolph Oscar was sitting in the front seat of a Grand Cherokee, and the truth was he felt less than fine. He was scared to death, and it was taking all his concentration to remain cool. Gripping his thighs with his hands in an effort to keep his hands from twitching nervously, he attempted to act casual, gazing at the scenery.

Oscar hoped he would survive the rest of the afternoon.

The driver wasn't so bad. The man was clearly an American, with a Mississippi accent and a calm demeanor, though he had a big black handgun nestled under his left armpit and sometimes, when he rested his left hand on the top of the steering wheel, the butt of the handgun poked out like a rabid rodent sneaking a peek at him.

It was the man in the back seat who had Oscar scared. He had dense, short-cut black hair and a huge pitted nose. It was the deformed mouth that made him hideous, as if his lips had been put through a meat grinder then mushed back into place.

When they pulled off Interstate 80 Oscar realized he knew where he was, and that made him feel slightly more at ease. It was a truck stop outside the Cheyenne city limits. They were heading for the rear of the mostly empty truck parking lot. The Southern guy parked the Grand Cherokee behind the truck. "Here we are, son."

They all climbed out of the Jeep and without a word the Southerner helped Oscar get his equipment out of the rear of the SUV. Oscar erected the tripod, then the Southerner helped him hoist the big camera into place. Oscar inserted a half-inch videotape cartridge, checked the settings on the camera, then looked around nervously. "I'm ready whenever you are."

The Southerner went to the rear of the semi truck trailer and used a key to unlock the oversize padlock, then he pulled the doors open, careful not to allow them to swing wide enough to allow anyone else in the parking lot to see within.

In the bright morning sun, Oscar saw the huge black block that was the missile battery. Mounted on the inside of the truck cavity were two of the slim, menacing shapes of the Patriots. He had been expecting to see them, but he had not anticipated how lethal they would appear to him.

These weren't just killing devices. These were weapons made for warfare.

"You sure you want me videotaping this?" he asked for the third or fourth time.

"Yeah," the Southerner said. "In fact, we want there to be no doubt. Get up close as you can without getting inside the truck. They got to know these are the real deal."

"Okay." Oscar started tape and rolled the tripod on its casters, getting a wide shot first, taking it all in, then moving in close to pan down the length of each of the two Patriot missiles. He focused on and held the series numbers painted near the tail fins.

This was going to be great footage. This was going to be a real shot in the arm for his career.

He took five minutes of tape before he turned the camera off. "Okay, I've got about all I can of the interior," he said. "I'm ready to tape your statement."

The foreign guy with the disfigured mouth stepped in front of the open trailer doors. "I will speak from here," he announced. "Pull the focus from the missiles to my face, understood? Point the camera at me only—do not get him in the shot." He nodded to indicate the Southerner.

"You remember what we said—this tape is not to be made public until noon today," the foreign guy said, meeting his gaze emotionlessly. "If anybody finds out about this meeting in the next four hours, your life will be forfeit, and the lives of your family. Do you understand?"

"Yes. Yes, of course." Oscar tried not to look into the man's eyes, but he couldn't help but allow his gaze to be drawn to the hideous mouth. When the lips moved, it was like looking at something alien. He saw the lips mouth the words, "Start now."

Oscar hit the record button and adjusted the focus slightly. "Okay. Tape is rolling."

Asad Cakmak looked into the camera and began to talk.

Stony Man Farm, Virginia

HAL BROGNOLA TOOK the unlit cigar out of his mouth just long enough to pop in an antacid tablet, chew it with a disgusted look on his face and swallow with an effort. On the wall display CNN was playing the tape for the umpteenth time in the past hour. The sound was muted, but that didn't matter. The man from the Justice Department had memorized every word.

"Last night the U.S. government attacked me at my home in Evergreen, Colorado. Without provocation they came and attempted to put a halt to our freedom fight. But we did not allow them to do so. We stood our ground against our oppressors, even when they shot us down in cold blood.

"We should have retaliated immediately. But mercy stayed our hands. Even if the U.S. government does not care to sacrifice its own people, we do not wish for innocent citizens of the United States of America to die needlessly.

"But the next time we will not be so patient. If the U.S. government forces our hand, we will fire one of our missiles at a U.S. city. We have the capability to hit ground-based targets. Hundreds of U.S. citizens may die. It is time for the U.S. government to do what is best for its people."

"I love the 'without provocation' part," muttered Yakov Katzenelenbogen.

That was when Cakmak finally got down to the meat of the matter.

"For years the United States has been a friend to our Turkish oppressors. We're calling on the U.S. to use its might to cut off Turkey from international trade and relations until such time as Turkey has freed the Kurd people from oppression. We have the right to be free. We demand to be free. Turkey has the responsibility to give us our freedom, and the U.S. has the influence to make it happen.

"Decades of peaceful negotiations have accomplished nothing. Now we will bring about our freedom by force. Now we have the tools."

Brognola ignored him. "I just got my ass chewed out in the Oval Office," he said. "The Man is not a happy camper."

"Because?" Barbara Price challenged.

"We stepped on some toes when we moved in on the Evergreen site. Which wasn't so bad until Pretty Boy made it public knowledge."

"Our blacksuits did a first-rate job of cleaning up in Evergreen before the army was called in to take the launcher, Hal," Price said.

"You can't expect us to erase the fact that the attack happened," Kurtzman said.

"The Man thinks we should be able to."

"He's wrong. Short of incinerating the lodge and the forest all around it..."

"I know. But the President is in a bad place here. And that puts me in a bad place. The FBI wants to know the identity of the team that came in and shut down Cakmak's facility at Evergreen, and they have every right to know."

"What's the President's strategy?" Katzenelenbogen asked.

"Plausible denial," Brognola said, holding his cigar in a single crooked finger, "which makes it even worse for him. That means he's lying to his own federal agencies. It makes it even worse that he is new on the job. You know this guy is still idealistic."

"We came out of there with two unfired Patriot missiles, which the FBI never could have retrieved," Price insisted. "They'd have holed the terrorists up in the lodge and tried to talk them out for the next eight weeks. It was targeted on the Denver capitol building, for God's sake."

"Yes. Of course. But the fact remains that the President is unhappy with this turn of events," Brognola said. "Keep in mind he is our license to operate."

"Don't tell me we're going to have to start keeping a low profile at the expense of saving lives," Price demanded.

"We're going to have to keep a low profile and continue saving lives," the big Fed growled.

"That's not always possible."

"We have to find a way."

"What way? Are you saying there's a better way we could have gone into Evergreen that would have kept a lower profile?"

"No. I've read the reports. We made no errors in Evergreen."

"So what are you expecting of us here, Hal?"

"I don't know. I'm just telling you where we stand, and it's not on very solid ground. This President doesn't like us. Doesn't like the idea of the Farm. The new guys never do. And every time we get him in trouble—whether we're actually responsible or not—he's going to come down on us. And if we keep getting him in trouble, we'll be out of business before we have a chance to earn his trust."

"I understand, Hal," Price said, her voice curt. "The last thing I want to do is endanger the Farm's existence. But I will not compromise the mission." She looked at him across the broad expanse of the table, and her beautiful eyes glinted with fire.

Brognola tapped the butt of the cigar on the table three times, daring himself to continue the discussion, then thought better of it. "How's this thing going overall?"

"To hell," Price said shortly. "Three of our men dead. I can't remember the last time the Farm took so many casualties in so short a period. That's not counting the Air Force man who died with our pilot in Turkey."

"What's Phoenix's situation now?"

"Sitting tight," Katzenelenbogen reported. "The Air Force is sending out another transport, ETA in forty-five minutes. They're using the time to get some answers out of their prisoner."

"This guy is really U.S. Army?"

"Harold Thorpe is an honest-to-God, genuine Benedict Arnold," Kurtzman said with a grimace. "He confessed. TAK paid him to betray his country and feed the organization information for the past five months. He was stationed in Incirlik. Managed to get a two-day leave that started just hours before the Incirlik attack by the True Army. In all the chaos, Incirlik didn't even realize he was AWOL yet."

"What's he told Phoenix so far?" the big Fed asked.

"That he's not the only American on the team. Not even the only military," Price said. "There are at least eight more soldiers out of Incirlik and an unknown number recruited from Hickam Air Force Base on Oahu. Probably more he doesn't know about. Worse, Thorpe believes there's at least one upper-level U.S. Air Force officer involved."

Brognola's cigar drooped. "Huh. How upper-level?"

"Another unknown."

"This guy doesn't really know a hell of a lot, does he?"

Katzenelenbogen nodded. "That's to be expected. The True Army is proving itself to be a pretty intelligent bunch. They'd have seen their U.S. military recruits as their weakest links and given them precious little in the way of real information."

"So what I want to know is, does Phoenix have enough to go on? I've got to promise the Man that we're progressing, at least."

"Definitely," answered the Stony Man's tactical adviser. "The intel they got from Thorpe told them locations for at least three more staging sites for Patriot launchers in Turkey. They can investigate."

"Doesn't sound like good intelligence to me," Brognola growled. "Those staging sites will be changed once the True Army realizes their security is compromised— and I'd bet my government pension that was five minutes ago. Phoenix is going to come up empty."

"No," Kurtzman said. "We've circumnavigated that problem. At least, we can do so with your help."

"My help?"

"Authorization to allocate."

Deliberately, Brognola withdrew the cigar from his mouth, leaned on his hand and narrowed his eyes. "Allocate *what?*"

CHAPTER TWELVE

Incirlik Air Force Base, Turkey

Colonel Lennard Grantly had a sinking feeling in his stomach as he strode across the asphalt, watching one of the smallest hangars in the U.S. section of the base swing open slowly. A four-man crew was taking the aircraft through her preflight checklist, including filling her expansive fuel tanks. Grantly watched from a distance, not eager to distract the men with his presence until their vital task was completed.

It wasn't a large aircraft, with a short, flattened stub of a body and a sixty-nine-foot wingspan, but she had the sleek, faceless appearance that made people look twice. She was the Darkstar, a High Altitude Endurance Unmanned Air Vehicle—HAEUAV—developed in the Skunk Works and operated by Lockheed Martin, along with the Boeing Defense and Space Group. She was designed to go where living human beings couldn't or shouldn't go, and then stay there for hours at a time. The Darkstar was designed for fully autonomous operation, including independent takeoffs and landings, making use of the differential Global Positioning System. She could feed a sustained data stream, operating at subsonic speeds at an altitude of forty-five thousand feet for as long as eight hours at a stretch while deploying her electro-optical payload. The Darkstar could fly in fair weather or foul, day or night. Most importantly, she could operate in the most dangerous skies of the world virtually unnoticed. Even if she was pinpointed—unlikely, given her low-profile radar signature—she could be shot down without loss of life.

Grantly didn't like the situation he was being put in. He had been ordered to quietly launch the Darkstar and put her trained, ground-based flight crew and remote pilot in contact with an agency unknown to him. He wasn't even being told what the mission was, although he was sure it involved the search for the perpetrators of the Patriot missile theft.

Every officer stationed in Incirlik was red faced over that one, and would do anything to help make that horrible situation go away. And quick, because those bastards were threatening to use the weapon on the Turkish people.

Grantly knew the relationship between the U.S. and the Republic of Turkey was already rocky, with the death of Turkish airmen when the Patriot was launched into the Turkish section of the air base. What would happen if ten innocent people in Ankara were killed? Or a hundred or a thousand?

He watched the Darkstar roll out of the hangar and turn toward the runway. It was unsettling to think of the aircraft taking to the skies without a human in the cockpit.

But still, Grantly whispered as it accelerated down the runway, "Godspeed."

Behind him the flight crew started work on a second Darkstar.

ONE THOUSAND YARDS AWAY, in a small, windowless room, David Nicosia and Elizabeth Roman sat in acoustically insulated cubicles watching a pair of screens and panels of controls that gave them access to the Darkstar aircraft. Air Force pilots, both with aeronautical engineering training, were, by definition, redundant in their jobs. There was little for them to do, especially now, before the aircraft for which they were responsible were even on station.

Nicosia paid little attention to his partner, whose aircraft was already airborne, as he watched the readings from his own Darkstar. There was simply nothing for him to do. The aircraft was built to operate without human operators. He and Roman were simply safeguards built into the system. At least, they were under normal circumstances. For this operation they were also designed to serve as liaisons.

Nicosia turned on the cargo-fixed optics and showed himself a display from under the wide, rounded nose of his Darkstar. It looked cool to watch the ground speed under the belly of the beast during takeoff. From a proximity of just a couple of feet he watched the smooth concrete floor of the hangar pass under the Darkstar and become the asphalt of the taxiing area. He could even see the feet of one of the Air Force technicians when he moved in close, then walked away again.

"Ground control here. We're ready when you are, Eyes."

Nicosia's gaze swept over his feedback systems one last time. "Everything's A-okay on my end," he reported.

Then the asphalt sped up to a blur as the aircraft taxied across the tarmac to the runway, where it paused as the computerized pilot and the air-traffic-control computer exchanged messages. Nicosia's Darkstar silently received the okay for takeoff. It accelerated quickly, and Nicosia observed the runway on his display turn into impressionist streaks of color without texture. Then came the moment he loved, when the Darkstar became airborne, and the image on his screen suddenly drew back, his perception distancing from inches to thousands of feet in just seconds. The Darkstar jumped into the air over Incirlik, and the air base transformed from a vast landscape below the aircraft to a toy town. The last thing Nicosia saw before the Darkstar banked away was the ugly black scar on the asphalt, which was all that was left of the Patriot strike launched during the terrorist raid on the air base.

That black scar marked the place where innocent Turkish airmen had been killed. Struck down in flame.

That's what the mission was about, Nicosia reminded himself.

Soon the small, unmanned aircraft had climbed to twenty thousand feet and was heading east-southeast, deeper into the Turkish interior and around the city of Diyarbakir.

He glanced over at Roman. She was leaning back in her chair, watching her displays. There was nothing for either of them to do for the time being but wait.

"You have any idea what's going on?" she asked.

"No. All I know is these people aren't Air Force."

"I don't think they're even military," she said in a low voice. They hadn't been expressly forbidden to talk about the mission with each other, but there was no point in taking chances.

"Whoever they are, they've clearly got clout," Nicosia said.

Roman nodded, folding her arms on her chest. Nicosia

thought she looked beautiful, even in her Air Force uniform and boyishly short haircut. She looked up at him, and Nicosia realized he'd been staring. He'd seen her a couple of times in her civvies and she'd just about taken his breath away.

"I think it's CIA," she said in a whisper.

"Who else could it be?" He shrugged. "But if it's CIA, why don't they just come out and say so?"

"Maybe the Turks would freak out if they found out the CIA is operating here."

"They said they wanted us to cooperate fully. Doesn't that mean Central Intelligence?"

"Who knows? Maybe they think the CIA's a bunch of spies and they'll be opening the door on their own security if they let 'em in."

He grimaced. "Nothing we can do about it. I just do as I'm told."

"Yeah," she replied, grabbing her first of many cups of coffee that would see her through the mission. Then she stabbed at the telephone on her desk and started opening the outgoing networking protocol that would put the feeds they were receiving from the aircraft into the DOD net.

"Well," she said, "they have to be on our side if they have access to our systems, right?"

Nicosia snorted.

Roman's contact was in the U.S. That much she knew from the phone contact she was making. She heard multiple clicks and pauses before somebody picked up at the other end.

"We're ready when you are, Airman Roman," said a man's voice on the phone.

Christ, they even knew her identity.

"It's out there."

"We've got your feed," the man replied. "Now we've got Airman Nicosia's. From this point we'll be able to communicate on the system."

That meant they were not to call that number anymore. No more voice contact. Only messages keyed in over the network. "Understood."

"I know this is irregular. Thanks for cooperating."

"No thanks needed, sir," Roman said, feeling, unreasonably, as if she liked the faceless stranger on the line. He sounded a lot like her father. "We want the bad guys stopped as much as you do."

Stony Man Farm, Virginia, U.S.A.

STONY MAN FARM HAD humble beginnings and an even more humble locale. The quaint Virginia farmhouse that was its home was adequate for the antiterrorist operations that transpired there during the early days. After years of expanding scope, it became crowded with equipment, then incapable of holding all the communications, defense and computer hardware required to keep it at the forefront of antiterror activities—electronic hardware that wasn't even dreamed of in the early days of the Farm.

Recently, the Farm had gone through a major expansion. Now more than ever, the men and women who operated the facility had the tools to do what needed doing.

The Annex sat on forty-eight acres that had once adjoined the old eastern boundary of the Farm. It had been planted with apple trees, which were now well past their prime. Recently, as far as the locals knew, the land had been converted to a pulpwood plantation. The apple trees were cut down, and fast-growing varieties of poplar were planted, ideal for concealing a new network of sensors, digital video cameras and other warning devices protecting the new perimeter.

Dominating the new tree farm was a wood-chipping facility erected on a knoll close to the old perimeter fence. This was a one-stop wood-processing plant. After the trees were cut down, they were dragged to the plant and ground into wood chips.

Aboveground the plant consisted of a single-story, flat-roofed, concrete-block building. Inside, the chipping mill took up about half the space, and an office took up the other half. The mill side opened on the building's north end to allow trucks to bring wood in. A two-story wood-chip silo adjoined it.

It was an efficient, all-encompassing operation. It also made ideal cover for the new Stony Man Farm facilities—in fact, everything about the building's appearance was deceiving.

In truth, sections of the flat roof could be retracted to expose a battery of antiaircraft weapons, should the need for them ever arise. The concrete-block facade of the building hid six-inch armored concrete walls, similar to the protective barriers used in missile launch sites.

The outer skin of the wood-chip storage silo was composed of special plastic sheeting over electromagnetically invisible composite material. While an inner chamber of the silo could, in fact, be used for the storage of wood chips, the interior was primarily used to house the antennae needed by the Annex's global communications net. Data link transmitters allowed the Annex to shoot signals to local mountaintop retransmission sites. The links carried any and all digital communications, including video, audio and data. All this was in addition to a small dish antenna mounted on the office half of the building, looking like a satellite TV antenna.

The floor of the chipping plant was three-foot-thick reinforced concrete, below which was the hidden two-story subterranean Annex, home to the new Computer Room, Communications Center and Security Operation Center, where defense of the Farm, if needed, could be coordinated. A thousand-foot-long tunnel connected the Annex to the old farmhouse. It was tall enough to allow walking between the buildings, although usually a small electric rail car, designed to accommodate Aaron Kurtzman's wheelchair, was used for transport. The original farmhouse remained home to the primary offices and living quarters for the Farm.

Aaron Kurtzman's Computer Room and the adjoining Communication Center had been expanded to double their size in the Annex, and massive new data-storage capacities, measured in terabits, allowed the Annex to have more data on hand than in past years. Where once it had been forced to go online with the global nets to retrieve data as needed, now that data was automatically and constantly procured and stored on-site.

The key to this functionality was the Stony Man Spider, a one-of-a-kind software application designed by Kurtzman and his cybernetics staff, Akira Tokaido, Carmen Delahunt and former Berkeley University professor Huntington Wethers. Tokaido's vast hacker expertise had been especially valuable in the design of the SMS, making it an unparalleled Internet cataloging robot.

Like other spiders widely used by search engines on the Web since the first World Wide Web Wanderer was created in 1993, the job of the SMS was to travel the world's networks identifying pertinent data and downloading it. Roaming the Web, randomly and following directives from the staff, it identified by keyword searches those Web sites and proprietary networks pertinent to Stony Man Farm databasing. It parsed the Web page addresses contained on the page and followed each link recursively. As it followed each link, it started the process all over again, prioritizing the links automatically. Unlike any other spider in existence, the SMS had the best security-hacking capability built into it. It could automatically locate security systems, identify them by type—including packet-filtering firewalls, circuit-level and application-level gateways and stateful inspection firewalls—break through and rifle the contents of the secure network, without leaving a trace that it had even been there. The SMS was so good at its job it had even cracked high-level corporate and governmental defense-system security on its own.

When the Spider failed to break in to a system, it sent notification to Tokaido, who was seldom stymied. Once he'd gained entrance, he'd reprogram the SMS with whatever new tricks allowed him to get into the stubborn system.

In the end few electronic systems on earth were safe from access by Stony Man Farm, and all the gathered data was downloaded into hard drive banks that were measured in the thousands of gigabytes each.

But sometimes all the knowledge in the world wasn't enough. Akira Tokaido and Carmen Delahunt were seated at high-definition displays at one end of the Annex's Computer Room, watching the images transmitting in from the pair of Darkstar robotic aircraft stationed over Turkey.

"What are we looking at?" Kurtzman asked.

Tokaido shrugged. "Pastureland."

"See anything of interest?"

"Nothing that survives close inspection," he said. "But I can tell you how many sheep are grazing north of the village of Besni. And how many are male."

Kurtzman had extracted thousands of images of Turkey taken by U.S. spy satellites since the theft of the Patriot missiles from Incirlik. They would have required months for manual inspection. Digitizing them, he had them analyzed by computer for images that matched the profile of the possible missile staging sites.

Most importantly, the sites had been prioritized by proximity to the last known staging sites, those provided by the U.S. Army traitor Harold Thorpe.

The resulting matches of possibles had still numbered in the hundreds, which had been reduced by only fifty percent by manual inspection. Now, as much as possible, they would attempt to get close-up views of those possible missile sights using the Darkstar robotic aircraft. Stony Man fed the GPS coordinates of its hundreds of possible results to the Darkstars, which coordinated and cooperatively—and automatically—optimized a search pattern that would allow the aircraft to rephotograph them all.

That had taken three more hours. The images had been transmitted to the Farm quickly at first, and Tokaido and Delahunt had been strained to be able to keep up with the flow.

In most cases the high-resolution photo had shown that the target was a mundane object. In a few cases there had still been doubts.

"I've got something," Delahunt reported. "Look at this, Aaron."

On half her screen was a blurry image, dated just minutes earlier, of what was clearly a semi truck with a cargo that resembled the Patriot launch battery. Photographs of the launch systems, taken from every conceivable angle, were tacked to the wall above their workstations. Delahunt pointed to one of the images, then tapped her screen. There was clearly a strong resemblance between them.

"I'm moving in for a closer look," she said. "Give me another two minutes."

"Pull up the original source photo," Kurtzman requested.

Delahunt keyed in to request the electronic version of the satellite image that had originally steered them onto this target. It opened on her screen below the Darkstar image, a blurry close-up obviously taken from miles above Earth. Kurtzman wasn't interested in seeing the image itself, just its date and time.

"Less than twelve hours old," he said. "How far is it from Phoenix's strike in Gecidi?"

"Roughly 110 miles," Delahunt said.

Kurtzman exhaled heavily, afraid to be too optimistic. "We'll see what we see," he said hopefully.

Text streamed into the small gray message window: "Roman: D2 is on station, Carm. Here comes yr pic."

The photograph that materialized onto the screen was as clear as the image from a news chopper hovering a hundred yards above a traffic accident. There was a collection of small hills, a copse of dense forest growth and the twin paths of a seldom-used vehicle trail through the grass. Then, in the middle of a small clearing was a parked semi truck cab. Two men stood a few paces away, guns dangling on straps from their shoulders, looking at the cargo—a missile launch battery, elevated on hydraulic lifts at a sharp angle, aiming into the skies of Turkey.

More text appeared on Delahunt's message window:

"Roman: Hey Carm, I think we found what we were looking for."

Kurtzman grimaced. "I think we did."

Gilroy, California

THE AIR SMELLED like garlic, of all things. More of it was processed in this part of California than anywhere else in the U.S.

"This is making me crave pizza," Schwarz said.

"I don't even smell it anymore," Blancanales said. They'd been in town for more than twelve hours. "But anything would be better than another burger."

"No kidding," Schwarz grumbled. He'd had three fast food burgers in the past twenty-four hours. "My sweat is beginning to taste like special sauce."

"Yeah, well, keep your eyes on the fries, my friends," Carl Lyons said. "We've got more activity."

A quarter mile downhill, at a cluster of campers and pickup trucks, a large black Lincoln Town Car and a local police car pulled up slowly, attracting suspicious attention from a group of men gathered around the open hood of one of the vehicles, a twenty-year-old Ford with heavily rusted body panels, telling of years spent in wetter, colder climates than central California.

The Town Car parked away from the makeshift neighborhood, as if uncomfortable being in the presence of blue-collar vehicles. The two men who emerged were twins in their dark suits, abbreviated haircuts and sunglasses.

"Feds," Blancanales murmured.

"Ya think?" Schwarz asked. "How could you make them in those nifty undercover disguises?"

Blancanales snorted. "Those cops are more undercover," he said, nodding at the two Gilroy officers that emerged from the squad car.

Unseen from their vantage point in the scrub well uphill of the small transient community, Able Team watched the Feds and their local law-enforcement support give a lesson in bad intelligence gathering and poor people skills. The police officers took the lead, approaching the band of men gathered around the pickup truck like Western toughs out to scare a local rancher. One hooked his hands in his gun belt as he delivered a short speech. The second officer stood back, arms folded on his chest, the late-afternoon sun mirrored on his glasses. The Feds watched from a distance, emotionless.

Schwarz was wearing a pair of headphones tied into a long-range listening device. The pickup dish was mounted on a tripod staked into the ground and was pointed downhill on the Kurdish transients. It was wired into the Hummer that had brought them from Mendocino, where every word was being fed to the Farm. After hours of listening, they had come up with nothing. If the small band of Kurdish migrant workers knew anything about TAK activity in the area, they weren't discussing it, even among themselves.

There had already been a visit earlier in the day by San Francisco–based FBI looking for intelligence. The Kurds had told them nothing.

What Able Team and the FBI both knew was that two of the men in the small community, brothers, were once members of the Turkish People's Liberation Army of Kurdistan. Both emigrated to the U.S. in the late 1990s. Their continuing ties to the pro-Kurdistan movement and other ARGK members was unknown. What was sure was that they were distant cousins to Asad Cakmak.

"What's that cop saying, Gadgets?" Lyons asked.

"About what you'd expect an arrogant asshole to say to people he thinks are lower than dirt," Schwarz said. "He wants them to talk or walk. They either provide the Feds with the information he's looking for or he'll drive them out of town like unwanted vermin."

"Nice," Blancanales said. "Any of them talking?"

"Course not. Now the Fed's going to prove he's even more of an asshole than the local PD," Schwarz added, pressing the headset closer to his ears. Below, one of the men in dark suits stepped forward and began speaking. "Oh, this is how you get things done. Revoked emigration cards. Now he's threatening to deport the husbands only."

"Threatening to break up families always gets you the cooperation you're looking for," Lyons said acidly.

"Gadgets," Blancanales said, "focus over at the rear end of the back camper."

Blancanales was pointing at the most dilapidated of the trailers, an ancient camper without much paint left anywhere on its aluminum shell. Schwarz walked the mounting arm of the tripod in an arc, then adjusted the alignment of the pickup dish as he homed in on the conversation going on there. A young woman was on a cinder block step, facing in through the open screen door and clearly agitated. Schwarz focused the sound dish on her and heard her speaking clearly.

"...nothing to fear." It was the voice of the woman, turned metallic by the long-range pickup. "They are trying to save lives."

"So is Cakmak," retorted the voice of a man, even more distorted because he spoke from inside the camper.

"Cakmak is a murderer," the woman retorted, and Schwarz could tell, despite the strange quality of her voice through the headphones, that she was struggling to keep her composure. He put his binoculars to his eyes. Now he could see her just as clearly as he heard her. She was a young, beautiful black-haired woman, with dark eyes that flashed with emotion. Her shapeless flannel work shirt and dirt-crusted jeans couldn't hide her lithe, strong figure.

"Don't say those words!" the man ordered.

"I will say it because it is true. He is a murderer—a murderer of children."

"He is a Kurdistan patriot!"

"If Kurdistan must come into being by the blood of children, it does not deserve to exist."

"I will not listen to this."

"*They* will listen," the woman said suddenly, and slammed the screen door, turning away. She didn't get far. The door was caught before it was even closed, and a dark-haired man in his late fifties stomped out. He was upon the young woman in three strides, grabbing her small wrist in a giant hand and pulling her off her feet. She shouted, almost a scream, but he clamped his other hand over her mouth, covering half her face. Her eyes were wild with fear and rage as she was dragged back to the camper. For a moment Schwarz thought she could see him, hidden in the bushes a thousand feet uphill, and was silently pleading with him for rescue.

Then she was dragged into the camper and was gone.

HEDIPE DEMIR FELT her body being lifted off the ground and she landed on the thin cushion of the mattress so hard the entire camper rattled. The mattress of her bed was only two-inch-thick foam, well used, and wasn't much cushion at all. She lay there gasping painfully for a long minute.

When she looked up, her father was sitting at the tiny

table with a single finger wrapped around the handle of a coffee mug, glaring at her, daring her to speak.

"So you are as prone to violence as they are, these patriots you speak of," she challenged.

"Violence has its purpose."

"Were you a killer, too?"

"You know I was."

"Were you a killer of children?"

The man said nothing, but the intensity in his eyes turned to chagrin and he examined what floated in his cup.

"You shame me," she said. "You and this terrorist with the weapons—you shame the Kurdish people."

"It is a fight for freedom," he hissed.

"You are creating a legacy that the world will remember long after the dreams of a free Kurdistan have died."

Now her father looked up at her, shock on his face, as if she had said something powerful that had never occurred to him before. It was merely a blatant ugly truth. Kurdistan might never come into being, but the Kurd people could very well end up with a reputation as killers and thugs that would endure forever. Hedipe could see this future as clearly as if it were accepted history—a time when to be Kurd was so profoundly negative that her people deliberately distanced themselves from their culture and their heritage, and their heritage vanished as a result.

She lay staring at the wall, deliberately facing away from her father. He sat at the table drinking his coffee. It was an hour later when he rose, left the camper and came back a minute later. He tried to shake her shoulder, but she moved it out of his hand.

"They have left. You can get up now."

She didn't speak. Her father left again, saying as he let the screen door slap closed behind him, "Start on dinner."

Turning onto her back, she stared at the ceiling. Her father would be going to join the circle of men that gathered in the center of the small village of transient Kurd agricultural workers. He would go to find out what the others had told the agents that had come asking questions. She knew what they had told them. Nothing. The group was close-knit. But more importantly, there was nothing that the others knew to tell the agents. Only her father and his brother—and their families—knew anything about the activities of the True Army of Kurdistan.

Hedipe thought about what she should do. To go behind her father's back and tell the U.S. government what she knew would be a betrayal of her family. She could very well be banished from all she had ever known.

But it might save the lives of innocent people.

When she came to that realization, she knew what she had to do.

CHAPTER THIRTEEN

Hedipe Demir emerged from the scrub a mile downhill, along the roadside. She intended to follow it down to the highway, then hitchhike into Gilroy or maybe even flag down a state trooper. Then she could tell what she knew to the authorities. They would listen to her once they knew the identity of her family.

But she wasn't going to let herself be seen until she got to the highway. There were a few trucks among her group. If her father found her missing, he might send someone after her.

She wished she had a watch. She guessed it had been half an hour since she'd stolen out of the camper and entered the brush. Her father would be returning to their home any minute now, expecting to find dinner ready. Instead he would find an empty camper.

She loved him. He was her father. But she knew what she had to do. She knew she was doing the right thing.

"Hedipe?"

She almost screamed. She was so startled she backed suddenly into a dried bush and felt the sharp branches scrape at the skin of her bare arms and face. The slim figure stepped up and grabbed her by the arm just above the elbow. His fingers were strong, but somehow more gentle than the heavy hands of her father, and he managed to keep her from toppling into the shrub.

"Who are you?" she demanded.

"Call me Gadgets."

"Gadgets who?"

"It doesn't matter."

"How do you know my name?"

"That doesn't matter, either. I am here to help you."

"Help me do what?"

The man held up a black plastic electronic device the size of a deck of playing cards and pressed a button. Hedipe was startled again, this time because she heard her own voice coming out of the device. It was metallic, like the sound of voices out of tin-can telephones she and her friends had played with when they were young.

"Were you a killer of children?" she heard herself say, and she realized it was the last argument she had with her father—maybe the last time in her life she would ever speak with him.

"You were spying on us?"

"Yes," the slim man said. "You know why."

She nodded. "Yes."

"I think you have something you can tell us."

The young Kurd woman appraised the slim man with a wary eye. He was dressed in desert camouflage, with sandy-brown boots. He had a mean-looking handgun tucked under one arm, and there was a knife on his belt, just behind his right hip, that looked as if it could be used to gut and skin an elephant. He was certainly a soldier of some kind. He wasn't a Kurd, but he was one more man of violence. So why did she get the impression she could trust him?

"I will speak to you," she said, "but first you must

tell me what you aim to do. Is it your intention to stop the True Army before it kills more innocent people?''

"Yes," Hermann Schwarz answered without hesitation. "We've dedicated ourselves to putting Asad out of business. If you have good information, you might be able to help us do it."

Now Hedipe Demir noticed a huge, flat-topped vehicle coming slowly down the hill road. It certainly wasn't one of the vehicles belonging to her people. The slim man glanced at it briefly and didn't look at it again as it rolled to stop behind him. There were two more men inside, both watching without malice.

"If I do not choose to go with you?" she asked.

"I'm not going to force you, if that's what you want to know," the man who called himself Gadgets said with a slight grin.

Hedipe looked back, through the brush, in the direction of her people and her father, whom she was probably leaving behind forever. "All right," she said quietly, then turned her head away. "I'll go with you."

The back seat door to the Hummer was being held open for her. The tall, slim man was smiling. As bad as she felt, she couldn't help but smile in return.

SHE LOOKED AT the big sheet of unfolded paper spread out in front of her.

"I am sorry, but I cannot make any sense out of this."

That wasn't what the man in the front seat wanted to hear. He gave some sort of significant look to the one who sat with her in back, the one who called himself Gadgets.

"You don't recognize any of these landmarks?" Gadgets urged her. "Here's the spot where we picked you up. Here's the highway. Here is Gilroy. North and south." His hand moved over the map, pointing out places as he explained the legend.

She shook her head. "I have hardly ever seen a map before. It is too hard for me to understand."

"But you know this area?" the man in the driver's seat probed. He was an intense figure, with the look of a man ready to strike at any second. Actually, he was what Hedipe considered an archetypal American soldier. The other man in front looked Mexican, stocky and powerful, and hadn't yet said a word.

"I know the area," she assured them. "I can take you to this place."

"How far?" Gadgets asked her. "How long would it take to get there from here?"

"By car—" she shrugged "—less than an hour."

The driver breathed long and low, very concerned about something. Maybe he didn't trust her. She looked at him and found him looking at her back-seat companion.

"Hedipe, give us just a minute, would you?"

The three men got out of the vehicle, which was now parked off the highway just outside Gilroy. They met at the front of the car and conferenced quickly. Then a dashboard light came on at the same time the driver, the intense one, started talking into a headset he'd pulled out of nowhere. She realized he was radio linked to somewhere. The one she thought of now as her friend, the one who called himself Gadgets, gave her a smile.

Ankara, Turkey

WHEN THE CALL to prayer issued from loudspeakers, it was heard in every corner of the sprawling metropolis that served as the governmental and economic center of

Turkey. Dogan Bir's forehead wrinkled in distaste. In his opinion the racket was a disturbance of the peace. If he had the political clout he'd issue a call for it to be banned. He smiled when he thought about the strict Muslim community's reaction to such a ban.

His secretary, a slight, short, dark-skinned young man, slipped through the double doors of his office and closed it behind him, grasping his hands low in front of him in what Bir considered to be a distinctly feminine gesture.

"Mr. Yilmaz has arrived. He's brought other men with him—businessmen that I recognize."

Bir considered this. So Yilmaz came with a contingent. That was interesting. "Show them in."

The secretary's face puckered in concern. His boss clearly wasn't getting the point. "I wanted you to be forewarned that there are many of them, sir. Five or six men. Some important men, if I recognize them correctly."

"So you leave them sitting around in the waiting room? Show them in! And bring coffee."

The secretary nodded, chastised, and pulled the door open again, making a valiant attempt at a welcoming smile. "This way, gentlemen."

He was a competent secretary, Bir thought. Just highstrung.

Cengiz Yilmaz came through the door at the head of a column of men that Bir quickly realized was a who's who of Turkish manufacturing and trade organizations. This wasn't a contingent; it was a lynch mob.

"Good morning, Mr. Yilmaz. Good morning, gentlemen." Bir wasn't so impolitic as to disdain shaking hands warmly with all his guests. He spread smiles throughout the room and didn't have a single one of them returned.

"Find seats, please, if there are enough of them to go around," he quipped. "I'll have the boy bring in chairs from the outside office. And where's the coffee?"

Bir could see that Yilmaz was quickly losing patience as he bustled throughout the room, supervising his secretary's efforts to get all his guests seated and served. That was fine with Bir. He was enjoying himself. "Now," he announced finally, "I think I'll have a cup myself." He proceeded to pour himself a cup of coffee, stir in a mound of sugar and head back to his desk like a harried party host finally finding the time to sample his own refreshments. He collapsed into the chair behind his desk with a sigh and a huge grin.

"So, it's good to see all of you gentleman today. My networking quota will be satisfied for the rest of the month, I imagine."

"Can we get down to business, Dogan?" Yilmaz demanded.

"Of course. You just caught me a little off guard, is all, Cengiz. If you had called ahead, I could have been a little better prepared to receive so many guests. If an earthquake brings down the building right now, the economy of the nation won't recover for years."

His ebullient mood and deliberately poor taste in jests sent a current of uneasiness throughout the gathering of businessmen. Just as he expected. Dogan Bir smiled into his cup of coffee, taking a gigantic swallow and satisfied that he had effectively deflated Yilmaz's efforts to intimidate him by showing up with his gang of heavy hitters. "What can I do for all of you?"

"We are here to discuss the ongoing debacle with the rebels," Yilmaz said, "and what the government is not doing about it."

So that was the gist of it, Bir thought. "I'm a trade official. There is nothing I *can* do about it."

"There's not going to be any trade at the rate we're going," Yilmaz retorted angrily.

"Exactly," another suited man, Recai Tantan, stated flatly. He was the founder and chief operating officer of one of the country's largest textile conglomerates. "We're in trouble. The entire country is in trouble because of these rebels."

"I understand that," Bir said.

"This is playing havoc with our European Union entry negotiations. Are you aware how much ground we've lost?" Tantan demanded.

"I think you're overestimating the impact of these events."

"The impact cannot *be* overestimated. These rebels have timed their strike just when it is most vital that the nation have a good image among the other EU nations. They're opening old wounds, stirring up fresh resistance to this country because of our history of so-called human rights. We cannot afford to look heartless and oppressive in the eyes of the other European nations, Mr. Bir!"

"I'm very aware of that, Mr. Tantan," Bir said levelly. "But we cannot hide the fact that the Kurd rebellion exists. All we can do is handle it in a manner most acceptable to the human-rights activists."

"The problem is that we've perpetrated no acts against the Kurds recently, and yet we're still being cast into the role of violent oppressors of Kurdish freedom," Yilmaz explained.

"And we'll continue to be as long as the Kurds are vying for freedom," Bir added. "That's the legacy of our history with our Kurdish people."

"It's unfair that we should be punished for the efforts

we've undertaken to protect our nation's integrity," Yilmaz declared bitterly. A chorus of agreements and shaking heads answered him.

Bir continued playing with them, baiting them. He was really enjoying himself. "The official stance of the government is to behave as the EU citizenry would ask—guarantee the Kurdish people the rights they demand."

One of the businessmen snorted angrily. Tantan rolled his eyes to the ceiling.

"And you can see how effective a policy that is," Yilmaz stated. "We've bowed to their every whim. We gave in endlessly to European demands to treat that criminal Abdullah Ocolan in what they would term a 'humane' manner. Look where it's gotten us. As soon as we're ready to embark on serious negotiations to enter the economic union, Ocolan's puppies start a new campaign to smear our image."

"Every time we start getting closer to joining the EU, the Kurds are going to find a way to stall the process, and in the end it will be years or decades before the thing can be done," explained a new voice, one of the elder statesmen of the Turkish metal-manufacturing sector. "The pattern is plain to see. We'll have to give in, make concessions to the Kurds, just to get back to the bargaining table. We will never achieve acceptance into the EU until we have made the ultimate sacrifice—surrender to the Kurds half our acreage for their own sovereign nation. They cut Turkey in two and bankrupt us to capitalize their new government."

Yilmaz nodded. "That's exactly right. We're entering a vicious circle. We need to extricate ourselves now, before the die is cast and escape is impossible."

Bir sat back in his chair, slightly slouched, shrugging

with a grimace. "I hear your words. I agree with what you are saying. Believe me, I understand your frustration. What I do not understand is what I can do about it."

"Don't play games with us, Dogan," Yilmaz shot back, and his brow had grown out over his eyes, leaving them dark and menacing. "We need you to put a stop to this. Now."

"I ask you again—how?"

Yilmaz sat back, thought about his next words carefully and said, "The men in this room represent a coalition that will fund efforts to put a halt to the current wave of violence against the Turkish people."

For the first time since the meeting had begun, Bir was taken off guard. "Really?" he asked. "Surely you know that there are substantial Turkish and U.S. efforts under way to accomplish that same goal."

Yilmaz waved the notion away. "Token efforts. Our goals and methods will be seriously intent on stopping the terrorists by using their own methods. We go after their own people. We hold their families hostage the same way they're holding all of Turkey hostage."

"That's the kind of human-rights maneuvering that put the nation of Turkey in the bad graces of the European Union," Bir replied.

"This will not be the acts of the nation of Turkey," the old metal manufacturer answered in a level voice. "Just as the terrorists are independent representatives of their people, the Kurds, we go to war with them as independent representatives of our people, the Turks. We strike at their heart. We take away their women and children. When they lower their voices, we'll give them back their families."

Bir thought about that, looking from face to face, then

a new grin grew on his mouth. "But I am a trade official. What you are engaged in is claimed to be a private enterprise. So I have to ask you for the third time, gentleman—what do you want from me?"

"Your access to government intelligence," Yilmaz replied, and for the first time he was smiling, as well. "Specifically, a list of Kurd targets."

Singapore City

"SPECIFICALLY," said Yilmaz on the tiny television screen, "a list of Kurd targets."

"This is rich. This could not be better."

"I assume you are interested in making the purchase?"

Nouri Bakir nodded, then said aloud, "Mr. Bir, tell me why you are selling."

"Why not?" Bir said, wearing a grin like a happy dog and leaning back in the cushioned chair in the private airport lounge. Much nicer, he noted, than the furnishings at the airport in Ankara. The Singapore Air flight, first class, had been nice, too. Maybe he would retire to Singapore. The meeting in his office had been just a few hours ago. He had been lucky to find that the only Lufthansa flight to Singapore was leaving at about the time he would reach the airport—if he raced there. He had called Nouri Bakir from the plane.

He had known Bakir for years, a contact he had always known would pay off handsomely some day.

"Won't the tape be incriminating to yourself, as well as to all these other men?" Bakir asked.

"Not at all, Mr. Bakir," Bir said. "The camera was set up to get everyone in the room except for the person behind the desk. Me, of course. Also, you'll note that the office is decorated in a deliberately nondescript manner. There's nothing unique about it. Nothing to prove it is my office. Thirdly, before I hand you the videotape I will have electronically removed my own voice—without, of course, altering the voices of any of the other men present in the room.''

"I see," Bakir said with a nod. "Now, I must ask you this, Mr. Bir. Why do you think I am even interested in purchasing this recording?"

Bir nodded, smiling, as if he had been expecting the question. "I'm not one hundred percent certain that you would be, Mr. Bakir. But after the meeting you see in the tape, I set about uncovering the facts that these gentlemen asked me for. They wanted me to find out as many identities as could be located of the Kurds behind the recent missile hijackings in Ankara."

Bir paused. Bakir said nothing, nodding slightly. Behind him, his trio of massive Indonesian bodyguards stood as still as statues, walling off Bakir and Bir from the rest of the airport activity, as if enclosing them in a private room.

"The name at the top of the list of those suspected of funding the activities of the True Army of Kurdistan was, well, you, Mr. Bakir."

Bakir said nothing, made no reaction whatsoever.

"If I am mistaken—"

"How much are you expecting me to pay you for this videotape?"

"One million U.S.," Bir answered without hesitation. "I won't negotiate."

"You're not a man with scruples, are you, Mr. Bir?"

"That's why they came to me in the first place," Bir said with a grin, waving at the small camcorder. "They knew I'd get done what they asked if they paid me the right price."

"But now you come to me?" Bakir asked without accusation.

"If you buy this tape, I plan on retiring."

Bakir nodded. "I see. What else would you do for the right price?"

Bir smiled and leaned forward, elbow on his knees, and nodded to Nouri Bakir. "Whatever needs doing."

"Good. Then I will pay your price for the tape. One million dollars U.S. Tell me where you want the cash deposited. And I will pay you that much again to perform one more task."

"Which is?"

"Give these men the information they asked for."

Bir was slightly stunned, and his face froze as he pondered it. "You want me to help these men locate the families of suspected True Army terrorists?"

"Yes," Bakir said without emotion. "This tape of yours will not officially come to light until after the attacks have been made. Their Kurdish victims will become our martyrs." Bakir nodded as if to himself. "At the right moment, when sympathy for my slain people is at its peak, we'll send this tape to every broadcast-news outlet in the world."

CHAPTER FOURTEEN

The young Kurdish woman, Hedipe Demir, pulled the binoculars from her eyes and squinted, trying to relax some of the tension out of her eyes, then rubbed the back of her neck, numb from hours scrunched in the same position. She glanced at Carl Lyons, sitting at her side in the driver's seat of the Hummer. Her tension had been growing in the past twenty minutes, as if she expected the men to demand quicker results from the stakeout. So far there had been nothing.

"What's the closest phone your father is likely to have used to make his contact?" Lyons asked her.

"I don't know. You may have noticed a gas station a mile onto the highway after we left the mountain road. That's the nearest public phone."

"Nobody in your community had a phone?" he asked.

"There was one or two cell phones," she explained. "My father is not the best-liked man among the village, nor the best-trusted. Whether he would try to use one or not—it depends how urgent he is."

"If he suspects you're going to rat on his friends, he'd consider the situation pretty urgent," Lyons guessed. "If he realized you were gone half an hour after you left the village, and made a call within ten minutes of that time, that's about forty minutes. Our man could easily have flown the coop.''

"Yes,'' she agreed tentatively, as if expecting him to get into a rage. He felt her tension and gave her a quick look and a small smile. He still didn't like having her along, but he had to admire her willingness to throw away everything she knew to help protect the lives of strangers.

"Movement,'' said Rosario Blancanales.

Demir put the binoculars back to her eyes and watched the dark figure emerge from the tiny, two-room house. He walked to the curb and up the street, heading uphill. He didn't look back or around, acting like any normal man out on a stroll.

"That is the man my father was friends with,'' Demir said. "I don't know his name.''

"Who does he live with?'' Lyons asked.

"Nobody as far as I know.''

They watched the man walking up the street. One thing was clear—he was in a hurry.

"Shouldn't we be following him?''

"In a moment,'' Lyons said at about the moment that the man disappeared from view. They were parked around the corner, with another tiny, ramshackle old house half hiding the Hummer. "Pol, want to do a little breaking and entering?''

"Sure. I'll sneak around, go downhill and come up toward the back of the house. Nobody'll see me coming or going.''

"That's a priority. Remember, we need to remain unseen.''

Hedipe was getting worried as the man slipped out of the rear of the Hummer, crossed the street and descended into the prairie plants and shrubs that grew along the outskirts of the small neighborhood outside the town of Gilroy. He descended the steep sides of the hill and was lost from sight.

"What's the matter?" she asked. "Why aren't you going to arrest that man?"

"It's not that simple," Lyons said.

She stared at him for a moment. "You don't believe me," she said. "You think I don't know what I'm talking about."

"Not at all," Lyons said. "But what good would arresting him do right now?"

"It would stop him from firing the missile!"

"He's not working alone, Hedipe," Schwarz said from the back seat. "If we arrest him now, his companions will know we're close on their tail. They might be panicked into pulling the trigger. The last thing we want to do is force their hand."

"There's even more to it than that," Lyons explained as he put the transmission into gear and started the Hummer rolling slowly to the corner, then turning up the street after the walking Kurdish man. "We're trying to stop missiles that might be planted all over the United States. We want to get information that will help us locate all of them. We can save more lives than just the intended victims of the terrorists based here in California."

Demir considered that. Then she nodded. "I understand."

"Don't worry. We'll do everything we can to stop this bastards from blasting a crater in downtown Gilroy," Schwarz said.

"Able Two here," said Blancanales in their headsets.

"Go ahead," Lyons said.

"I'm approaching the rear of our friend's house."

"Any signs of other occupants?"

"Negative."

Demir was silent as she listened to the one-sided conversation she was hearing. She was worried about the man—what was it they called him, Pol? She didn't even know the name of the man in the seat beside her, and Gadgets in the back seat—that was most obviously an alias, too. Still, she liked these men. They came across as ethical, and determined. She wouldn't want to see any of them get hurt. But here this man Pol was sneaking into the house of a suspected terrorist, alone and acting as if it were all in a day's work.

"I'm inside," Blancanales reported in a low voice. "Not a nice place he's got here. Neat and tidy this guy ain't. But there's nobody else here."

"Anything useful?"

"Not unless you're one of those artists who makes sculptures out of garbage." After a moment Blancanales added, "I've got a passport."

"Let's get a picture and fingerprints."

"Already done."

A quarter mile ahead of them, the man from the house walked into the door of an old street-corner convenience store, the kind of place that had existed for years as a neighborhood market. Lyons steered the Hummer around a corner and parked it on the shoulder. In the back seat Schwarz had just enough of a view of the entrance to watch it. He aimed his binoculars at it as Lyons conversed with Blancanales.

"That's about all I'm going to get out of this place," Blancanales was sighing. "Not too productive, I'm afraid."

"Maybe not yet," Lyons said. "Let's put our bugs in place and see what he will say for himself."

"I'm doing it now."

"Our man is out," Schwarz reported.

"I heard that," Blancanales said. "He coming back this way?"

"Yeah. But he's in no hurry."

Lyons put the Hummer in gear again and pulled away down the side street, then turned right again, putting an entire block of houses between the Hummer and the home where the Kurd man lived. They saw him in glimpses between the buildings as he strolled along with a bag of groceries.

"I'm out," Blancanales reported. "I'm hiding out downhill of his backyard. Let me know when I should move out."

They watched, pulling ahead to keep their suspect in view as often as possible. He strolled past his house and kept walking, heading down the long slope of the street. Lyons pulled out behind him when he was another quarter mile down the street, and Blancanales emerged from the weeds to rejoin them in the Hummer.

"Don't tell me I wasted my time," he said.

"He's definitely got somewhere else to go," Schwarz said.

As they sat there, waiting for the walker to put enough space between them so they could move on behind him, Demir watched Blancanales pull a laptop out of the rear of the Hummer and touch a button that brought it to life instantly. He extracted the Polaroid PDC from his pocket. It was a powerhouse of a digital camera, far removed from the instant cameras the company was known for. The PDC had 128 megabytes of CompactFlash memory. It enabled him to take and store eight or more 3.1 megapixel images, then change out the memory for additional storage. The high level of detail in the images would make every word of the photo-graphed passport legible when it was analyzed at Stony Man Farm.

Blancanales plugged the camera into the rear of the computer, extracted the images he had just taken, and e-mailed them via the cellular modem. Next out of the computer case came the Hewlett-Packard CapShare, which allowed him to scan a translucent card of finger-prints. He saw Hedipe watching him and explained, "I'm sending these photos and these fingerprints over a cellular modem to our central office," he said. "They're tied into the nationwide fingerprint databases and should be able to pinpoint our man using automated fingerprint-identification systems. Even if he doesn't have a U.S. criminal record, they might be able to ID him through some of the international databases."

"Why do you need that if you have the passport?" she asked.

"That'll be a fake," Schwarz said. "Even if it was issued legitimately, it was probably obtained using forged documents under fake names. But tracking it may give us more leads on his ID."

"Sounds like it would take a long time to do that," she said.

"We typically leave the hard-core investigating to somebody else," he said.

"He's heading into those trailers," Lyons announced. "I'm going to move in closer."

Lyons allowed the Hummer to coast down the long incline of the street until he was just close enough to watch the Kurd knock on the door of one of the trailers, a boxy-looking house trailer in pale yellow with faded white shutters. The door opened, and the Kurd stepped up inside the trailer. The door closed behind him.

"I think we're on to something here," Lyons said, staring through his binoculars."

Schwarz, also examining the trailer through field glasses, agreed. "Yeah. Something's not right."

"Why?" Demir asked. "What do you mean?"

"Look at the trailer," Lyons said, pointing at it. "Notice what is different about it?"

Demir stared at it, then grabbed Lyons's glasses out of his hands and used them to look at the big aluminum box over a quarter of a mile away. Then she turned her attention to the collection of eight other house trailers, all in various stages of age and disrepair, scattered in wide weedy plots around it. The makeshift neighborhood was surrounded and in some places engulfed by the weeds and shrubs, and had a view of the descending hillside and the long valley below.

"Yes," she said. "For one thing it was put in position not long ago. There are muddy tracks still there from when it was put where it is now."

"Right," Lyons agreed. "All we have to do is figure out when the last good rain was around here and we'll know how long the trailer has been in that position. We just need to have our people research local weather."

"You could just ask a local," she said, giving him a sideways glare. "I can tell you how long that trailer's been where it is. We had a downpour an hour after dusk yesterday."

"She's right," Schwarz agreed. "There's still muddy stains on the grass from the tires. It was moved in near the end of the storm or not long after the rain stopped."

"Midnight or later," Demir clarified. "There's also something funny about the shape of the trailer."

Lyons looked at her. "What do you mean by that?"

"It's not right," she said tentatively. "It's too tall.

Another thing—I've never seen a house trailer with the door at the end like that. Usually the door is in the middle, so that you enter in the middle of the house.''

Lyons lifted his glasses out of her hands while she was still peering through them and he reexamined the house trailer himself.

"She's right," Schwarz said.

"Stop saying that," Lyons grunted. "What's with the windows? Can you make out anything, Gadgets?"

"No. They've got some really heavy-duty blinds on them. Or maybe they just boarded them up from the inside."

"Think this is it?" Blancanales asked.

Lyons nodded slowly, then said finally, "Yeah. Yeah, I do."

"Those a-holes knew what they were doing," Schwarz said. "They put the thing right in the middle of a town. Nobody would think to look for it here."

"What are you saying?" Demir asked.

"We're saying that isn't a house trailer," Schwarz explained. "It's one of the Patriot missile truck-based launch systems. They've walled it up so it looks more or less like a house trailer, and who would question it?"

"Why would they do such a thing?" she asked.

"To hide in plain sight close to their target. The Patriot's got a range of about seventy kilometers—that's just over forty miles. From here they can strike downtown Gilroy or any number of local cities, as far away as Monterey or even Carmel-by-the-Sea. Not that the target really matters. These people don't want to annihilate any specific people or group. As long as a large number of humans are slaughtered, they'll be happy.''

"Yes, and the more the better, from their point of view," Blancanales said. "The more people that get killed if and when they launch that thing, the more nationwide attention it gets, and the more willing the U.S. people will be to give in to their demands."

"Then Carmel would make an ideal target," Lyons suggested. "There's lots of famous, high-profile people living there. Murdering a bunch of movie stars and wealthy businessmen will get them more attention than killing average Americans."

Demir nodded grimly, the horror of it affecting her. "We've got to put a stop to them!"

"We plan to," Lyons said. "Step one is to get inside."

Turkey

AYVALIK DIDN'T EVEN qualify as a town. A collection of hovels ten miles south of Cudi Mountain, and a rock's toss from the south bank of the Dicle River, Ayvalik was the settlement for a small population of Kurdish extended families.

Two facts were significant about the village. One was its proximity to the three-corner intersection with Iraq and Syria. When the need arose, as it sometimes did in years past when the Turkish People's Liberation Army of Kurdistan had been active, with several members based in the village, a safe international haven was a sprint away.

Another fact that had gone unnoticed by the few outsiders that passed through Ayvalik in recent months was that there wasn't a single able-bodied adult male to be found. All the adults were female and/or elderly.

Nobody noticed because nobody outside the village cared.

Until the name Ayvalik had floated to the top of the

list being put together by Dogan Bir from his intelligence sources.

Bir felt a sort of thrill as his detective work began to pay off. Using access he had purchased from a friend in Ankara intelligence circles, he had quickly assembled a pages-long list of the ARGK's most active and violent members prior to its 1999 dissolution, then culled from it those who were suspected of ongoing violent activities against Turkey. He began comparing the known addresses of the immediate families of those suspects.

Several of those families had coalesced in the past eighteen months in the small, strategically located village of Ayvalik, a five-minute car ride from the borders of Iraq and Syria. Bir found this significant, but not damning without further evidence. He called in a favor from an army general. The man routed a border patrol into the village, where they stopped under the pretense of making a temporary fix on a broken water pump. While one man worked, the two others wandered around looking for a bar. They didn't find one. Ayvalik was too small to support one. But they'd accomplished what they had set out to do: scope the population.

"No men except for the grandfathers sitting in the shade," the general had reported in his phone call to Bir.

"Good! Good!" Bir laughed at his own successful detective work and thanked his general friend profusely. The general, who didn't consider Bir a friend at all, had slammed down the phone and hoped to never hear from him again.

Bir supposed he could have gone back to Nouri Bakir for the location had he required it, but he felt the need to be especially careful around the Kurdish business mogul. The man appeared to have definite ideas about what

lines he would and wouldn't cross. He seemed to have
no ethical compunction about facilitating Bir's attack on
his own people, but had failed to volunteer any of the
necessary information, as if taking that step would have
been distasteful.

Bir didn't care if Bakir wouldn't get his hands dirty.
Bir, conversely, loved to get his hands dirty. It excited
him and he was good at it. It had brought him to where
he was today in the government bureaucracy. But all his
past exploits—petty blackmail, questionable contract
manipulation—were small potatoes. Now he was taking
steps into the big leagues.

Bir's next step was to call his good friend Cengiz
Yilmaz, the manufacturing head who had visited his office. Yilmaz was ecstatic that Bir had not only come up
with the required Kurd targets so quickly but was also
eager to take responsibility for organizing the paramili-
tary action himself. Yilmaz was another man who was
less than eager to get his hands dirty.

Yilmaz gave Bir contact information for a team of
Iranian mercenaries who would be willing to take the
job. All Bir had to do was make the appropriate phone
calls.

"It has been all coordinated, Cengiz," Bir said.
"Your little project is arranged."

"When will it happen?" Yilmaz asked tensely.

"It might be happening right now. I'm keeping CNN
International turned on in my office. I suggest you do
the same."

THE SHEEP TRUCK ROLLED down the single dirt street of
the village and stopped. One man got out of the passenger door, speaking into a handheld radio. He was dressed
in desert fatigues without labels or insignia to tie him to

any nation or army. The ancient proprietor of the only shop in town, a small market and grocery, glared at the man.

"I think he's an Iranian," he blurted to the gang of old Kurds who shuffled into his establishment, eager to discuss the stranger.

"How do you know?" one of the old men demanded.

"I heard him talking into that radio."

"What is he doing here?" one of them demanded. "Why is he acting so oddly?"

The stranger's behavior was indeed odd. He marched all the way down the road until the buildings ran out, peered between houses, eyeing the women and children and speaking nonstop into his radio.

"They are Turkish soldiers," one of the old men said. "They've learned we are the families of the True Army freedom fighters."

"You are blind!" the old shopkeeper responded. "These men are not in army uniforms. They're dressed like beggars."

"The truck that was in here this morning was army. They reported back. Now they've sent in disguised troops to gun us all down or take us prisoner."

The old man wasn't one hundred percent accurate, but he hit the mark closer than his companions. Still, he didn't experience any satisfaction when the man marched into the small shop and pulled a gun on them, ordering them into the sheep truck.

The women poured into the street when they saw their fathers and grandfathers being manhandled. They screamed accusations and threats at the gunner. One of the women emerged from her shack carrying an old shotgun. The Iranian gunner showed no fear. Standing between her and the truck full of old men, he knew she wouldn't shoot. Half the buckshot would have gone into her own people.

The automatic rifle in his hands was trained inexorably onto the gathering of women. "Give me the shotgun or I start shooting your neighbors."

She did as she was told, but she started shouting. "Cakmak will kill you for this. He is my brother! He will hunt you down and cut your throat!"

The gunner didn't even respond to the threat. He gestured into the truck bed with his rifle. The woman screeched wordlessly and impotently, and then she climbed into the back of the truck with the old men.

It took ten minutes for every man, woman and child in the village of Ayvalik to be herded into the livestock truck. Then the man with the gun spoke into his radio again.

Then they waited. The villagers could now see dust rising out beyond the village. Minutes later a trio of desert-camouflaged Jeeps drove out of the scrub land beyond the village. One of them stopped at the truck, and the villagers could see a bloodied body lying inside.

One of the women screamed and would have descended had she not been held at bay by the gunner. Then the Jeep driver got out and lifted the body out of the vehicle. The boy wasn't even a teenager. He had been shot in the knee as he tried to escape the gunmen by hiding in the scrub outside the village. Although he appeared unconscious, he groaned in pain when he was deposited roughly inside the truck at the feet of his sobbing mother.

The drivers of the three Jeeps and the gunmen from the truck were laughing now. An easy job accomplished. They were speaking in a tongue that only one of the Kurds could understand.

"Iranians," muttered the old shopkeeper.

"Why Iranians?" demanded one of the women.

They had known they were in danger. That was why Cakmak and the others had stationed them at a location so close to the international borders. But they had always expected the threat to come from the Turks. What interest did the Iranians have in them?

The steel gate was clanged into place. The black vinyl tarp was pulled over the top and sides of the truck bed, and the interior instantly grew torrid. The smell of old sheep dung grew pungent. The truck lurched away from the village, leaving it empty of life.

Behind them the Jeeps followed, ready to gun down anyone who attempted to escape.

The convoy rolled east for hours, then crossed the border into the hilly wastelands of western Iran.

CHAPTER FIFTEEN

The Dicle River, at the point it passes the small Turkish city of Bismil, is not impressive. Brown year-round, often less than a hundred yards across, it looks like any of the hundreds of thousands of small rivers coursing through Central Asia and every ice-free continent on the planet. From all appearances there's nothing exceptional about it.

Appearances are deceiving. The Dicle River is one of the most important waterways in the history of civilization. As it flows south, into modern-day Iraq, it becomes the Dijlah—the Tigris, which, along with the al-Furat, or Euphrates, formed the Fertile Crescent. Five millennia ago in this geographically vital spot on the Arabian Peninsula, the cast-off seedlings of Egyptian's infant civilization took root. A protoliterate period, ending in 3100 B.C., saw the development of the region's first cities and early writing, and by 2350 B.C. the Sumerians were speaking the earliest Semitic languages. Under the unification of King Sargon of Akkad, the first identifiable personality in all human history, these people rose to become only the second civilization ever.

The rivers, by bestowing fertility on the land and giving human beings the freedom to do more than simply struggle for food, were thus the most important element in bringing about the advent of human intellectual and cultural advancement.

But the people along the Dicle River at the Turkish city of Bismil didn't seem to care about its historical significance. To them, Sargon, Babylon and the Sumerians were very old news. They had day-to-day worries and concerns. The Dicle was their most important resource, making the city an important port for locally produced wool and live sheep. Most of their livestock went upriver, to stockyards in Diyarbakir. Wool, too, went to that city's processing mills.

Bismil was geographically important for another reason. It sat on what some considered to be the outside northwestern boundary of the geographic zone claimed as Kurdistan by the Kurdish people of Turkey, Syria and Iraq.

"Your target is eleven miles to the east of Bismil, which makes us think that's the target—or Diyarbakir, which is still within range of the Patriot," Barbara Price reported over the speakerphone.

Phoenix Force had rented a civilian Land Rover in Mus, then augmented their supplies with a shipment of munitions from Incirlik brought in by the investigative team that shipped in to quietly clean up the destroyed Air Force Hercules. That team would also be charged with returning the body of the Stony Man pilot and his Air Force copilot to the United States.

David McCarter wondered who would get the task of informing the next of kin. The Air Force would take care of their own man. In fact, the Stony Man pilot was likely Air Force or Navy himself. Telling his family about his death in the field would surely fall to whatever military branch he had originated from. The parents and siblings, maybe even wife and children, would be told nothing about his assignment, only that he had died doing his duty.

That would have to be enough.

They'd driven southeast, along a main highway that took them to Bitlis, then southwest again, through Baykan.

"You'll turn south onto a local road after you cross the Batman River. That road will take you to Bitlis."

"The *what* river?" Hawkins asked from the back seat.

"You heard me," Price said, then she read off a set of GPS coordinates. "That's where you'll find the Patriot."

"I hope you guys are keeping a close watch on that baby," Gary Manning said.

"Count on it. We've got eyes in the sky over her right now."

"Any danger of our friends on the ground noticing that they are being observed?" McCarter asked.

"Not the surveillance we're using."

Encizo nudged Hawkins as the Land Rover carried them onto an old concrete bridge. A rusted metal sign stood unsteadily on one of its two original legs at the side of the bridge entrance.

"Batman River," Encizo read.

Hawkins snorted. "I'll be damned."

GARY MANNING WAS justifiably proud of his exceptional skills as a marksman, but just now he was wishing he didn't have the responsibility.

The problem was easy enough to understand. There were ten men hanging around the Patriot missile in the three-acre valley below the cliff on which Manning was stationed. Phoenix Force was charged with the unlikely task of hitting them hard and fast enough to knock them down and secure the missile before the missile could be fired.

"What's your reading on our chances?" McCarter asked him in a near whisper.

"Damned slim," Manning shot back harshly. Then he gave McCarter an apologetic look, but the Phoenix Force leader got the point. Manning wasn't feeling optimistic.

There were simply too many targets.

Manning was parked on his stomach behind a bipod-mounted Walther WA-2000, a portable, high-tech sniper's rifle. For a carefully planned sniping operation in the field, there were few pieces of equipment superior to the WA-2000. Manning found it to be an efficient, accurate weapon. He had the gun sighted at two hundred yards and had managed to plant himself on the hills at just over that distance from his targets. He adjusted his sights to accommodate the bullet's rise of just over an inch. The Schmidt & Bender 2.5 ×x 10-power telescopic sight gave him up-close-and-personal access to his targets.

None of which made him feel any better about the success of the mission.

"Explain to me again why we just can't bomb these bastards out of existence?" he demanded.

"Good question," McCarter admitted. He was less than satisfied with the answer he had received himself. He dragged on the headset as he strode downhill toward the Land Rover.

"How's it look?" Price asked when he radioed in.

"Not good, Stony. We've got ten men on the ground around this thing—that we know about. There's a pair of vehicles, including a van, parked nearby. There could be more bad guys inside."

"What's your strategy?"

"To take these guys out with any degree of confidence before they have a chance to fire that Patriot," McCarter said. "We call in some F-15s out of Incirlik and blow this entire hill to oblivion before they even know we've figured them out."

"That's a negative, Phoenix."

"Listen, Stony, we're in a bad place here."

"You've got Gary staged to pick them off?" Price asked.

"Yeah, for what good it will do," McCarter said. "He's damned good at his job, but even Striker wouldn't be able to take down one hundred percent of the targets fast enough to guarantee a successful probe."

"What's the terrain look like?" she asked. "How fast can the rest of you move in on them?"

"Fast!" McCarter said testily. "Very fast. Now ask me if it will be fast enough to stop the launch of that missile."

There was a moment of silence. "Fast enough?" she asked.

"I don't know," he shot back.

More silence.

"I'll get back to you," Price said.

Washington, D.C.

"WHAT DO YOU want me to do here, Hal?" demanded the President of the United States.

Brognola had thought that was obvious. "Call an air strike, Mr. President."

"Call an air strike. In Turkey. As if it's that easy."

"Ask the Turks to make the strike, then. It doesn't

matter who blows the hill as long as the hill gets blown.''

Brognola knew he was sticking his neck out on this one. It was just his luck that the Man was in a foul mood and wasn't happy about being pulled away from a lunch with a couple of cabinet members. The man from Justice had taken his usual seat in front of the President's Oval Office desk, but the Man hadn't taken his seat behind it. He just leaned on the edge of the desk, a clear sign he wasn't giving the big Fed a lot of time.

"Mr. President, my team is on-site at this minute and is more than ready to go in and do its best—"

"Then why can't they just go?"

"Because, sir, they judge their chance of success here as less than twenty percent.''

"I thought your guys were good?"

Brognola stiffened. "My men are the best antiterrorist special-operations commandos on the planet, as a matter of fact.''

"Then what is the problem? Send them in. Take some prisoners.''

"That isn't their primary goal,'' Brognola reminded him. "The men they are up against are sitting on a United States Patriot missile, ready to launch at the push of a button as far as we know. I guarantee you my men can get into the valley, take down some of the terrorists and come away with living, breathing prisoners. I cannot promise you they can stop that missile from flying. That's what we're worried about, sir—Turkish civilian casualties.''

The President folded his arms on his chest, thoughtfully, then shook his head. "Do I have to remind you that we're talking about just one of a dozen missiles remaining at large in Turkey?''

"No, you certainly do not," Brognola replied icily.

"And unless you have a lead you're not telling me about, we have no idea where the rest of those missiles are. Is that correct?"

"Yes, Mr. President."

"Now how do you plan on tracking them down without intelligence gathered at the scene now?"

"I don't know. I guess I'm taking a less long-term view."

"Maybe you should change your perspective, Hal. We've got to account for every single one of those Patriots."

Brognola was thinking furiously. "Yes, sir."

"Got any other options?"

He shook his head slowly. "I don't."

"You send your men in. Take down those terrorists and ground that missile and send me a report when the job is done."

"We'll do our best, Mr. President," Brognola said. He couldn't help reiterating, "I've already told you what the outcome may be."

"I don't want to hear it!" The Man strode to the door and wrenched it open so fast he startled the pair of Secret Service agents in the adjoining reception area and they jumped into defensive postures looking for a threat. "Now I'm going to go finish my lunch!"

Bismil, Turkey

MANNING COULDN'T afford to get fatigued. He had turned on his back with his fingers laced behind his head, staring at the blue sky and clouds, as if he were relaxing on a summer's day after a picnic lunch. In actuality he was anything but relaxed. Beside him Calvin James was on his stomach with field glasses in front of his face, keeping an eye on the activity around the launcher.

The Patriot missile launcher control consisted of a phased array radar and an engagement control station, all computer-operated and driven by a powerful portable generator. The control system was capable of operating a collection of up to eight launchers, each with four missiles ready to fire. The Kurds had a single box of four, which was more than enough to cause heavy damage and death to ground-based targets. Three men are typically required to operate the battery in combat situations. There were currently three figures hovering around the control station, moving without urgency.

"What's the status on the torque tube handles?" asked McCarter, standing on the hill ten feet below them.

James was peering at the handles, his view too angled to get a clear view. "Three are locked. One is unlocked."

"One missile live," McCarter said quietly. "You sure they're not ready to launch that puppy?"

"How can I be sure?" James asked. "It doesn't look like it. In fact, they just finished dinner. I'd say they're getting ready for something." He trailed off.

"Is there activity?" McCarter asked.

"Yeah. Nothing urgent, but I'd guess they're expecting something to happen. They're packing up some of their supplies into the van. If I was to guess, I'd say they just had their last meal at this spot and they're planing on clearing out in the near future."

"Well, they aren't going to get the chance for that," McCarter said.

Manning propped himself up on his elbows. "Tell me the Man's gonna wipe this spot clean."

"That's a negative, mate. We've been given the job, and the job requires us to come out with prisoners capable of leading us to the rest of the Turkish missiles."

"That sucks," James declared to no one in particular.

Manning dropped his head back on the ground. "I hope Hal read the Man all the disclaimers, because I sure have a bad feeling about this."

"I know." McCarter shrugged. "It's a bloody stump of an assignment, but we're elected to do it."

"Phoenix One, you read me!" Hawkins's voice suddenly burst into their headsets from fifty yards downhill, at the Land Rover.

"Phoenix One here. Go ahead."

"We've got another vehicle approaching. Repeat, one vehicle. Definitely civilian. I'd say these guys are about to get company."

McCarter saw the possibilities instantly. "How far?"

"Couple miles. Moving at top speeds of no more than twenty miles an hour on the dirt road."

McCarter's brain went into a whirlwind of strategizing. "Gary, stay put and keep watch. Let me know if those guys start getting worked up, Cal."

McCarter gestured with a nod and he and James jogged quickly back to the Land Rover, where Hawkins and Encizo were watching the slow-moving vehicle, a small red Fiat, lurching over the old dirt vehicle trail that led to the clearing.

Encizo grinned. "He's having a hell of a time of it."

CALVIN JAMES DIDN'T particularly like hiding in bushes, but it was all part of the job. The tall black commando adopted a low crouch, then, not even consciously, went through a quick limb-by-limb relaxation exercise that made his body almost limp, freeing his senses to every sound and movement in the vicinity.

Now he could hear the approach of the Fiat, just a hundred feet up the trail. Maybe the True Army terrorists in the valley beyond the hill would hear it, too.

For this plan to work it had to be lightning-fast and flawless, and it had to take the driver of the vehicle completely by surprise. It had to work without the driver being killed or even getting knocked unconscious.

James breathed easily, as if he were meditating, and the Fiat's tiny engine buzzed as the driver revved his way out of a crater in the road. The Phoenix Force commando bounced slightly on his feet. His hands were empty. He was thinking about a book he had read years ago by an obscure Chinese martial artist, Wang Xuan Jie, and his emphasis on perfecting the natural instinct. James was a black belt in tae kwon do, and interested in any theory or philosophy that would help him advance his skill in the art. Now the vehicle was twenty feet away and accelerating. James's mind was filled with the image of the road just in front of him. Another small dip, then a flat surface, then another, deeper trench in the road. The Fiat went through the first pothole fast, and the driver braked when he was almost out of it, the underside of the vehicle hitting the ground with a brief crunch.

The driver swore and cautiously pushed himself with a short surge out of the dip, seeing the next pothole and braking hard. He descended into the second pothole and momentarily came to a complete stop at the bottom of it. That was when James felt the natural instinct to move.

There was a flash of movement and a dark shape flashed out of the brush near the vehicle so quickly the driver didn't have time to turn his head and focus on it. It slammed into the side of his head with a knock that sent him flopping onto his side. Through the daze he saw the hand that had knocked him wrench the stick out of gear, then yank the door open and extract him from the car by his ankles. He hit the earth on his back, the breath pushed out of him, and gasped painfully as he felt his handgun removed from the holster on his stomach. It had happened so fast he was still trying to understand the sequence of events when he found himself staring down the muzzle of an M-16 held in the hands of a short-haired black man, who wasn't even breathing hard.

Three minutes later the Kurd was again behind the wheel of the Fiat, with two passengers tucked in the back seat.

CHAPTER SIXTEEN

Manning watched the Fiat come around the side of the cliff and into the valley. James and Encizo had directed the driver to park as far away from the cliff as possible.

The plan was a series of simple surprises. Take the True Army terrorists off guard with sniper fire from above. Surprise number two would come when McCarter started firing from the west face of the cliff as he made a rapid descent. Surprise three: Hawkins, firing from the rocks and bushes at the side of the trail from the eastern entrance. Finally, cleanup would come from Encizo and James, who would exit the Fiat when the terrorists' attention was drawn.

Manning held the pistol grip and placed the stock against his cheek, peering into the Schmidt & Bender scope and adjusting the tilt of the weapon on the bipod by less than a millimeter as he lined up on his first target. The man was nearest to the steps at the rear of the launcher, idly watching the Fiat park and casually holding on to the stock of the AK that dangled on one shoulder.

The Walther WA-2000 sniper rifle had a thirty-six-inch-long bullpup design with a barrel fluted longitudinally to facilitate cooling and for minimal vibration during firing. It wasn't suppressed, and the sound of

Manning's first shot reverberated through the canyon, pushing the weapon hard into his shoulder. He ignored the pain as he quickly lined up a second target without even bothering to confirm that the first shot was on target.

But it was. The 220-grain round had slammed through the upper rib cage of the gunner at a sharp downward angle, creating a tunnel of shattered bones and torn tissue that exited through his spinal column in a plume of gore. The terrorist was dead before the sound reached him. A second target broke for cover and tripped over his own feet at the same moment the second blast shook the valley, but became still on the earth with a large bloody hole in his side. A third man made a running dive to get himself underneath the body of the launcher when the third round smacked him into the earth like a bug getting swatted onto the sidewalk in midflight. There was a massive wound in his leg, and he twitched as high-pressure arterial spurts fountained out of the wound. He was drained dead in seconds.

Manning paused to survey the valley, which was suddenly devoid of movement, and he spotted a pair of gunners' heads appearing momentarily above the roof of the black van.

"Phoenix One, it's your move," he radioed.

"I'm moving," McCarter responded. A second later there was a burst of gunfire from the west side of the hill, and Manning spotted McCarter making a wild, barely controlled run down the steep open side of the hill, his M-16 rattling out a barrage of rounds that slammed into the side of the van.

The Phoenix Force leader strafed the pair of gunners without remorse, pinning them to what they thought would be the protective side of the van with multiple gunshot wounds. McCarter didn't even watch them go down, peripherally spotting movement at the base of the cliff where a dense stand of shrubbery showed one or more gunners in hiding. One of them stood, already leveling and firing his Kalashnikov. He emptied the weapon's magazine in four seconds of intense fire, all the while trying to catch up his deadly stream of rounds to McCarter's downhill plummet. The gunner snatched at the magazine as he descended into a crouch, reversed it, and slammed it back into the AK. He never had the chance to fire the refreshed weapon. McCarter aimed at the base of the bushes and unleashed a torrent of full-auto fire from his M-16 A-2. The 5.56 mm rounds ripped up the vegetation like a shredder and chopped through the gunner twice at hip level, sprawling him on his back. McCarter heard a short scream. That wasn't his gunner—at least he didn't think so—which indicated a second man behind the bushes.

Ahead of him, twenty paces away, another gunner moved behind the cover of rock-fall boulders at the base of the cliff. McCarter had to move, and he chose the route the new gunner would least expect—he bolted directly at the bushes he had just been firing into, diving to the ground nearby. Of the two men sprawled behind the cover, one was dead and the other moaning and writhing with a hideously mangled left eye. The Briton's round had taken the eyeball out, yet somehow managed to avoid damaging the brain fatally. McCarter reached out with both hands and fired a single mercy shot, this time impacting and destroying the man's brain and turning his life off instantly.

FALAH TALABANI CRAWLED on his elbows behind a low rock shelf to the old Mercedes, where Adel Nerweyi was holding the radio in front of his face.

"Where's Murad?" he demanded.

"They are getting him."

"Who are these people? Where did they come from?"

Nerweyi pointed in the direction of the Fiat. "Barzani brought them in."

Talabani nodded. "The fool allowed himself to be carjacked."

Nerweyi looked surprised. "He did not betray us?"

"Not deliberately. Look. They have him handcuffed to the steering wheel. You think if he sold us out he would even have allowed himself to be brought here?"

Nerweyi shrugged. "Whether it is through stupidity or intent, he still betrayed us."

Talabani heard a voice come on the radio and snatched it out of Nerweyi's hand.

"Freedom One here—report!" demanded the staticky voice of Jalal Murad, second in command to the leader of the True Army of Kurdistan and de facto TAK commander in Turkey while Cakmak was in America.

"Freedom Eight here. We're taking fire," Talabani reported.

"Who's attacking?"

"Unknown. We've only seen one of them and they're not in identifiable uniforms. Light haired. Probably an American, but I can't even guess about the others."

"How many?" Murad demanded.

"Unknown. We've seen two so far. They've put a sniper on top of us. Between him and the other man, they've knocked out three or four of my men and they've got us pinned down."

There was another blast of sniper fire from above. Talabani craned his neck to see where it was directed, then spotted one of his men slumping over in his hiding place. "We can't move," he declared into the radio in frustration.

"You know what you need to do, Freedom Eight," Murad insisted. "If they know where you are, then they came for prisoners. They want intelligence on all our activities."

"I know."

"They could easily have called in air bombardment that would have taken out you and your men before you even knew you were under attack. The only reason they are going in manually is to get prisoners who will talk."

"I know!"

"You will follow the directives of the True Army," Murad said. "And you will live forever as a hero of Kurdistan."

"Yes," Talabani replied, but his voice had a new and thoughtful quality.

"You must strike a blow for Kurdistan!" Murad insisted.

"Yes."

But for the first time in years, Talabani's dedication was being called into question. He had faced death in battle again and again as a member of the Turkish People's Liberation Army of Kurdistan, and had lived the violent life of an outlaw since joining the extremist faction that eventually coalesced under Asad Cakmak as the True Army of Kurdistan. But those dangers had been incurred in true battle.

What he was being asked to do now was simply commit suicide.

Nerweyi crawled back from the front of the car. "There's just the two of them! I swear it!" he exclaimed.

It was time to pass the buck.

"Adel," Talabani said, "Murad commanded that you fire the weapon."

Nerweyi stared at him in bewilderment. "I can't reach the missile. Not with that sniper up there."

"You know the plan. We will provide cover for you to reach the missile and get to safety again."

"How will you provide cover against a sniper you can't see?" he demanded, and then understanding dawned on his face. "It was you. Murad doesn't even know who I am—he commanded that you be the one to fire the missile!"

The Sarsilmaz Hancer 9 mm handgun appeared in Talabani's fist out of nowhere, and he pulled it in tightly to his ribs to keep it steady and to keep it out of Nerweyi's reach. Just five feet separated the two men. Talabani wouldn't miss. "You have two choices, Adel. Take your chances and come out a hero, whether you live or die, or die right now in shame."

Nerweyi's eyes blazed red, and he spit out the worst insult he could come up with. "Traitor!"

But there was resignation in the word, too. Talabani knew he would do what needed done. Nerweyi climbed to his feet and bent low as Talabani growled into the radio for his other surviving men.

"Nerweyi is making a run for the missile. Be ready to provide cover in ten seconds."

"WHAT ARE THESE GUYS doing?" McCarter asked.

"Not a thing at the moment," Manning replied from the top of the cliff. "We've got them pinned down."

"Stay sharp," McCarter advised. "We haven't halted their momentum. They'll make a move any moment."

"I'm counting on that," Manning replied, adjusting

his firm grip on the WA-2000. Then he adjusted his aim minutely as a figure broke from cover and zigzagged across the open ground. At the same moment three more figures began firing up the side of the cliff, their rounds thrashing at the vegetation and the rock wall, seeking out the sniper. Manning pulled back as a burst of fire sliced through the grasses around the WA-2000 and one of the rounds pinged off the barrel.

"This is Phoenix Three—I'm cut off!" he said into the radio.

"I can't move. They've got me covered, too," McCarter reported.

"Phoenix Two here. We're on it."

Simultaneously, Encizo and James propelled themselves out of the back doors of the Fiat, hugging the rear bumper and finding targets. The gunners that hemmed in Manning and McCarter hadn't expected them.

Encizo founded one easy target, a gunner crouched between the rock and the cliff, aiming for McCarter's cover behind the rock-fall boulders. Gunfire from the Cuban's M-16 took the gunner in the shoulder and slammed him into the cliff wall before dropping him out of sight. James' targets were trickier. Two men were peering over the hood and trunk of one of the parked cars, laying an uninterrupted volley of rounds into the cliff where Manning was hiding.

James slipped a round into the M-203 grenade launcher mounted under his M-16 A-2 and triggered it. The 40 mm high-explosive round shot at the car as a third figure wove an erratic path across the open ground. James watched in amazement—the 40 mm had to have singed the hairs on the man's nape.

The round impacted the car and there was a flash and a crack of white fire as the blast tore into the gas tank from just inches away, igniting it instantly. The two gunners behind the vehicle were blown away in a maelstrom of fire, and the wall of superheated air billowed after the running man, smacking him down to the ground just in time for Encizo's rounds to sail over his head.

The gunner was up again in a flash, clapping at the orange tongues of flame on the sleeve of his shirt as he bolted for the staged Patriot. Encizo targeted the runner, but the terrorist somehow sensed him or glimpsed him out of his peripheral vision and whirled on him with amazing speed, already squeezing the trigger of this Kalashnikov. Encizo was forced to flatten behind the tire of the Fiat and he shouted, "Cal!"

James saw it coming and threw himself into a backward dive as the automatic AK-47 fire cut across the Fiat, shattering the back windshield and chopping into the skull of the driver, who was frantically wrenching at the handcuffs securing him to the steering wheel. He screamed and went silent, and the running gunner managed to stumble behind the control structure containing the Patriot's engagement control station.

Hawkins decided he had waited long enough for McCarter to call him into the battle, and he stepped out onto the path up the mountainside and stared down the barrel of the M-16 A-2. At the same instant McCarter shouted for him in the radio, while the Phoenix Force leader himself jumped into the open for a clear shot at the man at the launch controls. Encizo and James scrambled to their feet, trying to aim at the figure behind the metal support girders. They all fired within the space of a second, the torrent of rounds raining on the launch system.

But only Hawkins had a clear shot, and he lined it up carefully, breathed and squeezed the trigger with the calm demeanor of a yoga instructor, putting a single 5.56 mm tumbler through the chest of the Kurdish terrorist who slumped on a control monitor.

For a fraction of a second, David McCarter had a vision of a scene from an old slapstick science-fiction movie in which the bad guy gets killed but his slumping body hits the launch lever on the control panel and the spaceship accidentally gets blasted into orbit.

But nothing happened, except that the gunner flopped out of the control station and slammed into the dry earth.

There was sudden silence.

Then all hell broke loose.

CHAPTER SEVENTEEN

Talabani laid down a steady stream of fire as Nerweyi bolted suicidally across the open ground to the engagement control station, and at the back of his head niggled a sudden sense of shame and regret. It should be him out there, risking his life for the great cause of Kurdistan.

Then he saw chaos descend on the scene as more commandos materialized, seemingly out of nowhere. Two from the Fiat. Another stepped out from behind the rock against the cliff. Where in the name of God had all these men come from?

Then Talabani knew Nerweyi's brave attempt had been a failure. The last man to appear calmly and efficiently took down his comrade with a single shot through the heart. He watched Nerweyi's already dead body tumble to the ground.

The time for desperate measures was upon him. For some reason the cowardice and reluctance that had infected him a minute ago had dissipated. All that was left was the old fanatic fury. He would do what needed to be done. It didn't matter if he or any of his men lived to tell the tale. All that mattered was the making of the great statement of the True Army of Kurdistan.

Talabani drew his secret weapon out of the pack at his feet.

For months he had been coveting the MM-1 like a man on a lifeboat hides away a crust of bread from his starving companions. It had cost him plenty, but he had known it would get him out of some of the worst situations he could expect to be in. It was his passage to freedom. Right now, all he considered was that it just might keep him alive long enough to put one Patriot missile into the air.

All twelve chambers of the bulky MM-1 multiround Projectile Launcher were loaded. The weapon had a huge revolving cylinder, holding twelve grenades. Talabani grabbed it by the forward pistol grip, hefting the twenty-pound weapon to his stomach. He aimed almost straight up the cliff side and fired the first HE grenade. The range of the MM-1 was 130 yards, more than sufficient to plant the 40 mm bomb on top of the cliff and blow the sniper to kingdom come.

MANNING SAW it coming. He recognized the distinctive outline of the projectile launcher the moment the Kurd stepped into view, aiming it uphill. He saw the flash and swore to himself as he scuttled backward, away from the cliff edge as fast as he could move.

It wasn't fast enough, and he'd moved just five feet before the 40 mm round slammed into the side of the cliff, mercifully short of the target. The round detonated with a crack that pulverized the rock into sand and shook the cliff underneath his body. He wondered for a moment if he would feel the entire cliff face begin collapsing underneath him.

HAWKINS KNEW what the second target would be. Encizo and James were sitting ducks. The Fiat might give them some cover from Kalashnikov rifle fire, but it would disintegrate under the blast from an HE round. Without considering his actions, he stepped out from his cover and spotted the Kurd with the projectile launcher, just a small sliver of his head and arm visible as he lined up on the Fiat. Hawkins triggered the M-16 A-2 in full auto, cutting a swath of noisy rounds over the top of the car hiding the Kurd gunner. Not one of them scored, but the rounds weren't wasted. The Kurd ducked for cover and his second HE went unlaunched.

Hawkins was about to radio for Encizo and James to get the hell out when McCarter beat him to it. "Phoenix Two and Four, move your asses!"

"We're ahead of you," Encizo responded as they scrambled away from the Fiat and bolted for a more distant jumble of boulders. Then, over the distance, Hawkins heard a loud Kurdish word issue from the man behind the vehicle. He didn't recognize it, but he knew it was a profanity.

That terrorist was angry. Hawkins's instincts told him things were about to spin out of control.

The man behind the vehicle stood, in plain view, spotted Hawkins and launched another HE directly at him. It happened so quickly the Phoenix Force commando didn't have time to return fire. He launched himself off the steep rocky trail into open space over the steeply declining ground, flying through open air with his arms waving wildly to maintain his midair stability, then plummeting into a five-foot stand of grass and shrubs. The round slammed into the rock wall against which he had been standing and detonated with a crack. Hawkins heard it as he descended into a wild roll, his speed escalating uncontrollably for a handful of seconds, the deformities in the terrain and the rocks cracking and ripping at his body as he was chased downhill by the licking tongues of flame and a storm of rocky shrapnel that sliced through his clothing and cut through exposed flesh. Then the incline ended in a dip and he rolled to a stop, limp and expecting a sudden burst of pain from some hideously wounded part of his body.

Before he had time to feel it, there was another grenade blast. Then another.

"HE'S FIRING BLIND," James said.

Manning had moved back to the edge of the cliff, as dangerous as the position was, and saw it all happen. The Kurd behind the vehicle fired wildly, first at Hawkins, who vanished under the cloud of fire and dust, then at McCarter's nearby opposition, then in the direction of James and Enciso, then back at McCarter. Manning heard the bray of noise coming out of the terrorist, a long, drawn-out shout of frustration and fury.

Then the Kurd was running, into the open, brandishing the MM-1 like a room-clearing assault rifle. He fired on the run, toward McCarter and Hawkins, then jogging backward to send another round flying after James and Enciso. There was no precision in his aim, and his targets were obscured by the billowing dust of previous explosions, but he was just as likely to score a hit out of chance.

Now he turned and sped directly at the control station, and Manning dragged the WA-2000 sniper rifle into a new position and rose from his stomach onto his knees. He lined up, firing almost straight down the cliff face, tracking his target through the scope on the run and instinctively triggering a round. He missed by chance—the Kurd below halted to fire off another of his rounds at McCarter's position, and the bullet thumped into the dry ground at his feet. The Kurd stared at the tiny crater for a fraction of a second before understanding its meaning, then whipped up the MM-1, aiming up the cliff face.

"Gary!" Manning heard through his headphones. It was Encizo. Somehow the little Cuban commando was still able to see what was happening in the field of fire. "Gary, get out of there!"

Manning fired another round as the Kurd sneered at him through the Schmidt & Bender scope and triggered an HE that rocketed almost straight into the sky. The sharp angle of the fire spoiled both shots. The HE passed within arm's reach of Manning as it passed the edge of the cliff then sailed overhead. Manning's round creased the front of the Kurd's pant leg before cutting into his shin and burrowing through his foot.

The Kurd screamed and collapsed, then the sound of his agony was washed away as the HE round deposited itself on the earth forty yards behind Manning and blew. The Canadian curled into a ball with his arms shielding his head, waiting out the precious second and a half for the pelting rain of earth and pebbles to cease, then pushed himself back onto his knees, manhandling the WA-2000 into target acquisition, only to feel his heart freeze in his chest.

The Kurd was at the control station, dragging himself into a standing position in front of it. The MM-1 was discarded on the blood-muddied dirt at his side.

The terrorist's hands were moving on the controls.

Manning triggered the WA-2000 and felt the sniper rifle jump in his hands. He quickly reoriented the Schmidt & Bender scope and spotted the Kurd clinging with one hand to the edge of the command panel, his body swinging without balance as if he were dangling by one hand from a skyscraper window. A mass of blood had replaced his other shoulder.

But he was still alive, and he regained his balance. Manning jammed the WA-2000 to his shoulder. The Kurd jabbed at the panel and the rifle jumped in Manning's hand. A plume of smoke materialized at the base of the cliff.

Manning heard himself whisper, "No!"

But the Patriot was airborne.

Stony Man Farm, Virginia

BARBARA PRICE AND Aaron Kurtzman watched the image on the huge, high-definition display screen that dominated one end of the Annex Computer Room, transmitted by the patiently circling Darkstar aircraft. The puffs of dust that had been the blasts of HE rounds were nothing compared to the sudden cloud of smoke that filled a quarter of their screen where the launcher had been.

At the same instant, over the radio feed from Phoenix Force, one of the commandos whispered, almost intimately, "No!"

Price and Kurtzman stared at the screen silently. Behind them Carmen Delahunt said quietly, "Oh, Jesus."

There was nothing more they could do. There was no way the missile could be stopped. It moved too fast for the Darkstar to track it. They didn't have the radar facilities on-site in Turkey to watch it.

Doubtless, the U.S. and Turkish air forces in Turkey would have spotted the sudden flicker of fast movement on their security missile-tracking systems.

If the missile had been a long-range weapon, there would have been time for antimissile measures—perhaps—to be taken. Maybe even another Patriot could have been deployed to knock the TAK-launched missile out of the air.

But the fact was that the Patriot was a short-range weapon. Even at its maximum range it was in the air for just around two hundred seconds.

The PAC-3 launched outside of Bismil didn't even have that much total flight time. It was in the air just 130 seconds—no more than a blip on the screens of even the most sensitive missile-tracking instruments.

Price and Kurtzman could do no more than wait for the news of the impact.

Diyarbakir, Turkey

THE GOVERNMENT operations in the port city of Diyarbakir, on the Dicle River, were dominated by the fifty-four-year-old Government Center, where the officials in charge of the city, as well as the province of Diyarbakir government, had administrative offices. The five-story building contained nearly one hundred rooms and offices. It employed nearly 350 people, but the number of human beings within those walls on any given day of normal government operations could double or triple that, with local citizens visiting to conduct governmental administrative and legislative business.

There were 809 people inside when the U.S. PAC-3 Patriot missile penetrated the fourth floor of the building while descending at a twenty-nine-degree angle. The detonation of its ninety-kilogram HE warhead shook the foundation, bringing down most of the fourth and fifth floors in a sudden rumble of violence. As the explosion tore into the third and second floors, gas-fed piping ignited, feeding flames that traveled throughout the rooms, consuming paper, wooden desks, windows coverings and trapped people.

The screams of the dying were heard on the streets

below, but only one of the four stairways up from the ground floor was passable, and it was closed off at the top by a conflagration as impassable as a wall of solid concrete. Of the two elevators in the building, one was trapped between floors and transformed into an oven. The three occupants suffocated in the heat almost instantly. The other elevator stopped with its doors locked open on the first floor, where it had been when the missile struck. It refused to respond to the frantic summons of those on the floors above who saw it as the only means of escape.

Just when it was thought there was no way to get to the upper stories, arriving firefighters heard the sounds of frantic pounding on the roof of the stalled elevator. When the roof door was opened, dozens of smoke-blackened, burned people began pouring out. Many had received severe wounds from the elevator cables that had torn their hands open as they slid down. Several others lay dead on the roof of the elevator, killed when they fell during their attempted escape.

Two hundred and thirteen people had been on the first floor when the missile struck, and every one of them escaped the building. Another 134 people managed to fight their way down from the second and third floors, either through the elevator shaft or by hurtling themselves out the windows.

Those on the fourth and fifth floors died without any chance of escape.

The True Army of Kurdistan had achieved its first major victory.

CHAPTER EIGHTEEN

Gilroy, California

The old man's gray wool trench coat looked as if it had been through several previous owners, none of whom had bothered to have the garment cleaned. It was too long for the hunched, heavy figure, and the bottom hem dragged in the mud.

The man had a canvas sack slung over one shoulder, bulky with personal items, and his combat boots were worn and shabby. A single big toe protruded from one of them.

The old man was looking for lunch. He moved quickly between the trailers, paused at the corner of one, then stepped furtively to the garbage can. With a swoop he had the lid off and was pawing around inside. He found a white plastic garbage bag and cursed under his breath about people who packaged their trash.

Alfred Boyd heard every word of it. Boyd hated bums, and the last thing he wanted was some lousy bums hanging out in his neighborhood. Not that his neighborhood, a small park for house trailers and other manufactured housing, was all that high class a place, but he wanted to keep it at least as nice as he could.

On the other hand, the thought of confronting the homeless man made his stomach turn.

He watched, hoping the homeless man would leave, but the bum headed for the next trailer—the big trailer that had been towed in earlier in the week. The one that belonged to the foreigners. Not Mexican foreigners, but some other kind of foreigners Boyd couldn't identify. Again, the homeless man cowered briefly next to the trailer before walking quickly to the garbage and pulling open the can.

The bum found a pizza box. He opened it, pulled out a slice of pizza, rolled it up carefully like a dinner roll and placed it in the front pocket of his trench coat.

Then—and Boyd almost threw up when he saw it— the homeless man licked his fingers.

That was all he could stand. He limped to the door, throwing it open so hard the flimsy aluminum slapped against the side of his trailer home. He grabbed his old cane, which he kept just inside the door, and brandished it in the air.

"Hey, you bum! Get the hell out of here! We don't welcome no bums here!"

The homeless man regarded him without interest and scrounged deeper into the trash can.

"I said get out of here! I'm calling the police! You hear me?"

The homeless man gave him a scowl and muttered something in Spanish. Boyd cursed under his breath. He should have known—a Mexican foreigner bum!

But at least the guy took his threat seriously. He was hobbling toward the front entrance to the trailer park.

Boyd locked the door behind him and limped to the phone. He was going to call the cops anyway. Lord only knew what a Mexican foreigner bum was capable of.

THE GILROY POLICE Department squad car rolled up and down the drives briefly, seeing nothing suspicious, before it paused in front of the trailer door where Boyd stood pointing his cane.

"He went that way," Boyd said excitedly. "Not five minutes ago."

"We just came from that direction, Al," said the driver, Officer Clairborne. "We didn't see him."

"He must have been hiding. He was a damned Mexican. They're sneaky!"

Clairborne's partner, Jesus Gutierrez, leaned across the seat so Boyd could see his face. "Yeah, you can't be too careful with those damned sneaky Mexicans. You never know where they'll pop up."

"HOW'S THE RECEPTION from my bug?" Blancanales asked, stripping off the filthy trench coat and stuffing it into a plastic garbage bag along with the canvas sack. He twisted it closed and tied it tight, hoping to seal in the aroma.

"Unknown," Lyons reported. "We caught a few words, then the cops showed up and our friends inside went quiet. I think they're watching the activity."

Out the window of the small, empty apartment, situated over an old liquor store in a fifty-year-old building, Gadgets Schwarz was adjusting a small antenna and a tripod-mounted lens that was linked electronically to his laptop. The LCD screen on the laptop was displaying a highly magnified view of the trailer that they suspected of housing the Patriot missile launcher. The blurry squad car was in the foreground. The laptop was recording the images for transmission via the cellular modem to Stony Man Farm in case further analysis was needed. The audio transmitting device was also tied into the laptop. So far, Schwarz couldn't be sure he was getting an adequate feed. He held the headphones tighter to his ears, listening to the background noise. If what he was hearing was the ambient noise inside the trailer, then the bug was working exceptionally well. "Come on," he said out loud. "Say something."

As if obeying, there was a sudden voice speaking over the headset, and Schwarz smiled to the others. "Clear as day," he reported.

They had heard it, too, via the stereo speakers on the laptop. "Fine, but what did they say?" Lyons asked.

It was Hedipe who spoke. "They are making fun of the old man who called the police," she reported.

More speech came through the speakers. "This is already the second time he called the cops in the past twenty-four hours," Hedipe explained. "They think he is a senile old goat."

The members of Able Team exchanged glances. "You're pretty useful to have around," Schwarz said.

"Thank you. Every woman likes to feel useful," Hedipe commented dryly.

"If you don't mind, I'm going to plug you in to our headquarters so they can listen in on your translation," Schwarz said, and tapped a command to tie in the omnidirectional microphone he had plugged in the laptop.

"You don't have Kurd translators on your staff?" She sounded mildly surprised.

"Uh, no," Schwarz said.

"Seems like you would, under the circumstances."

Schwarz grinned and shrugged. "You're right. I guess we blew it. Mind helping us out of this jam?"

She smirked. "Not at all."

Hedipe began translating again as more conversation occurred in the trailer. The man who called himself

Gadgets quickly explained over the microphone, to whoever was on the other end, that Hedipe would be doing the translating in real time.

But so far the talk was mundane.

The terrorists were making lunch.

BLANCANALES WAS CATCHING a catnap on the floor while Lyons paced slowly around the room. Hedipe and Schwarz were on their eighteenth poker hand, with Schwarz down a cool twenty grand. The occupants of the trailer had been watching a courtroom television show for an hour when one of them spoke again.

"I think I'm learning Kurdish for 'How about another beer?'" Schwarz said.

"Obviously not," Hedipe said. "What he said was, 'Time to report in.'"

Lyons stopped and Blancanales opened his eyes, but lay where he was. The room was silent as they heard slight beeps coming through the audio feed. It sounded as if someone was dialing a cell phone. The television volume was muted at the same time.

There was a short salutation, a pause, then a short word. The conversation was over already.

"He said something like, 'Hello, this is Loyalist Four,'" Hedipe said. "Then it was just 'Okay' and he hung up."

The next bit of conversation was brief. "They've been ordered to keep waiting and stay vigilant," Hedipe said.

"Not much to go on there. Was that time enough to trace the call?" Lyons asked Schwarz.

Kurtzman had heard the question on his end of the line and a minute later relayed an answer through the private line into Schwarz's headphones. Schwarz grinned. "Time enough."

Lyons wasn't exactly smiling, but he wore the expression of a feline with a rodent tail dangling out of one corner of its mouth.

Stony Man Farm, Virginia

THE PHONE THAT WAS being called turned out to be a satellite phone, using the satellite system launched by the Globalstar consortium and allowing global communications from virtually any location. The system was highly secure compared to the ubiquitous cell phones, which allowed the pirating of phone calls by just about anybody. Still, the security was breakable. Kurtzman and Tokaido had the outgoing call identified in minutes. Decrypting the messages going to and from the phone would happen soon after it was used the next time.

The next time was less than a minute later, when the phone dialed out an 011 number, directing the call out of the U.S. That left Tokaido with a dilemma.

"Destination or decryption?" he asked quickly, hands poised above the keys. In just seconds he would be able to commence work on one or the other. Not both.

"Decryption," Kurtzman replied. "The destination is useless unless we know what the call is about."

Tokaido watched his window of opportunity open as the audio signals began bouncing back and forth between the callers. A straining, squealing sound like bad electronic feedback leaked out of his computer speakers.

Whoever was on the other end was also using a Globalstar phone. Not that it made the decryption process any easier. Tokaido's hands brought up application after application. Although automatic software was multitasking furiously, he still exercised manual control as he watched the results displays. It took him eighteen seconds to achieve decryption, and suddenly the electronic squealing sound became the crystal-clear sound of voices. What they said was gibberish to him.

"That's Kurdish!" Kurtzman said, but he knew Tokaido knew it. "Get in the destination."

"I'm way ahead of you, boss." As the voices were automatically recorded on the hard drive, Tokaido was changing gears, trying to pinpoint the location to the receiving Globalstar phone, tapping into the network of forty-eight low-earth-orbiting Globalstar satellites and tracking their signals. But it seemed like just seconds later that the call was being disconnected, just as the tracking software appeared to be homing in at lightning speed on a destination. Tokaido felt like a fisherman grabbing at a slippery, record-setting northern pike that slipped the hook and slithered in his hands. For a long, long second he didn't know if he was going to lose it over the side or haul it victoriously into the boat.

Then, almost anticlimactically, a small set of GPS coordinates appeared on his computer screen. No blinking red message. No triumphant beep. It was a success just the same.

"I am *good* at this job," Tokaido said out loud.

Kurtzman rolled over a few feet and stared at the results on Tokaido's monitor.

"My friend," he said, grinning and clapping the young man on the shoulder, "that's why we pay you the big bucks."

HAL BROGNOLA HAD BEEN feeling like hell. The footage out of Turkey of the catastrophe at Diyarbakir depressed him every time he saw it, and it was all over the television.

Then he walked into the War Room and things looked

better immediately, and they hadn't told him anything yet. But they were on to something. He could read it in their eyes and feel it in the very mood of the room. He wasn't at all surprised that a major breakthrough had been made.

It was a smaller group that assembled now. Price and Kurtzman, along with tactical adviser Yakov Katzenelenbogen.

"Give me the bad news first, if there is any," he asked even before he had his aft end resting on his chair.

Price said, "The bad news is we haven't disabled any more Patriot missiles. The good news is that we are on the right track. We've managed to pry open a True Army communications leak big enough to supply us with the locations of some or all of the unaccounted-for Patriots."

"Turkish or North American?" Brognola asked.

"Both."

Brognola nodded slowly. "That is good news. Where and how was this leak uncovered?"

Price briefed the big Fed on recent West Coast activities. "The phone led to none other than Asad Cakmak. He's still here in the United States, as expected, leading the U.S. end of the operation," Kurtzman explained.

"You'd have thought he would want to personally oversee the Turkish end of the operation," Brognola commented.

"Not when you consider that he sees the U.S. part of the operation the more vital of the two," Katzenelenbogen offered. "He knows that if the U.S. becomes completely dedicated to his cause, we will bring tremendous pressure on Ankara.

"In fact," he continued, "I have a feeling the primary target for both ends of the operation is the U.S. Here in

North America he's putting a massive number of U.S. citizens in harm's way—essentially taking the entire country hostage. In Turkey his use of U.S. weapons puts the responsibility for any innocent deaths onto U.S. shoulders. The weight of this double burden, quite frankly, is going to be unlike anything the people of this nation have ever known. Look at the degree of reaction we're seeing already.''

''You don't have to tell me about that,'' Brognola said. ''The disaster in Diyarbakir has Turks around the world screaming mad, and well they should be. There's already been impromptu anti-U.S. protests in nine major Turkish cities, including Ankara and Istanbul. The President is taking flak from all over the place.''

They all knew what that meant. If the President was taking flak, then Brognola was taking flak from the President.

''He should agree this is good news,'' Price reasoned.

''I'm not going to tell him,'' the big Fed snapped. ''I'm going to save it for a while. Maybe just a few hours or maybe longer.'' Then he added in a lower voice, ''His expectations for a quick, clean resolution to this problem will become even more unrealistic when he knows.''

''CNN's reporting he'll address the nation in a few hours,'' Kurtzman said.

''The President isn't giving in to the True Army. He's going to take a hard-line stance when he addresses the nation. What's our current status?''

''We're employing Hedipe Demir as our translator. She's on stakeout with Able now, but we're feeding her everything we get for translation.''

''Can we trust her?''

''We believe so,'' Price said. ''Her involvement came by chance. There's no way she could have been set up to run into Able. They're confident she's sincere about wanting the terrorists stopped. She and Gadgets have developed a rapport.''

"Good for them. What about the missiles they're sitting on?"

Katzenelenbogen said, "Able is confident that they'll have ample warning before the thing is fired up. At the very least they'll hear generator noise, and it'll take time for them to activate the hydraulics to position the battery. Able will have time to rush the place and put a stop to it before that happens. Our hope is they'll get a chance to disarm the thing without the on-site operators knowing about it.''

"For what purpose?"

"We want to be able to monitor them for as long as possible. They're helping fill in our intelligence gaps. If we can be sure their weapon won't fire, then we can just keep sitting on them, listening in, without putting anyone at risk.''

"Are you telling me we have a way to disarm that missile from a distance?" Brognola demanded.

"Not at all," Katzenelenbogen said. "Somebody is going to have to sneak inside that trailer.''

Denver, Colorado

MACK BOLAN HAD spent hours doing nothing, accomplishing nothing.

And he was miserable doing it.

He retreated to Denver, checked into a hotel and slept while he could, downing acetaminophen to cut the pain without thinning the blood and exacerbating the bruising. The mass of black on his shoulder where the bullet had slammed into him would look ugly for a few weeks, but it didn't compromise his range of motion. He would be able to use it when he needed to. It just hurt like hell.

He had enough of sitting on his butt and contacted Price to inform her he was heading back to California, where he intended to meet up with Able in Gilroy. At least he could be in on the stakeout. That would be something. Hell on earth was defined by the Executioner as inactivity.

At five in the morning he was packing away a huge meal at an all-night diner when he got another call from Price.

A new phone call had come in to the terrorists in Gilroy. It had come from Cakmak. The fiasco at the lodge in Evergreen had been discussed. The failures of Jalal Murad and the Turkish end of the operation were mentioned.

"They mentioned that another vehicle is en route to the next staging areas. We know where it is."

"In my part of the country?" Bolan asked.

"Close enough that you might be able to catch up with them."

"Where?"

"As of five minutes ago they're on Interstate 76, headed northwest just outside the city of Sedgewick."

"Do we know if it is Cakmak's rig?"

"We don't know," she said. "His locale is still an unknown."

"Doesn't matter. It's something at least. I'm on my way."

Bolan dropped a ten next to the plate to pay for his five-dollar breakfast and was out the door.

BOLAN'S METHOD of transport was a big Ford Excursion SUV, rented out of an all-night agency in Denver. It had a big 6.8-liter, ten-cylinder engine with automatic transmission. At three hundred horsepower, it gave him more speed and power than he needed on the highway. Within minutes he was pushing it onto Interstate 76, heading north through Colorado and getting on Interstate 25 north.

"I've got the Wyoming State Police keeping an eye on the rig," Price said when he called in.

"What happens if they decide to get involved?"

"I've asked them not to, but it's a risk we have to take," she replied. "It's not like we have much choice. Somebody's got to keep them pinpointed until you can catch up with them."

"Who are you posing as?"

"When I contact the troopers I'm from a branch of the Justice Department, Domestic Transport Security Agency. You've probably never heard of it."

"I haven't," Bolan admitted.

"'Cause I made it up. But for right now they're happy to be helping out the Feds. I just hope they stay happy and don't involve anybody who knows better before you get to that truck."

"We also have to hope they don't make themselves known by the truck drivers," Bolan said. "If they figure out they're being trailed, who knows how they'll react?"

"If I had my druthers, I'd have left Jack with you to provide you air transport."

"He's best left where he is," Bolan said. Grimaldi was on station in Denver with the Stony Man Farm blacksuits, prepared to fly them anywhere the suits were needed.

Price informed him that he was less than sixty miles behind the rig, and that it had turned off the interstate heading north on U.S. Highway 20. Without the uninterrupted progress possible on the interstate, they would surely lose ground compared to Bolan.

He pushed the big SUV up to twenty miles per hour faster than the posted speed limit—and, as dawn broke, kept an eye out for the very same state police that were helping him out.

HE CAUGHT UP with the rig ten miles outside Fort Laramie, Wyoming, just as the truck was exiting from U.S. 26 onto U.S. 85, heading northwest toward South Dakota. The big truck accelerated to fifty-nine miles per hour and stayed there, determined to look normal. Bolan paced it for a while, keeping his distance, then sped up and passed it at a leisurely pace, examining every inch of the rig as he did so.

When they cruised by a parked trooper, Bolan slowed, trying to look like the part of the guilty motorist, and fell back again, behind the truck. He had precious minutes to go before his proximity started looking suspicious to the nervous truck drivers. As he drove he took out the suppressed Beretta 93-R and aimed it out the window, keeping the gun held close to the body of the Excursion, making it difficult to see by the drivers of the rig, even if they were watching him closely in their rearview mirrors.

Ahead the road curved to the left slightly, giving Bolan a prime opportunity, despite the fact that another car was in the oncoming lanes and would surely be able to see the big gun when they drove past him. He had to shoot fast. Concentrating, squinting in the morning sun, he accelerated on the rear of the semi truck and fired the 93-R one time before he passed around the big rig and was on his way, quickly withdrawing the handgun.

As the Excursion put distance between himself and

the rig, Bolan was satisfied that the maneuver had gone off about as well as he could have hoped for. The single 9 mm round had gone into the rearmost tire, so cleanly the tire hadn't shattered into a mess of rubber scrap, and exited from the side wall. It was rapidly deflating, and soon the drivers would realize they had a problem. They'd eventually be forced to pull over and take care of the tire—or risk looking mighty suspicious as they drove down the highway trailing rubber parts as the tire disintegrated.

A small truck stop was ahead, less than a mile. Better and better. The truck would likely make use of it for the tire change. Bolan accelerated fast and took the exit into the truck stop, parking behind the building and watching the highway, just in case his judgment was wrong.

It wasn't. The truck crept into the parking lot at a meager twenty miles per hour, the drivers taking it easy on the bad tire. When they parked, the driver stepped down and headed for the service bay.

Bolan was out of the Excursion by then, moving to the opposite edge of the parking lot, where a phone stood. Beyond it was a field of corn. The truckers in the rig couldn't see him, but anybody in the greasy spoon inside who happened to be looking out the window at the right moment might. Bolan looked at the window, barely able to make out the silhouettes of the diners inside. When none of them was looking, he slid into the cornfield and began hiking.

It took him all of ten minutes to circle the big parking lot, but the cornfield gave him cover until he was within ten yards of the rig. He watched it for a minute or two. The passenger was out of the cab, stretching his legs but staying close while the driver was standing in front of the truck bay negotiating with a mechanic. Bolan hoped their sense of urgency would prevent them from taking the time to investigate the reason for the flat. A small hole entering from the tread and exiting the tire's sidewall would be tough to attribute to anything other than a carefully fired bullet.

The more he thought about it, the more Bolan realized such a discovery was almost inevitable. The tires on the truck looked virtually unused. The well-funded True Army had a penchant for new equipment, specifically so problems like this could be avoided, and the drivers would want to know how a big rig's tire could have gone bad so soon. They'd look into it.

Bolan suddenly knew he had just minutes, maybe seconds, to get onto the truck. He gambled, waiting for the passenger to look away. After pacing for a few minutes the man stopped and circled the front of the cab and disappeared.

With a quick glance toward the repair bay Bolan bolted for the truck, running on his toes over the gravelly edge to the parking lot, and stopped at the ladder bolted to the rear end.

Without a second thought he ascended the ladder and flattened himself on the roof of the cab.

CHAPTER NINETEEN

The truck was ready to hit the road again in under half an hour. When the truck was rolled into the bay, Bolan had peered over the side of the roof to witness the driver and his passenger examine the tire with the mechanic who changed it. The mechanic couldn't figure out what could have made the hole. The idea that it was a bullet never occurred to him, and the customers didn't bring it up, but the glance they exchanged in the mechanic's presence was full of suspicion. As soon as the mechanic was back at work, the passenger pulled the front of his sweatshirt out of his pants to give easy access to the handgun that had to have been tucked there, then he left the bay.

He was gone for ten minutes. When he came back the tire was being remounted. He shook his head and shrugged for the benefit of the driver. He'd patrolled the truck stop and seen nobody suspicious.

By then Bolan had planted his homing device. It was essentially a cellular handheld computer with a GPS device built in, augmented with several long-life batteries coupled in series. All Bolan had to do was phone it when he needed to get its coordinates. He didn't even bother to hide it. Using a two-part adhesive, he glued the device to the roof of the truck body.

The adhesive had firmly set by the time the truck started rolling out of the repair bay. Bolan descended the ladder and stepped onto the parking lot, quickly affecting a casual stroll before he became visible in the truck's rearview mirrors.

Just in case they were watching him in their mirrors, Bolan entered the diner and strolled up to the counter.

The truck pulled onto the highway and was gone from sight.

The soldier realized then that there was a well-worn waitress standing on the opposite side of the counter staring at him expectantly. "Can I get you anything, honey?"

"No, thanks."

The waitress was mystified as he turned and left again.

Southeast Turkey

"WHAT DO YOU PROPOSE to do about it?" demanded Asad Cakmak from the staticky speakerphone sitting in the middle of the parlor. Around the phone were eight men, all members of his True Army. All well trained and highly effective soldiers. But right now Cakmak was struggling to keep them under control.

"They took our families," Mehmet Dilence retorted, slamming the butt of his rifle on the wooden floor. "They even took your sister, Asad."

"I know this—" Cakmak retorted.

"They killed my father! They left his body laying by the side of the highway just before they went into Iran. They killed three of our people! Even one of our young men! They shot him in the legs, then dumped his body!"

Cakmak wouldn't have tolerated being interrupted under any circumstances had he actually been there in person. He was having trouble getting control of the conversation now. He was speaking to the group from western America. The connection wasn't a good one—full of noise. Even worse, there was a second-and-a-half delay, so everyone was talking on top of everyone else.

The murmurs of discontent were starting to rise into a chorus of rebellion, and Cakmak knew everything was about to go to hell. He had to exercise his authority. "Not another word!" he thundered, and his voice was well beyond the capabilities of the speaker. It emerged as an irate buzz. But his men shut up.

"Now listen to me. Does anyone actually have a plan?"

There was a murmur of conversations.

"Does anyone even know where to start looking for our people?" he probed.

"Iran!" one of the young soldiers blurted. It was the kind of thing the others would have laughed at under normal conditions.

"I think it would be a waste of our time to go wandering around western Iran until we happen to stumble across our people," Cakmak said, attempting to sound reasonable.

"So we forget them? Our mothers and wives and children?" someone exclaimed.

"No!" Cakmak retorted. "I am convinced that the Turks are responsible for this outrage, so we hold them responsible. We make the release of our people one of our demands."

"The Turks haven't given in to any of our demands so far. Why do you think they will start to anytime soon?"

Cakmak started talking quickly. "We knew that the Turks would not be forced to give in to our demands instantly. We have to apply pressure and keep it on. Maybe for weeks at a time. Soon we will have the U.S. pressuring the Turks as well, especially if we accuse the Turks of terrorist tactics. The Americans hate that kind of thing. I am convinced that we are going to start seeing real progress very soon. But only if the True Army stands together and stands firm! Right now all I am hearing is the whining of dogs!"

The parlor was filled with silence. No man looked at any other man, abashed and angry.

"You will see Turkish troops going into Iran to rescue our people even as they begin acceding to our demands for territory," Cakmak said. "I promise you, we are holding all the cards in this game."

THERE WAS NO BETTER antidote to depression than activity. That was how James looked at it. Phoenix Force, to the man, considered the raid in Bismil an utter failure. They had gone in to stop the launch of the stolen Patriot and take prisoners for interrogation. Instead the missile had been launched. In the nearby city of Diyarbakir an unknown number of innocents were dead. And they had come away with not one prisoner. The terrorists were annihilated.

Nothing to show for it but a large number of corpses.

"Goddamn it, we did the best we could and I don't want to hear anybody say anything different," David McCarter stated afterward.

James knew that McCarter was silently blaming himself for the raid's dismal results. He was telling himself he should have strategized the attack better, differently somehow.

When James stepped back and thought about the attack himself, replaying it in his head, he searched for his own failures. When could he have made a break from the Fiat and taken down the maniac who had fired the missile? Surely there had been opportunities.

His practical mind told him there weren't, and that any such action would have been no more than a desperate gamble. He would have succeeded only in committing suicide. The raid as a whole, from a purely practical point of view, had gone about as well as could be expected.

So why did he feel he had just carelessly allowed a building full of innocent Turks to die?

An hour after the raid ended Phoenix Force departed the scene, a few minutes in advance of the Air Force cleanup-and-recovery crew. Price had contacted them with what she called her "shopping list."

"Able's come through in a big way," she said. "We've got intelligence on some of the Turkish Patriots. Maybe all of them." She gave them a location name, and Manning, at the wheel of the Land Rover, turned them southwest again.

"What fallout are you seeing from the Diyarbakir blast?" McCarter asked.

Price wasn't about to go there. "The President's going on TV tonight. He's going to hard-ass it. By the time he does, it would be a good idea to have another launcher secured."

She knew they were blaming themselves, and was glad to effectively present an option for them to redeem themselves in their own eyes.

By God, James thought, they wouldn't allow another one of those missiles off the ground.

Silently, he vowed that he would stop it if he had to throw himself in front of it personally.

Nobody else in the Land Rover was talking, either.

THEY HAD MADE good time across the southeastern end
of the country, along the imaginary border of what the
Kurds considered to be Kurdistan, for an hour and a half
after sundown. It made sense that they weren't going
deeper into Kurdistan—TAK wouldn't bomb any city
where it might inflict substantial casualties on its own
people.

The intelligence said the targets were any of several
mosques in the city of Gazi Antep, targets that had been
scouted out well in advance. Spotters would be stationed
in the city watching each of the locations. When the time
came to launch a missile, the spotters would be polled.
Whichever mosque turned out to have the highest number of inhabitants at the moment the fire decision was
reached would be designated the target.

Then it was simply a matter of plugging in the appropriate GPS coordinates and launching the Patriot.

From the perspective of a mass murderer, a mosque
was an excellent target. People were never willing to
give up their worship, despite warnings issued by the
government about gathering in large numbers. A good
target, in the form of a house of God, would always
present itself.

No. Not this time. Calvin James found he was gritting
his teeth.

Then the Land Rover rolled to a stop, and filled with
terrible determination, the five members of Phoenix
Force silently deployed.

THE PHOENIX FORCE WARRIOR, dressed in a blacksuit
and with his face smeared with nonreflective battle cosmetics, was virtually invisible in the night, but no more
so than his Caucasian counterparts. When James and
Manning crossed the open dirt road a quarter of a mile

to the north of their objective, they were twin shadows. Once into the sparse growth of scraggly trees on the side of the road, they double-timed it, jogging parallel to the road with their weapons in front of them in both hands. Their pace ate up the distance in seconds, the only danger coming from an ankle-twisting depression in the path hidden by the darkness.

Then they crouched at the edge of the eight-foot chain-link fence and peered at the building inside.

"Phoenix Four here," James radioed in a whisper. "We're at the fence."

"Stony One here. Report, Phoenix."

"Phoenix One here," James heard McCarter radio. "Team One and Team Two both at the perimeter."

"Any idea you're looking at?" Price asked.

"Negative, Stony. Not a house. And this fence isn't new. Some sort of factory, maybe."

Calvin James was scanning the structure with his field glasses, trying to make out the unusual nature of the building he was seeing. What he saw looked like a wealthy man's house at the front, but with a large, low, rectangular addition abutted to the rear. Behind that was an open-air pavilion, where a roof of light wood or canvas covered a framework, about an acre in size. Bundles were hanging from the framework—big masses of something. Was it wool?

As James heard McCarter describing the scene in the best terms he could to Stony, his field glasses traveled farther behind the framed pavilion. Some sort of crops were growing back there.

Then he figured it out. "Phoenix Four here," James radioed during the next pause. "That's tobacco. This is a factory for making cheroots and/or rolling cigars."

Silence answered him for a full five seconds. At his

side Manning reexamined the buildings and the fields with this bit of knowledge, and on the south end of the building he was sure the others were doing the same thing.

"Phoenix One here. Cal's got it right. We've got a tobacco field in the rear. Then an open-air area for drying and holding tobacco. It looks full, too. In front of that is a low building where they must do the processing and rolling of the tobacco."

"Phoenix Four here. You've got to hand it to them. That's an ideal spot for the launcher. They just cleared out the tobacco in the middle. It's covered on all sides by the drying tobacco and over the top by the tarp, which they yank down when they want to launch the missile."

"Yeah," agreed Manning in a whisper at his side, the whole scenario coming clear.

"Stony One here. So what's between you and the tobacco-drying pavilion?"

"Phoenix One. There's the rub. It's bare ground, a good fifty feet of it."

"Can you burn the pavilion?" Price asked.

Another moment of silence, as all five sets of ears listened to the night. James heard it. A faint rumble that sounded like the growl of a rabid dog destined to attack and kill.

"Phoenix One here. The generator appears to be in operation."

That answered Price's question. If the generator wasn't functioning, then the Patriot launch system was minutes away from being fired. Prior to a launch the generator would have to be started, the control system booted and the radar engaged. Plenty of time for Phoenix Force to blanket the pavilion with incendiary grenades and take down the operators. Since the generator was operating, the missile was in a much higher state of readiness. For all they knew, the target coordinates had been entered and the torque tube handles unlocked, meaning the missile could be fired with literally no more than the push of a button.

McCarter spelled it out for Price, who didn't need to be told. "If we try an incendiary attack on those blokes and we don't manage to put them down instantly, one of them could very well get that bastard launched. That's not an option, Stony."

"Agreed. What's the alternative?"

McCarter said, "We send in one man, nice and slow, with the rest of us covering him. If there are hidden security electronics, one man will have a better chance of getting by them than the whole herd. He gets to the launcher, puts it out of commission, then we all help with the cleanup."

"Phoenix Four here. I'm your man," James radioed just before Manning could break in to volunteer.

"You called it first. But T.J. and Rafe both want the job."

James ignored that. "The tobacco fields offer the closest concealed approach to the building, so I'm betting that's where they're watching hardest for intruders. Anybody who isn't on duty at the launcher is probably in the front house, so a frontal approach is out of the question. I should go in from the side. Right from where I'm now."

"Agreed," McCarter said. "Phoenix Three, you'll have to be our primary eyes."

"Understood," Manning said.

"You see any sign that Cal's in trouble, you let us know and we'll come up with a distraction on this side."

"Do we know if this fence is electrified?" James inquired.

"Phoenix Five here. You could grill a steak."

Manning reached into James's backpack and pulled out a collapsible shovel, then yanked out his own. "Let's dig a hole, buddy," he said with a grin.

It took them five minutes to scrape a thin depression from under the bottom of the chain link, then they insulated the bottom edge by attaching a hard rubber sleeve that extended four inches up from the bottom of the fence. After that, they were protected enough so they were able to work more quickly. Fifteen minutes was all it took for the depression to become a passageway.

James stripped off his equipment before lying on his back. The hot fence was gigantic over him. He inched his head under it, then Manning grabbed his feet.

"Keep those knees locked," the big Canadian advised.

"You better believe I will."

Then Manning put all his strength into pushing the black Phoenix Force commando through the opening. James's back scraped in the dry dirt of the hole, and he had to inch his shoulders along to stay moving while keeping his body ramrod straight. He was three-quarters of the way under the fence in just seconds. Manning stopped. Caution dictated he get no closer to the fence, but James was now able to inch his shoulders forward, then pull his shins and feet through the opening. He was inside.

Manning pushed his equipment through after him.

At the house, the addition and the pavilion there was no sign of movement in the darkness. No lights came on; no alerts were audible.

"Phoenix Four here. Here I go."

CHAPTER TWENTY

Calvin James moved across the empty ground, watching the structures for any sign of movement. He was getting worried.

"Phoenix Four here. Any response?"

"Phoenix One here. We're seeing nothing, Cal."

"This isn't right."

"I know it. Maybe this is the wrong bloody place."

James cursed silently. This had to be right. It was an ideal spot, and Stony had been very confident of Able Team's intelligence. But if the True Army had a Patriot stowed here, where was the security system? He could see why there wouldn't be armed guards roaming the place—too obvious. But surely they had to have something.

Lights came on suddenly. The low addition to the house blazed with light that shot out of the grimy windows like searchlights in the black night, and a moment later a string of light bulbs illuminated throughout the pavilion rack after rack of tobacco leaf-bunches hanging. Then there was a shout and a tramp of feet coming from the direction of the house.

James was standing in the middle of nowhere, with no cover in any direction, when he was alerted. He bolted forward, toward the closest possible cover, which was the leaves hanging in the pavilion itself. Ten fast, long strides brought him into a crouch under the edge of the canvas roof, and he listened to the conversation that was going on just twenty feet away. There were demands from two men approaching the pavilion on foot. Another man spoke, much closer—it had to be a guard stationed in the middle of the pavilion, at the missile launcher. James didn't understand a word, but he guessed the newcomers were demanding to know if the guard had noticed anything unusual. The guard was replying in the negative. The voices rose and James grimaced. He was pretty sure they were accusing the guard of sleeping on the job. The guard began denying it vigorously.

During the conversation, James was searching for a hiding place. He only briefly considered tucking himself in among the bundles of drying leaves—they didn't hang all the way to the ground. In the illumination from the string of bulbs they would see his legs and feet without trouble if they happened to crouch to look.

But that was his only option when he heard the men come through the racks, and he just managed to get buried in the leaves when one of them walked within a yard of him and turned on a flashlight, shining it into the dark, open ground that surrounded the buildings. James guessed he had triggered some sort of motion detection system on the way in. It was a relief. Now he was certain this was the right place.

James grabbed one of the four-by-four support poles for the canvas roof and shimmied up. The roof was supported by a wooden framework, also four-by-fours. It looked strong but ancient, but James didn't have time for an inspection. He would just have to hope it held. He pulled himself into the roof and straddled one of the wooden beams that climbed at a slight incline to the apex. He was guessing that the water from a good strong rainfall had to weigh as much as he did, so the roof should hold. But it wasn't a theory he'd be willing to bet money on.

His biggest challenge was to keep the roof from shaking so much the occupants would notice. He wasn't even sure where they were at the moment. Maybe all three of them were out searching the open ground. Maybe there was a fourth man that hadn't spoken, who was even now aiming a gun at the strange shape making bulges in the canvas of the roof.

When he had dragged himself to the center of the roof, he rested with his chest and stomach against the beam and his arms and legs pressing into the canvas. He pulled the knife off his hip and cut through the fabric as quietly as he could.

Below him, as clear as day under the lights, was the Patriot launcher. James was almost directly over the control panel.

"Phoenix Four here. Eureka."

"Thank God," McCarter radioed. "T.J.'s got you spotted on infrared. You safe up there?"

"For the time being. The pavilion looks abandoned at the moment."

"We can see two of them out here on our side. They're flashing their lights all over the place. We're under cover unless they decide to search outside the fence."

"Phoenix Three here. I've got one on my side, too."

"If they see our digging, they'll know somebody is inside," James said. "Otherwise they might be tempted to shrug it off as a rabbit."

"Yeah. Maybe," McCarter said, registering doubt. James was doubtful, too, and he made his decision.

"I'm going in now."

"Stay put, Phoenix Four. My guy's going back to the pavilion," Manning reported.

James watched in silence as one of the men returned to the pavilion and pushed his way into the open area in the center. He peered under and around the missile launcher, then stopped to look under the hanging leaves of tobacco.

James knew that if he happened to glance at the ceiling of canvas above him he would almost surely notice the protrusions of arms and legs through the material. He lifted his limbs, but that meant he was supporting himself only on the four-inch-wide wooden beam under his sternum, stomach and crotch, which quickly became painful. His muscles started to ache. He controlled his breathing and focused out the pain and strain, while below him the other two men entered the pavilion. They were worried about the disturbance, and the man who appeared to be the guard on duty was especially high-strung, transferring his AK-47 from hand to hand and sweating so profusely James made out the sheen on his forehead.

One of the men issued a set of very stern orders to the guard, who nodded constantly. Finally, the other two men left, walking back to the house.

The lights went out, and James exhaled in relief as he was able to rest his arms and legs again on the canvas. Below, in near pitch darkness, the guard began walking slow laps around the launcher. Finally he stopped near the control panel, illuminated by its small LCDs, and lit a cigarette, blowing out clouds of sweet smoke and visibly trying to relax.

James's combat knife cut inch by inch through the canvas until the opening was five feet long, the sound buried under the puttering of the diesel generator powering the launcher. Then he slipped through the opening and hung by one hand, picked his moment and dropped. He brought the handle of the big Randall fighting knife down on the base of the guard's skull with tremendous force. James rolled to one side and was back on his feet with his handgun aimed.

He had no need for it. The guard was slumped on the ground.

James didn't have the time to determine if the guy was alive or dead. He secured the man in plastic handcuffs, wrists and ankles, then jumped to the rear end of the rectangular container from Lockheed Martin that acted as a shipping, storage and firing cartridge for the Patriots. He grabbed the torque tube handle and locked it. The missile couldn't be fired until it was unlocked again.

Only then did he radio. "Phoenix Four here. I'm down and securing the missile."

"Affirmative."

During the long hours in the jet from the U.S. to Turkey, they had all gone through a two-hour video exercise on the disablement of the Patriot.

"Torque tube handles are locked, and I'm powering down the engagement control station." He quickly shut down the computer's operating system and turned off the power supply.

"Affirmative!"

James heard the enthusiasm in McCarter's voice. He felt it, too. The huge weight on his shoulders was growing lighter with every step of the process that took this Patriot launcher further and further from being fired.

"I'm removing engagement-control-station wiring and power supply cables," he narrated as he pried open an access panel and snatched out a handful of bound, heavily insulated wires, then chopped savagely through the CPU power line with the combat knife. "How's my cover?"

"No sign that they even know you're there."

He stepped quickly to the generator, found a cable and sliced it in two, then jabbed the blade of his knife under the control panel for the generator and dragged it against the electromechanical control terminals protected underneath. "I'm turning off the generator permanently."

"I don't recall that being a part of the video, Cal," McCarter said. "Don't you think that's overkill?"

"I'm improvising. This missile is disabled!"

Oglala National Grasslands, South Dakota

BOLAN HAD BEEN relieved to get out of Wyoming. The possibility of the state troopers getting suspicious and interfering was real and potentially disastrous. Now they were in South Dakota where the state police didn't even know about the pursuit—unless the Wyoming troopers had become wise to the Stony Man deception and phoned ahead to their South Dakota counterparts. Bolan had no contingency for that, and he wouldn't concern himself with it unless it came to pass.

He had followed the truck's GPS signal cross-country for hours. It bypassed Rumford, Provo and Edgemont, and was well on its way to Custer, passing into and out of a spur of the Black Hills National Forest, when it abruptly slowed to turn off the state road. Bolan was three miles behind it, and by the time he exited the highway the GPS display showed the truck was proceeding onto a dirt road that wasn't in the system's topographical database. The dust was still hanging in the air. Bolan didn't need the computer to track it.

He'd had all day to consider his options when the truck finally reached its destination. Sure it was almost home, he pulled the Excursion off the road and watched the progress the vehicle made on the GPS monitor. When it came to a halt he was certain it was there, and he was prepared to follow on foot, grabbing his pack and extra hardware.

He marched a hard mile and a half through the slowly rising Black Hills and found himself looking down at a ranch in a narrow valley. He heard the beeping of the truck in reverse as it was maneuvered through the open end of a horse barn, until just the front grille could be seen. Over the sound of its idling Bolan heard another engine starting up.

Pack in hand, he hurried down the slope, keeping low in the prairie grasses but sure he was sticking out in the bright afternoon sun like a red-and-white archery target. He scanned the ranch as he moved fast, looking for guards, watching for surveillance systems. Suddenly, his long, slow afternoon had turned into a life-or-death emergency. Was it the generator being started? What if the True Army was planning to fire the Patriot immediately?

Unbidden, Bolan's mind summoned up the image of the map he'd been staring at on the GPS. In the vicinity were a handful of small round dots on the electronic map—Custer, Hot Springs, Fairburn, Keystone. All were close enough for the Patriot to reach. Each dot represented tens of thousands of people.

Bolan had heard about the Patriot strike in Turkey.

The dead were still being counted. Maybe more than three hundred. He wouldn't let that happen here.

He raced through the shoulder-high prairie grass and emerged onto hard ground, then twisted and sprinted to his right, putting himself in the best blind spot he could find in a hurry. He was out of sight of the nearby ranch house, a large, one-level structure. He was taking a chance that perimeter alarms had been turned off during the entrance of the truck. He reached the corner of the horse barn and came to the closed shutters over a stall. Peering through the seam, he could see the truck inside. Were men working where they would notice the shutters opening? The bright sunlight outside and the shadowy interior made it impossible for him to tell. He had to take another major risk, and damned soon his luck would run out. He jimmied the shutter latch, pulled it open and slithered through, landing heavily on the hard-packed earth inside.

The stall was clean of horse droppings. In fact, the smell inside was musty and dry, as if it hadn't seen a horse for a long time. Bolan rose into a crouch and listened for sounds of alarm.

Footsteps approached the stall. Bolan slipped between the whitewashed boards that separated the stall from its neighbor, then into a third stall. This was deeply shadowed and gave him a partial side view of the engagement control station.

The footsteps had stopped at the stall and moved to the window that had served as Bolan's entryway. They grabbed it and pulled it shut with a slam, then left.

His eyes becoming accustomed to the darkness, Bolan soon saw how rapidly the walls of the trailer had been removed. The big corrugated-aluminum panels were being manhandled to the back end of the barn and leaned against the wall, underneath a twenty-foot-square opening covered with four hinged plywood panels, reinforced with two-by-fours. The quad-capacity missile cartridge on the launcher was pointed directly at it. That was the way out when the Patriots were fired.

Bolan's sense of emergency faded to simple urgency. The doors were closed, which meant the launch wasn't happening this minute.

Another plus—now Bolan could retreat to a hiding place outside the grounds and still have a way of knowing when the launch was eminent. But could he extricate himself from the barn again? It had been a huge risk getting in, and it would be just as big a risk getting out. It would be foolish to even attempt it while three people were inside with him. It was a minor miracle they hadn't noticed him coming through the window.

He counted just three men inside the barn taking care of the preparations of the launcher. Two were dark-haired older men, the ones stacking the aluminum panels, while the third was a young man with light, straight, sandy hair, who slumped himself on a stool in front of the engagement control station and folded his arms, staring at the panel.

The sandy-haired man looked toward the front of the barn, and Bolan saw the light from the front entrance got shut out as the big door was rolled shut. A fourth man entered his field of view.

"Where's Asad?" the sandy-haired man asked, speaking with a slight New England accent and standing up to get in the face of the new arrival.

"He is on his way." The new arrival, on the other hand, was struggling with his heavily accented English.

"Did you tell him I'm not doing his dirty work?"

"Yes. He did not think it was a funny joke."

The man made a derisive, wordless sound. "He can go to hell! He's the one who's being funny if he thinks I'm going to act as his trigger man. It's not what I was paid for."

"But you were paid very well, Sergeant Cole."

"And I performed my service very well, Mr. Celik. I was paid to instruct, not operate. That was the deal, and that's the only way it is going to go."

Celik shrugged and walked away. Cole huffed and sat heavily on the stool, glowering at the screen.

Bolan got himself comfortable on the hard dirt floor of the stall, intending to wait it out for the moment. Cakmak was coming and that was good news. The soldier was being handed the opportunity to cut the head off this vile snake at the same time he took down the last renegade launcher in the United States.

He only had to sit there and wait for the enemy to come to him.

"Striker here. Read me, Stony?" He was on a headset connected to a portable phone, but his voice so low he doubted it was getting through.

"Can you speak up, Striker?" Aaron Kurtzman asked him.

"Negative. Here's my coordinates." He quickly read off the last GPS reading from the bug on the truck trailer. "Repeat it, Bear, so I know you've go it right."

Kurtzman read the coordinates back correctly, and Bolan provided him with a succinct report on his situation.

"What is Cakmak's ETA?" Kurtzman asked.

"Unknown. How fast can you have G-Force and the blacksuits here?"

That took some conferring. Apparently, Phoenix

Force was up to its eyeballs in its own situation at the moment, and Price was giving them her attention.

"Two hours," Kurtzman said. "They're en route. Is that sufficient?"

"Who knows?" Bolan said. "They could plan on sitting here for days. Or they could be planning to launch any minute."

CHAPTER TWENTY-ONE

Turkey

The small charge cracked in the quiet darkness. When
McCarter, Hawkins and Encizo rose from behind the
protection of the low ditch, they found the fence peeled
back like the wrapping on a candy bar and marched
through.

Shouts came from the house, and an instant later the
lights in the addition and the pavilion blazed back to
life. The two Kurd soldiers who had come out to investigate James's disturbance emerged again from the rear
of the addition, calling for the guard.

James was waiting for them, pressed against the wall
alongside the door, with an unobstructed view of their
backs. He struck hard and fast, cracking the butt of his
M-16 against the skull of the nearer man, then leveling
the weapon into the abdomen of number two. Number
two froze when he found himself companionless and
trapped. He raised his arms. James shoved the rifle out
of his hands, then grabbed the terrorist by the collar and
dragged him away from the open door. More footsteps
were coming.

James's prisoner shouted and twisted wildly out of his

hands. The M-16 spit a single round that cored him through the fly of his trousers, sending him to the hard ground with a heavy thump.

The Phoenix Force commander pulled away from the windows as the familiar report of the AK-47 erupted from inside, shattering window glass and sending a brief hail of crystals over the two fallen Kurds. He chanced a look when the firing stopped, then pulled sharply back again to avoid the next burst of fire. The gunners inside were crying a name continuously, and James gathered one of the men he had just neutralized was the man in charge. Now the Kurds were leaderless and unsure of their course of action. Which was ideal.

"You pissed somebody off," Hawkins said as he fell into a crouch at James's side.

Encizo and McCarter were right behind him. The Briton held up a flash-bang grenade for the others to see. "On three."

McCarter crept under the nearest window and waited for a pause in the firing, then stood just long enough to sight the gunners and lob the grenade at their feet. They started firing, then pulled up short when they realized what was suddenly bouncing on the hard-packed dirt. There was a short outcry.

The Phoenix Force warriors didn't hear the outcry, but even with their fingers in their ears and their eyes squeezed shut they could hear the screech of the grenade and see the flash of light. Then they were storming into the low building where the gunners were now groping along the ground, clawing at their eyes.

James and Hawkins were already cuffing the pair as Encizo and McCarter raced through the low building, past worktables and piles of dried tobacco. A Kurd blundered through the narrow door at the end of the building and gaped in surprise. Encizo didn't even slow down, twisting like a cat and slamming his stocky torso into the gunner. The gunner was a gaunt, short figure, and he felt as if he had run into a concrete column. The gun flew out of his hands and he ricocheted off the wall before collapsing, stunned like a bird that just bounced off a window. His arms were wrenched behind his back and his wrists cuffed.

McCarter was through the door, spraying fire. A pair of figures retreated before his audacious offense, scrambling through the lower level of the house and crashing through the front door in full panic. Another burst of fire cut them down, chopping into their shins and feet. One of them hit the hard ground forehead first and was instantly limp. The other thrashed and screamed, trying to get a grip on the mutilated flesh and bones of his feet.

Something impacted his chest like a thrown brick, and he flopped onto his back, the air exploding from his lungs.

Gary Manning said, "Shut up."

The terrorist struggled for breath, staring up into the face of a man who he knew would shoot him dead without the slightest hesitation. The gunner couldn't have spoken if he tried, and he wouldn't have dared if he could.

Stony Man Farm

THE CONFERENCE CALL included Price, Kurtzman and Katzenelenbogen on one end, Brognola on the other. The big Fed was sitting in his Washington, D.C., office.

"Okay, tell me you've got good news."

"We've got good news," Price said. "Phoenix just took down a launcher."

"The intelligence we got through Able was good, then," Brognola said with a sigh. "That's encouraging. How many missiles still unaccounted for in Turkey?"

"Three Patriots, one launcher," Kurtzman said.

"There's more and it gets better," Price added. "Within the past hour we've gotten more intel through Able. Their communications system is really turning into the True Army's Achilles' heel."

"For as long as they don't know we have access to it," Katzenelenbogen warned. "Sooner or later it's going to become obvious to them they've got a leak."

"We'll just need to move fast enough so they don't have time to come to that conclusion," Brognola stressed.

"That may be easier said than done."

"What's the status of Able's launcher?"

"As of this moment, still live," Price said.

There was a moment of silence. "We're taking a chance every minute that it sits there in a ready-to-fire state," he said.

"We're quite aware of that," Price retorted, allowing a small measure of the strain to leak through in her voice. "So is Able."

"I know. I understand the pressure you're under. I take it Able is prepared to move on a moment's notice if it becomes evident the order has been given to launch the missile."

"Yeah. They're standing by like firemen."

Brognola said, "We've had no opportunity to shut it down? I thought we had a strategy, Bear."

"They're baby-sitting it twenty-four hours a day," Katzenelenbogen reported. "There's been no opportunity for Able to get inside without raising hell."

"So the only choices are to keep the California terrorists under constant watch and risk a launch, or take them out of commission and lose our intelligence source on the rest of the operation.''

"Maybe not that cut-and-dried," Price said. "Able's come up with a plan. It's a little far-fetched.''

She explained it to Brognola, who actually laughed.

"Could such a thing work?''

"It has before," Katzenelenbogen said.

"Well, tell them to give it a shot," the big Fed said. He added, without humor, "What do we have to lose?''

Gilroy, California

BLANCANALES THOUGHT this was about the worst part of the job. He'd been ordered to extract the filthy old trench coat from the plastic bag and to go out in public wearing it again.

But it was four in the morning, and he wasn't likely to be seen. Even the neighbor in the adjacent mobile home, the old man that called the police on him, wasn't stirring.

The job was a risky one. Getting caught wasn't what he was worried about. The risk was in alerting the inhabitant of the faked mobile home that somebody was on to him.

The Kurd and his companion were working in shifts of twelve hours. As a security measure they returned to the small house, a few blocks away, for sleeping during off hours.

Blancanales was sure whoever was on duty wasn't supposed to be sleeping, but that's exactly what was going on by the sound of the snoring coming over the bug. Either that, or he was already on to Able's surveillance and bluffing them.

Time to find out. Blancanales got down on his knees, then on his back, clutching his pack to his chest. He scooted himself underneath the body of the fake mobile home, wincing against the sound his body made scraping on the gravel.

He was in pitch blackness and had to work by feel, but the device Schwarz had monkey rigged for him was simple to operate. The toughest part was finding an entrance point for the tubing. He moved himself around until he saw what he was looking for. A small glimmer of light coming through the body panels from the interior above.

They had been counting on the probability that the terrorist would have done a less-than-perfect job when it came to putting a floor on their makeshift mobile home. Sure enough, there was a gap in the plywood. A gap was all Blancanales needed. He pulled out the four-foot roll of plastic tubing and inserted it through the hole, feeding out the entire length. At the other end was a small compressed canister of nitrous oxide. As he twisted open the spigot on the canister, the pressure forced the contents through the plastic tube. Blancanales dragged the gas mask over his face.

"I'm gassing him now," he whispered into the radio.

"Copy that," Lyons replied. "We're monitoring him. No change."

Five minutes later Blancanales reported, "The canister is empty."

"He's still snoring away, Pol."

"I guess that's a good sign. See if he responds."

"Here we go."

As Blancanales scooted out from under the trailer, he heard the phone ringing inside. That was Lyons, using the number they had extracted from their phone tap. It rang fifteen times as Blancanales moved into a small copse of trees at the border of the mobile home park, where Schwarz waited in the blackness.

"No answer. All signs point to success," Lyons radioed.

"Affirmative," Schwarz radioed. "I'm going in."

Schwarz pulled on his own gas mask and picked the lock on the flimsy door in fifteen seconds, his ears straining for the slightest sound of a warning from Lyons, who was monitoring the heavy breathing of the sleeper inside. No warning came. He let himself inside and closed the door behind him.

He could barely move. The interior of the mobile home shell was filled by the huge cartridge for the Patriot missiles. The only nod to comfort was a sleeping bag unrolled on the floor, hugging the floor of the truck bed. There was a small portable television and a lantern running off the power feed from the trailer park's power supply. Food wrappers and beer cans littered the floor. One man lay sprawled on the sleeping bag. Schwarz nudged him with his foot while covering him with his handgun.

"Hey, wake up. Why don't you clean up this pigsty?"

No response.

"Sounds like he's asleep," Lyons radioed.

"I think I'll make certain," Schwarz responded.

"How're you going to do that?"

Schwarz put one foot on the sleeping man's stomach and applied sudden pressure. The Kurd grunted out his breath and lay gasping, but his eyes remained curiously closed.

"He's asleep," Schwarz reported. "I'm getting to work."

Confident that he was well covered, with Lyons and

Hedipe Demir watching the street from the apartment and Blancanales close at hand outside, Schwarz holstered the weapon and crawled through the dark interior to the engagement control station. It took him fifteen minutes to access the primary CPU and plug in, feeding in the new operating-system software from the laptop. It had been designed by Tokaido to give the appearance of normal operation, but redundant systems ensured the final-ignition and launch sequence could never be initiated.

Next he moved about the interior, planting a half-dozen new bugs and even a pair of tiny video pickups.

"You've been in there twenty-eight minutes, Gadgets," Lyons warned him.

"I'm wrapping it up," he reported. They had estimated that, minimally, the dose of nitrous oxide would keep the terrorist unconscious for half an hour. But he was showing no sign of waking when Schwarz left the fake mobile home and locked the door again behind him.

Five minutes later he and Blancanales were back in the apartment that served as their base of operations. Blancanales quickly brought all his new audio and video devices online. They would be able to see eighty percent of the interior of the fake mobile home when the lights were on, including an over-the-shoulder view of anyone attempting to operate the Patriot engagement control station. He brought up the audio devices, and the computer speaker played the sound of the man's snoring from four different microphones.

"Quadraphonic sound," he announced.

"How many missiles were actually in the launcher?" Lyons demanded.

"Just three," Schwarz said.

Lyons frowned, feeling suddenly dejected. He had hoped they could strike another four Patriots off the list.

That left another four live missiles floating around North America.

Four missiles could do a hell of a lot of damage, and end a hell of a lot of innocent lives.

CHAPTER TWENTY-TWO

Stony Man Farm, Virginia

"What's that?" Kurtzman asked, nodding at the computer screen.

"Santa Cruz, California," Barbara Price said. "I'm on the city Web site. This is their boardwalk."

Kurtzman examined the photo. It was a summer day, with the sun glinting off the ocean. On the boardwalk, past T-shirt stands and fudge shops, strolled a light crowd of tourists, and he could make out a family, with a little girl eating cotton candy. Nearby was a pair of lovers walking hand in hand. It was about as perfect a picture of summer Americana as you could get.

"You thinking about taking a vacation?" he asked.

Price shook her head, and then suddenly Kurtzman understood.

"The Gilroy Patriots," he said.

"Yeah. Gadgets just sent me the GPS coordinates he found on the launch computer. It was aimed to hit right here." She tapped the image on the screen and added, "I just wanted to see what it looked like."

Kurtzman said, "If they launched that thing in the middle of the afternoon, with lots of people out on the boardwalk…'' It was a thought he didn't need to finish. Each of them mentally envisioned the resulting scenario of destruction and death.

"These guys deserve whatever they get,'' he finally said quietly.

Black Hills, South Dakota

CEMAL CELIK APPROACHED the car in a quick walk when it came to a halt in front of the ranch house, and he was wearing an oddly apprehensive expression. Asad Cakmak stepped out of the car and demanded, ''What's wrong?''

"We have a situation.'' Before Cakmak could demand a less vague answer he added, ''Don't look around. There's an intruder on the premises.''

The statement was so unexpected that Cakmak did something he almost never did—he froze, and it was an act of supreme will to keep himself from craning his neck over his shoulder to find this intruder.

"I saw nothing unusual on the way in. Don't you have the army on alert?''

"No,'' Celik said, and now he looked almost bemused. "I didn't want to alert him. You see, the intruder doesn't yet know we know he is here.''

CELIK BEGAN narrating rapidly. ''The launcher arrived a little ahead of schedule, and we positioned it in the barn. Before I left the house to supervise the staging, one of our security men pointed out a strange anomalous signal coming out of the compound somewhere. I decided it must be coming from the truck itself. I thought maybe one or both of our drivers had sold us out. So I had the rig and the cargo container body panels surreptitiously searched. While they were dismantling the roof, they found it—some sort of handheld computer, still operating, with GPS capabilities. I had it shut down immediately. I had the video system on the camp closely monitored while the search was taking place, just in case one of the drivers tried to sneak out of the grounds. Instead, they caught a man entering the grounds.''

Celik gestured at the lower left display screen on the bank of four. The security man stationed there touched the play button, and the monochrome image showed a slow scan of the grounds to the rear and side of the barn—and there, picture perfect in the afternoon sunlight, was a man emerging from the prairie grass and moving fast through the open. He disappeared under the overhang when he flattened against the barn.

''Where did he go next?'' Cakmak demanded, amazed at the intruder's audacity.

''We never saw him leave the barn,'' Celik said.

''You lost him?''

''No, I mean that he never reappeared.''

''We have had two sets of eyes on the screens every minute since he went in,'' the security systems operator added. ''We have even had another man fast-forwarding through the tapes since this time marker. I am confident that he is still hiding in the barn.

''Because I knew you were arriving soon, it seemed best to allow you to take charge of ferreting him out— and make the decision whether we should stay here at all.''

Cakmak nodded. ''Yes. He will have support with him.''

''So why is he waiting to call them in?'' Celik asked. ''Why did he sneak onto the grounds at all? If he planted the GPS tracker on the truck, then he already knows what it contains. His behavior is confusing.''

Cakmak barked, ''Roll the tape again.''

The operator quickly rewound the tape and again played the five seconds of footage showing the dark man creeping onto the ranch.

''Can you obtain a better image of his face from this tape?''

The operator shrugged, ''I can get a close-up, but the quality will be poor.''

''Do it.''

He fiddled with the controls for a moment before increasing the size of the image, and its graininess. ''That is as good as I can make it.''

''That is good enough. It is him.'' Cakmak pointed accusingly at the blocky pixels on the monitor. ''It is the same son of a dog that attacked the lodge in Colorado.''

Celik paled. ''Which means his backup team is nearby. So why haven't they attacked us?''

''His goal is not to apprehend the launcher—not solely. He wants me, too. He wants to make sure I am present before he stages his attack,'' Cakmak said.

''So do we try to take him out?''

Cakmak was thoughtful. ''He's got us by the testicles.''

''What? He's the one who's in the precarious position,'' Celik protested.

''No! He's in the barn somewhere and we don't know where. He's a skilled warrior. He may have put himself in a position to have a clear shot at the controls of the launcher. One good shot and he could put us out of business.'' Cakmak seethed. ''I warned the U.S. government about interfering—I warned them! Now I make good on my threat!''

"You're going to fire the missiles.''

"We will have Cole act as if he were shutting the launcher down, but in reality he will bring the launcher online and fire it before our spy knows what he is doing.''

Celik looked worried again at the mention of Cole. "There is another problem.''

ALREADY THE CREW was at work, quietly, on the exterior of the barn. Climbing an extension ladder, they attached two lengths of chain to the doors designed to allow the Patriot out of the barn. They worked in absolute silence.

Inside the ranch house, Cakmak said, ''I'm asking you to please do this favor for us, Clive.''

Clive Cole was taken off guard. The terrorist leader had never used his first name and had never said "please" to him—or to anyone.

"I won't do your dirty work, Asad,'' he said, shaking his head. ''I agreed to train your men in the operation of the launchers. You want me to do more training I will. But I will not push the button myself.''

"I know you have misgivings, Clive,'' Cakmak said. He was sitting on a chair at the big knotty-pine dining table, which was left over from the former residents of the ranch. No matter how relaxed and confident he tried to look, Cakmak's ruined mouth made him into a monster. Cole had trouble even looking at him. ''But we're in a situation here. We want that missile launched in the next ten minutes, and we want it done in a clandestine manner....''

"Clandestine manner?'' Cole demanded. ''What's that supposed to mean?''

"And—if you will let me finish—we're willing to pay you a substantial bonus if you will agree to do it."

Cole smiled. His greed had taken him this far. He had five years of his Air Force salary already sitting in his hometown bank in Newburyport, Massachusetts, courtesy of the True Army of Kurdistan. "How substantial?"

"We will match the amount we have already paid you. That is double our original agreement."

"Holy shit!" he hissed. "For ten minutes' work?"

"That's right. You walk out there right now and fire one Patriot, and then the extra cash is yours."

Clive grinned. "You got yourself a deal."

Washington, D.C.

NEWS ANCHOR ALLAN SACKHEIM grabbed the phone out of his assistant's hand.

"Sackheim here. Is this a joke?"

"No joke, Mr. Sackheim. I am Asad Cakmak. I am the man responsible for the theft of the Patriot missiles from the Hickam Air Force Base in Oahu, Hawaii."

"How do I know it's really you?"

"You don't. Shut up and start recording, unless you want me to give this scoop to ABC news instead."

"No. I'll listen to you, Mr. Cakmak." Sackheim gestured frantically for his assistant to flip on the Lanier tape recorder he kept ready on his desk, electronically connected to the phone line for crystal-clear recordings. "Tape is rolling."

"My name is Asad Cakmak, leader of the True Army of Kurdistan. I am still in possession of seven U.S. Patriot missiles and two missile launchers, configured to strike targets on the ground. I have promised that no one would be hurt by me if the nations of the United States of America and the Republic of Turkey cooperated in the formation of an independent Kurd state on Turkish, Syrian and Iraqi soil. I have also warned these nations against interfering with my efforts.

"The U.S. has not followed that directive. The American government endangered the lives of its own innocent citizens by aggressively interfering with me and my undertaking. Yesterday, I gave the U.S. a warning and it went unheeded. At this very moment a U.S. agent has infiltrated my compound in South Dakota. In retaliation for this betrayal, I will, within three minutes, fire one Patriot missile at a city in South Dakota. Within six minutes one hundred or more U.S. citizens will be dead or dying."

Sackheim had been struggling to stay quiet, but he finally exploded. "Don't do it! There has to be another way."

"This is the price the United States pays for betraying *me*."

There was a click.

Black Hills, South Dakota

BOLAN HAD BEEN in the barn for an hour and was feeling increasingly like a trapped tiger. His consolation was that dusk was just a couple of hours away and offered a better opportunity to get out of the barn unseen. There was no sign that a launch was eminent. The trio of guards stayed at one end of the barn, strolling in and out of the small door there, rifles dangling carelessly on their shoulders.

Cole appeared again and began fiddling with the controls, then got up and began a visual inspection of the systems.

Everything was as it had been when Bolan first laid eyes on the launcher. Like most of the systems the Stony Man teams had located, it was kept in a state of readiness. One of the Patriots was unlocked even now, just seconds away from firing. But they wouldn't risk firing the Patriot with the plywood doors closed, would they? The Patriot might blast its way through unscathed, but it just might throw it off course enough for a crash.

Bolan didn't like this and he didn't know why. Was Cole acting too casual? Was he *trying* to look as if he were just going through maintenance procedures? The warrior got into a crouch and had the MP-5/10A3 in both hands, ready to fire if the need arose.

Conflicting motivations were careening around in his head. He needed Cakmak to shut this operation down. Where was Cakmak? Why hadn't he arrived yet? But if he were to go on the offensive right now, he could clear out the barn and plant an HE under the launch system, rendering it inoperable. He couldn't let that missile launch.

He was as indecisive as he had ever been in his life, an unfamiliar state for the Executioner.

Cole had something plastic in his hand—it was a spray bottle. He was cleaning the glass on the engagement control station monitor. He looked relaxed. So why were Bolan's instincts telling him to attack hard and attack now?

Barbara Price came onto the open connection he was maintaining with Stony Man Farm. "Striker, are you there?" she demanded.

"Go ahead."

"Listen carefully—somebody just called into the NBC affiliate in D.C. He claimed to be Asad Cakmak. He said that a U.S. agent had infiltrated his compound in South Dakota, and in retaliation he's launching a missile—*right now.*"

Mack Bolan, the soldier of countless missions, actually felt his blood run cold. "Not if I can help it."

Bolan stood, leveled the MP-5/10A3 and was tossed back to the ground when an explosion cracked open the end of the barn. The wooden brace that held the big plywood doors disintegrated and wooden shrapnel ripped into his face and hands as he went down. Only when his head was slamming into the ground did his searching eyes locate Cole. He had placed himself behind the protection of a stall wall at the farthest end from the big doors.

Bolan's face was a hideous mask of fresh blood when he pushed himself to his feet, his teeth showing in his rage, and he leveled the submachine gun at the American missile operator, who sprinted back for the engagement control station. He was out of Bolan's line of fire, and the warrior knew what he was about to do. He shouted as a distraction, "Stop!"

Cole's face peered around the body of the launcher as Bolan was coming for him. Cole withdrew.

When Bolan came to a sudden stop, with the gun leveled on Cole, it was too late. There was a rush that sizzled in the air, a huge torrent of smoke and flame, and a Patriot slid into the sky and out the gaping opening in the end of the barn.

Then it was gone as if it had never been, leaving behind smoke and silence.

Cole didn't know who the armed man was, but he knew the enraged mask of an executioner when he saw one. The gambles he had taken, he realized suddenly, had been utterly foolish. What good was wealth when you were dead?

"How many people did you just murder?" The voice came from the bloodied gunman, as cold as the grave.

"Don't blame me!" Cole protested feebly. "It's not my battle! Cakmak's the one!"

There was a rattle of gunfire when a small army stormed through the open main doors at the far end. Bolan returned fire, nearly blinded by anger, sweeping down a trio of gunners in one brutal torrent of fire, then crouched behind cover when the MP-5/10A3 cycled dry. As he changed out the magazine, there were evenly spaced bursts of fire from the AK-47s, designed to keep him down, then the first fresh wisps of smoke reached his nostrils. It was distinct from the lingering exhaust of the departed Patriot—Bolan detected gasoline and wood smoke. The barn was being burned down around him.

A few shouts were followed by the rush of the semi truck engine, and Bolan suddenly knew the reason he was being held at bay. They wanted to save the launcher and the Patriots that remained cocooned inside.

Cole was nowhere to be seen.

Bolan berated himself for the launch that had occurred. He wouldn't allow one more of those weapons to be used. He would put that launcher out of commission or die trying.

Pulling a high-explosive grenade out of his pack, he lobbed it up and out into the center of the barn, aiming blindly at the truck cab. The blast came, and he pushed himself to his feet the moment he estimated the percussive shock wave had traveled past him, landing the barrel of the submachine gun on the wooden wall in front of him and triggering at the exposed bodies still recovering from the detonation. He cut down two figures who had been knocked to their knees, then directed the fire into the tires of the semi cab as it ground into gear and the engine struggled to pull it away. The HE bomb had landed badly and had done no more than dent body panels. The truck and trailer lunged forward, and Bolan aimed for the controls on the launcher. Without it, the entire thing was useless, and a single well-placed bullet could do it. The 10 mm rounds careened off metal supports and punctured sheet-metal panels before a trio of gunners with AKs rounded the corner and unleashed on him.

Bolan ran for cover, first behind the end of the departing truck. The position was tenuous. If he stayed on the truck's rear, he'd run right into the line of fire of the gunmen at the door. He ducked away, sighting the ladder for the loft, and scrambled up while he was still hidden from their view. When the truck was out the door and Bolan was visible to the gunners again, he was already ducking away from them into the loft. A pair of 7.62 mm rounds buzzed at his heels like angry wasps.

When he returned into their field of view, the men were still in the doorway, but they were no longer firing the Kalashnikovs. Instead they were upending bright red five-gallon plastic jugs of gasoline, creating a lake of flammable liquid that spread from one side of the wide entrance to the other. Beyond them the truck was moving out of his sight. It was getting away from him.

Bolan fired the weapon, aiming for the steel door frame. He didn't see the spark when the bullet hit, but the inch-deep gasoline in the guide channel erupted at once, flowed overground to the men with the gasoline cans and sprang at them before they even knew what was happening. One dropped his can, splashing himself with more gasoline and erupting in a fireball. Another man panicked, tripping and falling in the sheet of flame. As he jumped to his feet, his gasoline-sodden back caught fire and he screamed, landing on his stomach and thrashing until his body was completely engulfed. Only one man got free, slapping at the flames wearing gloves of fire, and the burning spread to his shirt when he frantically beat his hands on his chest. He finally fell and rolled, extinguishing the flames.

Bolan wasn't getting out the front doors. He rushed across the empty loft to the front of the building, to a small, shuttered window, slamming the butt of the H&K submachine gun into it. When it flung open, a group of running men below him stopped short. Bolan recognized one of them, the same ruined face he had seen for an instant in the lodge in Colorado. Asad Cakmak.

Cakmak knew him, too.

A scathing burst of gunfire drilled into the side of the building and through the window, driving Bolan to the floor before he fired a shot. When he was up again seconds later, the group was clambering into the rear end of a nondescript utility van, which was already moving. When the last of the men was inside, it accelerated away in a cloud of dust.

The interior of the barn was filled with billowing smoke, and the fire was eating through the walls at ground level. Bolan dropped the submachine gun out ahead of him before he pushed his big frame through the small window feetfirst. He hung by his fingertips from the window frame, then dropped, feeling the ground crash into his feet and dropping into a sky diver's roll that managed to save his ankles. By the time he was on his feet, he had snatched up the H&K again, but there were no targets for him. The last of the TAK vehicles was disappearing around the mountainside.

CHAPTER TWENTY-THREE

"G-Force!"

"I'm here, Sarge," Jack Grimaldi said into the radio.

"What's your location?"

"Five miles out from your position and coming fast with reinforcements."

"Too late for that—it's all gone to hell. I want you to be on the watch for a launcher. It's on the move. They managed to fire one of the Patriots, but the others are still in the battery."

"Your device still tracking that launcher, Sarge?"

"Negative. They removed the body panels, and I didn't give them time to put it all together again."

"You mean those assholes are driving around with a fully visible missile launcher? How far do they think they're gonna get?"

"Not far at all. I don't think they've even stopped to lower the hydraulic lifts. They'll pull over and put those missiles in the air the first chance they get. They're going to blow their entire load at once."

Grimaldi muttered a curse under his breath. "I'll keep an eye out and let you know when I spot them."

"STONY, TELL ME what happened to the missile."

"Reports are coming out of Custer, South Dakota,

Striker. It hit a municipal building in town,'' Price said. "We may have dodged the proverbial bullet."

"Explain," Bolan demanded as he reached the top of the ridge and jogged down the other side to the parked Excursion.

"It's Sunday and it's late afternoon. Little or no business being conducted inside."

As Bolan slid behind the wheel and cranked the big V-10 engine to life, he felt a surge of relief. If the report was accurate, that meant the loss of life would be minimized. Innocent people would have been killed, yes, but at least not tens or hundreds of them. "They must have planned on launching it during the work week and didn't have the chance to change targets."

"You think this guy Cole had the opportunity to set up the firing sequence for more launches?"

"Maybe, maybe not. I can't take the chance."

On the radio Grimaldi spoke. "Striker, I have your truck in sight."

GRIMALDI PULLED BACK on the stick and banked the CH-53E Super Stallion military transport helicopter to circle above the semi. From two hundred feet up there was no mistaking the big black battery on the truck trailer below. The driver was bringing up a cloud of dust as he swerved recklessly through the Black Hills.

"He's still on the move?" Bolan asked over the radio.

"Looked like he was sitting still when I spotted him, but he started up again when I made my presence known," Grimaldi reported.

"Don't let them stop, whatever you do," Bolan ordered. "Harass them. Fire at them from the air. Do whatever you have to but don't let them stop that vehicle. We can't give them the time to launch those Patriots!"

"Understood, Sarge," Grimaldi said, then turned to the man hovering at his shoulder and listening in on his own headset. "You heard the man, Mr. McDonald. Let's make that trucker's day a bad one."

Blacksuit One climbed into the rear of the Super Stallion shouting orders, and a moment later a young SEAL sharpshooter clambered to a side door of the helicopter, harnessing himself directly in front of it as his commanding officer pulled it open. The steady thrum of the three T64-GE-416A engines became a staccato thrumming. Below them on the wildly swinging landscape the semi appeared, careening at a hard angle through a narrow turn in the road.

The SEAL was an experienced marksman, but shooting from a moving helicopter at a fleeing truck on a crooked road could never be an easy task. He shouldered the U.S. M-21 Sniper Weapon, aimed, instinctively compensated for the movement of the vehicles and fired a single 7.62 mm bullet. A small shiny spot appeared on a black support strut of the launcher.

"Good," McDonald said. "Keep them scared. But don't incapacitate any of them. If they stop, they might try something stupid."

The young SEAL looked at him as if he'd lost his marbles. "I'll do my best, sir, but I think you're asking for impossible accuracy."

"Do your best. You know the consequences if we let them or make them fire a missile."

"Yes, sir."

BOLAN SPOTTED the hovering Super Stallion and twisted the wheel to take a narrow, overgrown vehicle path through the rocky hills. Finding himself facing a steep incline, he yanked the wheel in the other direction, but gravity dragged the three and a half tons down the dusty trail instead of allowing it to swerve to the side, and the walls of the tires plowed up weeds and crumbling dirt. Bolan cranked the gearshift into reverse and stood on the gas as a ten-foot wall of rock reared up in front of the truck. The trick slowed it just enough to enable the treads to make a successful grab at the ground. The SUV swerved hard and missed the rock wall with a yard to spare, then bounced on the steplike flattened rocks that brought the path down to the next level in the road. He'd made good use of the shortcut. Now the helicopter was so close Bolan had to lean into the windshield to see it, but the semi was still hidden behind the hills.

"I see you, Sarge," Grimaldi radioed urgently. "You better put the pedal to the metal, 'cause these guys have stopped and I think they are getting desperate."

"You on top of them?" Bolan asked.

"More or less. They've tucked themselves halfway under an overhang. You can get at them. You've got nothing but open road between you and them now."

"I'm on my way."

The Excursion rushed to life as Bolan steered the vehicle into a straightway and stomped hard on the accelerator, spewing dust behind him. Rounding a gentle curve at high speed, he spotted the semi halted under a rocky section of loose earth and rock. It looked as if the hill underneath it had been blasted out recently, probably for the express purpose of getting the big rig through the narrow road in the first place.

They were going to be trapped. He would be on top of them before they managed to reverse and get the angle they needed to thread that needle.

Then his satisfaction transformed to dread when he realized they weren't even going to make the attempt.

A dark-haired, swarthy man climbed out of the passenger door and ran to the driver's side, carrying an automatic rifle, which he aimed at the driver's door. The figure behind the wheel of the semi ducked out of sight as he simultaneously lurched the truck backward, turning the wheel so that the cab careened at the gunner, who scrambled back and triggered his weapon at the window and door.

The truck rolled a couple more feet, then stopped. The driver was dead.

Bolan guessed what had just happened. The driver had been eager to escape. To the fanatic with the rifle, escape wasn't an option. He wanted to go out in a blaze of glory.

Another man emerged from the cab with his hands in the air. It was Cole, being ushered at gunpoint out of the truck. He was going to fire the rest of those missiles or be shot.

"G-Force, better clear out of there," Bolan said. "You don't want to be in the line of fire if those Patriots start flying."

"Affirmative. I'll try to land some backup for you nearby."

Bolan didn't bother answering. He had no doubts that this would all be over before the blacksuits could join him. Bolan stood on the gas and aimed at the truck with one hand while he groped behind his seat with the other, dragging out the M-202 A-1. It had been part of the cache of hardware he had received from the Blacksuits in Colorado. He braked and twisted the Excursion, bringing it to a heavy stop on the dry dirt road, then stepped out, placing the SUV between himself and the pepper of automatic fire from the terrorist's AK. The Kurd was shouting at Cole, and Bolan's quick glance over the hood of the SUV showed him Cole fumbling around in the engagement control station.

Bolan had no idea how long it would take him to get the weapon ready to fire. He couldn't even be sure that it was still fireable after its rough ride through the hills. Surely there had been potential to damage the controls, the cartridge hydraulics. Would any of it matter?

He couldn't take the chance. He was going to put that launcher out of commission now. He shouldered the M-202 A-1 Multishot Rocket Launcher, leaned his body against the front end of the Excursion for better stability and sighted on the missile battery.

He couldn't see Cole, hidden in the control station, and the Kurd terrorist was only partially visible.

Bolan changed his mind. He tilted the sights of the M-202 A-1 over the top of the launcher and triggered the weapon.

The first 66 mm rocket streaked two hundred yards through the open air until it slammed into the earthen wall just an arm's reach above the top of the extended missile cartridge. At one-second intervals three more rockets fired, slamming into the hill explosively. The burst of the incendiary warheads blanketed the Patriot battery in fire and flying earth, hiding the Kurd terrorist and the traitorous American.

Then the earth began to move as the unstable overhang of rock and dirt succumbed to the explosive removal of its base soils. There was a single shout of terror from underneath as tons of soil slid and collapsed, crashing into the launcher cartridge and pushing it away like a giant hand. The cartridge tilted, teetered precariously, then collapsed on its side as tens of thousands of pounds of earth piled onto the truck bed.

Then there was a strange silence. Even the thrum of

the Super Stallion's rotors had died to a slow and distant idle. By the time the blacksuits appeared with Jack Grimaldi, the dust was clearing enough for Bolan to investigate.

The top of one tire was visible, as were the four ominous black openings at the top of the toppled missile cartridge. The truck cab was buried up to its windows. The rest of the truck bed was under a pile of rubble eight feet deep.

A single human hand protruded from the top of the pile.

Bolan got onto his knees and peered inside the cartridge openings. Three missiles were inside.

All the Patriots in North America were now out of the hands of the True Army of Kurdistan.

Bolan didn't experience much of a feeling of relief. Cakmak still lived. He still possessed missiles in Turkey. Innocent people were still at risk of being slaughtered by these madmen.

This war wasn't yet over.

CHAPTER TWENTY-FOUR

The CH-53E Super Stallion was airborne again a minute later, winging out over the Black Hills National Forest at near to the aircraft's maximum speed of 170 knots—about 195 mph—and definitely above Sikorsky's recommended maximum cruising speed of 150 knots. With the Stony Man Farm blacksuits left behind to secure the area pending the arrival of the Army cleanup team, the transport helicopter was flying nearly empty.

"There's Cakmak," Bolan said, pointing far ahead and below at a small convoy of cars trailing a billow of dust through the hills.

"Which one?" Grimaldi asked.

Bolan was concentrating, picturing in his head the chaos at the moment the True Army was piling into cars back at the ranch. Had he witnessed Cakmak, specifically, entering one of them? The mental image solidified.

"In front—the Jeep. Stay back."

Grimaldi pulled on the stick, taking the Super Stallion up another thousand feet while slowing her to match the automobiles' speed.

"They're going to split up when they reach the highway," Bolan noted, glimpsing the thin line of South Dakota 89 coming up fast.

"How sure are you about Cakmak being in that Jeep, Sarge?" the Stony Man pilot asked.

"Not as sure as I wish I was."

"We want to call in the state troopers."

Bolan's mouth hardened into a grim line. "They're not equipped to deal with terrorists with automatic weapons," he said.

"We can't let them get away," Grimaldi protested.

"You're right." Bolan raised Barbara Price and briefed her. "They're splitting up now. We're on the Jeep with Cakmak, heading south on SD 89. Two cars are going north. Don't clue the troopers in on Cakmak. He's mine."

"Understood. What's your plan?"

"I don't have one yet."

"We've got a .50-caliber machine gun back there," Grimaldi pointed out. "We can hover ten feet outside of their weapon's range and blast them to hell."

"I think we let them survive for the time being," Bolan said.

"You finally going soft on me, Sarge?" Grimaldi asked with a grin.

"Hardly, Jack. But I'm wondering what Cakmak's plans are."

"Three words—run like hell."

"Yeah, but where to?"

Grimaldi thought about that as they spied Interstate 18 approaching. "Back home?"

"Maybe. If he's truly given up on the North American theater of his operations, then why not go back to Turkey and try to salvage what's left there? But there's an alternative. Join his people in California, which as far as he knows is still secure."

"We let him do either of those things?"

Bolan was thoughtful. "It's a risk. But our progress is attributable to the intelligence we've been getting out of Able's stakeout. We can't trash that information source at this point."

"Makes sense, Sarge," Grimaldi growled, "but it sure would be a lot more satisfying to send that bastard to hell right here and now."

Bolan said nothing, but he couldn't have agreed more.

"Stony," Bolan said into the microphone, "where's the nearest airfield?"

"Just a second. Edgemont Municipal Airport is about fifteen miles from your current position."

"Looks like we're headed that way," Bolan said. "How big a facility?"

"Nothing big about it. One dual asphalt runway, one turf runway. No fuel, no tower. They've got a sock on a stick and that's about it."

"How long's the asphalt runway?"

"Thirty-nine hundred feet."

"That would give them room to get a business-size jet off the ground," Bolan commented.

"A small one," Grimaldi added.

Bolan thought hard and fast. "Jack," he ordered, "get me to that airport in a hurry."

For the second time in ten minutes the Super Stallion was being pushed to its limits, and they swept out over the Edgemont Municipal Airport. Among the collection of private prop aircraft that was lined up in the grass they easily made out the distinctive lines of a small single-engine jet. For the moment, the area around it appeared deserted. Bolan took the stick while Grimaldi examined the jet.

"Cessna," the small Stony Man pilot announced. "Citation CJ1. Quick enough, but we're not talking about a long-range piece of work. Maybe thirteen, fourteen hundred miles. That's a lot of stops for gas between here and the Middle East.''

''Radar?''

''Sure, but not exactly long-range stuff. What do you have in mind, Sarge?''

''I'm thinking of allowing Cakmak to get away in his business jet.''

''Really?'' Grimaldi sounded incredulous. ''Then what?''

''We follow him to his next stop, see what happens next. Maybe we follow him all the way home.''

''Not in this we don't,'' Grimaldi said. ''This baby kicks ass, but she's not going to keep up with any jet, even a suit shuttle.''

Bolan grabbed the radio, and before he spoke into it he said, ''Jack, get us out of sight.''

Stony Man Farm

THE COMPUTER ROOM WAS packed. Katzenelenbogen, John ''Cowboy'' Kissinger and Kurtzman, whose cybernetics staff was ensconced in one corner rifling through the contents of a hard drive from a computer the blacksuit team had found during their search of the house in South Dakota. At another end of the office, with one hand over his ear, was Hal Brognola, talking to the President of the United States and trying to put the best spin possible on the events of the past hour.

''Striker, what's going on?'' Price said.

''I'm on Cakmak's trail and I'm certain he's about to make a run for it in a small jet based at Edgemont Municipal Airport.''

''What are you doing about that?'' Price asked.

"Nothing."

Price thought she had heard wrong. "You're doing nothing? You're letting him get away?" She flipped on the speakerphone so the others could hear both sides of the conversation. Brognola had finished his own call anyway.

"You know we need to keep him communicating with the TAK base in California," Bolan said. "We still have live missiles in Turkey to locate."

"At the price of letting Cakmak get away?"

"For the time being, yes," Bolan stated in a voice that didn't easily invite an argument.

Price wasn't intimidated easily by anyone, including the Executioner. "I don't see how you can pull this off, Striker. Jack can't keep up with that aircraft."

"That jet isn't going more than fourteen hundred miles without stopping to refuel," Bolan said. "No matter which direction it heads, it'll be on radar. We just follow it on the FAA radar net. We also try to beat it to its destination. I want to be on the ground if and when Cakmak disembarks. It's likely he'll switch to a longer-range aircraft if he's headed home."

"Head home!" Brognola exclaimed. "Why would he do that?"

"Cakmak is the man in charge. TAK is his baby. As far as he knows, he has one undiscovered base in the U.S., but he also has the opportunity to salvage his operations in Turkey. I think he'll go back to where he can be of some use, take charge of that end of the operation and restrategize. We still don't know where the remaining Turkish missiles are. If we keep him alive and kicking—and communicating with his Turkish people—we may find out more."

"Striker, why not take Cakmak down now, while

we've got him in our sights, damn it?" Brognola demanded.

Katzenelenbogen spoke up. "Three potential scenarios if we shut down Cakmak and leave the Turkish end of the business leaderless. One, the surviving members of the True Army of Kurdistan disappear, abandoning the Patriots they've still got. They will likely be found and recovered, eventually.

"Two, TAK disappears and takes the missiles with them. The United States is left sitting around looking foolish and waiting for the other shoe to drop. The political embarrassment the U.S. is now suffering would last for as long as those missiles remain unrecovered— maybe months, maybe years."

"And three, Katz?" Bolan asked, although he said it as if he already knew the answer.

"Three," Katzenelenbogen said, "TAK melts into the woodwork, but only after firing all the missiles they have left in one last display of rebellion."

Brognola put an antacid tablet into his mouth, scowling at the tabletop. "I've got to admit I don't like the sounds of options two and three."

"Option one is the least-likely possibility," Katzenelenbogen stated. "These guys are ruthless and without regard for human life. They've demonstrated that to everyone's satisfaction."

"So we wait out Cakmak," Bolan insisted. "We dog his trail all the way to the missiles if that is what it takes."

Brognola nodded. "I guess there's not much of a choice. This is against my better judgment, but I agree we should allow Cakmak to go free for now. But, Striker, don't allow that son of a bitch to slip through your fingers."

"Hal, he's at the top of my list."

Brognola said nothing. The Executioner's list, he knew, was a dangerous place to have one's name included.

CHAPTER TWENTY-FIVE

Over Southern Minnesota

"Going back home to lick your wounds?" Nouri Bakir snarled from the phone.

"Returning to personally coordinate our attacks," Asad Cakmak retorted. He was flopped in the fully reclined chair just behind the cockpit of the Cessna, five companions in the seats behind him. There was an air of gloom in the cabin. These weren't men who took well to running away with their tails between their legs.

They had been watching the news networks ever since their hasty departure from Edgemont Airport, hoping for a miracle. But there were no reports of a second missile attack in South Dakota. It was clear the launcher had been overtaken and disabled before another Patriot was launched. What was worse, the missile they did launch had killed just one man, a janitor at a Custer government building. A petty triumph.

Cakmak had chosen the target because, during the week, it was packed with people, from off-the-street citizens to local politicians. A strike would have potentially killed hundreds, a real stab into the heartland of America.

Cakmak was exhausted and disheartened, but he refused to allow Bakir to sense that.

"What attacks?" Bakir demanded derisively. "You've lost all your weaponry."

"Not at all," Cakmak retorted, trying to sound reasonable, to control his anger. Bakir was the one man he couldn't afford to lash out at.

"Tell me your plans."

Cakmak didn't really have any. He hadn't thought that far ahead. He improvised. "I declare a new ultimatum in the U.S. They enact full sanctions against the Republic of Turkey and all countries engaging in trade with Turkey until the independent nations of Kurdistan is created."

"More ultimatums." Bakir sighed. "The U.S. will not accede, of course."

"Of course. So we launch our remaining missiles and get some major media coverage, and at the same time we declare a new ultimatum in Ankara. Kurdistan now or pay the consequences."

"You think the Turks will give in?"

"It's possible," Cakmak said.

"Not even remotely," Bakir said. "They know your firepower is greatly diminished. They'll choose to ride out the worst you can throw at them and be done with the affair."

"Not after they see the devastation we can conjure up in California. We'll videotape it and send the tapes to all the news outlets, including Turkey's. The people of Ankara will watch the Santa Cruz, California, boardwalk explode into flame a hundred times a night on television. They won't dream of allowing that to happen in their own city."

"The people will decry it, but the politicians won't

care and they won't give in. Think about it from their perspective, Asad.''

"If we launch those missiles, there will be an hour of death and destruction followed by years of political repercussions!'' Cakmak protested.

"But it will be all cleanup work. On the other hand, if they allow Kurdistan to come into being they'll be accused of betraying the very nation they lead. The financial implications alone for Turkey will be staggering. To the politicians it will be an ongoing disaster, as opposed to a quick one.''

Cakmak sat up, getting angry again. "Are you saying we can't win?''

"We could have once. If I didn't believe it I never would have funded the True Army. But not anymore. Our coercive potency is too compromised.''

"You can't tell me to put a halt to everything here and now! I won't do it!''

There was a moment of silence on the line. Incongruously, Cakmak detected the sound of a splash in the background, like someone jumping into a swimming pool. Where was Bakir, anyway? Was he sitting in some resort while the True Army fought in the trenches?

"I would not suggest you stop, Asad. I'm just saying we may not be able to achieve our goals in this one final stroke. We will need to reassess our timetable. Come up with a new strategy. A new way to convince the world that Kurdistan is inevitable.''

Cakmak was the quiet one now, contemplating his failure, an unaccustomed feeling. He didn't like it. Defensively, he said, "I'm not convinced we cannot pull a victory out of this mess.''

Another sigh. "I like your confidence, Asad. Do what you can. If nothing else, you will send a very firm message to the people of Turkey—that the True Army is serious in its conviction.''

"HIS NAME IS Nouri Bakir,'' Yakov Katzenelenbogen stated.

Bolan stared at the image on the small computer monitor in the rear of the Airbus Industrie A300-600, hastily reappropriated after discarding the Super Stallion. With Grimaldi at the helm, they were making excellent time across the northern Midwest states. At the moment they were just ninety miles south of the Cessna and on the same heading. In less than an hour they might, or might not, be descending on any of the airports in the Minneapolis–St. Paul area.

"Don't know him,'' Bolan said.

"No reason you should. He is the world's richest Kurd, but his businesses are mostly legitimate,'' Katzenelenbogen said. ''Made a small fortune in tobacco, then branched out into textiles and made a bigger one, then pieced together his own conglomerate. Now he's into some of everything, including extensive business dealings with lots of Turkish companies.''

"Isn't he shooting himself in the foot by funding an anti-Turk terrorist group?''

"He would be if the news got out. He doesn't intend to allow that to happen. He's kept a very low profile and maintains his distance from his Kurd comrades. In fact, we've got pretty reliable information that he's been at his home in Singapore for weeks.''

"Makes it tough for the media to tie him to the whole thing,'' Bolan observed.

"Right. But we've got him locked in as the source for the cash. He's put up tens of millions just in equipment for his little pet army, and he's spent several million more to hire himself the best inside people at the U.S. Air Force in Hawaii and Ankara.''

"He's trying to buy himself into a position of power," Bolan remarked. "He funds the formation of the True Army, TAK does his dirty work, then he steps into a high-ranking position when a Kurdistan government bureaucracy is created."

"Cheaper than running for election," Katzenelenbogen said.

"Has IDing this guy as the money man helped us out at all?"

"That's what I was coming to. Bakir hasn't done a perfect job of keeping himself perfectly separated from the True Army. We've uncovered a most important link—maybe."

"Tell me."

"One of Bakir's trading companies is Format Trading, a subsidiary of Reference Trading. There's such a thing as a Format Trading corporate air fleet, ostensibly for use by Format Trading corporate executives. Problem is, there are no Format Trading corporate executives. It's run entirely by Reference Trading execs, who have their own planes. So who's using the Format fleet?"

"Asad Cakmak?"

"Looks like it. They own a Cessna Citation CJ1, which has been filing flight plans all over the Mid-Northwestern states in recent days."

"So how does that help us?"

"Because we've located another Format Trading aircraft, a 707-320 Intercontinental fitted as a cargo jet. Right now it's sitting on the ground in Minneapolis. This is Boeing's long-range model. Four thousand miles at a jump, Striker. They could get to Ankara with maybe one stop for gas."

Bolan considered that for all of ten seconds. "You hearing this, Jack?"

"Got it," Grimaldi said from the cockpit.

"How fast can you get us on the ground in Minneapolis?"

Bolan could almost hear the grin on Grimaldi's face. "Pretty damned fast."

"I guess what I really want to know is, how far in front of the Cessna?"

"We're not that far out. Fifteen minutes. Maybe twenty. Depends on how fast we get clearance and how slow they get it."

"We can pull some strings on that count," Katzenelenbogen said.

"Give me all the time you can without making them suspicious," Bolan said.

"You're not telling me what you have in mind, Striker," Katzenelenbogen said.

"You'd just try to talk me out of it, Katz," Bolan said.

Minneapolis–St. Paul International Airport

JACK GRIMALDI SET the Airbus on the tarmac and taxied into the cargo terminal, maneuvering among Federal Express and Airborne cargo jets. Katzenelenbogen and Price had been working fast to set up the scenario that took place, but it went off without a hitch.

Grimaldi parked the jet at the assigned loading bay, which just happened to be a stone's throw from a 707-320 Intercontinental, white with a dark purple Format Trading logo.

A crate was waiting for Grimaldi's plane on the loading bay. He had no idea what it contained, but they were to go through the ruse of actually loading it onto the jet to keep up appearances in case somebody on the Format plane was suspicious.

Bolan marched down the ladder, wearing a brimmed cap to shadow his face and hoisting his pack on one shoulder. He was carrying a sheaf of paperwork, and it looked as if he was simply going into the bay office to get the appropriate signatures and hand out the requisite receipts.

Grimaldi waited. From the cockpit window he watched the slow-paced loading activity going on at the 707-320 Intercontinental.

But he didn't see Bolan again.

"G-Force?" It was Price.

"Go ahead."

"You might as well take off. We just got a call from Striker. He hitched a ride on a different plane."

"Understood. Let's hope they don't throw him out halfway."

CHAPTER TWENTY-SIX

Ankara, Turkey

The footage was grisly and Dogan Bir was fascinated. It was a hillside bunker with narrow, long openings along the wide concrete face. The faces in these windows were angry and submissive.

The camera operator walked up the hill to the open side of the bunker. After pausing momentarily to show two masked gunmen guarding the prisoners with automatic rifles, the camera was directed inside the concrete structure. It took a moment for the automatic iris to adjust from the bright sun outside to the gloom inside.

"...released just one hour ago. The footage is believed to come from mercenaries holding the hostages in the mountains of northern Iraq or eastern Iran."

At first it looked as if all the prisoners were women. Then it became clear that the children were huddled in the rear, hiding behind their mothers, while the old people were laid out at one end of the bunker, as if all dead or nearly so. Two of the old men were bloodied, their chests opened with gunshots, the wounds indistinct in the poor lighting and shaky videotaping.

"The hostage-taking was just the latest wrinkle in an intercontinental crisis that climaxed with the launch of

U.S. Army Patriot missiles in both North America and Turkey. Although the U.S. target, in Custer, South Dakota, was an almost totally abandoned government building, a similar target in the city if Diyarbakir, Turkey, was crowded with government employees and local citizens. The official death toll in Turkey is at 255 and still climbing.

"Opinions already fiercely divided over the issue of negotiation with the True Army of Kurdistan have been further complicated over True Army assertions that the nation of Turkey bears responsibility for the kidnapping of the hostages, which many are calling a terrorist act in and of itself. However, Turkish officials have denied complicity with the mercenaries accused of taking the hostages."

The news station was replaying the tape. It would be seen again and again throughout the day, Bir was certain, until interest waned or something new came along to top it.

Bir opened his desk and withdrew a box of tiny digital camcorder tapes, copies of the tape he had shown his new friend, Nouri Bakir. He would make the round of the news outlets in town, dropping the tapes in mail slots and leaving them anonymously at media-outlet reception desks. It would be all over the news in two hours.

When the videotape proved that Cengiz Yilmaz and his unofficial consortium of high-level businessmen had stooped to terrorist methods to combat the True Army, they would be shamed into ruin—and maybe arrested— by this time tomorrow. Bir could also foresee a new Turkish movement arising that would proclaim the businessmen heroes for taking a proactive stance against the terrorists.

Things were really getting complicated.

Dogan Bir was enjoying every minute of it.

BOLAN SPENT HOURS cramped into a tiny partition he had constructed for himself among the cargo crates packing the big transport jet. Then, with indomitable patience, he crawled his way atop the wooden crates and found he had less than eighteen inches of space to move between the top of the crates and the roof of the interior of the fuselage. There were probably air-safety standards being violated by cramming in this much cargo, Bolan considered.

Maybe he should arrest Cakmak for violating FAA regulations.

He saw lights ahead, and as he crawled he eventually heard voices. When he reached the end of the cargo section he found himself perched looking over the back wall of a passenger area. It was fitted with eight chairs worthy of the first-class section of a passenger jet. A movie was running on a video screen without sound.

Below Bolan's perch, within arm's reach, was Asad Cakmak, mastermind of all this terror. Bolan felt a huge temptation to simply reach down and end him here and now. One good downward stroke would pierce the bony shield of his skull, allowing the Randall fighting knife to penetrate to the hilt. Then a quick twist, just as insurance, and Cakmak's brain would be rendered unusable, and the terrorist leader would be out of the picture.

The risk was too great. Bolan was certain a madman like Cakmak would have left instructions to be carried out should he meet his demise—and those instructions would almost surely call for more mass murder.

The Executioner's justice would have to wait a little while longer, but without a doubt it would come.

He stayed in his cramped, prone position atop the crates, listening to the conversation among the terrorists, eager for the intelligence that would end Cakmak's usefulness. But the location of the final cartridge of Patriots was never mentioned, only the plan to launch them in one sudden and ultimate deadly barrage if and when the Kurdistan cause looked hopeless.

The only stop en route was in Reykjavik. The aircraft landed, taxied, refueled and took off again without delay. Bolan watched the hours pass and estimated when they would be over the Balkan states. Almost exactly when he had estimated it, the pressure change told him the 707-320 Intercontinental was descending.

Bolan, hovering like a malevolent spirit over the heads of the terrorists, heard one of them say the word *Izmit,* and then he knew where he was. Three hundred miles east-northeast of Ankara, Izmit was one of the most populous Turkish cities but well outside of the territory claimed by the Kurds. Why here?

Maybe the location was critical because it *was* so far out of Kurdish territory. Security would naturally be tightest in the Kurdish regions of Turkey.

A pair of customs agents boarded the plane when it was resting at the cargo gate at Izmit, their dour expressions melting to smiles when they were inside the aircraft. Cakmak and his companion's passports were stamped perfunctorily, and a wad of U.S. bills was accepted by the agents without discussion.

Bolan had been stuck in his hiding perch for an interminable wait, listening for intelligence that never came. He still didn't know where the last Turkish missile battery was. But he was sticking with Cakmak from here on out. The terrorist leader would take him to the weapons.

The last leg of the flight took under an hour. This time

there were no customs checks when they landed. With the Format Trading jet's paperwork already cleared, it was free to move about the country of Turkey.

The aircraft powered down and the passengers got to their feet, showing the weariness of the long flight. Bolan dropped into the passenger area just after the pilot and copilot were the last to leave the aircraft, and did a series of quick stretches to overcome the extended cramping resulting from forced inactivity. He did a quick series of checks out the small windows, then moved into the cockpit for a better view of the layout.

The dark landscape was gently rolling for miles and virtually empty. Nearby long, low buildings were unlit except for a pair of white security lamps that illuminated the loading dock at one end. A sign nearby showed the same Format Trading logo Bolan had seen on the jet when he boarded it—this time in Turkish. The windows of the expediter's office were glowing a dirty yellow.

Distantly, over a fanged range of mountains many miles away, he could make out a haze of light that might be coming from a large city.

Istanbul? Samsun? Based on their flying time from Izmit, it could be any of a half-dozen Turkish urban areas. Bolan would know that soon enough. There was something else beyond the shipping warehouse, vast and sprawling, but too indistinct to make out in the darkness.

With the way out apparently clear, he opened the side hatch and crept onto the wheeled ladder to the desert floor.

Throughout the flight, uncertain of the radio facilities on board, Bolan hadn't taken the chance of using any of his electronics. Finally, he was able to reach out and touch someone. He dialed up the secure line on the field-toughened Qualcomm headset Globalstar phone, listening to it go through a series of terrestrial cutouts in North America. Then Aaron Kurtzman answered, already aware who it was on the dedicated line.

"Striker here."

"Cripes, we've been waiting forever for you to call in."

"It's been a long flight," Bolan said. "They didn't even provide pretzels." Bolan powered up the GPS on his watch and for the first time determined his location. "Here's my coordinates, Bear. It's a Format Trading facility, by the looks of it, forty klicks outside Ankara."

"Ankara," Kurtzman said. "No surprise there. A high-visibility target from the True Army's point of view. Do you know if the Patriots are there?"

"Negative." Bolan looked around him. Lots of darkness out there. He thought he could make out a perimeter fence a half-mile away, presumably enclosing the entire airfield. There had to have been landing lights, but they were off now. "I'll keep you abreast of the situation as I move in," he reported. "I assume Phoenix is standing by."

Kurtzman laughed. "Standing by? You should hear those guys complaining! They've been stuck in their hotel doing nothing for hours. I thought they were going out onto the streets to take down some hashish peddlers just for something to do. Able's in even worse shape. They've been sitting on their thumbs for two solid days."

"They'll both get the opportunity to do some good soon," Bolan replied.

"They're nearby. We'll have them in the air in ten minutes, Striker. After that, fifteen minutes to get to you."

"Fine. Just have them keep in mind that this facility

has just about the best ground-to-air defense system available. They'll need to get in around it.

"Understood. Keep in touch."

"I'm moving in."

Bolan crept down the steel stairs and crouched at the bottom, looking under the aircraft for signs of maintenance crew or guards. There weren't any. How good would the security be at this facility? Would it have been beefed up in recent days? Would there be simply a perimeter guard of some type, watching the fence, or were there more electronics watching the grounds inside?

Bolan donned night-vision goggles as he started through the blackness toward the building, his eyes peeled for sensors and not seeing any. He removed the goggles when he was near the loading bay, an oversize roll-up door that would allow a truck to actually pull inside the building. That, Bolan thought, was an unusual way of unloading cargo. But an ideal arrangement for bringing in a missile launcher. Just pull it inside and shut the door, and it was out of sight.

Bolan briefly considered that if there was a launcher inside, it had been the first one put into position. No matter what side of the city they were on, they would probably be less than a two-hour drive from the Incirlik air base.

The soldier crept up against a wall of the building that had a set of eight small windows. They were blinded, blackened on the inside.

His next goal was the roof. He pulled out a grappling hook and thin nylon cord out of his pack and launched it at the top of the building. It landed with a metallic thud, and Bolan retracted the slack until he felt it catch on something. He put his weight on the line, waited a moment, then began a quick hand-over-hand ascent.

At fifteen feet there was another bank of windows, but these weren't blacked out. Bolan dangled in front of them, making a quick loop for his foot on the line, allowing him to stand in the position almost effortlessly. Then he leaned into the window, cupping his face to block the dim glow of the loading-bay lights coming around the corner.

Inside there was a truck, although he wasn't immediately certain it was the launcher. He allowed his eyes to adjust fully, and then he was sure.

"Stony?"

"Standing by, Striker."

"I have the launcher at this locale."

"Understood. Phoenix will be joining you soon."

"Good to know, Stony. I hope there'll be nothing for them to do when they get here."

"Leave them some scraps, Striker."

Bolan climbed another five feet before he gripped the edge of the building and pulled himself onto the gravel roof. The grappling hook had dug into the softer undersurface of the roof itself, and Bolan contemplated leaving it there as an exit, should he need one. He decided it was better to cover his tracks as he went.

The roof was a jumble of enclosures, heating and air-conditioning units, motor assemblies for the cranes inside, lots of exhaust fans. Bolan could again make out the big shape, which he had observed from the aircraft steps. It was a quarter mile away now, and he was sure it was a jumble of collapsed buildings. It had the indistinct lines of a ruined city that wasn't just old, but ancient. Was Format Trading sitting on the site of a medieval Ottoman town? Maybe it was even a Hittite settlement. Three-thousand-year-old Hittite ruins dotted this part of Turkey.

Bolan didn't have time for sight-seeing. His first step was to find the Patriot exit door. There had to be a way to open the roof for the firing of the missile. If the roof couldn't be opened, the missiles couldn't be fired.

The soldier moved silently, finding the door he wanted. It was aluminum, thirty feet wide, on two six-inch wheeled tracks. He pulled a pocket-size tool set and used a screwdriver to extract two screws from the track mount. He found it easy to work quietly. The track was new and the screws free of corrosion. Next he threaded the screws through the chain links just before and after the cog wheel, tripling them to keep them from stripping off when the door was activated and the chain tried to move. It might not stop the door permanently, but it would sure wreck the works if somebody flipped the on switch. The cog and the chain would jam, and the door would be stuck in place.

But the door was just flimsy aluminum, and there was nothing that was going to stop Cakmak from simply having it torn out of the roof when he wanted those Patriots put in the air.

So the next step was to get inside and disable the launcher—then disable Asad Cakmak.

When the lights started coming on, Bolan doubted it was going to be as easy as it sounded.

CHAPTER TWENTY-SEVEN

The security lights were everywhere, as if installed by a paranoiac. The first ones to blink on were floodlights planted in small domes atop the air handlers and exhaust fans, coming on in the blink of an eye and turning Bolan's dark lurking place suddenly into a wide, exposed field in which he stood out like a Mongolian camel standing in a baseball diamond. Before the warrior could react to his sudden exposure more lights came on—on the sides of the buildings, sixteen-thousand lumen high-pressure sodium security lights tucked against the building eaves began blinking on one after another, until the grounds around the building were blanketed with harsh white light.

Bolan didn't know what security sensors he had tripped, and it no longer mattered. He was already running for the far side of the roof, yanking the grappling hook from his belt and stooping as he slid onto his knees, jamming the steel talon into the soft, tarry subsurface of the roof and driving it in deep with the heel of his hand. Now he heard the first noises, the voices of men shouting. Bolan peered over the edge and found the ground on his side of the building empty and brightly lit. A less-experienced soldier would have succumbed to the temptation to stay where he was, temporarily out of sight, rather than descend into the wide-open field without cover. Bolan knew better. If they were on to him, his perch was no protection. They would swarm up after him, and Phoenix Force would find nothing but his quickly chilling corpse when they arrived.

Bolan looped the nylon line around his right forearm as he swung himself bodily off the roof, feeling the sudden incendiary heat as the line scorched through the flesh of this hands at high speed, his two hundred pounds of densely packed mass carrying him to the ground in what was just slightly more controlled than a fall. His feet hit the earth heavily and he bolted.

He was too late. A pair of figures emerged from either end of the long building during the same heartbeat, and both ordered him to stop.

Bolan didn't obey. Instead, he grabbed at the Heckler & Koch MP-5/10A3 holstered on his back and whirled on the man to his right, triggering a quick burst of precision fire. The guard hit the wall as he fell onto his face. Then Bolan jumped forward suddenly, avoiding the quick shots coming from the second new arrival. The submachine-gun fire swept over the gunner and drove him bleeding into the wall, then dropped him.

The Executioner was alone again, but the gunplay had guaranteed that Cakmak knew he was here, so his immediate need was for good cover. The bright sodium lights were reaching far enough out into the night to show him the leading edges of the rocky ruins. He headed for them, feeling himself as brightly illuminated as a deer caught in headlights, knowing he was an easy target for a skilled gunner. More shouts came from behind him, but he didn't bother to look back. When the gunshots rang out, the ruins were getting close and he heard the bouncing of the rounds as they reached the rocks ahead of him.

Bolan bolted into cover behind a wall of skull-size rocks. It was seven feet high, protecting him completely—but for how long? Bolan peered out again. Men gathered at the building, which was now hundreds of yards away, conversing in two groups over the bodies of Bolan's victims.

They were deciding how best to pursue him. If Bolan were the man in charge, his first order would be to put the lights out. The lights were suddenly a hindrance to them. They would figure that out eventually.

It was time to get the lay of the land. As he moved back into the ruins, the walls and piles of bricks came together and started forming building foundations and actual rooms, and he found the earth sloping away beneath him. He climbed on top of one of the taller walls and discovered it was an ideal lookout point, high enough to see over the ruins and across the open ground to view the entire Format Trading warehouse and shipping building, but distant enough to be dark and invisible to the conversing guards. Unfortunately, he was also out of effective range of the MP-5/10A3 or his handguns.

In the other direction he was surprised to find acres of ruins descending slowly into a large bowl-shaped valley. The ruins were too ancient to be medieval. Bolan realized he was standing on the site of an ancient Hittite city. Many buildings were no more than piles of collapsed rubble. Others showed intact, strong-looking walls, the concrete in their seams spotted with regularly spaced rocks to indicate they were the work of twentieth-century restoration. But the abandoned atmosphere of the place told Bolan that archaeological work at this site had ceased long ago.

His warrior's mind, trained in chaotic jungles when he was a young man and on the countless missions that had come since, quickly assimilated the layout of the dead city, identifying likely hiding places and ambush points. His disadvantage might be that some of the men who would pursue him here would know the dead city better than he did. The advantage would be that he, the Executioner, had the skills and instincts to make the best use of this labyrinth of old stone.

Let them come.

CHAPTER TWENTY-EIGHT

Supreme General Asad Cakmak was trying to keep his face from growing red with shame.

There was one way and one way only an intruder could have made his way to this place within mere minutes of their arrival.

He had to have come with them.

Cakmak felt like a bloody fool.

He marched to the wall where the map of the compound was printed on a large white board that could be used with erasable colored markers, good for strategizing security exercises. This was the first time that there had been a need to use it for actual security measures. "I want four Land Rovers out to the perimeter fence on the far side of the ruins." He spit out the directions like staccato snare-drum taps. "I want sweeps run between the gate and this point here."

Edip Aslan nodded quickly. "At that rate we'll be passing by any given point on the far side of the ruins every minute or so. There's no way he can get through."

Cakmak pondered that. "That's my intent. You've run simulations on break-ins at this facility. What's the fastest anyone has ever got over the fence?"

Aslan smiled. "Five minutes, fifteen seconds for a team of eight men to get over the fence without simply blowing it up. Those simulations were run with men try-ing to get into the compound, not out. But it would not make much difference."

"Unless the man has explosives on him," Cakmak reminded him. "Then he'll need less than a minute to get through the gate."

Aslan's smile didn't waver, but he nodded in agree-ment. "You are right, General Cakmak."

Edip Aslan had been involved in the theft of the Pa-triot missiles, and had been placed in charge of the For-mat Trading facility, which had been operational as a legitimate shipping terminal as recently as ten days be-fore the operation began. To his dismay he had ended up sitting on his rear end since the day the Patriot battery arrived, with nothing to do but play cards with his men.

Not that he had actually allowed his men much down-time. There had been hours of training every day. End-less security patrols of the grounds. War games in the ruins. Target practice in the empty warehouse. Aslan was a ruthless military man. Although he would admit it to no one, he was a part of the True Army of Kurdistan more for the lifestyle of a militant terrorist than for the cause of his beleaguered people.

Aslan knew General Cakmak's grand schemes had failed again and again, that the TAK objectives were slipping from reach, and it was just fine with Aslan. It meant the war could continue. What was the satisfaction in a war that was won easily and quickly?

Right now he was just thrilled to finally be a part of the action.

Cakmak altered his orders. "Put two Land Rovers on the outside of the fence, two on the inside. If he blasts his way through, then we'll have vehicles there to run him down like the dog he is."

Aslan, for the first time, frowned. "General Cakmak, it sounds as if you know who this man is."

"I believe," Cakmak said, looking very unhappy, "we have met before."

Aslan saw that no further explanation was forthcoming, so he asked, "Is he the kind of man who will even attempt to escape?"

Cakmak looked sharply at his second in command. It was an obvious question, and one he should have asked himself several minutes ago. "No. He will not."

"Then what will he do?"

Cakmak nodded, his mind finally traveling in the right direction. Why did his strategy have to be led by this largely untrained dirt fighter? "He is an American agent and he is here with one overriding purpose—to put a stop to the firing of the Patriots. He is undoubtedly a part of the operation that's been at work here in Turkey and in America. If he is who I think he is, he was the man personally responsible for driving us out of our operations in Colorado and South Dakota."

"Personally responsible?" Aslan retorted. "How can that be? I thought there were whole teams of paramilitaries involved in the raids."

Cakmak nodded. "There were. But it was this one man who did the majority of the work to drive us away. He nearly killed me both times." Cakmak glared at the map, drawing his brow low over his eyes as he looked at the simple line drawing.

The Format Trading compound had been established nine months earlier for the very purpose of serving as a main launch point for one or more batteries of the Patriot missiles. Nouri Bakir had run it as a legitimate business. He had claimed the distance from the city of Ankara gave him the leeway to build his own landing field and therefore save money and time on the most expensive and potentially delaying factor in international shipping—the loading, unloading and ground-based logistics of shipping.

There were others who had thought the facility was a waste of time and money. It was expensive to build, especially the landing strip to accommodate the largest intercontinental aircraft. Without a hangar, Bakir's facility would be at the mercy of trucked-in repair and maintenance crews.

Bakir had publicly admitted the facility was a financial flop a few weeks earlier and announced its closing, moving the Ankara end of Format Trading's shipping business back to the Ankara International Airport.

All that was as planned. Now the facility was dark and ignored, and freed up for use by the True Army of Kurdistan. The property was dominated on one end by the runway and by the three large loading bays, each tied to a circular building where moveable racks of transported goods—from small crates to the largest shipping containers—could be stored and reloaded onto vehicles. There was even a rail spur, never used, that entered directly into Building Three.

These three circular extensions were the centralized loading and unloading centers, but reaching out behind them was the long warehouse where untold thousands of shipped crates could be stored.

The rest of the facility was mostly empty. There was a parking area for cars, and a four-lane road heading in and out of the facility. A small maintenance building for the fleet of vehicles used on-site. The rest of it was vast tracts of empty ground and the old, abandoned Hittite ruins.

The ruins had come with the facility. They were impressive and vast, ancient homes and city buildings that all dated from the century prior to the fall of the Hittite Empire in about 1190 B.C. They had been mapped by archaeologists, studied decades ago, and Nouri Bakir had made the politically correct statement that he would welcome further study in the future. But recent requests for access to the ruins had been denied, and for the time being they were abandoned.

Except for one man who was using them as his own personal hiding place.

"We have to take him down," Cakmak said, almost under his breath, for a moment forgetting he had been in the middle of a planning session with Aslan.

"My men know those ruins like they know their own mothers," Aslan declared. "We've been training there for weeks. One man? We can flush him out like a rabbit in the bushes."

Cakmak nodded. "Do it."

"You want to question him?"

"No need for that," Cakmak said. "What could he tell me that I would believe or find useful? It does not matter what agency he is with or how he gets his information. Just bring him to me so I can see his face and be sure that he is the same man who came after me in the United States."

"Right," Aslan said. "Face intact. The rest of him does not matter."

CHAPTER TWENTY-NINE

Bolan began giving names to the buildings as he moved among them to keep them straight in his mind. One building was full of unexcavated pots still half-emerging from the soil. It seemed like an ideal place to store grain, so he named it the Granary. Another building had a sunken area in the middle—maybe from excavation, maybe dating back to the original inhabitants. It became the Bath. One building had a long low stone table along one end, and then a wide open area dotted with smaller stone tables, configured more than anything else in Bolan's mind like a bar out of the Old West, so it became the Saloon. There was the School, the Grocery, the Temple and row after row of multiroom dwellings.

Fronting the city, looking off into the dark night away from Ankara, away from the warehouse and away from all things modern, was a pair of stone pillars set with very worn lions, disfigured by the passage of time. In Bolan's mind the Lion Gate became a symbol of the past, of forgotten greatness, well removed from the terror of today.

He wasn't trained in archaeology, and his guesses as to the purposes of the buildings might have been far from the mark, but it didn't matter. What mattered was having an infallible mental map of the place when the time came to use it as cover.

The time was now. As a small convoy of vehicles raced away from the warehouse and began performing a back-and-forth patrol along the three-yard chain-link fence that bordered the grounds, well beyond the edge of the ruins, and a patrol of two vehicles began moving between the ruins and the building, a twelve-man army marched toward the Hittite city.

They entered the city from the rear, as Bolan had, and immediately fanned out, slithering infallibly through the stone walls. The soldier watched them from the center of the city, invisible in the blackness atop a mass of stone. So they knew their way around the ruins. And there were twelve of them. At first glance, they had the advantage of familiarity and the strength of numbers.

Bolan knew that wasn't the case. He wasn't really against an army of twelve, but against twelve men one at a time, if that was how he could manipulate the coming battles.

Against any one man the Executioner felt confident of his own skills.

He slithered down from his rocky perch. He had another major advantage that he didn't believe his opponents possessed: night vision. The Kurd soldiers were heading into the ruins wearing visor-mounted flashlights.

He jogged toward the Temple, a long-columned building on the far side of the ruined city, near enough to the rear that he could see the patrols passing to and fro along the distant chain-link fence. He stowed his pack atop a seven-foot-tall broken column. Without it he had greater freedom of movement. Wearing a thin black shirt with a turtleneck, dark slacks and shoes, his body was invisible in the night. He had tied his pant legs tight to his shins to keep them from making noise as he moved, and careful application of combat cosmetics had turned his dark-tanned complexion into a wraithlike face that melded with the shadows.

Bolan was invisible, a specter.

He knew that by the time the men reached the Temple they would be scattered throughout the city, which was how he wanted it. Little time for an effective response to a cry for help. They didn't seem to be using a buddy system. When Bolan's first victim came to him, actually strolled within arm's reach of him, the man never even knew he was in danger.

The Executioner simply reached out through the blackness and grabbed him, like the arms of a spider reaching out of a hole to draw in an oblivious fly. This fly didn't even have time to buzz before his life ended. The Randall combat blade sliced into his throat when the electrical impulses of surprise were still flashing into his brain. Bolan's right leg clutched at the dying man's legs to keep them from kicking until he went limp.

Bolan tucked the corpse into a nook and moved on, keeping his feet on the small tufts of grass growing in the rocky dirt. The terrorists were making the mistake of walking on the rocks themselves—pebbles and stony detritus eroded from the building blocks of the city over the past thirty centuries. Bolan's jungle-trained ears picked up the sound as easily if they were stomping on dry leaves.

Following the crunch brought him to a second man, standing next to one of the houses adjoining the Granary, staring away as if he had heard something suspicious. If he had it was one of his own men, since he was looking directly away from Bolan. When the blade hit him, his body deflated like a punctured water bladder.

Number three went down just as silently, making a noise no louder than a snore from his nostrils as he vainly tried to open his jaw and at the same time turn on his attacker, only to find the life blood flowing out of his throat so suddenly he was drained of vitality in mere seconds.

Dawn was going to find the dead city full of the dead, Bolan thought, all neatly tucked away into alcoves and corners.

He dismissed that overconfidence. There were still nine men left roaming the ruins with him. Eventually, probably soon, he would have to chuck the silent stalker routine and the real battle would begin.

He heard nothing and no one. He'd cleaned up this part of the town. Time for a trip to the Saloon.

CAKMAK STOOD at the window of the warehouse security office, his command center. The room lights were off to more easily watch the activity that might occur outside the wide windows. He could see the building patrols pass below and saw the headlights of the fence patrol a mile or so out. The closest walls of the ruins of the Hittite city were just visible in the compound lights. He had seen his men enter there and disappear.

"What's happening?" he demanded impatiently.

"Not a thing, General," Aslan answered easily. "My men are making a slow and methodical search."

"Report, Gray Team," Aslan said into the radio.

"Gray Team Leader here. Nothing to report."

"Understood."

Aslan smiled confidently, as if no news was just fine with him. Cakmak wouldn't make an issue of it. Aslan supposedly knew what he was doing.

The minutes passed slowly.

"Gray Leader here," they heard the radio say. "Ten-minute report-in."

"Gray One here. All okay."

"Gray Two here."

"Gray Three here."

As the quiet voices reported, Cakmak took a pair of binoculars off the desk and used them to try to see into the ruins. They hadn't worked the first two times he had tried them, and they didn't work now.

He realized with a shock that the radio was silent, and he turned on Aslan, who was staring at the speaker as if it would answer the unasked question.

"Gray Leader here. Report in Gray Nine."

Another silence.

"Shit!" Cakmak said in a near whisper.

"Gray Leader here. Report, Gray Ten."

"Gray Ten here."

"Gray Eleven, report."

Silence.

"Gray Eleven, report!"

Cakmak had been having doubts that the man who had dogged him all the way from the United States was the same man who had nearly killed him in Colorado and South Dakota. Those doubts were now wiped away like the chalk marks on a slate.

"Gray Twelve, report!"

It was the same man, like a malevolent spirit pursuing him, inexorably homing in on him.

"Gray Twelve!"

And always finding him.

BOLAN KNEW the dawning confusion that would come with the discovery that three of their men were already missing. It would give him a short but prime hunting season. Men would be concentrating not on their surroundings as much as on listening to their commanders and getting control of the situation. He struck, and struck fast.

"Gray Four here," he heard just around the corner. "Understood, Gray Leader. I'm heading to coordinates three-dash-four."

Bolan heard the footsteps pick up their pace, and he moved fast, hooking his ankle in the path of the rushing terrorist and bringing him to the ground. Before the man had a chance to catch his breath, Bolan landed on his back with both knees, slamming his lungs shut. The man tried to gasp, then felt hands grip his chin and skull. Unable to make a noise, the terrorist's mind screamed in horror—he knew what was coming next. He felt the sudden movement....

Bolan heard the vertebrae snap and got to his feet. Four down. More voices thirty feet away. Jogging that way, he came to a wide avenue and paused when a pair of runners appeared ahead of him, coming right at him, their head-mounted lights swinging wildly about the stone walls and rocky ground.

He stepped back into the shadows and they ran right by, but then he stepped out again and brought the handle of his combat knife crashing into the back of the skull of the rear man, sending him flopping forward into the feet of the first runner. The first man cried out, a Turkish or Kurdish word Bolan didn't catch, and began berating his fallen companion in a hushed torrent of curses. As he got to his feet he realized his companion wasn't moving, just lying there, facedown in the rocks. His small light saw something black come out of the darkness, moving fast.

The sitting man's eyes went wide just before Bolan's knife handle cracked his skull.

The Executioner was satisfied. This battle was going well—but this was no time to get overconfident. The tables could turn against him in the blink of an eye.

"GRAY THREE! Gray Five! Give me a report!"

"Gray Leader, what's happened to your command?" Aslan demanded.

"I wish I knew! I think we've been ambushed. There's got to be more than one man out here. There's no other way we could have lost so many men so fast."

Aslan nodded. "I agree."

Cakmak grimaced. "I don't."

Aslan ignored him. "Gray Leader, regroup and light the place up."

BOLAN HADN'T BOTHERED taking a radio from one of his victims. He couldn't understand what was being said, so he had no clue that he had found the leader of the group. The man did have combat senses a little more finely tuned than his comrades. He whirled on Bolan as the warrior stepped up behind him, dropping the radio he had close to his lips and leveling the Kalashnikov.

But the Executioner struck too fast and too hard. His combat knife sought and found the soft spot in his throat just above the collarbone, and it entered with such force it sank to the hilt, throwing Gray Leader literally off his feet. If the blade hadn't killed him, the massive blow his head received when it slammed into the rock wall would have.

"GRAY LEADER, acknowledge!"

Nothing.

"Gray Leader!"

Aslan swore, then shouted into the microphone. "Gray Two, come in!"

"Gray Two here."

"You are in charge. Regroup Gray Team and light the place up!"

"Understood."

"All vehicles—leave your patrols and surround the city, headlights on. I want the place bright as day!"

BOLAN HAD FOUND precious little use for his night-vision goggles after all, but now he donned them as he crawled atop a conical heap of rocks and scanned the dead city. His display showed he wasn't the only one taking the high ground. Someone was standing on a broken corner of a wall maybe a hundred feet away with a big-barreled handgun. Bolan recognized it as a flare gun. They were going to illuminate the city from above in hopes of spotting him, and it might do the trick. He yanked out the Beretta 93-R and adjusted it to single-shot mode for increased accuracy, gripping his gun-hand wrist with his other hand for added stability, and fired.

It was a distant shot, made more difficult by the trickery of using night-vision optics to judge distance, but the shot scored. The man with the gun knelt where he was, and the gun went off in his hand, sending a cascade of sparks and flashing light into the ground. The flare bounced off the earth and zipped down a narrow avenue, ricocheting off walls and rocks and bounding into the air for a short, ten-yard arc before disappearing behind a wall that glowed with its light.

Long before the flare stopped its brilliant gyrations the gunner had taken another bullet and crashed to the ground. By then Bolan had spotted the vehicles moving in around the city.

Four men were still inside the city. Would these four get pulled out, or would reinforcements be sent in? Either way, it was time to put the killer-in-the-dark routine to bed. His watch told him it was nearly time for the arrival of reinforcements.

Time to put an end to this thing once and for all.

CHAPTER THIRTY

"We have aircraft approaching!"

Cakmak jumped out of his chair and ran to the stairway leading into the cavernous warehouse below the security office, where U.S. Army First Sergeant Alfred Maldin was monitoring radar tied into the engagement control station on the Patriot launcher. Around him were gathered three more U.S. military deserters, all trained on the Patriot missile launcher by the U.S. Army.

The soldiers had been ensconced here in the Format Trading shipping warehouse since the raid at Incirlik. They had joined the raid as it went down—as planned—but all had been recruited months prior to that day. Maldin had been the one to recruit them after he went on the True Army's payroll.

Maldin had himself been easy prey to the True Army. He was a bitter man in his late twenties who escaped his miserable life in the Florida Panhandle, where he grew up as what he considered white trash, only to enter the prison of military life, where he found himself stepped on and underappreciated.

But he did learn a skill, and the Army augmented his skills with training over and above his role in the missile battery, with the intent of promoting him to more-complicated and secret missile-operation positions. Negative reports from commanding officers had kept those promotions and transfers from happening.

He had been a sour grape ripe for the picking when he was approached personally by Asad Cakmak nine months earlier and offered one million dollars to take on what Cakmak called "the most impactful role you will ever have in this world." Maldin was to be instrumental in the operation of the Patriots, but also in training other operators to perform the special programming TAK wanted to fly the missiles at ground-based targets.

Maldin had deserted months prior to his lesser Army recruits, and helped in the meticulous planning that had gone into the raid and theft at Incirlik. Now he was in charge of the True Army's Turkish theater of missile operations. He had never been more self-satisfied.

And in a week, when the project was done, he would take his money—already in his Cayman Islands account, he had been sure of that—and go live the beach life, with plenty of women and booze to keep him happy in perpetuity. The rest of the world could go to hell.

But he wasn't on the beach yet. And in the past few days it had been looking less likely that he'd be squeezing sand through his toes in the near future.

"Two of them. Now three!" Maldin railed at Cakmak. "We're being attacked by half the goddamned Air Force!"

"Let me see." Cakmak shouldered him out of the way and glared at the radar screen, the multicolored display going red as the rage boiled into his vision. There were numbered targets floating through the display grid, blinking for attention.

BOLAN FOUND his way back to the Temple and retrieved the pack, then he backed into an alcove and listened to the shouts and engine noise coming from the vehicles outside the ruins. The light of their headlights couldn't reach him this far inside the stone walls, but a glowing haze hovered over the rocks, giving the slightest level of illumination to objects below.

Across the temple, hidden in his own alcove, Bolan's first victim lay in death gazing at him, as if accusing him of his murder.

Bolan ignored the corpse. "Stony?" he said into the Globalstar telephone as the line was picked up.

"Striker," Barbara Price said in a relieved breath. "Glad to hear from you. How is it going?"

"I'm minding the fort," he said, then related the events since he had hung up with Kurtzman.

"Sounds like you've been keeping them occupied."

"I needed something to do until Phoenix showed."

"They are there. As close as they can get anyway."

"You do realize this place is armed with an antiaircraft missile battery."

"It didn't slip our minds."

"So what's the contingency in case Cakmak decides to start launching Patriots?"

"Actually," she said, "we're hoping he does."

"THEY'RE MOVING in close," Maldin said excitedly. "Not that fast, but low. Man, they're gonna try to bomb the launcher!"

Cakmak shook his head. "Not if we take them down first."

"You want to swat them, man?"

"Yes. They think we wouldn't dare waste a single missile."

Maldin grinned ear to ear. "All right. Let's do it!" He jumped to a big industrial-size electrical control and stabbed at the green button. Above him the motor on the big roof opening began to rumble.

Then it strained and the door rattled violently. Maldin and Cakmak both stared at it as the motor suddenly birthed a brilliant electrical spark and grew silent.

BOLAN BEGAN to move cautiously through the ruins, heading back to the rear entrance he had used, closest to the warehouse. He was watching for the four remaining gunners he knew still lingered inside the Hittite city somewhere, at the same time listening on the radio frequency provided by Barbara Price. He reached the rear side of the city without seeing another gunner, then took up a position in the rocks where he could look out and assess the activity level on the grounds. He needed to be ready to move when the opportunity was presented.

Three more minutes by the estimates of the Stony Man Farm mission controller.

Four Land Rover Defenders were parked on this end of the ruins, facing directly into the city with their high beams blazing. Bolan made out the shapes of figures standing around the vehicles, watching the city. They weren't coming in, but they would make it difficult to get out. As soon as he stepped out of the rocks he would be the proverbial sitting duck, highly exposed to who knew how many gunmen. He'd wouldn't get ten paces before being cut down.

Time for Phoenix Force to supply him with an effective diversion.

MALDIN SHOUTED, "It's diving right at us!"

"What's taking so long?" Cakmak demanded.

Three of his men had been hustled onto the roof with bolt cutters.

"We found it," one of them shouted back. "The chain had been screwed together in the middle. The motor couldn't handle it and froze up."

"I don't care what the problem is—just get that door open now or we're all dead!"

Cakmak heard the crunch of the bolt cutters from above and the rattling as the chain was dragged away from the frozen drive. "How much time?" he demanded.

"Twenty seconds—maybe fifteen."

"You ready to fire?"

"I'm ready."

"Go as soon as the door is open."

"Understood."

There was another endless moment when there were no sounds from the roof, then, with a lunge, the door was pulled manually and it began creeping open with a sonorous rattle.

"All right, fire."

"We got to be sure it will clear the door!"

"How much time?"

"Ten seconds!"

"So fire!"

Maldin's eyes were locked on the slowly emerging square of sky above him. If the missile hit the door as it was launched, it might ricochet around in the warehouse and kill them all.

He fired.

NOW BOLAN HEARD the steady thrum of the aircraft, and so did everyone else. He didn't need to see their silhouettes to know all eyes were turning to the aircraft. Now he could make out the bright blinking lights come to life on the wings of the aircraft, and it materialized just a few hundred feet above the compound at a steep angle.

Then there was a flash of light pouring out of the roof of the warehouse and a huge billow of smoke as a tiny, thin shape streaked into the heavens and directly at the aircraft, as if there were a guide wire between the two of them.

The detonation was monumental, as if the air had been cracked apart by vicious lightning, but at the close proximity of a Roman candle detonation. Bolan had jumped to the ground outside the Hittite city at the moment of the explosion, running at the nearest of the vehicles as fast as possible. Now the men who had gathered around the Land Rovers were ducking for cover as debris rained all around them.

Bolan engaged in slaughter, triggering the coughing Beretta 93-R into the men as they knelt with their heads under their arms. He ignored the flying scraps of metal and flaming bits of plastic. If something substantial hit him he'd go down, whether he had his head covered or not. He preferred to be doing *something* if the end came in the form of the sky falling.

The two at his feet dead, Bolan jumped behind the wheel of the Defender, threw it into gear and pulled away in a hurry.

McCARTER HAD NEVER SEEN a sight quite like the cold gray image of the Darkstar swooping out of the sky like some mindless suicide bomber.

Then came the flash of light from the low, well-lit building and a streak of fire that jumped at the Darkstar in an eye blink. McCarter knew the time was now.

"Phoenix Three—out," he ordered, giving Gary Manning a shove that sent the commando hurtling out the aircraft doors and into the night sky. James was a heartbeat behind him, then Encizo, then Hawkins, and finally McCarter flung himself into the sky.

They dropped in close proximity, slate-gray shapes in the unlit night, plummeting toward the shadowy, strangely textured black square that dominated one end of the Format Trading compound. It had been described to them as the ruins of a Hittite city, three thousand years old. McCarter couldn't care less what it was.

The vehicles were gathered around it, a few on each of the four sides, but just beyond the vehicles was blackness, presenting a safe, unlit landing zone for his black-suited commandos.

Manning unfurled his black paraglider and steered for the darkness behind the three vehicles parked on the side wall of the city. He knew they had the place surrounded because Bolan was inside the ancient walls. He hoped Bolan was going to make use of the diversion being provided for him. Right now he couldn't worry about Striker.

McCarter was concerned any time he had to skydive his team into a hostile situation. Dangling in the air was about the most exposed place to be, and an air-filled chute was an easy target. Gunners on the ground simply had to disable the chute in order to kill the target.

The last to land, McCarter steered the sail across the open ground twenty yards behind the Land Rovers, ran out the energy of the landing, then twisted and wadded up the nylon material fast. He quickly joined the others in a low huddle, piling up their used chutes. They had landed unnoticed, but they were still out in the open. McCarter didn't like that one bit.

Incirlik Air Force Base, Turkey

IN THE TINY WINDOWLESS room, David Nicosia stared at the fuzzy collection of screens and error-message displays, feeling as if somebody had just run over his dog.

He got up. Why stay at his post now? He wandered over to Elizabeth Roman's acoustically insulated cubicle and leaned against the wall, watching her monitor her still-functioning readouts and displays.

She had to have sensed him standing there. "How was it?"

"Kind of like jumping under the wheels of a bus on purpose."

"This sucks!"

Nicosia couldn't agree more. "But we're saving lives."

Roman turned and grinned at him. So she did know how to smile, he thought. "I guess," she said with a laugh.

Then she turned to her screen and touched the headset, receiving her orders. "Time for me to die," she announced.

She transmitted her orders to the Darkstar, sending it on a predetermined flight path that would take it into a steep dive over the Format Trading shipping warehouse at an altitude of less than one hundred feet.

She turned on the cargo-door optics and nose optics and stared into them as the unmanned Darkstar aimed at the distant building and dived, increasing speed. They could see vehicles parked on the ground and one set of headlights careening wildly around the far end of the building.

Her heart was in her throat, her hands sweaty and shaking. Suddenly, she pushed back from her control panel and grabbed David Nicosia's hand, just as there was a flash of light and a huge billow of smoke from inside the warehouse.

Then they saw the Patriot. It was just for a split second of time, but they actually could see it, a tiny point of a nose borne up on a brilliant white flame. Roman's hand tightened on Nicosia's and she gasped.

The Patriot came at the screen in under an eye blink and embraced the Darkstar in white fire.

Elizabeth Roman's monitors went blank.

Format Trading Facility, Outside Ankara

"LET'S MOVE OUT, Phoenix," McCarter said as the blast of the second destroyed Darkstar rolled across the open ground. Darker than the night in their blacksuits and gear, they crept to the three Land Rovers, all of them all-terrain Defenders. The men who had been manning them and guarding the fence side of the ruins were now standing on their hoods, trying to see over the ruins to the crash site.

Using a prearranged game plan, Hawkins, Manning and Encizo each took a vehicle, creeping up on its rear end and rising up to peer in the back windows, while McCarter and James hung back, covering them. All three found their vehicle interiors empty and sent back hand signals. Then McCarter and James stepped forward.

"Hands in the air," McCarter ordered.

All the men whirled on the newcomers, and one of them acted without thinking, making a grab for the AK-74 hanging from his shoulder. There were three quick shots—Manning, Encizo and James each scored torso shots with a single round each. Any one of them would have brought the gunman down.

The five other True Army terrorists watched their comrade die like a hastily swatted fly. Their hands went in the air.

CHAPTER THIRTY-ONE

"Do *not* fire again!"

"They're gonna bomb us, man!" Maldin retorted with a wave of his hand at the moonlit cloud of white smoke visible in the air above them.

"I don't think so," Cakmak said. "There's something wrong here."

"You better believe there's something wrong—they want us dead!"

"Think about it. They might have been willing to call our bluff with the first aircraft if they were really desperate, but not with two. The U.S. doesn't just toss its soldiers' lives away...."

At that moment Cakmak knew the truth. "Drones. They sent us unmanned aircraft to make us waste our missiles."

"You mean we just blew up some robot planes?" Maldin said. Then he shrugged.

Cakmak looked disbelievingly at him, this stupid man who shrugged in the face of a humiliating defeat. Was Maldin the measure of Americans? If so, how could they have possibly defeated him? After such a promising start to this campaign—when he had successfully carried out the operation to rob not one but two U.S. Air Force bases—Cakmak had considered his great plan preordained to succeed. Now it was in shambles. Just one missile remaining in Turkey, just three in America.

"They've been making fools of us," Cakmak grunted, almost to himself.

This was all going to end very shortly. But it was going to end on *his* terms.

Gilroy, California

FOR THE FIRST TIME in two days, the phone in the trailer rang.

"Thank God." Gadgets Schwarz said, dropping his poker hand and moving to the laptop that had been set up as their impromptu bugging center.

The call was picked up on the second ring, and the sound of a distant voice said, "Cakmak here."

"The man himself," Schwarz muttered.

Blancanales and Lyons had moved to the window to watch the trailer with their binoculars.

Able Team had been alerted to the fact that Phoenix and Bolan were coming together in Turkey and something major was happening.

"Yes, General."

"The time has come, Hakki," Cakmak said in Kurdish. Hedipe Demir translated in rapid-fire English.

The man in the trailer in Gilroy suddenly grew excited. "The timing is good, General! It is afternoon here! The targets will be filled with tourists. Many people!"

"Do it now. I will wait. As soon as it is done, I will call my news network contacts in the U.S."

"Here they go," Blancanales said from the window. Hedipe went to the other window and watched, squinting into the afternoon sun.

Down the street a block away they could see the two

men race out of their trailer. As one of them started the car and left the doors open for a quick getaway, the other began yanking bolts from the body panels of the trailer enclosure.

"We should stop them," Demir said in a hushed voice.

"They can't harm anyone," Schwarz said calmly. "Those missiles can't fire. We saw to that."

"You sound pretty confident. You had better be right."

Schwarz looked at Lyons.

"We're right," Lyons growled. "Bear wouldn't make a mistake like that. But we do need to be ready to take these guys down when the truth comes crashing down on them."

As the commandos shrugged into gear, which was prepped and waiting, Hedipe stood at the glass and watched in awe at the possibility of what she might witness.

"Keep a running translation going for us," Schwarz said to her as the three of them hustled from the apartment.

She could see a single body panel being removed at the far end of the trailer, then saw the old man in the trailer across the drive emerge onto his front stoop, observing the flurry of activity with interest. If he was saying anything, Hedipe didn't catch it, although the numerous bugs Able Team had planted were feeding loud thumps and squeaks through the laptop speakers—the sounds of the dismantling in progress.

The engagement control station exposed, the man named Hakki worked with it in a flurry of hand movements. Then she saw him raise the small portable phone to his face and his voice came through the laptop. Hedipe translated into the radio mike. "They are ready to start the firing process."

Cakmak replied with a single short word, harsh and commanding. He was giving the order to launch.

Hakki touched a switch on the control panel, and the trailer roof began to push up as the pneumatics elevated the missile battery into launch position. The aluminum body panels slid off, flopping to the ground, and in a few seconds the black missile battery was there for all to see, as clear as day.

"You can't do that! I'm calling the police!" It was the sound of the old man coming through one of the still functioning bugs. He disappeared inside.

The man behind the controls nodded to his partner, who jumped onto the launch bed and made a series of quick adjustments, then jumped down again.

Hakki spoke again to Cakmak, his voice sharp and clipped with excitement.

Hedipe said, "He is firing missile one."

Hakki's hand moved on the engagement control station.

Nothing happened.

"Hakki?" Cakmak asked.

"There is something wrong!"

"Try again!"

"I am trying to fire! The system says it is ready, but when I push the button nothing happens!"

"Fire the others."

"Nothing. Nothing."

"Try again!"

"I am trying! The station says everything is good, but they will not fire!"

The other man spoke now. "We've been set up. We have to get out of here."

"Cakmak, we must leave!"

"You have to get those missiles launched! If you leave your post, I will kill you myself."

"I will not leave my post, General," Hakki said with a resigned air.

Then, from behind the old man's trailer, Hakki's peripheral vision spotted movement that shouldn't have been there. When he turned his head he faced a dark-complexioned, grizzled bull of a man coming for him with an M-16 rifle, eyes dark as night.

Hakki didn't even really notice the man as his fingers flew frantically over the controls. The man approached him calmly, but was clearly intent on using his weapon if he needed to.

In desperation Hakki kicked at the front panel of the control station.

The screen was still telling him all systems were go.

There were sudden gunshots. Hakki froze when he witnessed his comrade making a break for their car, firing into the street. In response came a brief burst of shots that cut the running man's legs out from under him and brought him crashing into the trunk of the car. He bounced off, covered in blood, and flopped to the ground on his back.

Hakki gazed openmouthed at the dead man, then at the man in front of him with the M-16.

"Give it up, bud," Blancanales said in a low, no-nonsense voice.

Hakki gave it up.

THE GILROY POLICE Department squad car came to an abrupt halt as it turned into the trailer park. David Clairborne and his partner, Jesus Gutierrez, said nothing. They just got out of the squad car and stared.

There, where just a couple of hours ago there had been a parked trailer house, was now a monster of a missile launcher, gleaming black in the afternoon sun. The body panels that had once covered it were strewed on the ground. The missile launcher's control panel was dark, the screen bashed in and dead, and next to it, trussed up on the ground like a calf, was a bearded man, his wrists and ankles linked together with plastic handcuffs. His partner was nearby, dead from blood loss with multiple gunshot wounds. On his front stoop, looking down on all of it, was the old man, Al Boyd, his mouth hanging open and his jowls drooping under his chin.

"Al," Clairborne asked incredulously, "who did this?"

The old man thought about it for a second, then he grinned and said, "I did."

CHAPTER THIRTY-TWO

Turkey

Bolan aimed the Land Rover at the set of ground-level loading-dock doors that were standing open, billowing white smoke. He slammed his foot on the gas and sent the Defender barreling into the interior of the warehouse, finding himself flying between towering shelving units for holding cargo, just inches of space on either side of the vehicle.

Bolan wasn't sure yet what was happening, although he was reasonably confident that there hadn't been people on the two aircraft that had just tossed themselves into the jaws of fiery death at the hands of the Kurdish madman. Still, there was a missile remaining, and Ankara was less than three minutes' flight time away. Any second Cakmak would get angry enough to throw all bets to the wind. He was going to realize he had been defeated. His diseased, murderous mind was going to decide he had nothing more to lose and one last, grandiloquent statement to make to the world.

Bolan didn't care what he had to do, but he was going to stop it. Somehow, right now.

He slowed the Land Rover and found himself in an

open, stadium-size area from which the shelving and overhead machinery had been removed. Above was the vast window to the sky that he had failed to keep closed. One hundred feet ahead of him was the waiting launcher and its caretakers, wearing U.S. Army uniforms.

Bolan experienced a surge of cold, quiet fury. He despised the murderers of the innocent. He knew nothing but loathing for those who coldly manipulated and ruined the lives of others. The images of three long-ago faces flashed through his mind—mother, father, sister.

How many mothers, fathers and sisters would die in flames in the city of Ankara as the last of the Patriots was used to further a madman's dreams?

How far down the ladder of human dignity did a man have to descend before he was willing to turn traitor to his country and allow himself to be made a slaughterer of innocents, and for no better an excuse than money?

The four soldiers around the missile launcher were looking at him, suspicious. Was he one of Cakmak's men? If so, what was he doing here in the Defender? Why was he just sitting there?

The Executioner swung the muzzle of the MP-5/10A3 through the windshield, then laid the weapon in the shattered opening as his feet crushed the pedal and he accelerated at the launcher. He triggered the submachine gun, cutting down a man fleeing to the left, another man on the right. One of the men drew himself into a ball as he dived into the cover of the engagement control station, trusting the control cabinets to protect him from the flying 10 mm rounds, while a man working on the missile bed clambered toward the far end, keeping the black missile battery between himself and the onslaught of gunfire. Bolan extracted the submachine gun from the window and stepped out of the Defender as he steered it into the control station, then hit the ground hard, rolling three times before pushing away from the spinning floor and landing on his feet.

Bolan didn't see the man in the control station grow wild-eyed with horror at the unmanned Land Rover rolling at him. He pushed up from the floor, trying to outrun the vehicle, but he was too slow. It slammed into the control station at the moment the man was between them. He was crushed instantly.

The Executioner was more concerned about the state of the control system, chagrined to see that the glowing panels appeared to be functioning normally. They had taken the crash in stride.

He never got the chance to issue the coup de grâce on the launcher. Above him he heard a doorway fling open and a figure appeared at the top of the steel stairs, covering him with an AK-74, the Russian autorifle firing 5.45 mm rounds.

Bolan didn't move. He stood where he was, his chest against an engagement control monitor, and gazed into the disfigured face of Asad Cakmak.

"Shoot me if you dare, Cakmak."

"It is you." The words were bitter on his tongue; he was spitting them down on Bolan. "I thought as much. I hoped as much."

"Glad you're happy to see me again."

"Step away." Cakmak gestured with the Kalashnikov.

"You'll have to kill me." And Bolan, gazing up through the barrel of the automatic rifle into the face of a man he knew was truly insane, smiled.

Cakmak's eye twitched. Inside he felt the high-tension wire of emotions—monumental anger and unbelievable frustration—mix with simple incredulity. Why wasn't this man afraid of him?

Maldin came limping out of the shadows, the only one of the four missile operators who had somehow managed to escape death. He looked wildly at Cakmak, then at the soldier with the submachine gun.

"You fucking maniac!" he ranted. "You son of a bitch!"

"You traitor," Bolan replied calmly.

"Kill him, General! Kill this son of a bitch!"

As he observed the two of them, Cakmak's question was answered. This was how he had been beaten by the Americans. Not by the likes of Alfred Maldin, a coward and an idiot, but by the likes of this nameless executioner: ruthless, shrewd and absolutely without fear.

"We have a Mexican standoff in the works, General," Bolan said. "You shoot me, you risk disabling the firing controls."

"I'll shoot you then, you son of a bitch!" When Maldin raised his hands he was holding a compact Russian Izh-75 automatic pistol. Bolan saw it coming and he stepped back and down, ducking for cover behind one of the missile cartridge's pneumatic cylinders. The 5.45 mm cartridge bounced off the control panel where Bolan had been standing, cracking the glass. Then the expansive warehouse filled with Cakmak's howl of rage.

There was a stutter of 5.45 mm fire from the AK-74 and Bolan watched through the machinery as Maldin whirled in a circle before dropping to the ground.

"Damned idiot!" Cakmak thundered as he stormed down the steel stairs, each footstep clanging. He held the weapon on Bolan's hiding place as he stomped close enough to the control station to see that the display, though chipped, was still operational.

"You shot me in the leg," Maldin almost sobbed.

"Next time I'll aim for the head."

"You son of a bitch," Maldin said weakly, and Bolan saw him aiming the Izh-75, this time at Cakmak. The Kurd general didn't know his danger until the shot was fired and the 5.45 mm round slammed into his back.

Cakmak spun and laid on the AK-74's trigger, firing into the wounded American, watching Maldin's body jump and twitch and then lie still, and still he kept firing until the cartridge was empty and the corpse was no longer recognizable.

Cakmak dropped the automatic rifle. It hit the concrete floor butt first and clattered noisily as he snatched the .45 Ruger from the holster under his left arm. The thrill of pain in his side was invigorating. Maldin had inflicted nothing more than a flesh wound. Now where was the American?

Bolan had moved away from the launcher and was standing in the open. The submachine gun hung on its strap on his back, and he covered Cakmak with the .44 Magnum Desert Eagle.

"We're evenly matched," Cakmak said.

"Don't fool yourself," Bolan answered coolly.

Cakmak moved, aiming the Ruger as he squeezed the trigger, confident he could bring aim and discharge together at the proper instant, but Bolan was faster. The Desert Eagle cracked out a round, and the black handgun jumped in his grip. Cakmak's gut was ripped open and he collapsed, feeling his hands lose his hold on the Ruger. Now opaque clouds encircled his vision, closing in his sight. He was going into shock.

He had to make his death matter. Somebody—he didn't even care anymore who it was—had to pay for the misery and bitterness that had been his life.

The truth was he had never cared. The war had never been about his people, his culture, the independence of the Kurds. It had always been a battle to exact revenge. He stumbled for the engagement control center.

The monitor was still glowing. The target was still set and simply awaiting his fire command. He reached for the launch switch.

Bolan was there, behind him, the hot muzzle of the Desert Eagle against Cakmak's spine. "You've got a lot of explaining to do, General. Don't take the coward's way out."

Supreme General Asad Cakmak a coward? Suddenly, he realized that it was true.

All he had ever been was a powerful coward.

It was a realization he couldn't live with.

He reached for the fire switch. Bolan pulled the trigger.

CHAPTER THIRTY-THREE

Calvin James jumped into the Land Rover alongside Hawkins, who was assigned driving duties. Land Rover two consisted of Manning at the wheel and McCarter playing gunner in the passenger seat. Encizo was assigned to bring up the rear—and keep out of sight until he saw he was needed. With a wave Hawkins stomped on the gas and steered the all-terrain vehicle around the corner of the ruins and into the plain sight of the next grouping of vehicles.

The four vehicles were still parked where they were supposed to be, but half the terrorists manning them were sprinting in the direction of the building where the rain of debris from the twin aircraft explosions had fallen. They had left behind a man for each of the Land Rovers, who were more intent on watching the commotion than keeping an eye on the ruins. They didn't even pay attention as the newcomer pulled up.

"Evenin', gents," Hawkins greeted them.

All four Kurds jumped like startled coyotes and two of them had the presence of mind and the poor judgment to snatch their AK-47 autorifles into play. In their haste they failed to notice the silent statue in the back of the vehicle. James triggered a brief burst from the M-16 that cut down the gunners before they knew what hit them.

The pair of survivors put their hands in the air. Hawkins tied them up, ankles and wrists, to the rear bumper of one of their own vehicles.

"Hurry it up, T.J.," James said, nodding toward the warehouse building a quarter of a mile away. "We've attracted attention."

As Hawkins got behind the wheel again he saw a small army of gunmen were marching in their direction on foot, while two of the Land Rovers that had been stationed there lurched toward them.

At that moment there was a new explosion, and a blast of orange fire could be seen over the shadowy ruins.

MANNING TWISTED the wheel hard to the right as a blast of autofire danced on the ground and spit past their tires. "Hang on!"

McCarter was doing just that, dropping into his seat and holding on to the roll-bar top of the windshield to keep from being tossed out.

"Give me a shot," McCarter directed.

"Coming up," Manning replied, twisted again to the left and suddenly presented the broad side of the all-terrain vehicle to the parked gunners. McCarter rose up in his seat, pushed his hip against the roll bar for stability and triggered the M-203 grenade launcher mounted under the barrel of his M-16 A-2. It was a tricky shot— 175 yards and still moving fast. The 40 mm HE round took its sweet time about coming down while a fresh barrage of 7.62 mm autofire rounds buzzed after their vehicle, trying to catch up. The rifle fire was closing in hard when the HE hit the ground an arm's length from the nearest vehicle and detonated with a crack. The vehicle was in flames and figures fled it, burning alive. The fire made a broad jump to the next vehicle, and the canopy and interior became an inferno with a rush of air.

As Manning pushed the engine to redline revs he steered in a broad arc to herd in the fleeing Kurds. McCarter put down an invisible line in the dirt with the throbbing M-16 A-2. One of the runners brought up his weapon to offer return fire and was cut down before his fingers reached the trigger. That was enough. The remaining men tossed away their weapons and put their hands on their heads.

"Phoenix Five here," Hawkins said over the radio. "We could use a little help."

"Phoenix Two here," Encizo returned. "I'm on it."

As McCarter and Manning made quick work of cuffing the surrendering terrorists together into a human chain nine bodies long, Encizo raced past them in his own vehicle.

JAMES AND HAWKINS decided their best short-term tactic was to stop and make a stand. Swinging the Defender to a broad-sided stop, they jumped out and put it between themselves and the approaching army.

The True Army foot soldiers made a foolhardy charge, and the two Phoenix Force warriors let them come on, waiting patiently until the unprotected platoon was well within range of the 5.56 mm rounds of their M-16 A-2 autorifles. The terrorists began slowing their approach when they realized they might be walking unprotected to their doom, and that was the moment James and Hawkins emerged from behind the vehicle to commence firing short, precise bursts that had a devastating impact. Grouped like amateurs in a tight knot, there was no way they could miss. Seven of them dropped, dead and wounded, before they had managed to flee back the way they had come.

Now it was time for the pair of Land Rovers to make their charge. They roared to life and swept out in broad arcs designed to bring them out and around the rear of the Phoenix Force warriors, leaving them fully exposed. They split apart, circled wide, and came back in from two directions—but by that time James and Hawkins had moved around to the other side of their cover, knowing they were out of range of the fleeing terrorists. The drivers stomped on the gas and aimed directly at the two men as if from mutual frustration.

James thumbed a buckshot round into the breech of the M-203 mounted on his M-16 A-2 and laid his arms carefully on the hood of the Land Rover, lining up on the oncoming vehicle. The driver was coming straight at him, accelerating over the uneven ground to near highway speeds as if to ram the parked vehicle. At ten yards James triggered the 40 mm round, and the effect was instantaneous and horrifying. The double-aught projectiles smashed through the windshield and ripped through the flesh of the driver, killing him instantly. The gunner just sticking his head out of the window took the blast undiluted by safety glass, and flesh and bone flew from his skull in pieces. The vehicle veered away and drifted to a halt.

The driver of the second vehicle had glimpsed the sudden demise of his comrades and swerved his vehicle in sudden horror just as Hawkins's HE round burst from his M-203. The Texan's aim had been dead on—it was the target that had failed to cooperate—and the HE traveled near parallel with the ground for almost forty more yards before smacking soil and erupting into flame. By that time the vehicle had been accelerating away from the deadly pair to regroup. But as the driver was slowing, confident he was now out of range of whatever the pair could throw at him, another all-terrain vehicle came ripping around the corner at speeds that sent dry dirt and weedy vegetation arcing away behind its tires.

The occupants saw at once that the maddened driver was in the same black combat cosmetics as the pair who had just wiped out their comrades and they opened fire. The driver of the careening vehicle acted content to ignore their barrage of autofire as he spun the vehicle to a stop, reached into his seat and pulled out another M-16 A-2/M-203.

The driver of the terrorist vehicle stood on the gas, and his tires spun in soft dirt, moving him nowhere for the longest second of his life as his two passengers shouted and pleaded for him to get moving. Then the tires gripped and the vehicle lurched forward—and in that moment the commando's M-203 belched fire. The round crossed the distance in the time it took for the car to move three feet, sending the cracking into the back seat instead of the hood, and it erupted into blinding white-and-yellow flames.

"STRIKER, come in!"

"Striker here, Phoenix One." Bolan realized that the sound of McCarter's urgent radio calls had been coming over his headset for several seconds and he had selectively tuned them out. "The General is out of the picture."

"What about the launcher? Still a threat?"

"Hold on, Phoenix One."

Bolan calmly aimed the Desert Eagle into the blood-smeared monitor and fired, then into the control boxes and CPU components.

The electronics were a mangled mess, beyond repair. The last of the weapons had been rendered unfireable. Finally, the peril of the Patriot missiles had ceased to be.

"Striker here, Phoenix One," Bolan said. "The missiles are no longer a threat."

"Yee-haw, Striker!" That could only be T. J. Hawkins.

"Nice work, Striker," Barbara Price added.

"You coming in for a landing, Phoenix?" Bolan asked. "There's still cleanup work to be done."

"Buddy, we're already here and mopping the floors. We dived in while Cakmak was busy wasting Patriots on the Darkstars."

"Where are you now?" Bolan asked, relieved at the confirmation that the destroyed aircraft were unmanned.

"Out in the backyard. We've rounded up eighteen or so Kurdish hardmen. They're surrendering in droves."

Bolan mounted the stairs and entered the silent security office, walking to the window and looking out on the well-lit grounds. Indeed, Phoenix Force had wasted no time. There were rows of terrorists sitting on the ground with their cuffed hands resting on top of their heads.

"Here come a few more to join the circus," he radioed to McCarter. "Look behind you."

Below he saw McCarter and the others turn around fast, but they were in no danger. The last four soldiers of the True Army of Kurdistan were emerging from the ruins of the Hittite city, arms held high, weapons held by the barrels, shouting for mercy and feeling lucky just to be alive.

EPILOGUE

Stony Man Farm, Virginia

Gadgets Schwarz used a bright red thumb tack to stick the *USA Today* cutting on the wall of the War Room. In the margin he had written in red ink, "Our hero." The cutting showed the picture of a slightly bewildered-looking old man in a wrinkled golf shirt and oversize stretch slacks, grinning toothlessly for the camera. The article read:

> Although law enforcement officials have their doubts, local resident Alfred Boyd claims personal responsibility for exposing and apprehending Kurdish terrorists who were holed up in the small town of Gilroy, CA, with a battery of Patriot missiles. The terrorists are believed to be a part of the group who recently threatened violence on U.S. and Turkish cities using Patriot missiles stolen from two U.S. Air Force bases.
> U.S. military officials have also expressed doubts that Boyd, eighty-two, could have single-handedly apprehended…

T. J. Hawkins strolled in with a cup of coffee and scanned the cutting. "Must be nice to get all the glory."

"While schmoes like you and me," Schwarz said grimly, "go totally unappreciated."

Ankara, Turkey

DOGAN BIR SLAMMED the suitcase closed with one sock still sticking out and struggled to force the latches closed. He grabbed his small collection of semivaluable jewelry and stuffed it into his pants pocket. What else? There was nothing else that he owned that was very valuable, nothing small enough to carry. He was going out into the world with nothing—nothing! He had maybe a week's pay in his pocket. His bank account was frozen. The account Nouri Bakir set up for him in the Cayman Islands had somehow disappeared, as if it had never been. Now he was a wanted man.

That son of a bitch Cengiz Yilmaz had sold him out. As soon as he and his petty little consortium of businessmen had been exposed from Bir's video tape and arrested, they had started singing like canaries and named Dogan Bir as an accomplice. Bir had expected that. But they had no evidence against him, and he could claim he knew nothing about the scheme.

But then Yilmaz had gone on Turkish television claiming Dogan Bir had been the money man behind the plan to stop the True Army by holding their families hostage.

The horror had dawned on Bir slowly—Yilmaz's lie had signed Bir's death warrant. The unpaid Iranian mercenaries would be coming after *him* for the money Yilmaz owed them. When he failed to come up with the money they wanted, his life would be forfeit.

He had to get well away from Turkey. Western Europe? He didn't think even that would be far enough. Maybe America.

But how in God's name would he get to America? Even getting out of the country was unlikely with his passport officially revoked during the investigation.

He slammed the door of his flat and strode fast to the elevator. It pinged on his floor when he was still twenty paces away and the shabbily dressed, dark-skinned man that emerged had murder in his eye. His blackened teeth grimaced when he saw Bir, and he held up a garrote.

Bir spun and ran for the stairs, yanking open the creaking emergency door and flying down the stairs. He lived in an expensive new apartment building with all the latest fire and earthquake safety features, including stairways at either end of the building.

It wasn't long before he could hear footsteps coming down after him. He dropped his suitcase and flew down flight after flight, gradually leaving his pursuer behind, until he breathlessly reached the first floor. He burst through the exit door and cried out as his feet caught on some unseen obstruction. His body was hurled heavily to the sidewalk and his breath was knocked out of him.

Before he could make his throbbing lungs function again, he was lifted up and carried off the sidewalk into an alley, where he was leaned against the wall, gasping painfully. Finally, as the breath came back, he saw that he was surrounded by three men, Iranians. A fourth man was approaching—the black-toothed murderer from upstairs.

"Dogan Bir," Black Teeth said, "you owe us some money."

"No," he gasped. "They lied to you. I had nothing to do with this!"

"We were told you were the money man."

"No!"

"We were told you would pay us for services rendered."

"No!"

"You know we had to let our hostages go. We didn't even get a ransom. Now somebody has to pay us for our time."

"I swear to you, I'm not the one!"

Black Teeth placed the garrote around his neck. "If you come up with our money, then I won't have to make use of this, Dogan Bir."

But in the end, the garrote was necessary.

Singapore City, Singapore

NOURI BAKIR STOPPED and stared at the man in black pants, black shirt and black hair, standing easily in the living room of his penthouse suite on the nineteenth floor of the Bakir Building.

Bakir was about to demand to know who the man was, what he was doing here, how he had bypassed the building's, and his personal, security. His words froze in his throat when he looked into the man's chiseled iron face and merciless eyes.

Those were the eyes of a killer. Not the murderers-for-hire that Bakir knew and employed, not the Kurdish fanatics he had funded, but a different kind of killer. He wanted to characterize the man as morally incorruptible, but was such a thing possible? An ethical murderer?

Suddenly, Bakir knew he was in danger more grave than ever before. Why was the man just standing there? Just looking at him?

"Who are you?" he blurted at last.

"I'm the man who just executed Asad Cakmak."

"Don't know him," Bakir blustered, trying to think fast.

"Your lies are wasted on me, Bakir," Bolan said in a low, steady voice. "I've read the files they're putting together on you in Washington and in Ankara. They're preparing to indict you for funding global terrorism."

"Ha!" Bakir blurted. "They'll prove nothing!"

"I know it."

"If they try to send me to jail, I'll have the courts locked up for decades. I'll never serve time."

"I know it."

More silence, pregnant with menace.

"So why are you here? What is your business?"

"Someone had to make sure you pay for the murders you sanctioned, Bakir."

"So you've chosen yourself to be my judge and jury?"

"And executioner," Bolan said simply, withdrawing the suppressed Beretta 93-R from his black leather jacket.

Bakir was visibly trembling, but he tried to look haughty and casual as he strolled to the teak bar, then he snatched at the Smith & Wesson .38 Special strapped under the sink. The straps were empty. The gun was gone.

Bolan gestured toward a pile of dismantled weapons on the couch cushions. With a sinking heart Bakir counted them and realized that every single gun he kept in the penthouse was there, rendered useless.

Bakir made a mewl of frustration. He wasn't a man used to being impotent.

"All right! What do you want from me?"

Bolan gestured again with the 93-R, this time to the

open window, looking out on Industry Avenue, 190 feet below.

"You can't make me do it!"

"If you don't do it, I will."

Bakir's mind was reeling. "This can't be the end for me!"

"It is."

"You don't understand—"

Bolan's hand twitched; Bakir jumped. Across the room a television came to life, showing taped news footage of bodies being pulled out of the wreckage of the government building in Diyarbakir, Turkey.

"I do understand, Bakir," Bolan said. "I understand it's time for you to pay for what you've done. The only decision left to you is how it happens."

Finally Bakir understood it, too, and with a look of bitter resignation, raised his eyes toward Bolan.

"Do you mind if I sit for a moment?"

Bolan thought that it wasn't too big a last request. He nodded.

Bakir moved to the couch and turned to sit. Then with the speed of a striking cobra, his hand darted toward his leg, grabbing a small pistol from an ankle holster.

Bolan watched as the tiny muzzle swung toward him. Far enough.

The triple punch from the silenced Beretta slammed Bakir against the backrest of the couch, the pistol flying out of his hand as a splash of crimson created a new pattern on the fabric.

The warrior's diamond-hard gaze was unreadable and his jaw muscles rippled as he slowly shook his head.

His work here was done.

The Executioner was blitzing on.

DON PENDLETON'S

STONY

AMERICA'S ULTRA-COVERT INTELLIGENCE AGENCY

MAN®

DON'T MISS OUT ON THE ACTION
IN THESE TITLES!

#61928-6	THIRST FOR POWER	$5.99 U.S.	☐
		$6.99 CAN.	☐
#61927-8	ZERO HOUR	$5.99 U.S.	☐
		$6.99 CAN.	☐
#61926-X	EDGE OF NIGHT	$5.99 U.S.	☐
		$6.99 CAN.	☐
#61924-3	BETRAYAL	$5.99 U.S.	☐
		$6.99 CAN.	☐
#61918-9	REPRISAL	$5.99 U.S.	☐
		$6.99 CAN.	☐

(limited quantities available on certain titles)

TOTAL AMOUNT	$
POSTAGE & HANDLING	$
($1.00 for one book, 50¢ for each additional)	
APPLICABLE TAXES*	$ _____
TOTAL PAYABLE	$ _____

(check or money order—please do not send cash)

To order, complete this form and send it, along with a check or money order for the total above, payable to Gold Eagle Books, to: **In the U.S.:** 3010 Walden Avenue, P.O. Box 9077, Buffalo, NY 14269-9077; **in Canada:** P.O. Box 636, Fort Erie, Ontario, L2A 5X3.

Name: _____

Address: _____ City: _____

State/Prov.: _____ Zip/Postal Code: _____

*New York residents remit applicable sales taxes.
Canadian residents remit applicable GST and provincial taxes.

GOLD EAGLE®

GSMBACK3

**Readers won't want to miss this exciting
new title of the SuperBolan® series!**

DON PENDLETON's

MACK BOLAN®

Power of the Lance

**THE
TYRANNY
FILES**

BOOK II

The Temple of the Nordic Covenant has the weapons, connections
and skinhead shock troops to fulfill their mad vision of a Reich
reborn. Bolan teams up with a Mossad agent in Germany in a race
to halt the slaughter of German Jews in a next-generation
Kristallnacht. Steuben and his fanatics are also planning an
assassination that will rock Europe—and set the stage for a rebirth
of the Nazi reign of terror.

Available in July 2001 at your favorite retail outlet.

Or order your copy now by sending your name, address, zip or postal code, along with
a check or money order (please do not send cash) for $5.99 for each book ordered
($6.99 in Canada), plus 75¢ postage and handling ($1.00 in Canada), payable to Gold
Eagle Books, to:

In the U.S.	**In Canada**
Gold Eagle Books	Gold Eagle Books
3010 Walden Avenue	P.O. Box 636
P.O. Box 9077	Fort Erie, Ontario
Buffalo, NY 14269-9077	L2A 5X3

**GOLD
EAGLE**®

Please specify book title with your order.
Canadian residents add applicable federal and provincial taxes.

GSB79

**A journey through the dangerous frontier
known as the future...**

JAMES AXLER
DEATH LANDS®

THE
SKYDARK
CHRONICLES
Book II

Judas Strike

A nuclear endgame played out among the superpowers created
a fiery cataclysm that turned America into a treacherous new
frontier. But an intrepid group of warrior survivalists roams the
wastelands, unlocking the secrets of a pre-dark world.
Ryan Cawdor and his band have become living legends in a
world of madness and death where savagery reigns, but the
human spirit endures....

Available in June 2001 at your favorite retail outlet.

Or order your copy now by sending your name, address, zip or postal code, along with a
check or money order (please do not send cash) for $5.99 for each book ordered ($6.99
in Canada), plus 75¢ postage and handling ($1.00 in Canada), payable to
Gold Eagle Books, to:

In the U.S.

Gold Eagle Books
3010 Walden Ave.
P.O. Box 9077
Buffalo, NY 14269-9077

In Canada

Gold Eagle Books
P.O. Box 636
Fort Erie, Ontario
L2A 5X3

GOLD
EAGLE®

Please specify book title with order.
Canadian residents add applicable federal and provincial taxes.

GDL54

James Axler

OUTLANDERS®

SARGASSO PLUNDER

An enforcer turned renegade, Kane and his group learn of a mother lode of tech hidden deep within the ocean of the western territories, a place once known as Seattle. The booty is luring tech traders and gangs, but Kane and Grant dare to infiltrate the salvage operation, knowing that getting in is a life-and-death risk....

In the Outlands, the shocking truth
is humanity's last hope.

On sale August 2001 at your favorite retail outlet. Or order your copy now by sending your name, address, zip or postal code, along with a check or money order (please do not send cash) for $5.99 for each book ordered ($6.99 in Canada), plus 75¢ postage and handling ($1.00 in Canada), payable to Gold Eagle Books, to:

In the U.S.	In Canada
Gold Eagle Books	Gold Eagle Books
3010 Walden Ave.	P.O. Box 636
P.O. Box 9077	Fort Erie, Ontario
Buffalo, NY 14269-9077	L2A 5X3

Please specify book title with order.
Canadian residents add applicable federal and provincial taxes.

GOLD EAGLE®

GOUT18

**Gold Eagle brings you
high-tech action and mystic adventure!**

THE

Destroyer™

#124 BY EMINENT DOMAIN

Created by
MURPHY
and SAPIR

THE
RUSTED
CURTAIN
BOOK II

Somebody's given America an eviction notice in Alaska—in the form of mass murder. Pipeline workers and dozens of U.S. troops are being slaughtered by a mysterious "ghost force" of killers. Remo and Chiun recognize the techniques—a bargain brand of Sinanju—which pose an alarming question. Who has trained an army of die-hard Soviet troops in the ancient, secret art of the master assassins?

Available in July 2001 at your favorite retail outlet.

Or order your copy now by sending your name, address, zip or postal code, along with a check or money order (please do not send cash) for $5.99 for each book ordered ($6.99 in Canada), plus 75¢ postage and handling ($1.00 in Canada), payable to Gold Eagle Books, to:

In the U.S.

Gold Eagle Books
3010 Walden Ave.
P.O. Box 9077
Buffalo, NY 14269-9077

In Canada

Gold Eagle Books
P.O. Box 636
Fort Erie, Ontario
L2A 5X3

Please specify book title with your order.
Canadian residents add applicable federal and provincial taxes.

GOLD
EAGLE®

GDEST124